Praise for *Darkness: Two Decades*

"This diverse 25-story anthology is a superb sampling of some of the most significant short horror works published between 1985 and 2005. Editor extraordinaire Datlow (*Poe*) includes classic stories from horror icons Clive Barker, Peter Straub, and Stephen King as well as SF and fantasy luminaries Gene Wolfe, Dan Simmons, Neil Gaiman, and Lucius Shepard. The full diversity of horror is on display: George R. R. Martin's 'The Pear-Shaped Man' about a creepy downstairs neighbor, and Straub's 'The Juniper Tree,' which chronicles a drifter's sexual molestation of a young boy, exemplify horror's sublime psychological power, while Barker's 'Jacqueline Ess: Her Will and Testament' and Poppy Z. Brite's 'Calcutta, Lord of Nerves' are audaciously gory masterworks. This is an anthology to be cherished and an invaluable reference for horror aficionados."
—*Publishers Weekly*, starred review

"Make sure you are in a safe place before you open it up."
—*New York Journal of Books*

"*Darkness* promises to please both longtime fans and readers who have no clue what 'splatterpunk' was supposed to mean."
—*San Francisco Chronicle*

"Eclectic . . . a complete overview of some of the best horror stories published in the last twenty years."
—*SF Site*

"I can't recommend this book highly enough and no, that's not just the rabid fanboy inside me talking. This is my serious critic's voice. I know it doesn't translate well in the written word, but trust me. I give my highest recommendation for this book."
—*Hellnotes*

Praise for *Hauntings*

"This anthology of 24 previously published dark fantasy and horror stories, edited by the ever-adept Datlow (*Blood and Other Cravings*), explores a variety of situations in which people encounter literal or figurative specters from beyond. . . . Solid entries by Neil Gaiman, Caitlín R. Kiernan, and Joyce Carol Oates capture the mood perfectly and will thrill fans of the eerie."
—*Publishers Weekly*

"Apt to entertain and disquiet the horror fans."
—*SF Site*, featured review

"Datlow once again proves herself as a master editor. Her mission to broaden readers' concepts of what a haunting can be is nothing short of a success, and the twenty-four stories on display run the gamut from explicitly terrifying to eerily familiar. Readers who wish to be haunted themselves should not miss this one. Highly recommended."
—*Arkham Digest*

"Award-winning horror editor Ellen Datlow offers readers a skillfully crafted, captivating collection with *Hauntings*, an anthology of twenty-four reprinted ghostly tales from the last 25 years of horror literature."
—*Rue Morgue*

"Ms. Datlow has assembled a formidable community of eminent genre artists working at the very heights of their literary powers to create this outstanding dark fantasy anthology. This is the best of the best—don't miss it!"
—*The Tomb of Dark Delights*

"I have a short list of editors that I will buy an anthology of, regardless of whether or not I have even heard of the writers it contains, and Ellen Datlow is at the top of that list. She has this crazy knack of consistently putting together stellar anthologies and *Hauntings* is no different."
—*Horror Talk*

"This collection is formidable. . . ."
—*True Review*

Praise for *Lovecraft's Monsters*

"Ellen Datlow's second editorial outing into the realm of Lovecraft proves even more fruitful than the first. Focusing on Lovecraftian monsters, Datlow offers readers sixteen stories and two poems of a variety that should please any fans of the genre."
—*Arkham Digest*

"[A]n amazing and diverse treasure trove of stories. As an avid fan of Lovecraft's monstrous creations, THIS is the anthology I've been waiting for."
—*Shattered Ravings*

"Editor Ellen Datlow has put together an anthology that will rock your liquid fantasies. Tachyon Publications has produced an excellent themed anthology. Lovecraft enthusiasts will plunge into the volume and be happily immersed in the content."
—*Diabolique Magazine*

"[A]n entirely enjoyable read. . . . For Mythos devotees I would highly recommend picking it up."
—*Seattle Geekly*

"*Lovecraft's Monsters* will appeal to fans of Lovecraft's work, particularly his Mythos stories, and to readers of dark fiction everywhere."
—*Lit Reactor*

"Datlow brings together some of the top SF/F and horror writers working today and has them play in Lovecraft's bizarre world. And that's a delight."
—*January Magazine*

Tachyon Publications
1459 18th Street #139
San Francisco, CA 94107
(415) 285-5615
www.tachyonpublications.com
tachyon@tachyonpublications.com

Series Editor: Jacob Weisman
Project Editor: Jill Roberts

ISBN 13: 978-1-61696-167-1

Printed in the United States of America by Worzalla

First Edition: 2014

9 8 7 6 5 4 3 2 1

THE CUTTING ROOM

DARK REFLECTIONS OF THE SILVER SCREEN

Ellen Datlow, Editor

TACHYON PUBLICATIONS

SAN FRANCISCO

ALSO EDITED BY ELLEN DATLOW

THE
CUTTING
ROOM

edited by Ellen Datlow

TSCONT

NTSCON

Acknowledgments

I'd like to thank Micaela Morrissette, Anna Tambour, Adam Nevill, and Stefan Dziemianowicz for their generous recommendations.

Also, thanks to Russell Farr, Jeremy Byrne, and Deborah Layne for ferreting out an electronic file of Howard Waldrop's story.

And thanks to Genevieve Valentine for her introduction and for her input regarding my preface.

Finally, thanks to Jacob Weisman and Jill Roberts at Tachyon.

INTRODUCTION
Genevieve Valentine

Horror always benefits from a certain kind of light. When Mary Shelley wrote *Frankenstein*, it was oil lamps. These days, it's the flickering dark of a movie theater. What is it that an audience of horror lovers craves?

Look no further than the camera.

Since the first nickelodeons, the development of motion pictures created a unique and influential visual language, a shorthand that has since played on film so often and for so long it's a dictionary of its own. Through the camera's eye, visual tropes became as eloquent as the inter-titles of dialogue. To iris in on a kissing couple meant their happiness was assured, but to linger on an open doorway was to invite trouble.

By now, the default state of the frame is suspense: show us a shot of an empty room, and we're already waiting for something to happen.

It's a long-established trick that horror directors figured out remarkably early. The first horror movie, the extremely short and incredibly goofy *Haunted Castle*, was made by director Georges Méliès before the turn of the twentieth century. (Setting a trend for horror flicks in the decades to come, it was almost immediately remade.)

Horror literature, designed to build dread on the page, developed its lexicon hand in hand with the emerging narrative technology of the movies. On both sides, the vocabulary of suspense changed and expanded in structure, imagery, and purpose.

And cinema's ability to translate fear on screen has created a stylistic feedback loop within horror, across all media. Any significant canon within a genre creates its own tropes, which increasingly enter the public discourse until they eventually become parodies of themselves. For a genre peopled with characters remarkably unaware of the dangers of splitting up in an abandoned castle, horror cinema is notoriously self-referential, from recreating individual camera shots to mocking tropes at work: one of the highest-grossing slasher flicks of all time is the semi-satirical *Scream*.

And in turn, the movies have become a fixture of horror literature itself. With a medium so inherently suspenseful, made through a fabulous alchemy into a series of atmospheric angles and special effects, horror writing could make good use of cinema's visual vocabulary and the beautiful artifice that modern readers can parse nearly as easily on the page as on the screen. (Scary stories about film itself were going to be inevitable.)

Horror literature skirts definition: varied in tone and subject, the horror aspect is often as much a mood as it is a chronicle of suspicious thumps. Still, it's interesting to trace signposts of the genre after movies swept the collective imagination. The visual lexicon of the movies helped contribute to a sea change in the consideration of brevity as literary merit; while Edgar Allan Poe and Stephen King are clearly from the same twisted branch of a single family tree, the effect of cinematic pacing and dialogue on their shared style of horror is evident in King's work.

And of course it has worked in the reverse, as works of horror are adapted to film by the dozen. Sometimes a film can even make the case for viewing a story as genre. Daphne Du Maurier isn't a writer traditionally thought of for writing horror, but when Alfred Hitchcock embraced the true scare potential of her story "The Birds," his film cemented the story as an iconic work of horror and reframed Du Maurier to later readers as a master of suspense.

Interestingly, for all their simpatico, the adaptation of horror to film is at times a tenuous proposition. Taking horror page to film is neither a foolproof formula nor an easy translation; horror literature is as open to interpretation as any other kind, and the same shorthand that makes film such an efficient conductor of narrative can trample some of the nuance that lives best in the written word. (In an ironic and ready example,

the thematic and psychological complexity of the first horror novel—
Frankenstein—has yet to be fully transported to the screen . . . unless one
were to combine individual elements from several different films.)

Sometimes, it turns out, only the written word will do. But with suspense
as an essential shared component of both dark cinema and dark literature,
and with the process of filmmaking being only a hairbreadth from the
supernatural, dark fiction can be a genre particularly suited for the silver
screen.

When it comes to horror, whether film is the medium or the subject,
there's always something sinister waiting just outside the frame.

PREFACE
Ellen Datlow

Everybody loves the movies. From the first moving picture publicly shown—a train running into the audience—the medium has maintained its hold on society's imagination. Writers have a complicated relationship with movies and moviemaking. Some write directly for the screen, others have had their work adapted for it, with mixed results. There have been many memoirs by screenwriters and other movie creators about their experiences in the industry, some positive, many negative. This might be primarily because while writing prose is generally a solo enterprise, writing for and working on movies is always a collaborative process, one during which compromises are made over and over again, often to the extent that the original piece of text that inspired the movie is unrecognizable to its author.

Surprisingly, there have been only a few major anthologies featuring movie horror and dark fantasy: the most prominent are David J. Schow's *Silver Scream*; *Midnight Premiere*, edited by Tom Piccirilli; *It Came from the Drive-In!*, edited by Norman Partridge and Martin H. Greenberg; and *The Hollywood Nightmare*, edited by Peter Haining.

Not only do I enjoy classic horror movies, but I've come to love stories about movies of all kinds, especially dark stories about the medium. The stories herein aren't about horror movies per se, although some of the classic horror movies and some imaginary horror movies do show up. *The Cutting Room* is more an exploration of the dark side of movies and

PREFACE

moviemaking, with views from both sides of the lens. As I was reading for this anthology, I became aware of several subgenres of movie stories:

The real life celebrity: What really happened to Marilyn Monroe or James Dean—were they murdered? Did they survive their supposed deaths?

Tales about actual, existing horror movies: The making of *King Kong*—with a sub-sub-genre about the fictional character Ann Darrow.

Protagonists or other characters who become part of a movie (by their own agency or not).

The effect of movies or a specific movie on the protagonist.

About the making of a movie (only sometimes of horror movies).

Protagonists obsessed with movies that may or may not exist.

In addition to the twenty-one reprints and two poems that I finally chose, I read more than 115 stories that were quite good, but just didn't make it into the mix. One story, "Tenderizer," by Stephen Graham Jones, appears for the first time.

Now, on with the show.

Ellen Datlow
November 7, 2013

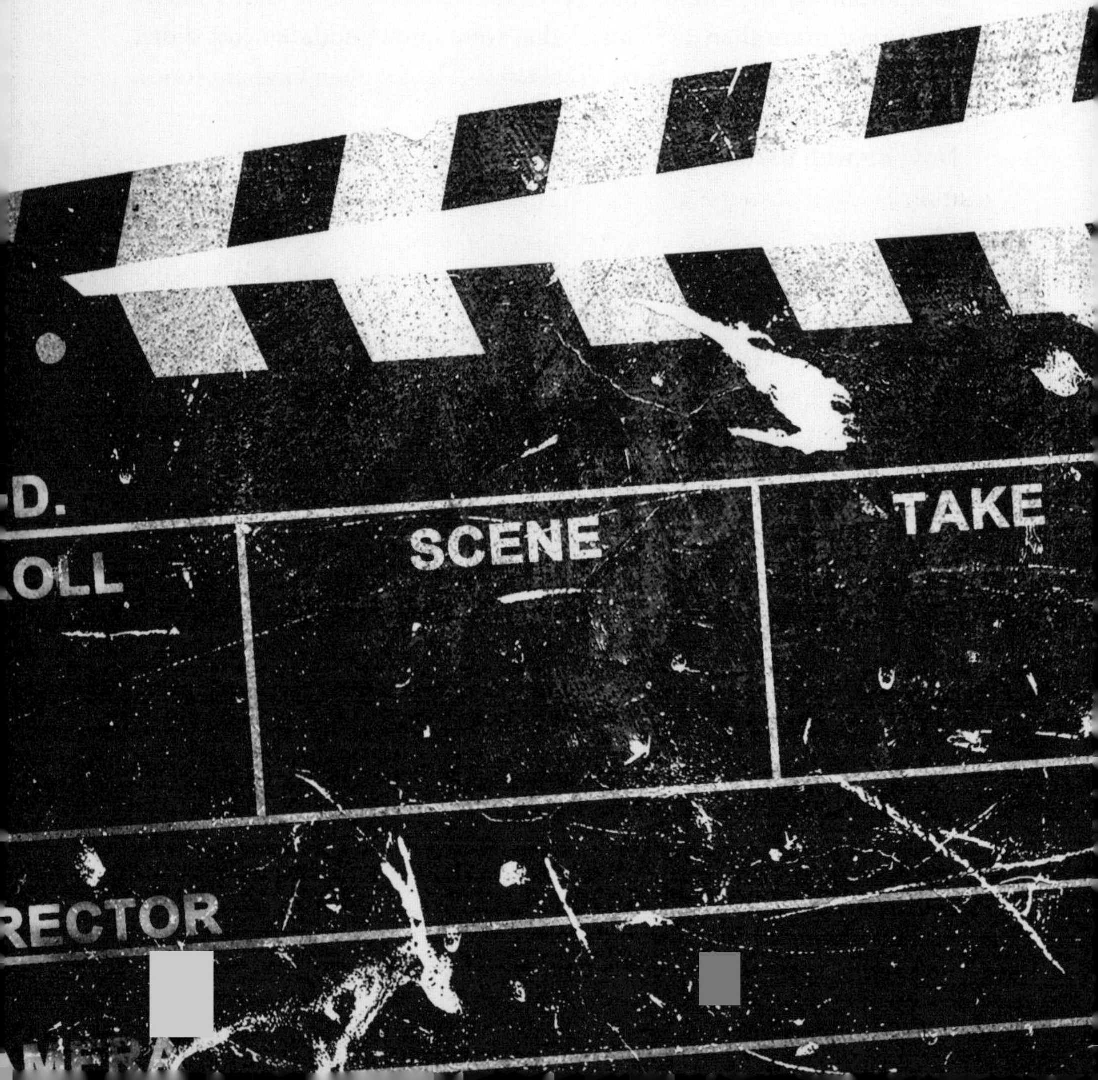
SCENE
TAKE

THE CUTTER
Edward Bryant

My memory is still intact. I remember the scene as well as I can recall any other episode from my childhood. The year was 1951 and I was six years old.

I was right there with the men—the scientists and the soldiers—as they cautiously crept through the dark, close tunnels of the Arctic base. The steady metronome of the Geiger counter clicked ever faster, eventually crackling into a ripping-canvas sound as the probe neared the metal storage locker.

Capt. Hendry paused a moment. The scientists, Carrington and Stern, exchanged glances. The tall, storklike newspaperman, Scotty, didn't look happy at all. The other men leveled their guns at the cabinet. There was something in there. Something from another world. It was ravenous for human blood, and it had already killed.

Capt. Hendry nodded. The man called Bob gingerly reached forward and flipped the door-catch. The locker opened as the music crashed to a climax and I jumped.

The frozen carcass of a sled dog rolled out and thudded to the floor. I stared. So did the men.

Dr. Stern looked disappointed. Dr. Carrington, I couldn't tell. Capt. Hendry smiled grimly and shrugged. Crossing to the other side of the room, he motioned for the rest of us to follow.

We were right behind him when he twisted the knob on the door to the next passageway. The door swung open without warning to reveal the creature standing on the other side. It raised its clawed hands and swiped at Capt. Hendry.

I wet my pants.

As I said before, it was 1951 and I was six. I hadn't read the publicity and hadn't heard Phil Harris sing about "The Thing" on the radio. I had never heard of John W. Campbell's story. I didn't care whether Christian Nyby or Howard Hawks had really directed.

All I knew was I had lived through a scene up on the flickering screen that had branded itself in my brain far deeper than anything that was to come until a few years later, when I sat in the same theater and watched Janet Leigh's dark blood swirl down the drain in *Psycho*.

Twenty years after I first saw it, I watched *The Thing* at a science fiction film festival in Los Angeles. I sat there as entranced as the first time, but now I didn't wet my pants. There was not even the temptation. The absolutely shocking scene I'd remembered wasn't there. Sure, there were the components—the dog falling out of the locker and the part where Kenneth Tobey's character opened the door to the greenhouse and there was the Thing waiting for him. But the juxtaposition that had left me with nightmares for months just wasn't there. I told a friend about it, but he laughed and reminded me that the human mind does that frequently with books and movies, not to mention the whole rest of human experience. We edit in our heads. We change things from reality. After a while, we accept the altered memories as gospel. It's a human thing.

Yeah. Right. What I didn't tell my friend was that I knew for a fact that I had once watched the scene I'd remembered. Frame for frame. I didn't tell him, but I'd known the man who'd re-edited the movie. Little had Hawks—or Nyby, for that matter—known. I used to work for that man. The cutter.

I had been there the final days. And worse, that last night.

"Well, Robby Valdez," said Mr. Carrigan. "You're early again." He paused and smiled. "You are always early."

I never knew what I was supposed to say, so I said nothing and simply stared down at my sneakers.

"So how's your family?" said Mr. Carrigan. My dad was still down in Cheyenne drooling over the new Ford Thunderbird he'd never be able to afford in a million years. He was supposed to be looking for work. I knew my mother was cleaning up after supper and thinking how much money she could win if she could just get on *The $64,000 Question*. My sister would be in her room listening to her Elvis Presley records and skipping her homework, humming through her cleft palate and dreaming of someone who would never want her. I had homework I needed to do, but I knew I'd rather be down here at the Ramona Theater helping out Mr. Carrigan. How was my sad family? Don't exaggerate, my mom would have cautioned me.

"Fine," I said.

Mr. Carrigan wasn't listening, not really. He was staring over my head and I guessed he was looking at the black crepe he'd draped over the posters for *East of Eden* and *Rebel Without a Cause*, bracketing the signed studio still of James Dean. "So senseless," he said softly. "Such a terrible waste."

"Did you ever do any work on those two movies?" I said, meaning the Dean pictures.

Mr. Carrigan looked mildly alarmed and darted quick looks around the lobby, but of course, there was no one here this early. The box office wasn't even open. The high school girl who ran the concession counter was probably still putting on her uniform and fixing her hair.

"Say nothing of that, Robby. It's our secret."

"Right," I said. I knew very well I was supposed to tell no one of Mr. Carrigan's genius for changing things. I never confided in anyone. Not even later, after the thing with Barbara Curtwood. After all, what good would it have done then?

"All right," said Mr. Carrigan. "Let's get to work. You get the fresh candy out of the storeroom and restock the counter. I've got things to do in the projection room." He smiled. "Oh, and I like the coonskin cap very much," he said.

"Davy Crockett," I said. "My aunt and uncle gave it to me. It's early Christmas."

"In September." Mr. Carrigan stopped smiling. "Thanks for reminding me. Barbara's birthday is soon. I should get her something nice."

I said nothing. I knew he was talking about Barbara Curtwood. He was in love with her. My mom talked about that. But then so did most of the people in town. Not about Mr. Carrigan and Barbara Curtwood, but about just her and how she ran around. She worked at the dress shop and spent—so my mom said to my dad—her nights either at the bars or somewhere else. I didn't know what the somewhere else was, because my mother's voice always dropped lower then and my father would laugh.

It hurt me to think about Mr. Carrigan and Miss Curtwood. Even at ten, I knew how much he loved her and how little she thought of him. About the only thing they had in common was the movies. She came to just about every show at the Ramona. Usually she came with a date. Every week or two, the man she came with would be someone brand new.

Even as young as I was, I had some idea that Mr. Carrigan was about the only man Miss Curtwood would have nothing to do with, and it pained him a lot. But he kept on. Sometimes he'd talk to me about it.

"Think she'd want a Davy Crockett cap?" I said. "I don't think she came to see *King of the Wild Frontier*."

Mr. Carrigan looked at me in a funny way. "I don't think so. Something a bit . . . more grown-up, perhaps." His mouth got a little pinched. "*King of the Wild Frontier*. Now *there* is a film I could have done something with."

"You didn't change it?"

He shook his head. "I was working on another project. A new thriller called *Tarantula*. I had to move the Disney film right along the circuit. But the monster movie, I was able to get my friend at the distributor's to send me a print early. I've been working on it."

"Oh boy," I said. "That's super. I've seen the ads for *Tarantula* in the *Rocky Mountain News*. I know it'll be good."

"It was good," said Mr. Carrigan. He looked down modestly. "Now it will be great."

"I'm sorry I can't think of anything right for Miss Curtwood," I said seriously.

"I'll come up with something." He went through the door to the projection room. I hauled a carton of stale Guess Whats over to the candy case.

———

It wasn't until I was an adult and moved away from my tiny hometown that I realized what a genius Mr. Carrigan must have been. Who else could have taken movies, including some really bad ones, and re-cut them into stranger, more ambitious forms? The score was sometimes a little choppy, but we were a small town and we didn't really notice or care. We were just there to be entertained. Little did we understand the novelty, the singularity of what we were seeing.

Nobody but me knew what Mr. Carrigan did. And nobody but me knew how he reversed all that work, re-editing the movies into their original form, painfully chopping and splicing the film back into the way it had been, more-or-less, and sending it on the bus to its next stop on the Wyoming small-town circuit.

I guess if he'd stayed in Hollywood, he could have become a star. I mean as a film editor. A cutter, he called it. But something had happened—I never knew what—and he'd come out here and started a whole new life. I always wanted to live in a small town, he'd told me. I'd grown up in one. I thought he was crazy for saying that. But he convinced me he was searching for the best of all possible worlds.

One thing about Mr. Carrigan, he was an optimist. That's what he called himself.

"Robby," he said to me many, many times. "You can alter reality. If you don't like the way things are, you can change them."

I remember I wanted to believe him. I wanted to change things, right enough. I wanted my dad not just to get a good job, but to keep it. I wanted my mom to get on a quiz show and win more than anybody. I thought, sometimes when I wasn't hating her, that I'd like my sister to be able to see Elvis on *The Ed Sullivan Show*. I mean *all* of Elvis, not just from the waist up like the camera showed. But I knew from a year of working after school and on weekends for Mr. Carrigan that it isn't often a person can really change things. And when you can edit something, sometimes the price is way too high.

We were showing a double feature of *Creature with the Atom Brain* and *It Came from Beneath the Sea* that Friday night. After Polly, the high school junior who was selling popcorn and candy, showed up and Mr. Carrigan turned on the marquee lights and people started lining up to get tickets, I stood off to the side in the lobby and just watched. I was supposed to be an usher if some of the older patrons needed help finding their seats. I didn't think this double feature would bring in a lot of old people.

There were some parents and a number of grown-ups who weren't here with kids at all. They were mostly talking about "Ike." I knew vaguely that President Eisenhower had suffered a heart attack and was in a hospital down in Denver. It made me feel sort of strange to know that the president of the whole United States was just a hundred seventy miles south of me.

Tonight people were wearing jackets. This September was more like autumn than Indian summer.

I noticed that the man with Barbara Curtwood had on a leather jacket that must have come off two or three calves. He was a big man and it was a large jacket. I didn't recognize him, which was a surprise since just about everybody in this town knew everybody else. Anyhow, he bought the tickets, escorted Miss Curtwood to the line at the concession counter, and then went into the men's room.

I realized Mr. Carrigan was standing right beside me. "Tell Polly to give Miss Curtwood her candy for free. Her soda too. Whatever she wants."

I stared up at him.

"Now. Do it."

I did it.

Miss Curtwood got a large Coke, a giant popcorn, and a roll of Necco Wafers. She didn't even blink when Polly told her it was a present from Mr. Carrigan. She turned from the counter, walking right by him, saying absolutely nothing.

"Barbara," Mr. Carrigan said.

She stopped dead still.

"Your birthday is coming up."

"So?" she said, staring down at him. She shook her hair back. Miss Curtwood was a funny kind of blonde. My mom said it came out of a bottle. She was tall and had what my friends later in junior high called "big tits." Tonight she was dressed in a checkered skirt with a white blouse and pink sweater. Some people thought she was pretty. Me, I wasn't so sure. There was something about her that made me want to run. She reminded me of the cruel witch in *Snow White*. The hair color was wrong, but maybe if the witch had bleached it—

Mr. Carrigan smiled at her. "I thought maybe—if you weren't doing anything—well, perhaps on your birthday we might have supper at the Dew Drop Inn."

Miss Curtwood actually giggled. Some of the people waiting to get popcorn stared. "You're kidding," she said, a little too loud.

"Actually," said Mr. Carrigan, "I'm not."

"You're at least ten years older than I am."

Mr. Carrigan smiled. "Perhaps twelve."

"You're an old pervert." More people stared.

Mr. Carrigan was starting to turn red. "I think I'd better go see about preparing the projectors."

Miss Curtwood sneered at him. "Nothing will change, you old creep."

People in the lobby started to mumble to one another. Parents hurried their children past the popcorn and into the theater.

"*Anything* can be changed," said Mr. Carrigan.

"Not how I feel about you."

"Even you could change."

"Not a chance," she said venomously.

"Something wrong, sweetheart?" It was the big man, her date, back from the bathroom. "Is this old square bothering you?"

"He owns the theater," I squeaked. Both of them glanced down at me.

"Go inside and see if anyone needs help finding seats," Mr. Carrigan said to me.

I looked from Miss Curtwood and the big man to Mr. Carrigan and back again.

"*Now.* I'll talk with you after the show." His voice was firm. I did as I was told. I noticed that Miss Curtwood and the man came into the auditorium about three minutes later. They took the stairs up to the balcony. The man was red-faced. Miss Curtwood had tight hold of his arm. The people downstairs pointed and whispered to each other.

I was glad when the lights went down, the curtains parted, and the previews of coming attractions began. But somehow I knew that when the double feature was over, I'd have a special mess to clean up by the big man's seat. There was. The floor was sticky with Coke, and bits of popcorn were scattered all over. Along with all the rest of it, there was something strange, half-covered by the Necco wrapper. It was like a deflated balloon, five or six inches long, with something gooey inside. I didn't want to touch it, so I used the candy wrapper to pick it up and put it in the trash. I also suspected I shouldn't ask Mr. Carrigan about it, although I thought I saw him watching me as I looked at the thing. But he didn't say anything.

After I'd finished cleaning up, Mr. Carrigan asked me to come to his office. He looked older. I'd never stopped to wonder before just how old he was. At that point in my life, I thought all adults were ancient. But now I realized Mr. Carrigan was at least as old as my father. He walked with a stoop I hadn't noticed before. He moved slowly, as though he were in pain. He asked me if I wanted a Coca-Cola. I shook my head. He asked me to sit down. I took the metal folding chair. He sat down then too, on the other side of the desk, and looked at me for a long minute across the heaps of paper, splicing equipment, film canisters, and the cold, half-filled coffee cups.

"I really love her, you know."

I looked back at him dumbly. Why was he telling me this?

"Miss Curtwood. Barbara. You know who I'm talking about."

I nodded, but still said nothing.

"Do you think I'm not entirely rational about this all?"

I kept perfectly still.

Mr. Carrigan grimaced. "I know I'm not. It's an obsession. I have no explanation for it. All I know is what I feel for Barbara is love that transcends easy explanation—or perhaps *any* explanation at all." He put his elbows on the cluttered desk, laced his fingers, and set his chin in the cradle. "She's not even what I want. Not really. I would prefer her to be shorter and more delicate. She's not. I love red-headed women. Barbara is a blonde. She is far too—" Mr. Carrigan hesitated "—far too buxom. And there is more which is less apparent. Barbara wished to have no children. She told me this. I would like a family, but—" He closed his eyes. I wondered if he was going to cry. He didn't, but he kept his eyes closed for a long time. "She is everything I should loathe, yet I find myself fatally attracted."

Another minute went by. Two. I stirred restlessly on the hard metal seat.

Mr. Carrigan looked up. "Ah, Robby. I'm sorry I'm keeping you. I simply needed to talk, and you are my only friend." He smiled. "Thank you very much."

"You're welcome," I said automatically, not really understanding what I had done for him.

"I'm going to see Barbara on her birthday," he said, still smiling. "She said so tonight."

"I'm glad," I managed to say, wondering if I should be crossing my fingers for him.

"Life is strange, isn't it, Robby?" Mr. Carrigan stayed seated and motioned me toward the door. "If you wait long enough, you can change things the way you want. If you want things badly enough. If you're willing to do what needs to be done."

Later, I tried to remember back, listening in my memory to tell if his voice had sounded odd. It hadn't, not as best I could recall. Mr. Carrigan had sounded cheerful, as happy as I'd ever heard him.

"She's going to stay after the last show on her birthday. And then we will go to the Dew Drop Inn for a late supper. She told me so. When her—friend—tried to argue, she told him to shut up, that she knew her mind and this was what she wanted to do. I must admit it, I was amazed." The smile spread across his face, the muscles visibly relaxing. He looked straight at me. "Thank you, Robby."

"For what?" I said, a little bewildered.

"For seeing me like this. For being someone who saw my happiness and will remember it."

I was *very* bewildered now.

"Good night, Robby. Please convey my best to your family."

I knew I was dismissed and so I left, mumbling a still-confused good night.

All these years later, I've come to live in Los Angeles, and it's where I'll probably die. Southern California drew me away from my small town. It must have been the movies. I walk Hollywood Boulevard, ignore the sleaze, the tawdriness, and pretend I move among myths. I tread Sunset and sometimes stop to look inside the windows of the restaurants and the shops. I soak up the sun, even while realizing that the smog-refracted rays must surely be mutating my tissues into something other than the flesh I grew up in.

No one ever sees me, but I realize that must be because they are akin to the figures moving on the flickering screen and I am the audience. But I am not only the audience, I control the projector. And, like Mr. Carrigan, I am the cutter.

Miss Curtwood's birthday was Friday, the first night of *Tarantula*. The crowd was large, but I didn't notice. I was just impatient to see everyone seated so that I could take my place in the far back row of the theater and watch the magic wand of the projector beam inscribe pictures on the screen.

I did see Miss Curtwood come down the sidewalk to the Ramona. I knew a ticket was waiting in her name at the box office. She was by herself.

Her friend, the big man in the leather jacket, arrived ten minutes later, just before the previews started. He sat on the other side of the theater from Miss Curtwood. I noticed. I saw Mr. Carrigan paying attention to that too.

Then *Tarantula* started. I forgot about everything else until the movie was done. When the jet pilots—Clint Eastwood, John Wayne, and the others—were strafing the giant spider, the Russians could have dropped their H-bombs and I wouldn't have noticed.

The lights came up and the crowd seemed happy enough. I know I was. The people drifted out and I lost track of the big man and his leather jacket. Miss Curtwood was one of the last to get up and leave.

She saw me and came across the row. "Where is Mr. Carrigan's office?"

"Back down the hall past the women's restroom, just before the door for the supply room." I pointed.

"This is very important," said Miss Curtwood. "Tell Mr. Carrigan to come to the office in twenty minutes. No more, no less. Do you understand?"

"I guess so."

"Do you or don't you?" Her voice was hard. Her blue eyes looked like chips of ice.

"Yes," I said.

"Then go and tell him."

I found Mr. Carrigan out in the lobby holding the door for the last of the patrons. I said to him what Miss Curtwood had told me to say.

"I see," said Mr. Carrigan. Then he told me to go home.

"But what about the cleaning?" I said.

"Tomorrow will be soon enough."

"But the pop," I said, "will be all hardened on the floor."

"The floor," said Mr. Carrigan, "needs a good mopping anyway."

"But—"

"Go," said Mr. Carrigan firmly.

I left, but something made me wait just down the block. I watched from the shadows between dim streetlights as Mr. Carrigan locked the lobby doors. The marquee light blinked off. Then the lights in the lobby. Another minute passed. A second.

I heard something that sounded like gunshots, five of them. Somehow I knew they were shots, even though they were muffled, sounding nothing like what I'd heard in westerns and cops-and-robbers movies.

For a moment, I didn't know what to do. Then I went down to the alley and felt my way through the trashcans and stacked empty boxes to the Ramona's rear emergency exit. As usual, the latch hadn't completely caught and so I slipped in. Past the heavy drapes, the inside of the auditorium was completely dark. I walked up the aisle, somehow sure I should make no noise. At the top of the inclined floor, I looked down the corridor and saw light spilling from Mr. Carrigan's office.

I called his name. No one answered.

"Mr. Carrigan?" I said again.

This time a figure stepped from the office into the light. It was him. "What are you doing here, Robby?"

"I heard something weird. It sounded like shots."

Mr. Carrigan looked very pale. The skin of his face was drawn tight across the bones. "They were shots, Robby."

"What happened?" I said. "Do you need some help?"

"No," he answered. "I need no help at all, but thank you anyway." He smiled in a funny sort of way.

"What do you want me to do?"

"Go home," he said. He looked suddenly tired. "Go home and call the sheriff and tell him to come down here to the theater right away. Can you do that?"

"Yes," I said without hesitation.

"*Will* you do that?"

"Yes."

"That's good. That's very good." He started to turn back through the pooled light and into the office again, but hesitated. "Robby, remember what I've said so many times about how you can change things for the better?"

"Yes," I said again.

"Well, you can. Remember that." And then he was gone.

I stared at the wedge of light for a few seconds and then walked back toward the rear of the theater. I didn't go outside. Instead, I just sat behind the screen, there on the dirty wooden floor, thinking about the larger-than-life figures I'd seen dance above me so many times.

After ten or fifteen minutes, I heard another shot. This time it was louder, but I guess that's because I was inside the theater.

I slowly walked back up the aisle. Once I'd reached the corridor, I turned toward the light. I looked inside. Then I went out to the lobby and put a nickel in the pay phone and called the sheriff. I didn't want to phone him from Mr. Carrigan's office.

My parents didn't want me to hear what was decided in the coroner's report, but that didn't matter because it was all over town. And besides, I'd seen it, and even at ten, I could figure some of it out.

Miss Curtwood had gone to Mr. Carrigan's office as she'd said she would, but she had been joined by the big man with the leather jacket. They had taken everything off, the jacket, her dress, everything. They had lain down on the desk together, after shoving all the things lying on it to the floor.

When Mr. Carrigan came into his office, they were both there to moan and laugh at him.

If Mr. Carrigan had laughed too, there was no way of telling. But the sheriff did know Mr. Carrigan had taken a .45 revolver out of a desk drawer and fired five times. Some minutes later, he had pulled the trigger a sixth time, this time with the muzzle tight against his right eye.

That was just before I'd phoned.

What I knew, and what none of the other kids at school knew, not even the sheriff's bratty daughter, was that most people in town didn't know everything that must have been in the coroner's report originally.

I remembered everything in detail, like a picture on the screen. I didn't know what it all meant, most of it, until long after. But the images were sharp and clear, waiting for my eventual knowledge.

The first thing I saw when I poked my head through the light outside the office doorway was the big man and Mr. Carrigan, each of them lying in blood with parts of their heads gone. But what I really remember was Miss Curtwood.

Now I know truly how much she had become as Mr. Carrigan really wanted her. Her hair was no longer blonde. It was wet and red. She was not a buxom woman any longer. Nor was she tall. Mr. Carrigan had carefully arranged her legs, but you couldn't ignore the sections that had been removed.

There were other changes I hadn't realized he had wanted.

September evenings are never as crisp and chilly in Los Angeles as they are back home. I miss that.

I just got back from visiting my sister and her family. After Mom and Dad died, she moved out here and married a guy who works at some plant out in Garden Grove. They have a son and a daughter. The son is what the doctors call disturbed. He goes to special classes, but mainly he sits alone in his room. God only knows what he thinks. The daughter has run away from home three times. The first time, they found her at Disneyland; the last two times, with one guy or another in the Valley. The family pictures look like my sister and me as kids.

Everything reminds me of something or someone else.

I bought a .45 revolver just like the one Mr. Carrigan kept in his desk.

There are times I carry it with me to the movies. I sit in the back row and wonder whether the things I see on the screen are edited just as the director planned. Then I go back to my Hollywood apartment and try to sleep. I am the cutter of my own dreams. The fantasies here have never worked out as I'd hoped.

Sometimes I think about changing my sister's life. And perhaps my own as well. After all, our parents' lives became better, thanks to a late-model T-bird and a drunken real-estate developer. With no dreams left to search for, I have only nightmares to anticipate.

The Thing waits for me on the other side of the door.

That which I've never told anyone. The knowledge that behind every adult smile is an ivory rictus. Skeletal hardness underlies the warm flesh. My mother told all her friends I was such a *happy* child. Anyone can be wrong.

I feel like I've built a cage of my own bones.

Mr. Carrigan was right, of course, in the final and most profound analysis. You *can* make anything better. Life can be changed. It can become death.

(for Warren Zevon)

THE HANGED MAN OF OZ
Steve Nagy

*K*nee-high grass dominated the scene, thick blades uprooting the foundation of a sagging cabin, pushing aside cobbles in the shaded road. Trees circled the clearing and an abandoned orchard lay behind the cabin, straight rows masked by weeds and windrows of dead leaves and forgotten fruit.

A pastoral display except for the people posed throughout—two middle-aged men, one dressed as a hobo, the second clad in a dirty threadbare uniform; an old woman sporting too much rouge and mascara, skinny legs visible beneath the hem of a little girl's dress; and a dead man, hanging from a tree, his feet twitching at odd moments in time with some unheralded tune raised by the wind whistling through the forest.

Obsession is an art form.

And if you're lucky it's contagious.

Denise and I got together for dinner and drinks at her place. Our first date, although we saw each other in the apartment hall every day. I lived in 2B. She had moved into 2C in February. I'd made great strides, starting with an occasional nod and shared rides to work. I'd eventually thrown out an off-the-cuff comment about her hair, which she'd shorn from its ponytail length to a flapper-style skullcap. Guys should notice changes like that; it's an easy way to score points.

15

After that first compliment, the progression from casual to intimate was natural. We left in the morning at the same time, talked about our days, compared notes on work. If you practice something enough, anything is possible. I knew the boy-next-door routine better than when to observe national holidays. And the Fourth of July doesn't change from year to year.

Besides dinner and drinks, Denise made me sit down and watch *The Wizard of Oz*.

"You've seen this before, Michael?"

"Lots of times," I said. "Not lately, though. Isn't it usually on around Easter?"

"Until recently," Denise said. "Ted Turner bought the rights and pulled it for theatrical release."

Oz? God save me. I already regretted the date and struggled to keep an interested expression as Denise gave me the inside scoop. It was like a psychotic version of *Entertainment Tonight*.

When I was in college I worked at a greasy spoon as a busboy. The chef was a compact Italian named Ricky Silva who came across as uneducated, unhealthy, and gullible. I stayed late one night, and I found Silva pouring over a stamp collection in a back booth. I questioned him about it, saying something crass because the idea of Silva as a philatelist didn't match my preconceptions. He told me there were an infinite number of worlds. Each existed next to the other, always overlapping and occasionally intertwining. Learning about his deeper reality forced me to change my opinion of him.

Denise and *Oz* were like that. The places she went and the things she did contained wholly unexpected layers. Up until now I'd only seen her "hallway" face.

But I wasn't in Kansas anymore.

The trivia litany went like this:

Buddy Ebsen—the original Tin Man—almost died from pneumonia, suffering a bad reaction to aluminum dust from his makeup, which let Jack Haley jump into his metal shoes.

The Cowardly Lion's costume was so hot Bert Lahr passed out at least a dozen times.

The Munchkins raised so much holy hell on the set that Chevy Chase mined that aspect for *Under the Rainbow*.

Shirley Temple led the pack for Dorothy's role. Probably because everyone considered Judy Garland too old and a poor box-office draw. The movie lost money, costing about $4.6 million and earning only $4 million the first time out.

Studio executives cut a groundbreaking dance number that showcased Ray Bolger. They believed audiences wouldn't sit through a "children's movie" if it was too long.

Faulty special effects burned Margaret Hamilton at the end of her first scene as the Wicked Witch. This was shortly after Garland arrived in Oz. Hamilton tried grabbing the ruby slippers, but was thwarted by the Good Witch, an actress named Billie Burke. Hamilton dropped below the stage and right into a badly timed burst of smoke and flame. . . .

It went on and on and on, everything you never wanted to know. Peccadilloes, idiosyncrasies; in other words, crap.

Then Denise told me a story about the man who hanged himself during filming—and she claimed the final print showed the incident.

"What? You're kidding me. I've never seen a dead guy."

Denise licked her lips, imitating a poorly belled cat. "Not everybody does. It's like those 3-D pictures where you cross your eyes."

"Prove it."

Denise paused the video. On screen, Dorothy and the Scarecrow were in the midst of tricking the trees into giving up their apples, frozen seconds before stumbling across the Tin Man.

"It's at the end of this section. I'll run it through once at regular speed. Let me know if you catch it."

She hit PLAY. Dorothy and the Scarecrow freed the Tin Man, did a little song-and-dance, fought off the Wicked Witch, and continued their trek. I didn't see anything strange and shrugged when Denise paused it.

"Nothing, right?" She rewound the tape to a point immediately after the witch disappeared in a cloud of red-orange smoke (this time minus the hungry flames), then advanced the video frame by frame.

Our date had progressed from strange to surreal, and I couldn't wait for an excuse to leave.

Then I saw *him*—the hanged man.

Dorothy, the Scarecrow, and the Tin Man skipped down the road. Before the scene cut away to the Cowardly Lion's forest, the jerky movement of the advancing frames highlighted activity inside the forest edge.

A half-shadowed figure moved in the crook of a tree about ten feet off the ground. I thought it might be one of the many birds spread throughout the clearing and around the cabin, but its shape looked too much like a man. The next frame showed him jumping from his perch. His legs were stiff, as if bound. Or maybe determination wouldn't let him go all loose and disjointed at this defining moment. Before his feet touched the ground, they wrenched to the right. Whatever held him to the upper branches swung his ill-lit body back into the shadows. I think I heard his neck snap, although with the tape playing at this speed there wasn't any sound. Even at regular speed I knew the only sound would come from the three actors, voicing in song their desire to see the Wizard.

My heart raced and for a minute I worried that its syncopated thrum might attract the Tin Man, prompting him to step into the apartment and take it for his own.

"I can't believe it," I said. "It's a snuff film."

"Awesome, isn't it?" Denise restarted the film. I couldn't picture her smile as kind; it seemed too satisfied. "I stay awake some nights," she said, "letting my mind experience what it was like. The studio buried the whole thing. Can you imagine the bad press? I even think Garland started drinking because of it."

On the television screen, Bert Lahr made his appearance. His growls matched the rough nature of Denise's monologue. As the film continued I offered small talk, made Denise vague promises that I would see her in the morning, and left as the credits rolled.

"I feel as if I've known you all the time, but I couldn't have, could I?"

"I don't see how. You weren't around when I was stuffed and sewn together, were you?"

"And I was standing over there rusting for the longest time. . . ."

I knew I was asleep, sprawled on my couch. The past five days had stretched me to the limit. I always had a headache. Aspirin and whiskey didn't kill the pain. My conversations with Denise were forced; she mentioned the movie at every opportunity.

We'd had a second date. I agreed because Denise invited two friends from her work. Stan and Lora were smokers, rail-thin and shrouded in a pall of smoke. I think Denise brought them along (one) so she could look good in contrast and (two) so she had some place to hide if things went sour. We hit a club and during a busy night on the dance floor I demonstrated I wasn't a klutz. I guess you could say it was the modern social equivalent of an army physical. Denise and Lora exchanged approving nods near the end and Stan loosened up enough so that he took a minute between shots of tequila and his chain-smoking to talk to me.

Between all the alcohol and nicotine, I got a contact buzz and found myself obsessing about the hanged man and the way he disappeared into the shadows. Denise was still attractive to me, but I couldn't forget how pleased she'd looked as she talked about the death.

My thoughts hid me beside the Tin Man's cabin, watching the trio skip past. I would move onto the road. The hanged man was visible ahead. They must have turned their eyes to follow the road as it bent to the right, because they didn't see him.

But I did.

Denise had seemed like her old self in the mixed company, and I assumed I was overreacting. So I agreed to a third date. Instead of a rerun with the mystery man in the trees, I got Stan and Lora again and a nice restaurant. I was almost happy when I saw their wan faces.

Almost. Denise and Lora left to powder their noses, and Stan asked me a question.

"How did you like the movie?"

"What?"

"You know what I mean. You look like you haven't had a good night's sleep in a while."

"How do you know that?"

"Denise is predictable. I'd be more surprised if she hadn't shown you the film yet."

I gulped my beer. "You've . . . seen him?"

Stan shrugged. "What about it?"

"The guy hanged himself. She seems so glad."

"Someone dies somewhere every second. Get used to it. Life will get a lot easier if you do."

Before I could ask what he meant, Denise and Lora returned from the bathroom.

I had the dream again the next night. It started at the same point. The Tin Man finished his dance, stumbled off the road, collapsed in a heap on a tree stump near the cabin. The others rushed to his side, Technicolor concern painting their expressions.

No one noticed me. I couldn't hear everything they said. It *did* seem to change night to night, probably because I couldn't remember the dialogue verbatim.

The Wicked Witch screeched at the three adventurers from her perch on the roof above, surprising me again. I crouched and prayed she wouldn't see me. She tossed a fireball at the Scarecrow and even from this distance I felt the heat. The Tin Man smothered the flames under his funnel hat, but not before the silver paint bubbled and blistered on the edge of his hat and on several of his fingers.

The Wicked Witch took off on her broom. Smoke billowed like a tumor in her wake. No trapdoors this time; my position offered an excellent view behind the cabin. Her flight left a rough scar across the sky that traced the road's path toward the Emerald City and beyond to the land of the Winkies.

"I wonder how many she'll kill when she gets home?"

I jumped from my crouch. The Scarecrow stood beside me. Dorothy and the Tin Man remained in the road. Instead of the concern I'd seen earlier, they appeared curious.

"What are you doing?" I glanced toward the trees. The Hanged Man swung from his rope, as solid as a mirage, flirting with the shadows. I turned back to the Scarecrow. "You're supposed to be on your way to the Emerald City."

The Scarecrow, who looked less and less like Bolger, dropped his gaze and shrugged. The simple gesture produced a sound reminiscent of dead leaves. "I'm not supposed to tell you," he said, his words more rustle than speech.

Dorothy and the Tin Man, poor doubles for Garland and Haley, edged toward the bend. "We have to go, Scarecrow," the not-Garland said. "There's not much time left and we're expected."

The Scarecrow joined them. "I'm not supposed to tell you, Michael," he repeated. "Talk to Stan." He glanced towards the trees one last time as he and his companions moved away. "Stay away from the Hanged Man."

I woke drenched with sweat. I don't know what happened after the three left. Maybe they found the Cowardly Lion, became a quartet, maybe not.

Stay away from the Hanged Man.

Even the memory of those words hurt.

Talk to Stan.

What was I involved in here? Were my dreams random subconscious processes? Talk to Stan? I didn't even know his last name. Denise introduced him by first name. I only knew Denise's—Fleming—because the apartment glued labels to the lobby mailboxes. When we met, we exchanged greetings and first names. Surnames never came into it because right from the start we were always personal.

Hours remained until dawn. I left the apartment and hit Kroger. The big grocery on Carpenter stayed open all night—and its video selection included *The Wizard of Oz*.

I wanted a copy because . . . because I wanted privacy. I'd need Denise soon enough to find Stan, if I gathered the courage necessary to broach the subject. The Hanged Man was a drug and I was a junkie. If I had my own copy, I might control the addiction. I'd first seen him with Denise and everything stemmed from that. I'd entered one of Silva's infinite worlds; privacy might let me create a new perspective.

The shadowed streets looked different than they did during the day.

The late-night wind didn't touch the trees. Each moved on its own, apple hoarders, ready for a rematch.

"Just wait," a voice rasped beside me. "It gets worse."

I shouted and slammed the brakes. My car swerved, shuddered to a halt, and stalled. I turned and found myself facing the Scarecrow.

"What do you . . . what do you want?" I tried sounding angry, but my voice shook.

My Scarecrow smiled and the maw formed by his mouth—old burlap, leather, and rotting hay—made my stomach turn. "I won't hurt you, Michael." He nodded toward the back. "But I can't speak for her."

I twisted in my seat and craned to look. A shape huddled there, its outline weird and broken by too many angles. I fumbled to turn on the overhead dome light, but the person in the back actually *cackled*, and I leaped from the car and into the deserted street.

I tripped before I'd gone half a dozen steps. Scrambling up, I looked over my shoulder, expecting pursuit—and saw nothing. The door was open and the dome light revealed the empty interior. The only sound was the chime that signaled the keys were still in the ignition.

This isn't happening, I told myself. *The Scarecrow was in the passenger seat and the Witch—yes, the Witch—was in the back.*

A soft noise broke the breathless silence. I saw something slowly swinging in the tree shadows across the way. I knew the noise was a rope creaking under the strain of a dead man's weight. I retreated to my car, more scared of what hid outside than of my elusive passengers.

The residential speed limit was twenty-five. I did at least fifty and ran every red light getting home.

Two hours more till dawn.

I shredded the box wrap and popped the tape into my VCR. My head throbbed with too many ideas, as if I'd overdosed on coffee and Tylenol. I let it play and tried to clear my mind. I tried to tell myself there was no place like Oz. And this time the scene ran the same as I remembered it from my childhood.

The Tin Man stumbled and landed on the tree stump. Dorothy and the

Scarecrow ran over to help. The Wicked Witch made her threats, threw her fireball, bolted in a puff of smoke. The three adventurers danced off down the road.

There wasn't any sign of the Hanged Man.

There was movement among the trees, but I could see it was a long-necked bird moving one of its wings. Was there something different on Denise's tape? I didn't consider myself gullible. Because I didn't trust my eyes, I rewound the tape and played it again, cursing myself for doing that.

The Tin Man collapsed on the tree stump. But he didn't resemble Haley. His fingers and hat were burned, warped by some tremendous heat, even though the fireball lay moments in the future. Dorothy and the Scarecrow ran to help him. But she looked middle-aged and the Scarecrow was the rotting bag from my car. Once, all three stared at me. The screen thinned to gauze as thin as the dust coating its surface.

And the Wicked Witch screamed to life on the roof—a gangrenous, misshapen version of Denise.

I stopped the tape.

I waited in my car for two hours before Denise exited the apartment. I didn't want to meet her in the hall. She had started the avalanche of fear that buried my senses, and I wasn't ready for a confrontation.

Stay away from the Hanged Man.

Talk to Stan. . . .

I stayed at least a block behind her. She worked at a department store in the mall and liked to arrive early. I parked in the side lot. She was inside by the time I walked to the front entrance. I hovered there, wondering if I was too late. Entering the store wasn't an option. If Denise caught me inside, I didn't have any excuses. She'd know I'd followed her. Besides, I worked at a union job shop, creating ads on a computer, and I caught hell when I missed a shift.

Ten minutes later, Stan entered the lot.

I ran over and hovered as he locked his car. I'm not sure what I expected from him.

"I need help," I said.

"What are you doing here, Michael? Don't you have to work?"

"I'm taking a sick day."

Stan nodded, lit up a cigarette. I could blame my imagination, but I thought his hands shook. "So? What are you doing here?" he asked again. He didn't seem in any hurry to get to work.

"The Scarecrow told me to talk to you."

Stan didn't laugh. His mouth twitched, though.

"You know about it."

He shoved past me. "You're crazy," he said, walking briskly towards the store.

I followed, grabbed his arm. I glanced around the lot to see if anyone was watching. No one was close.

"Don't call me crazy," I said. "The Scarecrow popped in and out of my car like a damned ghost and he brought the Wicked Witch along for the ride and I'm scared. This is all Denise's fault, and you know something. You asked me about the movie. Don't dare tell me you don't know what I'm talking about."

Stan jabbed his lit cigarette against my hand as I held his arm. I jerked it away, hissed with pain, put my mouth over the burn. Stan backed up and pinned a sneer on his pale face.

"Get away from me, Michael." He paused. "If you don't, I'll tell Denise."

I stood there, silent, and watched him leave.

This time I observed the speed limit on my way home. A ghostly Dorothy rode shotgun this time. Toto sat in her lap. I didn't recall seeing the mutt before. A taxidermist had worked him over, mounting him to a wood base, so he traveled well, no tongue flapping out the window, no prancing from one side to the other, nails digging into your thighs. The Scarecrow and the Tin Man held the rear seats.

All four were quiet, which didn't bother me. Maybe the daylight silenced them. I parked in my slot, killed the engine. When I climbed out, chaff and aluminum dust and the ripe scent of a dead dog floated through the empty interior.

The apartment hall was empty. I pressed my hands against the cold surface of Denise's door. The number and letter glimmered as each reflected the fluorescent light, incandescent with a promise like prophecy. I knew now that I *wanted* to see. The knowledge might release me.

My fingers ached where I touched the door, as if the wood sucked at my bones, robbing them of warmth. The 2C pulsed and my breath frosted the air, crystallizing inside my chest until I forgot to breathe.

Then my legs buckled under fatigue and gravity, and the door answered my weakness with its own, selling its solid soul so I could fall through into the reality that lay beyond.

Dry grass rustled beneath me as I fell to my knees. A brick-paved road ran past, its surface a river of yellow pus baked solid under a neon-strobe sun. Disease festered in the scabbed cracks, more efficient as a contagion than as mortar.

The Tin Man's cabin sat across from me, wearing its abandonment like a badge. The logs sagged, eaten by dry rot and unable to sustain their weight. Years had passed since glass sealed the windows and thick cobwebs, choked with dead insects, served as the only curtains. The stone chimney wore moss and ivy like a fur coat, its only protection against the cold. Large gaps riddled the roof's green slate like open sores. In the places where there were not yet holes the sun glinted off shallow pools of water.

I stood and crossed the road, glancing left and right along its bumpy length—no one was visible in either direction. Not the intrepid trio or their hanged observer.

Light fell through the rear windows and the roof, illuminating the room. The sun had almost died in the west, but it was enough so I could pick out the familiar details of Denise's apartment.

From the front window to the door, I picked out the vague outlines of furniture. A mildewed couch slumped on broken legs. Two rickety crates supported several planks that served as a table, with an apish skull still wearing shreds of flesh as a centerpiece. Instead of the entertainment center, a cauldron sat before the fireplace, its mealy contents still bubbling.

A mask hung above the mantle like a trophy stuffed and mounted by a hunter. The facial lines were soft, cheeks frozen in a perpetual smile, spawning dimples on both corners. But the eyes were empty and soulless, the mouth a toothless hole, and they sucked away whatever resemblance to humanity the mask ever possessed.

It was Denise.

I backed away from the cabin, dazed by what I'd seen. Before I knew it, I'd crossed the road to my original entry point, just as a dark shape moved across the cabin roof, catching my eye. The Wicked Witch froze, straddling the peak like an Impressionist vision of the Statue of Liberty, broom held high in place of a torch.

"It took you long enough, Michael," she said, her smile as uneven as the road. "I thought I'd need to send someone out after you again."

"I don't know what you're thinking, Denise, but I'm finished with these dreams."

She cackled. "Stubborn to a fault, Michael. I love that. The longer you doubt, the closer I get. Eventually, it will be too late. . . ."

I walked towards the cabin, my first steps tentative as loose bricks threatened to turn my ankles. I stopped once, crouched, pulled one broken piece loose, steeled myself against the slimy feel as I clenched it in my fist. I needed a weapon. I didn't think this ball-sized brick would hurt her, but it might serve as a distraction.

"You're right. I don't believe." Debris littered the yard between the cabin and the road and matched the landscape of my chaotic dreams. "You've drugged or hypnotized me. Whichever, I don't care. It's over."

From behind the trees the Scarecrow moved into the clearing. Dorothy and the Tin Man skulked in his shadow.

"Calling in your troops, Denise?" I asked.

Age lines shredded each of their faces, changing grins into something as old as the brown apples piled under the trees, something as calculated as the way the trees' prehensile branches reached out, straining against the roots that kept each woody demon in place.

"Her name isn't Denise," said the Tin Man, brandishing an axe that looked freshly honed. "I don't think she has one."

"Names don't matter here," the Scarecrow said.

"Is that why you told me to talk to Stan?"

The Scarecrow cringed, glanced at the Wicked Witch. His companions backed away. I looked at the Wicked Witch too, expecting her to nail his straw frame with a quick fireball.

"You warned him?" she asked.

"No! No! I was trying to prepare him!"

The Wicked Witch leaped off the roof, black dress billowing behind her like crows hovering around a fresh kill. She landed in the middle of the road, nimble as a black widow.

Forget the rock, I thought. I needed something bigger if I wanted to come out of this alive. I crouched beside rubble from the chimney, dropped my brick, and grabbed a discarded axe handle where it lay half-buried among the weeds.

The Scarecrow trembled, begged. "Please don't hurt me! Please!"

The Wicked Witch formed her hand into a claw. Eldritch flames sprouted from her bitten nails, knotted into a pulsing globe.

"I release you, Scarecrow! I give you your freedom—in death!"

She hurled the fire and the Scarecrow tried to block it with upraised hands.

The ball hit him and ate his body up in seconds.

The Wicked Witch stepped into the yard, blocked my way to the road, as the Tin Man and Dorothy circled the Scarecrow's smoldering remains. If I braved the apple orchard, I'd have to fight them both, one armed with an axe, the other with a dead dog.

"This is taking too long," the Wicked Witch said. "It's time for you to join me, Michael."

"I'm not going anywhere, Denise." I waved the axe handle before me.

"My name is not Denise. I can't remember my name. It's been such a long time since I heard it."

"But if you're not Denise. . . ."

My words trailed off. I let my eyes trace the lines in her face. I barely recognized the woman I'd flirted with in the hallway. She might be there under the thick cheeks, the warts, the bony chin and green skin, but there wasn't enough to convince me.

"Then . . . I must be the Wicked Witch!" she said.

I swung my weapon and reached for the roof. The handle cracked when it hit, cut my hands as it splintered. The Tin Man was nearest the cabin and he screamed. His voice squeaked. *You're going to need to oil more than that, buddy.* My blow shook the roof's remaining boards and the water puddles washed into the yard, striking the Tin Man. He scrambled into the road, metal limbs clanking, joints squealing from friction. The shower streaked Dorothy's makeup, washed her brown tresses blonde, knocked Toto from her arms.

The Wicked Witch smiled.

She raised her claws to meet the deluge running across her body, black rags clinging to her stick frame. The shape beneath was suddenly too skeletal and bulged in all the wrong places, cancerous and demonic. She licked the stagnant moisture off her lips with a leprous tongue, slurping at the algae.

"Yeah, right," she said. "Like no one's ever tried water before."

I ran but a tree stopped me. Not one of the apple trees. Those were back by the cabin.

The Wicked Witch screamed—"Get him! I won't lose two today!"— and I looked over my shoulder, trying to spot a pursuer. When I turned forward again, I ran face first into a lightning-split oak.

As I lay there dazed, my audience assembled.

"You can't get away, Michael," the Wicked Witch said.

"What do you want?"

"I was thrown out of my land a long time ago and I can never go back." She gestured at the forest, the ramshackle cabin, and the rotting orchard. "This is my home. This is my reality. This is my dream."

I shook my head. "A dream?"

Dorothy wiped her face and left fingerprints in the wet mascara and rouge. "More than a dream. We play our parts, we keep her from loneliness."

"Stan was one of us," the Tin Man said. "He served his time. When she tired of him, she let him serve her outside."

"Be quiet, beehive!" said the Wicked Witch, pushing him aside. "You'll learn my ways soon enough, Michael. You're going to replace him."

"You're crazy!" I pulled myself up against the split trunk. "I'll never do anything you want!"

"That's why I love you, Michael." She motioned towards the tree. "Lift him up."

A noose dropped over my head and cinched tight. At the other end, hidden among the leaves, an orangutan jumped into the air, guiding its descent with spread wings as it hauled the rope across a thick branch.

My neck snapped.

The Witch's obsession traps us here, and her magic forces us into these forms. When I dream I'm still in my old life, but it fades as her obsession burns, tarnishing the memory. She watches and we try to amuse her. When she tires, I may stop hanging myself. And someday I will escape.

Her madness is contagious.

DEADSPACE
Dennis Etchison

It was only his first morning there. But, very early, he was awakened by the ringing of a bell.

So soon? he thought.

Well, it was about time. . . .

He rolled over and fumbled the receiver out of its cradle.

The ringing continued.

He lay on his back for a moment while his senses reassembled. One of his legs tingled, as if he had slept with it twisted under him. He could hardly feel it. But he swung his feet down, climbed out of bed as best he could and went in search of the sound.

As soon as he opened the drapes and staggered outside, it stopped.

He squinted and tried to clear his head.

From the balcony of his room at the Holmby Hotel, he had an unobstructed view of a sea of evergreens rolling away in tufted waves toward Sunset Boulevard and the Palisades beyond. Above the treetops clouds parted like curtains framing an electric blue proscenium, clean and vibrant with promise. He stood with his hands on the railing, his face tipped back, and awaited the warming rays of the sun as it passed on its way to the Pacific.

Now the sound resumed, drawing his attention to the driveway below, where it became the distant bleating of an automobile security alarm.

He braced his arms and leaned forward. The alarm was cut off as a door slammed and a desperate woman in a white jumpsuit hurried to the carpet in front of the hotel, swinging a bulging Sportsac like a stuffed armadillo. A valet tipped his cap at her heels, opened the car door, slid behind the wheel, closed the door and guided her black Mercedes away from the curb and into the underground garage. As the sedan glided out and turned into darkness, the insignia of the hotel was revealed in the macadam beneath. The roof of the carport covering the loading zone was dull and weathered, but the inlaid coat of arms was readable even through the yellowed Plexiglas.

VAYA CON DIOS, read the circle of tiles. BEVERLY HILLS, CALIFORNIA.

He had not noticed it before. *Go with God?* he thought. Was that really what it said? Decipherable in its entirety only from above, the message must have been designed exclusively for visitors on high, like a mysterious hieroglyphic invitation to the gods of the Nazcas. Reeling from a sudden rush of vertigo, he grasped the railing with both hands and forced himself to step back.

He wondered if the management had considered the possible effect such a logo might have on guests of suicidal inclination. It was conceivable that someone on the upper levels would see the emblem as a target. An image came to mind of a despondent man hurtling down, executing a perfect swan dive as he crashed through the panes to take the place of the Mercedes dead-center on the mosaic. From this height a body would fall like a stone, straight as a plumb line. The thought left him dizzy.

He took a deep breath and lifted his face again to the morning light. Somewhere a radio was playing a transient popular tune; it came from the other side of the building, from the high-priced bungalows or perhaps the pool. Was that the sound of another telephone ringing? No, only the whine of a power saw fading in and out like static on the breeze. On a nearby balcony glasses clinked. A scent of orange juice ripened the air. He opened his eyes.

The sky remained clear above the trees, though the expanse of blue invited some new pattern to take up the slack. If more clouds did move in to clot the horizon, he would not be surprised in the least.

He was sure of only one thing.

Once, a long time ago, someone had taken from him something irreplaceably valuable. He couldn't remember what it was. And no one would admit it.

But now, today, all that was about to change.

He finished dressing. The message light on the telephone was still dark. He dialed the desk. No calls for him yet. He took out a pack of cigarettes, picked it open, set it down, fingered it again and dropped it into his pocket, then put it away in the drawer and made himself leave it there. Trying to shake a vague feeling that he was forgetting something vital, he slipped into his sandals and rode the elevator down.

There were no messages waiting at the desk and the lobby was empty. The soft pink cushions on the antique divans were still undented, and a copy of *Architectural Digest* lay unread on the polished tabletop near the mock fireplace; the photograph on the cover showed a room remarkably like this one but without the vase of fresh flowers to add a tropical touch to the decor. He left word that any calls be directed to the wet bar, and stepped out through the French windows as carefully as a visitor to a closed and extremely restricted movie set. He reminded himself that the contract in his suitcase would serve as his pass to the Holmby and places like it from now on. As soon as he had taken care of one very simple formality.

He followed the signs that pointed the way to the pool.

He passed a Latin maid in a spotless white uniform, her cleaning cart color-coordinated to match precisely the green of the walkway and the trim around the doors. He noticed that she was munching a crisp snack of some sort. The dining room was open but he was too edgy to hold down breakfast. The maid smiled at him familiarly. She knows, he thought. Already! Was that a copy of *Daily Variety* on top of her sheets and pillowcases? She must read the trades, he realized with satisfaction, and continued on under the stucco arches.

The walking path led him between discreetly-spaced cottages where the blinds were still drawn, heavy Spanish tile roofs ruddy and shimmering under the perpetual sun. Shamelessly large potted palms trembled in the belvederes, shading rows of shy hydrangeas that filled the dampened beds. In alcoves along the way photos of visiting dignitaries hung like icons; an oversized frame near a particularly isolated suite displayed signed glossies of Princess Grace of Monaco and her daughter Caroline, a memento of the final unpublicized stay. At once he recognized the haughty features of the former actress. He hesitated briefly to pay his respects, nodding and smiling back in reverence and complicity. Then he moved on, basking in the glow, his own chin elevated a few degrees.

Trusting the signs, he descended deeper into the most secluded portions of the grounds, levels he had never before penetrated without Joe Gillis at his side. The film star knew the junglelike terrain as intimately as a tour guide, had stayed here so often at the height of his popularity that he was now venerated by the establishment as an old and valued friend. The front table in the dining room would be his for as long as he lived, the headwaiter would never forget to hold the salad for the final course. After the first few business lunches Wintner began to envy such treatment, and longed for the day when it would be his by association. Tonight, whether or not Gillis stayed on for dinner, he would at last dare to request the front table for himself as if it were a foregone conclusion.

He was no longer sure of his exact location but pressed bravely ahead along the winding path.

At the bottom of a terraced embankment he came upon a workman carrying a load of lumber on his shoulders. The man was on his way toward a gazebo that overlooked the fishpond. Wintner passed him on the narrow footbridge without a word, pretending interest in the signs that labeled the subdivisions of flora. Hand-painted lettering identified each variety with the care of a horticultural exhibit, white crosses marked with both popular and scientific names staked into the soil or nailed to the trunks of the oldest trees. He paused to study the placards, like a tourist intent on memorizing every detail of a long-awaited trip.

A few seconds later he was startled by the wail of a buzz saw. The back of his neck bristled as if a stranger had screamed his name. He shot a glance back through the foliage and saw the carpenter busy cutting a hole in the roof of the gazebo. A plywood circle dropped out of a spray of sawdust and a clear spot of sky shone down like a blue moon. Wintner could not imagine what the hole was for. He turned away, picking up the pace as he crossed the bridge to the other shore.

On the far side the path took him by a grouping of bungalows completely hidden from the other bank. Their separate doorways connected to an elevated wooden deck, where a long table was already set for lunch. Each crystal water glass was topped by a cloth napkin folded into the shape of a bird. Reflected in the facets of the cut glass were inverted images of the adjacent pond, where just now a cloud of white light seemed to be descending, the miniaturized movement of a napkin unfurling from the skies like wings. Wintner focused past the glasses to the pond. There an enormous white swan glided up out of hanging vines, tucking its feathers and neck back into a pose as graceful as an arrangement of folded linen.

Impatient, Wintner climbed the bank and cut through a glade of Italian cypress. He came out into a totally unfamiliar area, dense and overgrown. Here a cluster of redwoods filtered the light into bands of premature dusk. He made a mental note of the turns he had taken so that he would not make the same mistake after dark. Maybe Joe Gillis could draw him a map. But that wasn't necessary. There were guideposts all around, situated conspicuously along every route in the botanical gardens.

Everywhere except here.

Quietly the shrubbery closed like a wound behind him. Now it was all the same. He turned, turned again, trying to find the sun. The tops of the redwoods spun.

He was tempted to call out for help, to ask someone, the workman, perhaps, for directions. No. He would never be taken seriously on these premises after that. Word would get out. He visualized the headline in Army Archerd's column tomorrow morning: PRODUCER CAN'T FIND HIS WAY TO SWIMMING POOL. And the sidebar: *Can He Find Financing for Gillis Project?* He would never live it down. He had gotten this far on his own, hadn't he? He couldn't give up now.

"Is that anybody?"

A queue of tiger lilies whispered at his back. He faced them. Their hungry orange throats seemed to be speaking to him. There was a suggestion of movement, a silken rustling, close and yet separated from him.

"Hello?" he answered.

"Oh! I thought so. Ec-excuse me." The lilies stopped moving and a giant, waxy jade plant shook and murmured with a female voice.

"I hear you," he said. "Only I can't—"

"Are you the carpenter?"

"Sorry to disappoint you." He concentrated and zeroed in on her thin, reedy voice. He thrust his hand between bamboo stalks, took a chance and stepped through.

And there. He was out. It was easy, after all. He felt foolish. "I didn't mean to scare you." He shaded his eyes. "I just stopped to—to admire the orchids." Were there orchids? He hoped so. He was still disoriented.

Her eyes widened but she stood her ground. She tilted her head diffidently and he could almost see the wheels turning behind her forehead, clicking into place as she arrived at a decision. The pool enclosure began a few yards farther up the path, a white enameled fence; through its bars a bright oval of water sparkled like an azure teardrop.

"Buy you a drink?"

"Hm? Oh, no. Th-thank you."

"Well, think I'll have one. Today's a very important day. It's—"

"I know. But I think you'll have to wait awhile longer."

"What?"

"The bar. It's not open yet."

He sighted past her. She was right. The wet bar was bare. The glasses had not yet been set out and there was no bartender in view. At her back the water was still and crystalline. She pulled a string and loosened her outer garment; the top sloughed off one tender shoulder. He settled back into the chaise and extended his legs so that one foot nearly touched her. She did not move away.

"Do you stay here a lot?" he said, already guessing the answer. Her skin was pale as alabaster.

"Hm? Oh, for the winters, mostly." She seemed distracted. "I had to come early this year. Sometimes everything takes so long. I wish it didn't."

"I know what you mean," he said sympathetically, choosing not to press her for details. When in Rome and all that. It was the way people spoke out here, a tantalizing game of one-upmanship. A game he must learn to play. A lazy breeze filtered through the windbreak, feathering the surface of the water. "I've been waiting a long time myself. I mean, I only checked in last night. But this deal has taken years to set up— longer, if you count finding the right script, lining up the backers . . ."

He let his voice trail off. No need to get ahead of himself. There was all the time in the world. She studied him impersonally, neither advancing nor retreating. He was sure he had said exactly the right things. He lay his head back against the white strands of the chaise and folded his hands confidently across his lap.

He felt at ease here. He had always known it would be this way. This place or something like it had been his destiny since the age of ten, when his life was changed irrevocably by so many glorious Saturday matinees. After that it was clear to him that film would be his life. He had never given up hope. And now it was as if this perfect setting had been arranged especially for his entrance. It had been a long time coming, but he was ready to assume his rightful place at last. The backwork was done; now he had taken the chair that was meant for him alone. It was right as rain. This empty position at poolside, this particular one and no other, had been waiting patiently all these years. He was here to stay.

The wafer of sun angled higher, warming the water. Ripples glinted through his eyelids like silver needles. He heard splashing and raised one hand to his forehead. Now she sat on the edge of the deep end and dipped water over her arms and legs. Her short robe lay nearby, deflated as a shed skin. While he watched she mounted the board and jackknifed into the pool, displacing a high, transparent bell of water. A spatter of droplets fell across his ankles. It was cool and refreshing.

She arched to the center, where she broke the surface with a gasp and a fleeting grin. Was she performing for him? He was alone to witness the audition. As yet no other sunbathers had shown themselves; only an empty cabana tilted in one corner of the enclosure, its tent flap snapping like a flag in the drafts. He enjoyed the privilege.

He sat up as she ascended from the shallow end. The conservative one-piece suit adhered to her slender body, glittered and bled water into a growing spot on the cement. He pushed out of the chair. She slicked her hair back from her narrow face; now, with darkened curls pasted to her skull, she appeared smaller, almost childlike. She clung there to the side bars, younger and more vulnerable than he had imagined. She could practically be my daughter, he thought. If my marriage had lasted. But then his life would have turned out altogether differently. For a while caring for Laurie had taken the place of his career. Now he was back on track. Without her he was free to resume the path that had led him here today. It was just as well this way—incomparably better, in fact.

"Where'd you learn to do that?" he asked. He left his sandals by the chair, approached the rim and squatted next to her.

She grimaced with embarrassment, as though afraid they would be overheard. Her eyes darted to the corner, where a clutch of hyacinths huddled in the shadow of an imposing queen palm. He was surprised at her shyness, and that made her even more appealing.

"You should see some of the girls who come here," she said self-consciously.

Was that why she was out so early? To avoid the competition? He pictured her withdrawing to her room as soon as the pool filled up, then sneaking out at the end of the day when once again there would be no audience.

"I've seen them," he said.

She trailed her feet in the water, hiding her toes. "How long are you staying?"

"Uh, well, that's hard to say. Until I close the deal, at least. But I'll be back. You can count on that."

"Are you an actor?"

"Me? No, no. I'm a—" He faltered; it was the first time he had dared to let the word pass his lips in casual conversation. "I'm a producer." Or I will be, he told himself, after today. "I'm here to sign my star."

"Your star?"

"My leading man." You know, he thought, the name, the one who brings the money into the box office. For my movie. She did go to the movies, didn't she? He had an urge to play his role to the hilt. It would be good practice.

"Joe Gillis," he said matter-of-factly. She blinked at him; incredibly the name didn't seem to register. He forced himself to go on, overriding his old insecurities. "The picture's called *Is Anybody There?* It was written for him. We start shooting in the spring—sooner, if we can find the right leading lady." He neglected to mention that they were already in contact with Susan Penhaligon's agent in London. No need to burst any bubbles so early in the day. Let her dream a bit, he thought. No harm in that.

He wondered if she could see his pulse speeding, the vein standing out on his forehead. She showed no reaction. The sun nicked the water in expanding circles. He remembered that he had forgotten his dark glasses. They were in his room, packed in the suitcase. He needed them; he needed to see the exact expression on her face.

"In fact," he went on, "I should be hearing from Joe right about now. He knows I'm in town. You know how it is with actors. They like to sleep late when they're not on call."

"Do they?"

This was a rare moment. He would remember this day for the rest of his life. The day it all came together.

"I could give him a call if I wanted to. I have his home number." Memorized, he thought. "As soon as he can make it over here to sign the contract, we're in business."

He didn't say anything about the answering machine. For seventy-two hours or more Gillis had let his Duofone take all calls. But surely that was to ward off distractions during the last stage of negotiations. For an Academy Award winner the phone must never stop ringing. But it would be back on the hook today. Either that or Gillis would show up here in person, pen in hand. He loved the script as much as Wintner's guarantors. And why shouldn't he? It would be the role of his career.

He looked over her head and savored the scene. The setting was made to order. Now the morning was officially beginning; a young Latino with a Walkman dangling from one white pocket entered the enclosure. Wintner watched him walk to the bar, carrying a tray loaded with cocktail napkins and swizzle sticks. He didn't need to bring the telephone; it was already plugged in by the cash register. Wintner stood.

It was time.

She raised her head. Her eyes were deep and shining. Drops of water evaporated from her complexion in the rising heat, leaving tracks of chlorination on her cheeks. Suddenly he was reluctant to leave her. What is it she wants from me? he wondered. Most likely nothing more than a few minutes of companionship before fleeing all the golden strangers. She's new to this, too, he thought. Like me, she's as pale as milk-fed veal. It takes one to know one. But for both of us all that will change in the next few hours.

He checked his watch. I can let her have a few more minutes, he thought. Besides, it will be better if I give Gillis a chance to call first.

He considered stripping down to his trunks and joining her for a brief swim. But he was not quite ready. His body, trim though it was, might blind her with its Eastern pallor. Feeling the first uncomfortable pangs of self-doubt since he had arrived, he flashed her an uneasy smile and knelt once more, gripping the lip of cement with his sandals.

"Did you hurt yourself?" he said casually, to compensate for the empty pause, and instantly regretted it.

Her eyes reluctantly followed his to her legs. There on the inner surface of her thigh was a glistening birthmark a few inches wide. It formed a rough outline of the North American continent. He looked away.

"It's all right," she said quickly. "It's nothing."

But she inched forward and dropped feet-first into the pool, moving out into the deeper water, covering herself to the neck.

"Sorry," he muttered.

She bobbed closer. "Did you say something? I can't hear you."

"I said, I think I'll make that call now." He showed her an all-purpose grin, unbent his legs and stood.

She treaded water, painfully alone in the pool.

"Look," he said on a last reckless impulse, "maybe we could have some lunch. Together." When she did not flinch he pressed it. "Let me see how long this takes. He probably won't be by till this afternoon. I'm going to try to get back to the room and catch a nap. You could meet me there later. Or I'll give you a call. My name's Stu Wintner, by the way."

"Maybe," she said uncertainly. She kicked and drifted closer. "It depends."

Here it comes, he thought. I should have known. "Are you here with someone?" He felt the compleat fool. "If you are," he added expansively, forced into playing it out, "I'd be pleased if you'd both join me."

"It's not that. But I don't know if I can get away."

"I understand."

"Do you?"

He backed off awkwardly and headed for the bar, where the young man in the white jacket was polishing a highball glass. "Nice talking to you," he called over his shoulder, and waved. "See you."

Good luck, he thought.

The young bartender took up a stainless-steel tool and began curling the rind off a lemon. Wintner sidled up and exchanged nods with him, as if they were old friends. He ordered a margarita and asked to use the telephone.

The answering machine was still on.

The world-weary voice on the other end had not changed. Like Gillis's films it would never change, at least not until the oxide wore away on the millionth playing, around the time his photographic image, equally unchanged and locked in the amber of celluloid, finally disintegrated and burned away with the last remaining frame of his last preserved film. With any luck that film would be *Is Anybody There?* His greatest, most memorable performance and his legacy for generations yet unborn. When he was gone, who could take his place? A kind of immortality. Wintner was jealous.

He left another message, reminding Gillis that he was waiting at the hotel. He contemplated leaving word with Gillis's agent in case the actor was out and called there first. But it was still early. He started on his drink and turned back to the overexposed brightness of the pool.

The girl was no longer in the water. Neither was she anywhere else that he could see. Somehow she had stolen away while he was on the phone. He hadn't heard a sound. If she had left wet footprints on her way out they were dry by now. There was no clue. He caught the bartender's attention. "Did you see. . . ?" he began.

The young man glanced up, munching on something round and white. As he bit down Wintner saw that it was hollow, like a shell.

"Never mind." For all Wintner knew she might be the daughter of an important guest. There was no need to make a total idiot of himself. He paid for the drink, laying down a nice tip.

Before he left the bar his curiosity got the better of him. "Can I ask you a question?"

The young man disengaged the tape player headphones from one ear. A faint cacophony of insect music hissed on the air.

"Where did you get that?" Wintner indicated the crisp snack. "At the restaurant? I've seen people walking around with them all morning. I guess I must be getting hungry."

The young man offered him a piece.

"No, no. I only want to know what it is."

"Día de los Muertos."

"I beg your pardon?" Does he speak English? Wintner wondered. He's not from around here; probably substituting for the regular man. He doesn't know—

Then he got a clear look at the object. It was a miniature skull, what remained of one, apparently made of spun candy. Most of the face had been eaten away, and the inner surface glimmered with loose granules of sugar.

"The Day of the Dead," explained the bartender. "You know, the second of November. It's a big celebration in Mexico. I have one more, sir, if you'd care to—"

Wintner held up his hand. "No, thanks."

The bartender shrugged, an expression of bemusement in his polished brown eyes.

California, thought Wintner, shaking his head.

Balancing the drink, he sauntered back to the deck chair. On the way he became aware of a muffled rustling. It was the cabana in the corner of the enclosure. The top billowed as the interior filled like an air sock. Then the breeze died and it collapsed inward and hung limp, nothing more than empty canvas, like the umbrellas over the white enameled tables. But the cabana was not anchored securely; when the wind came up again the pole creaked and the striped cloth puffed out in a simulation of breathing. At this angle the sun backlighted the upper half, transforming it into a glowing, translucent orange. Was that a distorted profile inside? Probably only a shadow of the fence rear-projected against the material. Still, it made him uneasy. He ignored it and returned to the chaise.

There, inserted between the plastic weave of the seat: a small square of paper. A cocktail napkin. He reached down to remove it, and noticed that it contained a handwritten note.

PLEASE HELP ME, read the shaky black letters.

He looked around.

Behind the bar, the attendant emptied his hands of the candy skull and resumed stripping the skin off a pungent lemon.

Now he was convinced that there was someone in the tent. Holding his drink in one hand and the flimsy note in the other, he walked back along the edge of the pool.

Wind ballooned the tent once more and moved on, leaving the sides sunken as empty cheeks. In the interval that followed he heard the rustling quite clearly.

It definitely came from inside.

He approached the structure, aware of the bartender's watchful eyes. He fought down a compulsion to peek directly into the opening and get it over with. Instead he stood there stiffly and shifted his feet.

A groaning.

Was it only the supports? He couldn't be sure.

Just inside the orange slit, two eyes locked on him. Startled, he stepped backward and almost fell. The eyes rose higher and the tent opened. A large woman lunged out, glaring at him. Before she drew the flap shut behind her he got a glimpse of something bathed in the unnaturally warm glow of the interior, something pale and nearly shapeless laid out on a white towel.

"Yes?"

He cleared his throat. "Can I be of any help?"

The woman stood guard at the entrance. Her bathing suit stretched to enclose her massive form, rolled black straps cutting into her doughy shoulders.

"You're new," she said. Though her protruding eyes did not move he knew that every detail, every inch of his body was being examined.

"Forgive me for bothering you," he said evenly. "But I didn't know . . ." He looked to the note as though it would explain everything. Unaccountably his hand shook. Already sweat ran from his wrists and blurred the lettering. He crumpled it and tossed it away.

Behind her something groaned.

"He gets cramps when I leave him in one position too long." She regarded Wintner warily for another moment, then abruptly stood aside. "He says he'd like to meet you."

"Are you sure?" Wintner was at a complete loss. He felt like he had stepped into a nudist colony without his papers.

The woman held out a wattled arm. The canvas curled open.

A man lay sweltering in the livid interior. Essentially he had no legs. One grew to the knee, one was a mere flipper. Ignoring Wintner, the woman sat and took the man's great grey head into her lap.

She proceeded to massage his temples. She wiped his forehead with a cloth. She took up a cotton swab and then, after she had painstakingly cleaned the whorls of one ear, used manicure scissors to snip at the salt-and-pepper hairs growing there. Wintner stood by, a spy observing a private ritual.

"We always come here this time of year," she said. "For the weather. We don't like the cold, do we, honey?" She kneaded his speckled shoulders, his jutting breastbone.

The old man rolled his head to the side, a mighty effort. His eyes were black as beads but with a tinge of blue-grey around the frayed pupils. His shortened body was scarred, folded in on itself at every joint and orifice. The stump-ends where his hands should have been were sucked in like navels, as though sewn to a point inside. His eyes searched Wintner's vicinity.

"Can I bring you something?" Wintner offered. "A cold drink? A glass of water? Anything?"

The grey head lolled in a swoon. The interior was sweltering; the sun transformed the walls of the tent into incandescent screens, the stripes a pattern of bars. Wintner itched to be gone.

He backstepped, feeling for the opening.

As if on cue the woman recentered the head on the towel, put down her tools and followed Wintner out.

He was instantly cooler. It was a sweatbox in there. Didn't she realize that? With his circulation so drastically shortened, the poor man's natural body temperature would be abnormally high to begin with; such confinement would become unbearable by midday. Was the tent a last resort to shield his condition from prying eyes? But wouldn't they do better in their air-conditioned room? Surely the man didn't care that there was a pool a few feet away, on the other side of the canvas barrier.

"Such a beautiful day!" she said. She inhaled deeply and shook her hair free. Moist curls flung jewels of perspiration into the glare. "I dream about this place all year long."

"Yes," said Wintner. He found his voice. "I was just on my way—"

"But you can't go. I won't let you." Her mood became generous, her lumpy face girlishly animated. "We must talk."

Wintner did not know whether he should feel flattered or threatened. Either attitude seemed absurd.

"Sure," he said. "But right now I'm expecting a call. I'll be back later, though. I—" and here he foundered, "I hope your husband feels better." How else to put it?

Her face sagged, the mere mention dragging her down like gravity. "It's Tachs-Meisner Syndrome," she said, her voice coarse again. "We thought he was safe from the bloodline. But since his fortieth birthday . . . One can only try to be as comfortable as possible, until the end."

"I'm sorry."

"You shouldn't be. We are almost free."

He nodded and stared at the cement. His feet were as pale as they had been the first day of summer on the sidewalks of the town where he grew up. He had never before felt grateful for his strong arches, his well-shaped toes. But now he noticed that his fourth and fifth toes were no longer perfect; distorted by years of proper shoes, they had grown inward—now they were mere knobs, the nails squeezed down to slivers and all but vanished, suggesting evolution to a lower form. How could he not have noticed until now? He was aware of a tightening. The concrete heated under his delicate soles, which had been pampered for so long that they were hypersensitive, less able to protect him from the real world. The taut skin covering his insteps wavered in a rising heat mirage. He detected a smell that was dangerously like burning meat. He needed to get away, back to his sandals and a patch of shade. But there was no shade here except in the tent.

"I'll stop by later," he suggested. "Do you take your meals in the dining room? Perhaps I'll see you this evening. I won't be alone, but you might enjoy meeting a friend of mine."

She shook her head. "There's no time. He needs me. Always." Her eyes filled with tears. "Every hour, every minute, every second!" she said with shocking bitterness, almost spitting the words. She gazed longingly at the pool as though it were an impossible distance away.

He moved off. "Well, I'm sure I'll see you later. This afternoon, probably. Good luck, Mrs. . . . ?"

"I was like my mother. I believed the dream. Young girls always do. We marry, thinking what a joy it will be. But somehow it changes." Her eyes distended above her puffy cheeks. "And now, God help me, it's too much!"

She lumbered toward Wintner to prevent his leaving, but too late. She stood there sadly, her fat bosom heaving, then wheeled around wearily and stooped to reenter the tent. Wintner could not avoid seeing the shapeless mass inside struggling to turn onto its side, the misshapen features, the ruined arms batting out for leverage. Resigned, the woman returned to her duties. She took up cotton and alcohol and began cleansing the pores on his neck.

Wintner retrieved his sandals and beat a hasty retreat.

The path was harder to follow than he remembered, but he hurried back faster than ever through the lush vegetation. Blood-red bougainvillaea dripped over arbors, huge ivy choked off plots of delphinium and quivered at the borders of the walk, eager to overgrow and split the painted cement. The table setting next to the hidden cottages remained immaculate and untouched. Below, in the botanical gardens, variegated plants were locked in a stalemate of symbiosis. He came to the gazebo, white as a lattice of crossed bones, and finally saw that the hole in the roof had been cut out to make room for a rapidly maturing tree; as he passed, heavily pruned limbs were already thrusting upward to fill the empty circle.

He realized that he could not call the girl from the pool even if he wanted to; he had forgotten to ask her name.

Now he would never know.

He remembered the last image of the man in the cabana, face crawling with sweat, mouth open on darkness in a desperate rictus. Wintner lay sprawled on the bed in his room and tried to put the memory out of his mind, but could not.

The morning lagged, the afternoon slackened until the sun came to a standstill above a blanket of smog. He made the call twice in the first hour, then every twenty minutes, then every ten. Each time Joe Gillis's voice droned the same prerecorded message. The actor's presence projected through the telephone to an extraordinary degree; even on tape his dark power was immediately recognizable. By midafternoon Wintner gave up leaving any word at all on the machine.

He pitied the man in the tent, but soon felt nearly as confined himself. The walls of his room narrowed in the lengthening shadows. He rode the elevator down to the lobby, which now seemed nothing more than a fey decorator's wet dream, hand-rubbed and unlivable. When he returned with a newspaper and a sandwich, the ceiling had closed in even more dramatically.

He considered renting a car. He had Gillis's address. He could simply drive over.

Why not?

He picked up the phone directory.

There was a knock on the door.

At first he didn't recognize her. She had put on a blouse and skirt; the lapels of the blouse, slightly too large, hung wide over the bathing suit so that she appeared childishly small, half-hidden in her loose clothes. She kept a reasonable distance and blinked at him from beneath dark curls.

"Were you sleeping? I can come back."

"No! No, please. I'm glad to see you. Come in."

"I got your room number from the desk." The young woman sidled in, visibly ill at ease. Did she notice what had happened to the walls and ceiling? "I hope you don't mind."

"Not at all. I could use some company." He moved his suitcase, pushed aside the unopened newspaper so she could sit on the bed.

"Have you heard from your friend yet?"

"I'll talk to him later. You know how it is in this business—hurry up and wait."

"Oh."

"Can I get you anything? I think there's a room service menu somewhere."

She tossed her curls, inexplicably amused. "No, but I'll be glad to get *you* something." She eyed the bottle of MacAllan Single Malt in his open suitcase. He had brought it to celebrate with Gillis. She reached for it. Before he could stop her she twisted off the seal with a flourish, an exaggerated bit of business she might have seen in a movie once. If she went to the movies. "Do you like it plain or with water?" she asked sweetly.

"No, really, I don't need anything." Then again maybe he did. It was not such a bad idea. Yet he felt oddly guilty. "You don't have to serve me. This was my idea, remember?"

"Was it?" she said. "That's all right. I enjoy it."

He believed she meant it. He leaned one arm back against the pillow and waited.

She removed the paper cover from one of his sanitized glasses and poured what she estimated to be a couple of fingers. She was trying so hard to learn the moves, to get it all down. She wanted to make it true, the way it would be on a bad television show. He was touched. The clothes, for example, were not quite right; he wondered where she had got them. He thought: She still accepts everything she was taught. She probably forces herself to go to the right places, do the right things, like staying at this hotel. And why? Is it worth it? She thinks it is. It may be all she knows. But what's the payoff for her?

He drank the Scotch down to the vapors while she sat on the end of the bed, one leg half-concealed under her.

"Did you hurt yourself?" He pointed to a small circle of cauterized skin on her shinbone. He had not noticed it earlier.

She made an attempt to cover it but her skirt was not long enough. "Oh, it's nothing. I don't mind anymore. It's only—only scar tissue."

Now he saw another mark an inch or two below her kneecap. She repositioned her legs nervously and her skirt hiked up. There were three, four, several more spots scattered along her calves, irregular patches of tissue, nearly round as if burned into her flesh by heated coins. Each scar covered a small concavity, suggesting that abscesses or tumors of some kind had developed there and been removed. They had healed well, but the indentations remained.

He had a hunch. "You didn't grow up on the beach, did you?" he asked.

She tilted her head quizzically.

Of course not, he thought. She was definitely not from around here. "My nephew had something like that. He was raised in San Diego. Surfer's knots, they were called. Calcium deposits. He had them removed, too."

"Oh, no," she said with forced casualness, "these were—were bone marrow transplants. Afterwards there's always an empty space." She smoothed the hollows with her hands. "They'll fill out, though. It takes time, but something else grows in. I'm sure that's what will happen with me. The doctor says you can't leave nothing where something used to be. Till then it's just deadspace."

"I see." He was careful not to show any revulsion. "Does it hurt?"

"It used to. After a while you don't notice it anymore. Now there's no feeling. There will be again, though. If not . . ."

Fascinated, he bent closer. He touched one of the spots with infinite care. It was softer than anything he had ever touched before. Her leg tensed, then relaxed slowly as if from an effort of will. He felt the silkiness of tiny hairs growing in around the scar.

She pressed his finger lightly into the gap and smiled with satisfaction. The fingertip filled it perfectly.

The sensation was unnerving. He was both attracted and repelled. He pulled away and sat back against the headboard.

"You look tired," she said.

He knew it was true. He hadn't slept well and the long day was taking its toll. His neck ached. His mouth was sour with the peaty taste of the Scotch and his eyes felt scorched. He wanted to close them. Until it was time.

"Why don't you put your feet up?"

"They are up."

"Oh. Then why don't you take off your shoes again? Here, I'll help you. Would you like another drink?"

"No." He felt himself slipping away. "I guess I am tired. All this waiting."

"I know."

How could she? She couldn't know what it was like. He didn't know what to do with her. To throw her out so soon would be rude. "Pour yourself one, if you like."

"I like your voice," she said. "And your face. It's gentle. Not like the other men who come here."

"Thanks."

"Are you very successful?"

"Sure," he said. "I will be. You'll see. You'll all see."

She came around and perched on the edge of the bed.

"You haven't read your newspaper yet," she said, as if acting out some women's magazine version of an idealized domestic scene. Why bother? Go home, he thought, to the small town you came from, marry some guy with a polyester suit and a regular income. You won't have any surprises, but you won't have any disappointments, either. Meanwhile practice on someone who can fill the bill. She could find someone else, couldn't she?

He was aware of her inching closer. He felt smothered, immobilized. What did she want from him? Somehow things had taken a turn toward the surreal. He didn't understand it. For now he felt too weary, too ineffectual to resist. That would have to change, of course. In another minute. As soon as she eased off. Then it would be time to call again.

She unfolded the newspaper and laid it across his lap.

He opened his eyes. "You're very kind," he began, "but you really don't have to—"

He saw the headline.

FILM GREAT FOUND DEAD

He snatched up the paper.

> HOLLYWOOD (UPI) Joe Gillis, one of
> the screen's most durable leading men for
> more than four decades, was found dead
> in his West Los Angeles condominium
> today, the apparent victim of a massive
> stroke.

"Jesus Christ," he said, "did you see this?"

"No."

He read on numbly.

> A security guard discovered the body
> early this morning, using a passkey after
> the actor's agent and friends became
> alarmed. Preliminary reports indicate
> that the star of such film classics as *Man
> Afire*, *La Carcel* and *Hole in the Wall* had
> been dead for at least several days. Police
> say the corpse, sprawled on the floor
> near an empty whiskey bottle and with
> the telephone only inches from his hand,
> had already begun to decompose. . . .

Wintner's eyes followed the story to the bottom of the page, then returned blearily to the three-column photo at the top and began again. He read the words over but they did not make any sense. It was some kind of sick, twisted joke.

He grabbed the phone, dialed 393-9058.

The receiver clicked.

"*Hi,*" said a reassuring voice.

"Hi, Joe," said Wintner, remembering to breathe again. "Listen, is this April Fool's Day or something? What's all that crap in the *Examiner* about. . . ?"

"*This is Joe Gillis. I'm sorry but I'm not in right now. If you'd care to leave a message, wait for the beep and I'll get back to you as soon as I can. And thanks for calling. . . ."*

"Hello?" said Wintner. The receiver began to shake in his hand. His fingers went cold, as though they were dying. The blood drained from the left side of his body and pounded in his ears. He could not hear whether or not anyone had picked up the other end. "Hello? Is anybody. . . ?"

She placed the glass in his right hand and poured.

The electronic beep sounded and, when he could not speak, clicked off into a dial tone.

She hung up the phone for him.

Dazed, he said, "I'm sorry, but something terrible's happened. I'll have to ask you to—"

"Is it so terrible?"

"*What?* Do you realize what this means?"

"Yes. I didn't think you knew."

"Why didn't you tell me?"

"That's partly why I came here."

"You did read it, then."

"No."

"Then how could you know?"

"I know he's dead." A maddening tranquility passed over her features. "I went to the room to get my towel, and when I got back he was—gone. He waited for such a long time. We all did."

"What the hell are you talking about?"

"My father. I believe you met him. Mother said you did. She's very strict with me, by the way. That's why I told you I wasn't sure when you asked me if I could—"

"Who? You mean the man by the pool? You mean that he's dead, too?"

He spilled the drink as he drained the glass dry. It went down like sweet fire but this time he could hardly taste it. She wiped the drops from his shirt, then poured herself a small one and sat sipping, watching him patiently.

It was too much. His head tilted back. His muscles were rubber. He felt his body, his legs, the bed and the floor dissolving and falling through while his mind continued to function, like the elusive Joe Gillis whose answering tape had stayed on as his stand-in even after he had gone, like the man in the cabana whose body, what was left of it, remained in place even as his mouth opened in a final wrenching paroxysm of terror.

"We all have to let go," she said, moving over him.

What would become of the actor after his tape was turned off? His number would be given to someone new, his furniture moved out and someone else's moved in. And then? Wintner was at sea, cast adrift.

"What happens now?" he said groggily, as the liquor anesthetized him.

"Now we're free," she whispered. He smelled the alcohol on her breath, close and sickeningly medicinal.

He saw the note in his mind, as if in a dream. It fluttered up on a dark wind. Was *he* the one, then? Wintner saw the man crawling like a living torso toward the opening and the light, struggling to speak, to scrawl one last plea before falling across the threshold to another country. HELP ME, PLEASE HELP ME . . .

"What did he want?" Wintner choked, as her hot breath filled the shrinking space around him. *"What?"*

"The same as anybody," she said. "The trouble was, Mother's too old to take care of him now. I couldn't help. She wouldn't let me. She says I've got myself to worry about. No one else could do it for her. It was her job, you see. You do see, don't you? Don't you. . . ?

"It's going to be easy from now on," she said, climbing higher, settling in. "You'll see. It's simple, so simple, I promise. . . ."

The morning sun was a burning penny in the sky. It blasted the canvas until the sides blazed with louvers of hot orange light.

She took down the top of her black bathing suit and lay prone on the bleached white towel, her elbows out and her small hands locked under her chin. When he glanced down it appeared at first that her arms were abnormally shortened, the bones already eaten away close to the body. But then she flipped her head to the other side and used one hand to touch a spot on the back of her neck.

"Here," she said, "between my shoulders. Can you get it, honey? It's starting to bother me."

So soon, he thought. He paused to peel off his T-shirt, then sat over her, kneading the hyaline flesh. He worked up slowly to a regular rhythm, soothing and mindless.

"Mmm," she moaned. "Feels so good. I love you to take care of me like this."

"Do you?" He didn't mind. It was easy, after all. So much easier. It gave him something to do now besides waiting.

A gust shook the tent. It was strong today, the first intimation of a full-blown wind, possibly even a rainstorm, what passed for winter here. The flap blew open. The sudden coolness raised bumps on his arms.

"Can you see my mother?"

He leaned back and peered through the gash of the opening. "She's at the end of the pool, by the diving board. It doesn't look like she's ready to go in yet."

"It's been too long," said the young woman wistfully. "It's like she has to learn all over again."

The woman was standing like an overgrown child, afraid to get her feet wet. There was no one else out yet; that, he thought, might make it easier for her.

"She's finally going to have some fun," he said.

"Oh, is she? I hope so! She deserves it. She waited so long. . . ."

"Shall we join her?"

"Not today. I'm not feeling well at all."

Of course, he thought. He heard the distant chime of glasses being stacked. "Maybe she's going to have a drink first."

"Mmm. That would be nice."

He stopped moving his hands and sat back to take a breather while the cabana grew brighter, the sides vibrating with an unearthly intensity, the threads of the canvas shimmering in bas-relief like the venation of a translucent membrane, like the projection of his own retinas on the screen of his eyelids when the light became too harsh and he had to close his eyes.

She took the opportunity to raise to her elbows and crawl forward a few inches. She put on his dark glasses and lifted the flap.

"Hey," she called, "can you do me a favor?"

Her mother turned from the bar and looked back blankly.

"Can you bring me something to drink?"

The mother nodded and said something to the attendant.

"I could use one, too," said Wintner.

"What?"

"I don't care," he said. "But tell her to make it a double."

She did. Then she crawled back into position so that he could continue taking care of her.

He did.

It went on like that.

CUTS
F. Paul Wilson

It started in Milo's right foot. He awoke in the dark of his bedroom with a pins-and-needles sensation from the lower part of his calf to the tips of his toes. He sat up, massaged it, walked around the bedroom. Nothing helped. Finally, he took a Darvocet and went back to bed. He managed to get to sleep but was awake again by dawn, this time with both feet tingling. In the wan light, he inspected his lower legs.

A thin, faintly red line around each leg about three inches up from the ankle. Milo snapped on the night table light for a closer look. He touched the line. It was more than a line—an indentation, actually, like something left after wearing a pair of socks too tight at the top. But it felt as if the constricting band were still there.

He got up and walked around. It felt a little funny to stand on partially numb feet but he couldn't worry about it now. In just a couple of hours he was doing a power breakfast at the Polo with Regenstein from TriStar, and he had to be sharp. He padded into the kitchen to put on the coffee.

As he wove through L.A.'s morning commuter traffic, Milo envied the drivers with their tops down. He would have loved to have his 380SL opened up to the bright early morning sun. Truthfully, he would have been glad for an open window. But for the sake of his hair he stayed bottled up with the AC on. He couldn't afford to let the breeze blow his toupee around. It had been especially stubborn about blending in with his natural hair this morning, and he didn't have any more time to fuss with it. And this was his good piece. His backup had been stolen during a robbery of his house last week, an occurrence that still baffled the hell out of him. He wished he didn't have to worry about wearing a rug. He had heard about a new experimental lotion that was supposed to start hair growing again. If that ever panned out, he'd be first on line to—

His right hand started tingling. He removed it from the wheel and fluttered it in the air. Still it tingled. The sleeve of his sports coat slipped back, and he saw a faint indentation running around his forearm, just above the wrist. For a few heartbeats he studied it in horrid fascination.

What's happening to me?

Then he glanced up and saw the looming rear of a truck rushing toward his windshield. He slammed on the brakes and slewed to a screeching stop inches from the tailgate. Gasping and sweating, Milo slumped in the seat and tried to get a grip. Bad enough he was developing mysterious little constricting bands on his legs and now his arm, he had almost wrecked the new Mercedes. This sucker cost more than his first house back in the seventies.

When traffic started up again, he drove cautiously, keeping his eyes on the road and working the fingers of his right hand. He had some weird-shit disease, he just knew it, but he couldn't let anything get between him and this breakfast with Regenstein.

"Look, Milo," Howard Regenstein said through the smoke from his third cigarette in the last twenty minutes. "You know that if it was up to me the picture would be all yours. You know that, man."

Milo nodded, not knowing that at all. He had used that same line himself a million times—maybe *two* million times. If it was up to me. . . .

Yeah, right. The great cop-out: I'm a nice guy and I have all the faith in the world in you, but those money guys, those faithless, faceless Philistines who hold the purse-strings won't let guys with vision like you and me get together and make a great film.

"Well, what's the problem, Howie? I mean, give it to me straight."

"All right," Howie said, showing his chicklet caps between his thin lips. He was deeply tanned, wore thick horn-rimmed glasses; his close-cropped curly hair was sandy-colored and lightly bleached. "Despite my strong—and, Milo, I do mean *strong*—recommendation, the money boys looked at the grosses for *The Hut* and got scared away."

Well. That explained a lot of things, especially this crummy table half hidden in an inside corner. The real power players, the ones who wanted everybody else in the place to see who they were doing breakfast with, were out in the middle or along the windows. Regenstein probably had three breakfasts scheduled for this morning. Milo was wondering which tables had been reserved for the others when a sharp pain stabbed his right leg. He winced and reached down.

"Something wrong?" Regenstein said.

"No. Just a muscle cramp."

He lifted his trouser leg and saw that the indentation above his ankle was deeper. It was actually a cut now. Blood oozed slowly, seeping into his sock. He straightened up and forced a smile at Regenstein.

"*The Hut*, Howie? Is *that* all?" Milo said with a laugh. "Don't they know that project was a loser from the start? The book was a bad property, a piece of clichéd garbage. Don't they know that?"

Howie smiled, too. "Afraid not, Milo. You know their kind. They look at the bottom line and see that Universal's going to be twenty mill in the hole on *The Hut*, and in their world that means something. And maybe they remember those PR pieces you did a month or so before it opened. You never even mentioned that the film was based on a book. Had me convinced the story was all yours, whole cloth."

Milo clenched his teeth. That had been when he had thought the movie was going to be a smash.

"I had a *concept*, Howie, one that cut through the bounds and limitations of the novel. I wanted to raise the level of the material, but the producers stymied me at every turn."

Actually, he had been pretty much on his own down there in Haiti. He had changed the book a lot, made loads of cuts and condensations. He had made it "A Milo Gherl Film."

But somewhere along the way, he had lost it. Unanimously hostile one-star reviews with leads like, "Shut *The Hut*" and "New Gherl Pix the Pits" hadn't helped. Twentieth had been pushing an offer in its television division and he had been holding them off—who wanted to do TV when you could do theatricals? But as the bad reviews piled up and the daily grosses plummeted, he grabbed the TV offer. It was good money, had plenty of prestige, but it was still television.

Milo wanted to do films and very badly wanted in on the new package Regenstein was putting together for TriStar. Howie had Jack Nicholson, Bobby De Niro, and Kathy Turner firm and was looking for a director. More than anything else in his career, Milo wanted to be that director. But he wasn't going to be. He knew that now.

Well, at least he could use the job to pay the bills and keep his name before the public until *The Hut* was forgotten. That wouldn't be long. A year or two at most and he'd be back directing another theatrical. Not a package like Regenstein's, but something with a decent budget where he could do the screenplay and direct. That was the way he liked it—full control on paper and on film.

He shrugged at Regenstein and put on his best good-natured smile. "What can I say, Howie? The world wasn't ready for *The Hut*. Someday, they'll appreciate it."

Yeah, right, he thought as Regenstein nodded noncommittally. At least Howie was letting him down easy, letting him keep his dignity here. That was important. All he had to do now was—

Milo screamed as pain tore into his left eye like a bolt of lightning. He lurched to his feet, upsetting the table as he clamped his hands over his eye in a vain attempt to stop the agony.

Pain! Oh Christ, pain as he had never known it was shooting from his eye straight into his brain. This had to be a stroke! What else could hurt like this?

Through his good eye, he had a whirling glimpse of everybody in the dining room standing and staring at him as he staggered around. He pulled one hand away from his eye and reached out to steady himself. He saw a smear of blood on his fingers. He took the other hand away. His left eye was blind, but with his right he saw the dripping red on his palm. A woman screamed.

"My God, Milo!" Regenstein said, his chalky face swimming into view. "Your eye! What did you do to your eye?" He turned to a gaping waiter. "Get a doctor! Get a fucking ambulance!"

Milo was groggy from the Demerol they had given him. In the blur of hours since breakfast, he'd been wheeled in and out of the emergency room so many times, poked with so many needles, examined by so many doctors, x-rayed so many times, his head was spinning.

At least the pain had eased off.

"I'm admitting you onto the vascular surgery service, Mr. Gherl," said the bearded doctor as he pushed back one of the white curtains that shielded Milo's gurney from the rest of the emergency room. His badge said, EDWARD JANSEN, M.D., and he looked tired and irritable.

Milo struggled up through the Demerol downgrade. "Vascular surgery? But my eye—!"

"As Dr. Burch told you, Mr. Gherl, your eye can't be saved. It's ruined beyond repair. But maybe we can save your feet and your hand if it's not too late already.

"*Save* them?"

"If we're lucky. I don't know what kind of games you've been into, but getting yourself tied up with piano wire is about the dumbest thing I've ever heard of."

Milo was growing more alert by the second now. Over Dr. Jansen's shoulder, he saw the bustle of the emergency room personnel, saw an old black mopping the floor in slow, rhythmic strokes. But he was only seeing it with his right eye. He reached up to the bandage over his left. *Ruined?* He wanted to cry, but Dr. Jansen's piano-wire remark suddenly filtered through to his consciousness.

"Piano wire? What are you talking about?"

"Don't play dumb. Look at your feet." Dr. Edwards pulled the sheet free from the far end of the gurney.

Milo looked. The nail beds were white and the skin below the indentations was a dusky blue. And the indentations had all become clean, straight, bloody cuts right through the skin and into the meat below. His right hand was the same.

"See that color?" Jansen was saying. "That means the tissues below the wire cuts aren't getting enough blood. You're going to have gangrene for sure if we don't restore circulation soon."

Gangrene! Milo levered up on the gurney and felt his toes with his good hand. *Cold!* "No! That's impossible!"

"I'd almost agree with you," Dr. Jansen said, his voice softening for a moment as he seemed to be talking to himself. Behind him, Milo noticed the old black moving closer with his mop. "When we did x-rays, I thought we'd see the wire embedded in the flesh there, but there was nothing. Tried Xero soft-tissue technique in case you had used fishing line or something, but that came up negative, too. Even probed the cuts myself, but there's nothing in there. Yet the arteriograms clearly show that the arteries in your lower legs and right forearm are compressed to the point where very little blood is getting through. The tissues are starving. The vascular boys may have to do bypasses."

"I'm getting out of here!" Milo said. "I'll see my own doctor!"

"I'm afraid I can't allow that."

"You can't stop me! I can walk out of here anytime I want!"

"I can keep you seventy-two hours for purposes of emergency psychiatric intervention."

"Psychiatric!"

"Yeah. Self-mutilation. Your mind worries me almost as much as your arteries, Mr. Gherl. I'd like to make sure you don't poke out your other eye before you get treatment."

"But I didn't—!"

"Please, Mr. Gherl. There were witnesses. Your breakfast companion said he had just finished giving you some disappointing news when you screamed and rammed something into your eye."

Milo touched the bandage over his eye again. How could they think he had done this to himself?

"My God, I swear I didn't do this!"

"That kind of trauma doesn't happen spontaneously, Mr. Gherl, and according to your companion, no one was within reach of you. So one way or the other, you're staying. Make it easy on both of us and do it voluntarily."

Milo didn't see that he had a choice. "I'll stay," he said. "Just answer me one thing: You ever seen anything like this before?"

Jansen shook his head. "Never. Never heard of anything like it either." He took a sudden deep breath and smiled through his beard with what Milo guessed was supposed to be doctorly reassurance. "But, hey. I'm only an ER doc. The vascular boys will know what to do."

With that, he turned and left, leaving Milo staring into the wide-eyed black face of the janitor.

"What are you staring at?" Milo said.

"A man in *big* trouble," the janitor said in a deep, faintly accented voice. He was pudgy with a round face, watery eyes, and two days' worth of silvery growth on his jowls. With a front tooth missing on the top, he looked like Leon Spinks gone to seed for thirty years. "These doctors can't be helpin' what you got. You got a *Bocor* mad at you, and only a *Houngon* can fix you."

"Get lost!" Milo said.

He lay back on the gurney and closed his good eye to shut out the old man and the emergency room. He hunted for sleep as an escape from the pain and the gut-roiling terror, praying he'd wake up and learn that this was all just a horrible dream. But those words wouldn't go away. *Bocor* and *Houngon* . . . he knew them somehow. Where?

And then it hit him like a blow—*The Hut*! They were voodoo terms from the novel *The Hut*! He hadn't used them in the film—he'd scoured all mention of voodoo from his screenplay—but the author had used them in the book. If Milo remembered correctly, a *Bocor* was an evil voodoo priest and a *Houngon* was a good one. Or was it the other way around? Didn't matter. They were all part of Bill Franklin's bullshit novel.

Franklin! Wouldn't he like to see me now! Milo thought. Their last meeting had been anything but pleasant. Unforgettable, yes. His mind did a slow dissolve to his new office at Twentieth two weeks ago. . . .

"Some conference!"

The angry voice startled Milo and he spilled hot coffee down the front of his shirt. He leaped up from behind his desk and bent forward, pulling the steaming fabric away from his chest. "Jesus H.—"

But then he looked up and saw Bill Franklin standing there and his anger cooled like fresh blood in an arctic breeze. Maggie's anxious face peered over Franklin's narrow shoulder.

"I tried to stop him, Mr. Gherl, honest I did, but he wouldn't listen!"

"You've been ducking me for a month, Gherl!" Franklin said in his nasal voice. "No more tricks!"

Maggie said, "Shall I call security?"

"I don't think that will be necessary, Maggs," he said quickly, grabbing a Kleenex from the oak tissue holder on his desk and blotting at his stained shirtfront. Milo had moved into this office only a few weeks ago, and the last thing he needed today was an ugly scene with an irate writer. He could tell from Franklin's expression that he was ready to cause a doozy. Better to bite the bullet and get this over with. "I'll talk to Mr. Franklin. You can leave him here." She hesitated and he waved her toward the door. "Go ahead. It's all right."

When she had closed the door behind her, he picked up the insulated brass coffee urn and looked at Franklin. "Coffee, Billy-boy?"

"I don't want coffee, Gherl! I want to know why you've been ducking me!"

"But I haven't been ducking you, Billy!" he said, refreshing his own cup. He would have to change this shirt before he did lunch later. "I'm not with Universal anymore. I'm with Twentieth now, so naturally my offices are here." He swept an arm around him. "Not bad, ay?"

Milo sat down and tried his best to look confident, at ease. Inside, he was anything but. Right now he was a little afraid of the writer stalking back and forth before the desk like a caged tiger. Nothing about Franklin's physical appearance was the least bit intimidating. He was fair-haired and tall, with big hands and feet attached to a slight, gangly frame. He had a big nose, a small chin, and a big Adam's apple—Milo had noticed on their first meeting two years ago that he could slant a perfectly straight line along the tips of those three protuberances. A moderate overbite did not help the picture. Milo's impression of Franklin had always been that of a patient, retiring, rational man who never raised his voice.

But today he was barging about with a wild look in his eyes, shouting, gesticulating, accusing. Milo remembered an old saying his father used to quote to him when he was a boy: *Beware the wrath of a patient man.*

Franklin had paused and was looking around the spacious room with its indirect lighting, its silver-gray floor-to-ceiling louvered blinds and matching carpet, the chrome and onyx wet bar, the free-form couches, the abstract sculptures on the Lucite coffee table and on Milo's oversized desk.

"How did you ever rate this after perpetrating a turkey like *The Hut*?"

"Twentieth recognizes talent when it sees it, Billy."

"My question stands," Franklin said.

Milo ignored the remark. "Sit down, Billy-boy. What's got you so upset?"

Franklin didn't sit. He resumed his stalking. "You know damn well what! My book!"

"You've got a new one?" Milo said, perfectly aware of which book he meant.

"No! I mean the only book I've ever written—*The Hut*!—and the mess you made out of it!"

Milo had heard quite enough nasty criticism of that particular film to last him a lifetime. He felt his anger flare but suppressed it. Why get into a shouting match?

"I'm sorry you feel that way, Billy, but let's face facts." He spread his hands in a consoling gesture. "It's a dead issue. There's nothing more to be done. The film has been shot, edited, released, and—"

"—and withdrawn!" Franklin shouted. "Two weeks in general release and the theater owners sent it back! It's not just a flop, it's a catastrophe!"

"The critics—killed it."

"Bullshit! The critics blasted it, just like they blasted other 'flops,' like *Flashdance* and *Top Gun* and *Ernest Goes to Camp*. What killed it, Gherl, was word of mouth. Now I know why you wouldn't screen it until a week before it opened: You knew you'd botched it!"

"I had trouble with the final cut. I couldn't—"

"You couldn't get it to make sense! As I walked out of that screening I kept telling myself that my negative feelings were due to all the things you'd cut out of my book, that maybe I was too close to it all and that the public would somehow find my story in your mass of pretensions. Then I heard a guy in his early twenties say, 'What the hell was *that* all about?' and his girlfriend say, 'What a boring waste of time!' and I knew it wasn't just me." Franklin's long bony finger stabbed through the air. "It was you! You raped my book!"

Milo had had just about enough of this. "You novelists are all alike!" he said with genuine disdain. "You do fine on the printed page so you think you're experts at writing for the screen. But you're not. You don't know the first goddam thing about visual writing!"

"You cut the heart out of my story! *The Hut* was about the nature of evil and how it can seduce even the strongest among us. The plot was like a house of cards, Gherl, built with my sweat. Your windbag script blew it all down! And after I saw the first draft of the script, you were suddenly unavailable for conference!"

Milo recalled Franklin's endless stream of nit-picking letters, his deluge of time-wasting phone calls. "I was busy, dammit! I was writer-director! The whole thing was on my shoulders!"

"I warned you that the house of cards was falling due to the cuts you made. I mean, why did you remove all mention of voodoo and zombiism from the script? They were the two red herrings that held the plot together."

"Voodoo! Zombies! That's old hat! Nobody would pay to see a voodoo movie!"

"Then why set the movie in Haiti, f'Christsake? Might as well have been in Pasadena! And that monster you threw in at the end? Where in hell did you come up with that? It looked like the Incredible Hulk in drag! I spent years in research. I slaved to fill that book with terror and dread—all you brought to the screen were cheap shocks!"

"If that's your true opinion—and I disagree with it absolutely—you should be glad the film was a flop. No one will see it!"

Franklin nodded slowly. "That gave me comfort for a while, until I realized that the movie isn't dead. When it reaches the video stores and the cable services, tens of millions of people will see it—not because it's good, but simply because it's there and it's something they've never heard of before and certainly have never seen. And they'll be directing their rapt attention at your corruption of my story, and they'll see 'Based on the Novel by William Franklin' and think that the pretentious, incomprehensible mishmash they're watching represents my work. And that makes me *mad*, Gherl! Fucking-ay crazy mad!"

The ferocity that flashed across Franklin's face was truly frightening. Milo rushed to calm him. "Billy, look: Despite our artistic differences and despite the fact that *The Hut* will never turn a profit, you were paid well into six figures for the screen rights. What's your beef?"

Franklin seemed to shrink a little. His shoulders slumped and his voice softened. "I didn't write it for money. I live off a trust fund that provides me with more than I can spend. *The Hut* was my first novel— maybe my only novel ever. I gave it everything. I don't think I have any more in me."

"Of course you do!" Milo said, rising and moving around the desk toward the subdued writer. Here was his chance to ease Franklin out of here. "It's just that you've never had to suffer for your art! You've had it too soft, too cushy for too long. Things came too easy on that first book. First time at bat, you got a major studio film offer that actually made it to the screen. That hardly ever happens. Now you've got to prove it wasn't just a fluke. You've got to get out there and slog away on that new book! Deprive yourself a little! *Suffer!*"

"Suffer?" Franklin said, a weird light starting to glow in his eyes. "I should suffer?"

"Yes!" Milo said, guiding him toward the office door. "All great artists suffer."

"You ever suffer, Milo Gherl?"

"Of course." Especially this morning, listening to you!

"Look at this office. You don't look like you're suffering for what you did to *The Hut*."

"I did my suffering years ago. The anger you feel about *The Hut* is small change compared to the dues I've had to pay." He finally had Franklin across the threshold. "I'm through suffering," he said as he slammed the door and locked it.

From the other side of the thick oak door he thought he heard Franklin say, "No, you're not."

"Missing any personal items lately, mister?" said a voice.

Milo opened his good eye and saw the big black guy standing over him, leaning on his mop handle. What was *wrong* with this old fart? What was his angle?

"If you don't leave me alone I'm gonna call—" He paused. "What do you mean, 'personal items'?"

"You know—clothing, nail clippings, a brush or comb that might hold some of your hair. That kinda stuff."

A chill swept over Milo's skin like an icy breeze in July.

The robbery!

Such a bizarre thing—a pried-open window, a few cheap rings gone, his drawers and closets ransacked, an old pair of pajamas missing. And his toupee, the second-string hairpiece . . . gone. Who could figure it? But he had been shaken up enough to go out and buy a .38 for his night table.

Milo laughed. This was so ludicrous. "You're talking about a voodoo doll, aren't you?"

The old guy nodded. "It got other names, but that'll do."

"Who the hell *are* you?"

"Name's Andre, but folks call me Andy. I got connections you gonna need."

"You need your head examined!"

"Maybe. But that doctor said he was lookin' for the wires that was cuttin' into your legs and your arm but he couldn't find them. That's because the wires are somewheres else. They around the legs and arm of a doll somebody made on you."

Milo tried to laugh again but found he couldn't. He managed a weak, "Bullshit."

"You believe me soon enough. And when you do, I take you to a *Houngon* who can help you out."

"Yeah," Milo said. "Like you really care about me."

The old black showed his gap-tooth smile. "Oh, I won't be doin' you a favor, and neither will the *Houngon*. He'll be wantin' money for pullin' you fat out the fire."

"And you'll get a finder's fee."

The smile broadened. "Thas right."

That made a little more sense to Milo, but still he wasn't buying. "Forget it!"

"I be around till three. I keep checkin' up on you case you change you mind. I can get you out here when you want to go."

"Don't hold your breath."

Milo rolled on his side and closed his eyes. The old fart had some nerve trying to run that corny scam on him, and in a hospital yet! He'd report him, have him fired. This was no joke. He'd lost his eye already. He could be losing his feet, his hand! He needed top medical-center level care, not some voodoo mumbo-jumbo . . .

. . . but no one seemed to know what was going on, and everyone seemed to think he'd put his own eye out. God, who could do something like that to himself? And his hand and his feet—the doc had said they were going to start rotting off if blood didn't get flowing back into them. What on earth was happening to him?

And what about that weird robbery last week? Only personal articles had been stolen. All the high-ticket stereo and video stuff had been left untouched.

God, it couldn't be voodoo, could it? Who'd even—

Shit! Bill Franklin! He was an expert on it after all those years of research for *The Hut*. But he wouldn't . . . he couldn't. . . .

Franklin's faintly heard words echoed in Milo's brain: *No, you're not.*

Agony suddenly lanced through Milo's groin, doubling him over on the gurney. Gasping with the pain, he tore at the clumsy stupid nightshirt they'd dressed him in and pulled it up to his waist. He held back the scream that rose in his throat when he saw the thin red line running around the base of his penis. Instead, he called out a name.

"Andy! Andy!"

Milo coughed and peered through the dim little room. It smelled of dust and sweat and charcoal smoke and something else—something rancid. He wondered what the hell he was doing here. He knew if he had any sense he'd get out now, but he didn't know where to go from here. He wasn't even sure he could find his way home from here.

The setting sun had been a bloody blob in Milo's rearview mirror as he'd hunched over the steering wheel of his Mercedes and followed Andy's rusty red pick-up into one of L.A.'s seamier districts. Andy had been true to his word: He'd spirited Milo out of the hospital, back to the house for some cash and some real clothes, then down to the garage near the Polo where his car was parked. After that it was on to Andy's *Houngon* and maybe end this agony.

It *had* to end soon. Milo's feet were so swollen he was wearing old slippers. He had barely been able to turn the ignition key with his right hand. And his dick—God, his dick felt like it was going to explode!

After what seemed like a ten-mile succession of left and right turns during which he saw not a single white face, they had pulled to a stop before a dilapidated storefront office. On the cracked glass was painted:

M. TRIESTE
HOUNGON

Andy had stayed outside with the car while Milo went in.

"Mr. Gherl?"

Milo started at the sound and turned toward the voice. A balding, wizened old black, six-two at least, stood next to him. His face was a mass of wrinkles. He was dressed in a black suit, white shirt, and thin black tie.

Milo heard his own voice quaver: "Yes. That's me."

"You are the victim of the *Bocor*?" His voice was cultured, and accented in some strange way.

Milo pushed back the sleeve of his shirt to expose his right wrist. "I don't know what I'm the victim of, but Andy says you can help me. You've *got* to help me!"

He stared at the patch over Milo's eye. "May I see?"

Milo leaned away from him. "Don't touch that!" It had finally stopped hurting. He held his arm higher.

M. Trieste examined Milo's hand, tracing a cool dry finger around the clotted circumferential cut at the wrist. "This is all?"

Milo showed him his legs, then reluctantly opened his fly.

"You have a powerful enemy in this *Bocor*," M. Trieste said, finally. "But I can reverse the effects of his doll. It will cost you five hundred dollars. Do you have it with you?"

Milo hesitated. "Let's not be too hasty here. I want to see some results before I fork over any money." He was hurting, but he wasn't going to be a sucker for this clown.

M. Trieste smiled. He had all his teeth. "I have no wish to steal from you, Mr. Gherl. I shall accept no money from you unless I can effect a cure. However, I do not wish to be cheated either. Do you have the money with you?"

Milo nodded. "Yes."

"Very well." M. Trieste struck a match and lit a candle on a table Milo hadn't realized was there. "Please be seated," he said and disappeared into the darkness.

Milo complied and looked around. The wan candlelight picked up an odd assortment of objects around the room: African ceremonial masks hung side by side with crucifixes on the wall; a long conga drum sat in a corner to the right, while a statue of the Virgin Mary, her small plaster foot trodding a writhing snake, occupied the one on his left. He wondered when the drums would start and the dancers appear. When would they begin chanting and daubing him with paint and splattering him with chicken blood? God, he must have been crazy to come here. Maybe the pain was affecting his mind. If he had any smarts he'd—

"Hold out your wrist," M. Trieste said, suddenly appearing in the candlelight opposite him. He held what looked like a plaster coffee mug in his hand. He was stirring its contents with a wooden stick.

Milo held back. "What are you going to do?"

"Help you, Mr. Gherl. You are the victim of a very traditional and particularly nasty form of voodoo. You have greatly angered a *Bocor* and he is using a powerful *loa*, via a doll, to lop off your hands and your feet and your manhood."

"My left hand's okay," Milo said, gratefully working the fingers in the air.

"So I have noticed," M. Trieste said with a frown. "It is odd for one extremity to be spared, but perhaps there is a certain symbolism at work

69

here that we do not understand. No matter. The remedy is the same. Hold your arm out on the table."

Milo did as he was told. His swollen hand looked black in the candlelight. "Is . . . is this going to hurt?"

"When the pressure is released, there will be considerable pain as the fresh blood rushes into the starved tissues."

That kind of pain Milo could handle. "Do it."

M. Trieste stirred the contents of the cup and lifted the wooden handle. Instead of the spoon he had expected, Milo saw that the man was holding a brush. It gleamed redly.

Here comes the blood, he thought. But he didn't care what was in the cup as long as it worked.

"Andre told me about your problem before he brought you here. I made this up in advance. I will paint it on the constrictions and it will nullify the influence of the *loa* of the doll. After that, it will be up to you to make peace with this *Bocor* before he visits other afflictions on you."

"Sure, sure," Milo said, thrusting his wrist toward M. Trieste. "Let's just get on with it!"

M. Trieste daubed the bloody solution onto the incision line. It beaded up like water on a freshly waxed car and slid off onto the table. Milo glanced up and saw a look of consternation flit across the wrinkled black face towering above him. He watched as the red stuff was applied again, only to run off as before.

"Most unusual," M. Trieste muttered as he tried a third time with no better luck. "I've never. . . ." He put the cup down and began painting his own right hand with the solution. "This will do it. Hold up your hand."

As Milo raised his arm, M. Trieste encircled the wrist with his long dripping fingers and squeezed. There was an instant of heat, and then M. Trieste cried out. He released Milo's wrist and dropped to his knees, cradling his right hand against his breast.

"The poisons!" he cried. "Oh, the poisons!"

Milo trembled as he looked at his dusky hand. The bloody solution had run off as before. "What poisons?"

"Between you and this *Bocor*! Get out of here!"

"But the doll! You said you could—!"

"There is no doll!" M. Trieste said. He turned away and retched. "There *is* no doll!"

With his heart clattering against his chest wall, Milo pushed himself away from the table and staggered to the door. Andy was leaning on his truck at the curb.

"Wassamatter?" he said, straightening off the fender as he saw Milo. "Didn't he—?"

"He's a phony, just like you!" Milo screamed, letting his rage and fear focus on the old black. "Just another goddam phony!"

As Andy hurried into the store, Milo started up his Mercedes and roared down the street. He'd drive until he found a sign for one of the freeways. From there he could get home.

And from home, he knew where he wanted to go . . . where he *had* to go.

"Franklin! Where are you, Franklin?"

Milo had finally found Bill Franklin's home in the Hollywood Hills. Even though he knew the neighborhood fairly well, Milo had never been on this particular street, and so it had taken him a while to track it down. The lights had been on inside, and the door had been unlocked. No one had answered his knocking, so he'd let himself in.

"Franklin, goddammit!" he called, standing in the middle of the cathedral-ceilinged living room. His voice echoed off the stucco walls and hardwood floor. "Where are you?"

In the ensuing silence, he heard a faint voice say, "Milo? Is that you?"

Milo tensed. Where had that come from? "Yeah, it's me! Where are you?"

Again, ever so faintly: "Down here . . . in the basement!"

Milo searched for the cellar door, found it, saw the lights ablaze from below, and began his descent. His slippered feet were completely numb now and he had to watch where he put them. It was as if his feet had been removed and replaced with giant sponges.

"That you, Milo?" said a voice from somewhere around the corner from the stairwell. It was Franklin's voice, but it sounded slurred, strained.

"Yeah, it's me."

As he neared the last step, he pulled the .38 from his pocket. He had picked it up at the house along with a pair of wire cutters on his way here. He had never fired it, and he didn't expect to have to tonight. But it was good to know it was loaded and ready if he needed it. He tried to transfer it to his right hand, but his numb, swollen fingers couldn't keep hold of the grip. He kept it in his left and stepped onto the cellar floor—

—and felt his foot start to roll away from him. Only by throwing himself against the wall and hugging it did he save himself from falling. He looked around the unfinished cellar. Bright, reflective objects were scattered all along the naked concrete floor. He sucked in a breath as he saw the hundreds of sharp curved angles of green glass poking up at the exposed ceiling beams. They looked like shattered wine bottles—big, green, four-liter wine bottles smashed all over the place. And in among the shards were scattered thousands of marbles.

"Be careful," said Franklin's voice. "The basement's mined." The voice was there, but Franklin was nowhere in sight.

"Where the hell are you, Franklin?"

"Back here in the bathroom. I thought you'd never get here."

Milo began to move toward the rear of the cellar, where brighter light poured from an open door. He slid his slippered feet slowly along the floor, pushing the green glass spears ahead of him, rolling the marbles out of the way.

"I've come for the doll, Franklin."

Milo heard a hollow laugh. "Doll? What doll, Milo? There's just me and you, ol' buddy."

Milo shuffled around the corner into view of the bathroom. And froze. The gun dropped from his fingers and further shattered some of the glass at his feet. "Oh, my God, Franklin! Oh, my God!"

William Franklin sat on the toilet wearing Milo's rings, his old slippers, his stolen pajamas, and his other hairpiece. His left eye was patched, and his feet and his right hand were as black and swollen as Milo's. There was a maniacal look in his remaining eye as he grinned drunkenly and sipped from a four-liter green-glass bottle of white wine. The cuts in his flesh were identical to Milo's except that a short length of twisted copper wire protruded from each. A screwdriver and a pair of pliers lay in his lap.

M. Trieste's parting words screamed through his brain: *There is no doll!*

"See?" Franklin said in a slurred voice. "You said I had to suffer."

Milo wanted to be sick. "Christ! What have you done?"

"I decided to suffer. But I didn't think I should suffer alone. So I brought you along for company. Sure took you long enough to figure it out."

Milo bent and picked up the pistol. His left hand wavered and trembled as he pointed it at Franklin. "You . . . you. . . ." He couldn't think of anything to say.

Franklin casually tossed the wine bottle out onto the floor where it shattered and added to the spikes of glass. Then he pulled open the pajama top. "Right here, Milo, old buddy!" he said, pointing to his heart. "Do you really think you want to put a slug into me?"

Milo thought about that. It might be like putting a bullet into his own heart. He felt his arm drop. "Why . . . how . . . I don't deserve. . . ."

Franklin closed his eye and grimaced. He looked as if he were about to cry. "I know," he said. "It's gone too far. Maybe you really don't deserve all this. I've always known I was a little bit crazy, but maybe I'm a lot crazier than I ever thought I was."

"Then for God's sake, man, loosen the wires!"

"No!" Franklin's eye snapped open. The madness was still there. "I entrusted my work to you. That's a sacred trust. You were responsible for *The Hut*'s integrity when you took on the job of adapting it to the screen."

"But I'm an artist, too!" Why was he arguing with this nut? He slipped the pistol into his front pocket and reached around back for the wire cutters.

"All the more reason to respect another man's work! You didn't own it—it was only on loan to you!"

"The contract—"

"*Means nothing!* You had a moral obligation to protect my work, one artist to another."

"You're overreacting!"

"Am I? Imagine yourself a parent who has sent his only child to a reputable nursery school only to learn that the child has been raped by the faculty—then you will understand *some* of what I feel! I've come to see it as my sacred duty to see to it that you don't molest anyone else's work!"

Enough of this bullshit! If Franklin wouldn't loosen the wires, Milo would cut them off! He pulled the wire cutters from his rear pocket and began to shuffle toward Franklin, sweeping the marbles and daggers of glass ahead of him.

"Stay back!" Franklin cried. He grabbed the pliers and pushed them down toward his lap, grinning maliciously. "Didn't know I was left-handed, did you?" He twisted something.

Searing pain knifed into Milo's groin. He doubled over but kept moving toward Franklin. Less than a dozen feet to go. If he could just—

He saw Franklin drop the pliers and pick up the screwdriver, saw him raise it toward his right eye, the good eye. Milo screamed:

"NOOOOO!"

And then agony exploded in his eye, in his head, robbing him of the light, sending him reeling back in sudden impenetrable blackness. As he felt his feet roll across the marbles, he reached out wildly. His legs slid from under him, and despite the most desperate flailings and contortions, he found nothing to grasp on the way down but empty air.

FINAL GIRL THEORY
A. C. Wise

Everyone knows the opening sequence of *Kaleidoscope*. Even if they've never seen any other part of the movie (and they have, even if they won't admit it), they know the opening scene. No matter what anyone tells you, it is the most famous two-and-a-half minutes ever put on film.

The camera is focused on a man's hand. He's holding a small shard of green glass, no bigger than his fingernail. He tilts it, catching the light, which darts like a crazed firefly. Then, so very carefully and with loving slowness, he presses the glass into something soft and white.

The camera is so tight the viewer can't see what he's pushing the glass into (but they suspect). Can you imagine that moment of realization for someone who *doesn't* know? Watch the opening sequence with a *Kaleidoscope* virgin sometime, you'll understand. The man pushes the glass into the soft white, and moves his hand away. A bead of bright red blood appears.

As the blood threads away from the glass, the sound kicks in. Only then do most people notice its absence before and discover how unsettling silence can be. The first sound is a breath. Or is it? Kaleidophiles (yes, they really call themselves that) have worn out old copies of the film playing that split-second transition from silence to sound over and over again. They've stripped their throats raw arguing. *Does* someone catch their breath, and if so, *who*?

There are varying theories, the two most popular being the man with the glass and the director. The third, of course, is that the man with the glass and the director are the same person.

Breath or no breath, the viewer slowly becomes aware they are listening to the sound of muffled sobs. At that moment of realization, as if prompted by it, thus making the viewer complicit right from the start, the camera swings up wildly. We see a woman's wide, rolling eyes, circled with too much makeup. The camera jerk-pans down to her mouth; it's stuffed with a dirty rag.

The soundtrack comes up full force—blaring terrible horns and dissonant chords. The notes jangle one against the next. It isn't music, it's instruments screaming. It's sound felt in your back teeth and at the base of your spine.

The camera zooms out, showing the woman spread-eagle and naked, tied to a massive wheel. Her skin is filled with hundreds of pieces of colored glass—red, blue, yellow, green. Her tormentor steps back; the viewer never sees his face. He rips the gag out, and spins the wheel. Thousands of firefly glints dazzle the camera.

The woman screams. The screen dissolves in a mass of spinning color, and the opening credits roll.

You know what the worst part is? The opening sequence has nothing to do with the rest of the film. It is what it is; it exists purely for its own sake.

But let's go back to the scream. It's important. It starts out high-pitched, classic scream queen, and devolves into something ragged, wet, and bubbling. If there was any nagging doubt left about what kind of movie *Kaleidoscope* really is, it's gone. But it's too late. Remember, the viewer is complicit; they agreed to everything that follows in that split second between silence and sound, between sob and catch of breath. They can't turn back—not that anyone really tries.

Here's another thing about *Kaleidoscope*—no one ever watches it just once; don't let them tell you otherwise.

The opening is followed by eighty-five minutes of color-soaked, blood-drenched action. (Except—if you're paying attention—you know that's a lie.)

The movie is a cult classic. It's shown on football fields, on giant, impromptu screens made of sheets strung between goalposts. It flickers in midnight double-feature theaters, lurid colors washing over men and women hunched and sweating in the dark, feet stuck to crackling floors, breathing air reeking of stale popcorn. It plays in the background, miniaturized on ghostly television screens, while burnouts fuck at 3 a.m., lit by candles meant to disguise the scent of beer and pot.

Here's the real secret: *Kaleidoscope* isn't a movie, it's an infection, whispered from mouth to mouth in the dark.

Hardcore fans have every line memorized (not that there are many). They know the plot back and forth (though there isn't one of those, either). You see, that's the beauty of *Kaleidoscope*, its terrible genius. It is the most famous eighty-seven-and-a-half minutes ever committed to film (don't ever let anyone tell you otherwise), but it doesn't exist. If you were to creep through the film, frame by frame (and people have), you would know this is true.

Kaleidoscope exists in people's minds. It exists in the brief, flickering space between frames. The *real* movie screen is the inside of their eyelids, the back of their skulls when they close their eyes and try to sleep. When the film rolls, there is action and blood, sex and drugs, and not a little touch of madness, but there are shadows, too. There are things seen from the corner of the eye, and that's where the true movie lies. There, and in the rumors.

Jackson Mortar has heard them all. Crew members died or went missing during the shoot (or there was no crew); a movie house burned to the ground during the first screening (the doors were locked from the inside); fans have been arrested trying to recreate the movie's most famous scenes (the very best never get caught); and, of course, the most persistent rumor of all: everything in the movie—the sex, the drugs, the violence, and yes, even the flickering shadows—is one hundred percent real.

"You know that scene in the graveyard, with Carrie, when Lance is leading the voodoo ceremony to bring Lucy back from the dead?" Kevin leans across the table, half-eaten burger forgotten in his hand.

Jackson nods. He traces the maze on the kiddie menu, and refuses to look up. Kevin is a fresh convert. Like moths to flame, somehow they always know—when it comes to *Kaleidoscope*, Jackson Mortar is the man. Jackson supposes that makes him part of the mythology, in a way, and he should be proud. But his stomach flips, growling around a knot of cold fries. He pushes the remains of his meal away, rescuing his soda from Kevin's enthusiastic hand-talking.

"And you know how Carrie is writhing on the tomb, and the big snake is crawling all over her body, between her tits and between her legs, like it's *doing* her, and she's moaning and Lance is pouring blood all over her?" Kevin grins, painful-wide; Jackson can hear it, even without looking up.

"Yeah, what about it?"

"Do you think it's real?"

Jackson finally raises his head. Sweat beads Kevin's upper lip; his burger is disintegrating in his hand. A trace of fear ghosts behind the bravado in his eyes.

"Maybe." Jackson keeps his tone as neutral.

The glimpse of fear gives him hope for Kevin, but Kevin's smile does him in. Maybe the kid sees more than the sex and drugs and blood, but that's all he *wants* to see. Kevin has seen *Kaleidoscope*, and wishes the movie was otherwise. That, Jackson cannot abide.

"Listen, I gotta get going." Jackson stands. "I got work to do."

"Oh, okay. Sure." Kevin's expression falls. Another flicker of unease skitters across his face.

Guilt needles Jackson—he can't leave the kid alone like this—but Kevin pastes it over with another goofy, sloppy grin. "Maybe we can catch a midnight screening together sometime?"

Jackson's pity dissolves; he shrugs into his worn, black trench coat, "Yeah, sure. Sometime."

Jackson squeezes out of the booth. Kevin turns back to his cold hamburger. Jackson wonders how the kid stays so skinny. As he pushes through the restaurant door, out into the near-blinding sun, Jackson tries to remember to hate Kevin for the right reasons, not just because he's young and thin.

Jackson steps off the curb, and freezes. Across the street, on the other side of the world and close enough to touch, Carrie Linden walks through a slant of sunlight. She glances behind her, peering over the top of bug-large sunglasses, which almost swallow her face. She hunches into her collar, pulls open the pharmacy door, and darts inside.

A car horn blares. Jackson leaps back, the spell broken. His heart pounds. No one has seen any of the actors from *Kaleidoscope* since the movie was filmed. There are no interviews, no 'Where Are They Now?' specials on late-night TV. It plays into the mystique, as though *Kaleidoscope* might truly be a mass hallucination thrown up on the silver screen. No one real has ever been associated with the film. The credits list the director as B. Z. Bubb and the writer as Lou Cypher.

It's been nearly forty years since *Kaleidoscope* was filmed, five years before Jackson was born (but long before he was *really* born). But Jackson knows it's her; he would know Carrie Linden anywhere.

Jackson has been in love with Carrie Linden his whole life. (Yes, he considers the first time he saw *Kaleidoscope* as the moment he was born.)

When Carrie Linden first appeared on the screen, Jackson forgot how to breathe. The scene is burned into his retinas; it, more than anything else, is his private, skull-thrown midnight show. He sees it on thin, blood-lined lids every time he closes his eyes.

Jackson refrains from telling anyone this unless he knows they'll really understand (and fellow Kaleidophiles always do). The problem—the reason he can't say anything to converts and virgins—is that the first part of Carrie Linden to appear on screen is her ass.

It's during the party scene. She walks across the camera from left to right. Long hair hangs down her back, dirty blonde, wavy, split ends brushing the curve of her buttocks. She wears ropes of glittering beads, but the viewer doesn't know that yet. They are the same beads used to whip Elizabeth in the very next scene, horribly disfiguring her face, but the viewer doesn't know that yet, either.

What the viewer knows is this: Carrie Linden walks across the screen from left to right. She climbs onto the lap of a man at least twice her age. She fucks him as he lifts tiny scoops of cocaine up to his nose, balancing them delicately on the end of an overlong fingernail.

The first time the viewer sees Carrie's face, she is sprawled naked on the couch. The camera pans up from her toes, pausing at her chest. Her breathing is erratic, shallow, then deep, then panicked-fast—a jackrabbit lives under her skin. Her head lolls to one side, her eyes are blissfully (or nightmare-chokedly) closed. A trickle of blood runs from her nose.

While Carrie sleeps, but hopefully doesn't dream, Elizabeth is whipped with Carrie's beads. Elizabeth screams. She's on her knees, and sometimes it looks as though she's stretching her hands out toward Carrie. Some viewers (Kaleidophiles, all) have made the comparison to various religious paintings. Elizabeth's face is a sheet of blood. When she collapses, her torturer steps over her, and drops the bloody beads around Carrie's neck. Almost as an afterthought he sticks his hand between Carrie's legs before wandering away. She doesn't react at all.

Jackson stares at the pharmacy door for so long that the woman he *knows* is Carrie Linden has time to conclude her business and slip out again, still darting glances over her shoulder as she hurries away. Once she's disappeared around the corner, Jackson dashes across the street, ignoring traffic. He yanks open the pharmacy door, and runs panting to the back counter. Luckily, Justin is working. Justin is a *Kaleidoscope* fan, too. (Aren't we all?)

"Hey, buddy. Here to get your prescription filled?" Justin winks.

Jackson ignores him, trying to catch his breath. "The woman who just left, did you see her?"

"Yeah. Dark hair and glasses? Not bad for an older broad." Justin's grin reminds Jackson of Kevin. He wants to reach across the counter and throttle Justin, who is skinny too, but old enough to know better. He's older than Jackson (not counting *Kaleidoscope* years, of course).

"Percocet," Justin says as an afterthought. He has no compunctions about confidentiality. If he didn't know the owner too well, he'd have been fired a long time ago.

"Can you get me her address?" Jackson asks. His mind whirls (like colors dissolving behind a credit roll while a woman screams).

"Sure." Justin shrugs. No questions asked—that's what Jackson likes about him. Justin consults his computer and chicken scrawls an address on the back of an old receipt.

"Thanks, man. I owe you!" Jackson snatches the paper, spins, and sprints for the door.

"Hey, who is she?" Justin calls after him.

"Carrie Linden!" Jackson slams through the door, answering only because he knows Justin won't believe him.

The name written over the address Justin gave him is Karen Finch. The address isn't five blocks from the pharmacy. Jackson runs the whole way, heaving his bulk, dripping sweat, legs burning, breath wheezing. It's worth a heart attack, worth the return of his childhood asthma, worth anything.

The street he arrives on is tree-lined and shadow-dappled. Cars border both sides of the road, dogs bark in backyards, and two houses over a group of children run in shrieking circles on an emerald lawn.

Jackson approaches number forty-seven. He's shaking. His mouth is dry in a way that has nothing to do with his mad, panting run. His heart pounds, louder than the dying echoes of his fist knocking against Carrie Linden's door. What is he doing? He should leave. But *Kaleidoscope* isn't that kind of movie. It isn't a movie at all. It's an infection, deep in Jackson's blood.

The door opens; Jackson stares.

Light frames the woman in a soft-focus glow, falling through a window at the far end of the hall. Her hair is dyed dark, but showing threads of gray (or maybe they're dirty blonde). The ends are split and frayed. She isn't wearing sunglasses, but shadows circle her eyes, seeming just as large. She is thin—not in a pretty way; her cheekbones knife against her skin. But she *is* Carrie Linden, and Jackson forgets how to breathe.

The second-most-famous scene in *Kaleidoscope* is the carnival scene. It's the one most viewers (not Kaleidophiles, mind you) rewind to watch over and over again. It's spawned numerous chat groups, websites, message boards, and one doctoral thesis, which languishes untouched in a drawer.

The scene goes like this: the characters go to a carnival—Carrie, Lance, Mary, and Josh, even Elizabeth, even though her face is horribly scarred (but not Lucy, because she's dead). The carnival is abandoned, but all the lights are on and all the rides are running. The night flickers with halogen-sick lights, illuminating painted rides and gaudy-bright games. The whole scene drifts, strange and unreal.

The gang rides the funhouse ride. But it's not just a funhouse—it's a haunted house, a hall of mirrors, and tunnel of love all rolled into one. The cars crank along the track, but jerk to a stop in the first room, as if the ride is broken. They wander through the ride on foot. And this is where the movie gets weird.

It fragments. Time stops. (Do any two viewers see the same scene?) The camera follows scarred Elizabeth; it follows meathead Lance. It follows Carrie Linden. Voices whisper, words play backwards, things slide, half-glimpsed, across the corners of the film, at the very *edges*, spilling off the celluloid and into the dark. (Is it any wonder the movie house burned down?)

The funhouse is filled with painted flats and cheesy rubber monsters loaded on springs. But there are also angles that shouldn't exist, reflections where there should be none.

There are odd, jerky cuts in the film itself, loops, backward stutters, and doubled scenes, as if bits of films are being run through a projector at the same time. It's impossible.

Everyone is separated, utterly alone. The strange twists of the mirrored corridors keep them apart, even when they are only inches away. And here debates rage, because something happens, but no one is quite sure what.

Maybe Carrie Linden steps through a mirror into the room where Elizabeth is raking bloody nails against the glass, trying to escape. Some viewers claim that it isn't really Carrie, because she stepped through a mirror too. (Inside the funhouse, is anyone who they used to be?) What follows is brutal. With eerie, cold precision Carrie tortures Elizabeth. Accounts vary. Is blood actually drawn, or is the pain more subtle, more insidious than that? (What did *you* see? What do you *think* you saw?)

What makes the violence even more shocking is that up until this point in the film, Carrie has been utterly passive. (Is it possible to watch her push a sliver of mirrored glass through Elizabeth's cheek and not feel it in your own?) Elizabeth's face fills with terror, but oddly, she doesn't seem to notice Carrie at all. Her gaze darts to the mirrors. Her panicked glances skitter into the shadows.

She looks straight at the camera, and tears roll silently from her eyes.

Four people leave the funhouse at the end of the scene—Carrie, Josh,

Elizabeth, and Lance. (Do they?) Mary is never seen again. Her absence is never explained. It's that kind of film.

The crux of the movie hangs here. Kaleidophiles know if they could just unravel this scene, they'd understand everything. (Do they really want to?) When she leaves the funhouse, what is Carrie holding in her hand? Was there really a reflection in the mirror behind Elizabeth's head? When Carrie leans down and puts her mouth against Elizabeth's ear, what does she whisper?

"Can I help you?" The woman's voice snaps Jackson back to himself. His skin flushes hot; panic constricts his throat.

The woman flickers and doubles. Carrie Linden (or Karen Finch) is here and now, but she is there and then too. Jackson shudders.

Something passes through the woman's eyes, a kind of recognition. It's as though all these years Jackson has been watching her, she's been looking right back at him.

"You're Carrie Linden," he says. His voice is thick and far away.

Her expression turns hard. Jackson sees the cold impulse to violence; for a moment, she wants to hurt him. Instead, she steps aside, her voice tight. "You'd better come inside."

Jackson squeezes past her, close enough to touch. He catches her scent—patchouli, stale cigarettes, and even staler coffee. Her posture radiates hatred; her bones are blades, aching towards his skin. When they are face to face, Jackson glimpses the truth in her eyes—she's been expecting this moment. Carrie Linden has been running her whole life, knowing sooner or later someone will catch her.

She shuts the door—a final sound. Jackson's heart skips, jitters erratically, worse than when he ran all the way here. Carrie gestures to a room opening up to the left.

"Sit. I'll make coffee."

She leaves him, disappearing down the narrow hall. Jackson lowers himself onto a futon covered with a tattered blanket. Upended apple crates flank it at either end. A coffee table sits between the futon and a nest-shaped chair. The walls are painted blood-rust red; they are utterly bare.

Carrie returns with mismatched mugs and hands him one. It's spider-webbed with near-invisible cracks, the white ceramic stained beige around the rim. The side of the mug bears an incongruous rainbow, arching away from a fluffy white cloud. Jackson sips, and almost chokes. The coffee is scalding black; she doesn't offer him milk or sugar.

Carrie Linden sits in the nest chair, tucking bare feet beneath her. She wears a chunky sweater coat. It looks hand-knit, and it nearly swallows her. She meets Jackson's gaze, so he can't possibly look away.

"Well, what do you want to know?" Her voice snaps, dry-stick brittle and hard.

Jackson can't speak for his heart lodged in his throat. There's a magic to watching *Kaleidoscope* (unless you watch it alone). The people on screen dying and fucking and screaming and weeping, they're just shadows. It's *okay* to watch; it's safe. None of it is real.

Motes of dust fall through the light around Carrie Linden—tiny, erratic fireflies. The curtains are mostly drawn, but the sun knifes through, leaving the room blood hot.

"All of it," Carries says, when Jackson can't find the words.

"What?" He gapes, mouth wide.

"That's what you're wondering, isn't it? That's what they all want to know. The answer is—all of it. All of it was real."

Jackson flinches as though he's been punched in the gut. (In a way, he has.) Should he feel guiltier about the cracked light in her eyes, or the fact that his stomach dropped when she said, "That's what they all want to know"? He isn't her first.

Carrie Linden's hands wrap around her mug, showing blue veins and fragile bones. Steam rises, curling around her face. When she raises the mug to sip, her sleeve slides back, defiantly and unapologetically revealing scars.

"Well?" Carrie's gaze follows the line of Jackson's sight. "Why *did* you come, then?"

She bores into him with piercing-bright eyes, and Jackson realizes—even sitting directly across from her—he can't tell what color they are. They are every color and no color at once, as if her body is just a shell housing the infinite possibilities living inside.

"I wanted to talk about the movie. I thought maybe. . . ." Jackson glances desperately around the bare-walled room—nowhere to run. In his head, he's rehearsed this moment a thousand times. He's *always* known exactly what he'll say to Carrie Linden when he finally meets her, but now it's all gone wrong.

I'm sorry, he wants to say, I shouldn't have come, but the words stick in his throat. His eyes sting. He's failed. In the end, he's no better than Justin, or Kevin. He's not a Kaleidophile, he hasn't transcended the sex and gore—he's just another wannabe.

Unable to look Carrie in the eye, Jackson fumbles a postcard out of his coat pocket. The edges are frayed and velvet-soft through years of wear. It's the original movie poster for *Kaleidoscope*, wrought in miniature. Jackson found it at a garage sale last year, and he's been carrying it around ever since. He passes it to Carrie with shaking hands.

As Carrie looks down to study the card, Jackson finally looks up. Like the movie, Jackson knows the card by heart, but now he sees it through Carrie's eyes; he's never loathed himself more. His eyes burn with the lurid color, the jumbled images piled together and bleeding into one.

The backdrop is a carnival, but it's also a graveyard, or maybe an empty field backed with distant trees. A woman studded with fragments of glass lies spread-eagle on a great wheel. Between her legs, Carrie lies on an altar, covered in writhing snakes. Behind Carrie, Elizabeth's blood-sheeted face hangs like a crimson moon. From the black of her wide-open eyes, shadowy figures seep out and stain the other images. They hide behind and inside everything, doubling and ghosting and blurring. The card isn't one thing, it's everything.

"I'm sorry." Jackson finally manages the words aloud.

Slowly, Carrie reaches for a pen lying atop of a half-finished crossword puzzle. Her hand moves, more like a spasm than anything voluntary. The nib scratches across the card's back, slicing skin and bone and soul. She lets the card fall onto the table between them, infinitely kind and infinitely cruel. Jackson thinks the tears welling in his eyes are the only things that save him.

"It's okay," she says. Her voice is not quite forgiving. For a moment, Jackson has the mad notion she might fold him in her bony arms and soothe him like a child, as though he's the one who needs, or deserves, comforting.

Instead, Carrie leans forward and opens a drawer in the coffee table, fishing out a pack of cigarettes. Something rattles and slithers against the wood as the drawer slides closed. Jackson catches a glimpse, and catches his breath. Even after forty years he imagines the beads still sticky and warm, still slicked with Elizabeth's blood.

Carrie lights her cigarette, and watches the patterns the smoke makes in the air, in shadows on the wall. They don't quite match.

"I'm the final girl," she says. The softness of her voice makes Jackson jump. He doesn't think she's even speaking to him anymore. She might as well be alone. (She's always been alone.)

"What?" Jackson says, even though he knows exactly what she's talking about. His voice quavers.

"It's fucking bullshit, you know that?" Her voice is just as soft as before, if the words are harsher. "I wasn't a helpless fantasy at the beginning; I wasn't an empowered hero at the end. I was just me the whole time. I was just human."

She stands, crushing her cigarette against the cupped palm of her hand without flinching. "You can stay if you want. Or you can go. I don't really care."

And just like that she's gone. Jackson is alone with Carrie Linden's blood-red walls and her battered couch, with her beads hidden in the coffee table drawer, and her autograph on a worn-soft postcard. When she walked onto the screen, Carrie Linden stopped Jackson's heart; walking out of the room, she stops it again.

He sees Carrie Linden doubled, trebled—bony-thin hips hidden beneath a bulky sweater; the curve of her naked ass, teased by long blonde hair as she saunters across the screen; a hunted, haunted woman, glancing behind her as she darts into the drugstore.

Jackson has sunk so low, he can't go any lower. (At least that's what he tells himself as he leaves to make it okay.)

At home, Jackson hides the postcard and Carrie Linden's beads at the bottom of his drawer. He covers them with socks and underwear, wadded T-shirts smelling of his sweat and late-night popcorn, ripe with fear and desire.

It doesn't matter how rare the postcard is, never mind that it's signed by Carrie Linden; he'll never show it to anyone, or even take it out of the drawer. The beads are another matter.

Everyone knows the opening sequence of *Kaleidoscope*, but it's the closing sequence that plays in most people's minds, projected against the ivory curve of their dreaming skulls, etched onto the thinness of their eyelids. It bathes the late-night stupors of lone losers curled on their couches with the blankets pulled up to their chins against the flickering dark. It haunts midnight movie screens in rooms smelling of sticky-sweet spills and stale salt. It looms large on sheets stretched between goal posts, while orgies wind down on the battered turf below.

It is the third-most-famous scene in cinema history. (Don't let anyone tell you otherwise.)

Carrie is running. Everybody else is dead—Lance and Lucy, Elizabeth and Josh and Mary, and all the other brief phantoms who never even had names. She is covered in blood. Some of it is hers. She is naked.

Ahead of her is a screen of trees. More than once, Carrie stumbles and falls. When she does, the camera shows the soles of her feet, slick and red. But she keeps getting back up, again and again. The camera judders as it follows her. It draws close, but never quite catches up.

Carrie glances back over her shoulder, eyes staring wide at something the camera never turns to let the viewer see. (Imagination isn't always the worst thing.) Carrie's expression (hunted and haunted) says it all.

There is no soundtrack, no psychedelic colors. The only sound is Carrie's feet slapping over sharp stones and broken bottles and her breath hitching in her throat. She's running for the grass and the impossibly distant trees.

The credits roll.

The screen goes dark.

But Carrie is still there, between the frames, bleeding off the edges, flickering in the shadows. She'll always be right there, forever, running.

LAPLAND, OR FILM NOIR
Peter Straub

A GENERAL INTRODUCTION

Our initial purpose is to discuss the effect, the *feeling tone* of headlights reflected on wet urban streets in Lapland, Florida. This is central to our discourse, the feeling tone of those reflections. By implication, then, rain; cars veering at great speed around sharp corners; unholstered pistols, brandished; desperate men; a sick, thrilled sense of impendingness. The immediate historical context plays a central role, as does a profound national sense of the shameful, the squalid, matters never acknowledged in the golden but streaky Florida light. You'd need a spotlight and a truncheon to beat it out of these people. Florida, it will be remembered, tends toward the hot, the dark, the needy, the rotting, the "sultry." The stunted and unnatural. Lapland, i.e., someone's (theoretically) warm yet not really comfortable, in fact impossibly dispossessing....

Steam rises through the grates.

We are in..
......................gulf coast..sempiternal
darkness...without surcease,
without hope for Silky's.....................

In Lapland, all the women are always awake. Even your *mother* lies awake

89

all the night through, drawing essential feminine nourishment from the bottomless communal well. Headlights shine in long streaks on the rain-soaked streets. Just outside the city limits, a gas station attendant named Bud Forrester rolls on his side in bed, thinking of a woman named Carole Chandler. Carole Chandler is his boss's wife, and she has no conscience whatsoever. Bud does possess a conscience, rudimentary though it is. He wishes he could amputate it, without pain, like a sixth finger no thicker around than a twig. In Bud Forrester's past lies a tremendous crime for which his simple duties at the gas station represent a conscious and ongoing penance.

During the commission of the crime, Frank Bigelow took two rounds in the gut, and he will never again void his bowels without whimpering, cursing, sweating. He walks with a limp, Frank. He isn't the kind of guy who can accept stuff like the whimpering, the sweating, the limping with every step of his beautifully shod feet. And when everything depended on where the money was, the money was lifting and blowing all across the tarmac, jittering through the air, like leaves, falling earthward in zigzags, like leaves. Bud Forrester always had a little tingle of a premonition that it was going to end this way. The other guys, they didn't want to hear about it. Bradford Galt and Tom Jardine, Bigelow had them hypnotized, *in thrall*. If Bud had tried to tell them about his little tingle, Galt and Jardine would have taped his mouth shut, bound his arms and legs, and locked him in a closet. That's the way these boys operate—on only a couple of very simple levels.

Frank Bigelow, though, is another matter. One night, over a lamplit table littered with charts and maps, he had observed a certain shine in the whites of Bud's eyes, and immediately he had known of his underling's traitorous misgivings.

One more detail, essential to the coils of the plot: Frank Bigelow also thinks endlessly and without.........upon Carole Chandler. These thoughts, alas, have darkened since he wound up impotent. Deep in his heart what he'd like to do is sic Tom Jardine on Carole; brutal, stupid Jardine is hung like a stallion (off-camera, the guy is always inventing excuses for showing off his tool) and while Tom makes Carole Chandler beg for more like the bitch she is, Frank would like to be watching through a kind of peephole arrangement. Trouble is, after that he would have to murder Tom Jardine, and Tom is one of his main guys, he's like one of the family, so that's out.

Every film noir has one impossible plot convenience: in this instance, despite his frustrated passion for wicked Carole Chandler, Frank Bigelow has no idea that Bud Forrester is employed at her husband's Shell station, because he sees her only at the Black Swan, the gambling club of which he is part-owner with Nicky Drake, a smooth, smooth operator. In Lapland, one always finds gambling clubs; also, drunken or corrupt night watchmen; a negligee; a ditch; a running man; a number of raincoats and hats; a man named "Johnny"; a man named "Doc," sometimes varied to "Dad"; an alcoholic; a penthouse; a beach shack; a tavern full of dumbbells; an armored car; a racetrack; a............; a shadowy staircase. These elements commonly participate in and enhance the effect of headlights reflected on wet urban streets.

THE WOMEN OF LAPLAND

When young, remarkably beautiful. When aged, negligible. This disparity passes without notice because few of the women of Lapland outlive their youth. They often hiss when they speak, or exhibit some other charming speech defect. Their reflections can be seen in rearview mirrors, the windows of apartments at night, the surfaces of slick wooden bars, the surfaces of lakes and pools, in the eyes of dead men. Carole Chandler likes the look of Bud Forrester, she "fancies" the "cut of his jib," but he strikes her as strangely inert, withdrawn, passive. Of course Carole takes these qualities both at face value and as a personal challenge. Nicky Drake wouldn't fuck this dame for, oh, a hundred million bucks, and his partner's obsession with her makes him............When Carole slinks into the Black Swan, handsome Nicky looks away and frowns in disgust.

Having the life expectancy of mayflies, these women dress like dragonflies, for like cigarette-smoking and cocktail-drinking the wearing of dragonfly attire is a means of slowing time. The most gifted women in Lapland live in virtual dog years, or on a 7:1 ratio. Time is astonishingly relative for everyone in Lapland. That it is especially so for the women allows them a tremendous advantage. They can outthink any man who wanders into their crosshairs because they have a great deal more time to do their thinking in.

In Lapland, no woman ever speaks to another woman, there'd be no point in wasting valuable time like that. What would they talk about, their feelings? They already understand everything they have to know about their feelings. In Lapland, no woman ever speaks to a child, for they are all barren, although some may now and again pretend to be pregnant. It follows that there are no children in Lapland. However, in a location error that went largely unnoticed, Frank Bigelow once drove past an elementary school. In Lapland, women speak only to men, and these interchanges are deeply codified. The soundtrack (see below) becomes especially intrusive at such moments. It is understood that the woman is motivated by a private scheme, of which the man is entirely ignorant, though he may be suspicious, and it's always better, more dramatic, if he is.

Lapland women all have at least two names, the old one that got used up, and the new one, which gets a little more tarnished every day. Carole Chandler used to be Dorothy Lyons, back when she lived in Center City and engineered the moral ruin and financial collapse of Nicky Drake's best friend, Rip Murdock, the owner of the Orchid Club, a gambling establishment with a private membership.

Rip, a dandy at the time, used to..............., and Carol/Dorothy, then a cocktail waitress at his club,...
....
............his beach shack...a moue.......
....a stranger with a gun..........
....
..........bloody rags............................
....
....off the cliff....................................
....
....arched an eyebrow.

Once in her life, every woman in Lapland gazes through lowered eyelids at a man like Nicky, or Frank, or Rip, or even Doc/Dad (but never at a man like Bud), and says, "You and me, we're the same—a no-good piece of trash." In every case, this declaration is meant as, and is taken to be, a compliment.

SOCIAL CRITICISM

In Lapland, the spectator observes a world characterized by deliberate dislocations, complex and indirect narratives, flawed protagonists, ambiguous motives and resolutions, a fascination with death....................
...."the blood in her hair, the blood on the floor, the blood in her hair"....................................
and an atmosphere of nightmare.

When Rusty Fontaine blew into town, he took a room at the Mandarin hotel and started spreading his money around. He was so successful at exploiting middle-class greed and veniality that in six months every square in Lapland owed him a fortune. To get out of debt, a consortium of the squares lured a banker, Chalmers Vermilyea, into an abandoned warehouse and, assisted by Rusty's luscious and treacherous female sidekick, Marie Gardner, persuaded him to embezzle...sprinkled gasoline over the corpse..off the cliff.

To the extent that Lapland is a style and not a genre, the vertiginous camera angles, broken shadows, neon-lit interiors, hairpin staircases, extreme high-angle long shots, graphics specific to entrapment, represent a radically disenchanted vision of postwar American life and values.

PSYCHOPATHS

Because paranoia is always justified in Lapland, psychopathology becomes an adaptive measure. Johnny O'Clock runs a gambling casino, the Velvet Deuce. He knew Bud Forrester in the war, when they fought across France, killing hundreds of Krauts in one bombed-out village after another. Forrester was his sergeant, and he always respected the man. When one day O'Clock stops for gas at a Shell station on the edge of town, he recognizes his old friend in the station attendant and, acting on impulse, offers him a job in the casino. Forrester accepts, thinking that he might escape his obsession with Carole Chandler. Unknown to Forrester, Johnny O'Clock was unable to stop killing after returning to civilian life and now, under the cover of his job at the Velvet Deuce, hires himself out as a contract killer. He intends to recruit his old sergeant into...............velvet gloves, his trademark

....

Frank Bigelow...steam rising through the grates...to the beach shack.....................................with the alcoholic security guard in a stupor.. aflame, the Dodge.....................................two corpses in the back seat and six thousand dollars in cash.

World War II, it must be remembered, serves as the unspoken background for these films and defines their emotional context. Eight percent of adult males in Lapland served as snipers in the war, and a good twelve percent have metal plates in their heads. These men drink too much and mutter to themselves. Because it gives them red-rimmed headaches, they detest big-band jazz, which they refer to as "that monkey music." They are prone to blackouts and spells of amnesia. They often marry blind women and/or nymphomaniacs. Unlike them, the former snipers display no visible emotion of any kind. The men with plates in their heads are completely devoted to the ex-snipers, who reward their loyalty with........... ....with onions.............................

Brace Bannister threw an old woman down the stairs. For pleasure, Johnny O'Clock shot Nelle Marchetti, a prostitute, in the head and got clean away with it. Norman Clyde existed entirely in flashbacks. Old Man Tierney poisoned a girl visiting from California and kept her severed hand in his pocket. Carole Chandler's husband, Smokey Chandler, molests small boys on "business trips" to Center City. Nicky Drake has assigned a number to everyone in the world. Carter Carpenter, the vice mayor of Lapland, sleeps on a mattress stuffed with human hair.

PRIVATE EYES

Most noncriminal adult males in Lapland, apart from the doomed squares, are either policemen or private eyes. It is the job of the policemen to accept bribes and arrest the innocent. It is the job of the private investigators to discover bodies, to be interrogated, to drink from the bottle, to wear trench coats, to smoke all the time, to rebuff sexual invitations from females with charming lisps and hair that hangs, fetchingly, over one eye. The private eyes distrust authority, even their own. Nick Cochran is a rich private eye, and Eddie Willis, Mike Lane, and Tony Burke struggle to make the rent on their ugly little offices, where they sleep on..........Frank Bigelow hired Eddie Willis to find Bud Forrester, but Johnny O'Clock followed Eddie into an alley behind the Black Swan and shot him dead. In Nick Cochran's penthouse, Nicky Drake persuaded Rusty Fontaine to.., but Marie Gardner, who was hiding on the............, overheard and..................
........................with Chalmers Vermilyea. Esther Vermilyea (no relation), made an anonymous call to Nick Cochran and...
....two corpses in the back seat and a man with a plate in his head...
....screaming and sobbing in the dark and rainy street.

Six thousand dollars blew away in the wind, and Tom Jardine.......................
for the first time since the landing at Anzio. Frank Bigelow could protect him no longer.

The armored car left the racetrack. The wrinkled old criminal mastermind known as Dad, whose................................had never left him, led Carole Chandler up the shadowy staircase and...
.............................with a new negligee from the Smart Shoppe.

THE ROLE OF ALAN LADD

Alan Ladd attracts the light.

THE OTHER ROLE OF ALAN LADD

He hovers at the edge of the screen, reminding you that you are, after all, in Lapland, and in some sense always will be. When he smiles, his hair gleams. The smile of Alan Ladd is both tough and wounded, an effect akin to that of headlights reflected on a dark, rain-wet street in downtown Lapland, his turf, his home territory. A sick, shameful nostalgia leaks from every frame, and it is abetted, magnified, amplified by the swooning strings on the sound track. The sound track clings to you like grease. You carry it with you out of the theater, and it swells between the parked cars baking in the sunlight, indistinguishable from the sounds in your head.

ALAN LADD CONSIDERED AS EXTENSION OF THE SOUND TRACK

His name is........................., says Alan Ladd, whose name is Ed Adams, or Johnny Morrison. *That man's name is.....................He is known as Slim Dundee and Johnny O'Clock, also.....................and.....................His names surround him like a cloud of flies. At the center of his names, he................... and...................A* speaking shadow rises from between the parked cars, and you wish for it to follow you home.

.........................., Alan says in musical italics, coming along steadily behind. Sirens flare. A man with a gun flees into a dark, sunlit alley. The hot white stripes of headlights reflected on rainy asphalt shine and shine and shine on the street. Beneath a car further down the block, an oily shadow moves, and the name of that shadow is.....................

Forget him, Alan says. *Forget IT.* Underneath his warm deep grainy voice, that of a tender and exhausted god, a hundred stringed instruments swoop and twirl, following its music. *Do it for my sake. If not for......sake, for mine. I know......can hear me, kid. Kiddo. Little guy.*

I always liked....., did you know that?

And at night, when.......lie in the bottom bunk with your face to the onyx window, only........awake in all the house, a streak of blond hair shines in the corner of the window frame, the music stirs like the sound of death and heartbreak, and when his wounded face slips into view, he says, *A lot of this is gonna disappear forever. If you remember anything, remember that it's.........fault..........mber that. Little guy. If you can't remember that, remember me.*

THE THOUSAND CUTS
Ian Watson

The Petrushka restaurant was a large dim cellar, with theirs the only table occupied. Ballets Russes murals writhed dimly on the walls: exotic ghosts.

As the waiter unloaded the chilled glasses of vodka, Don Kavanagh observed, "I don't think Russian restaurants are very popular these days."

"That's why we came," Hugh Carpenter said. "Bound to get a table."

"Don't blame me," said the waiter. "I'm a Londoner, born and bred."

"Maybe there's a good sketch there," suggested Martha Vine, who was the ugly sister of the team. "You know, restaurants run by the wrong sort of people. Such as an Eskimo Curry House. . . . Or, wait a minute, how about a slaughterhouse for vegetables. Wait, I've got it, protests at *vegetable vivisection!*"

Hugh dismissed the notion, and the waiter, with the same toss of his head. The whole sparkle of their TV show relied on cultivating a blind spot for the *obvious*.

"Not quite mad enough, darling." He cocked his head. "What's that?"

Don listened.

"A car backfiring."

"That many times?"

"More like gunfire," said Alison Samuels, shaking her impeccably corn-rowed red hair. She was beauty to Martha's beast.

"So it's somebody gunning their engine." Hugh grinned triumphantly. "Okay, where were we?"

Soon after, sounds of crashing and breakages, a woman's scream, and incoherent shouting came from the upstairs vestibule of the Petrushka . . .

"This isn't one of your practical jokes, is it, Hugh?" asked Martha anxiously. "Tape recorder upstairs? Is it?"

"No, it damn well. . . ."

At that moment, two brawny men wearing lumber jackets crowded down the stairs, thrusting the waiter, who was bleeding from the mouth, and the manager and his beige-blonde receptionist ahead of them. A third man stayed up top. All three were armed with machine guns.

"Stay where you are!" The armed man's accent was southern Irish. "You three, get to a table and sit down!"

The manager, cashier, and waiter did so, quickly.

The momentary silence that followed was broken by the approaching wail of a police siren.

"I take it," said Hugh loudly, "that we are all hostages in yet another bungled terrorist escapade?"

"Be quiet!"

Out of the corner of his mouth, Don murmured, "*Hush.* You're most likely to get murdered in the first few minutes. Then rapport starts building up. Just . . . meditate. Do nothing."

"Zen and the art of being a hostage, eh?" Hugh whispered. He sat still as a Buddhist monk.

A police loudspeaker spoke, close by. . . .

"Don't come any nearer!" cried the upstairs man. "We have hostages in here! We'll kill them!"

Lumber jacket number two ran to the kitchen door and kicked it open. . . .

Hugh's tongue moved inside her mouth. His finger traced the curve of her hip.

He pulled away instantly. He was naked. So was Alison. They were on the bed in his Chelsea flat. Outside was bright with June sunlight.

Alison gazed at Hugh, wide-eyed.

"But," she managed to say.

"But we're in the Petrushka, Alison. . . . I mean, correct me if I'm crazy, but I wasn't aware that I'm subject to bouts of amnesia! I mean . . . how the hell did we get here? I mean, you *can* tell me, can't you?"

"Hugh. I . . . I can't tell you anything. We're in the restaurant. Those IRA men are . . . at least . . . I suppose that's what they were. But we aren't. We're here."

Hugh sat up. Dumbly he stared at a newspaper lying on the yellow shag-piled carpet.

The headline was: Petrushka Siege Ends Peacefully.

He read the story, hardly understanding it. But he understood the accompanying photograph of himself with his arm wrapped round Alison's shoulders, both of them grinning and waving.

"Just look at the date! June, the *ninth*. This is next week's newspaper."

"So we're in the middle of next week." Alison began to laugh hysterically, then with deliberate irony she slapped her own cheek. "I must remember this trick next time I visit the dentist's. . . . Why can't either of us remember a bloody thing?"

"I wish I could remember us making love."

Alison started to dress.

"I always wanted us to get into bed," Hugh went on. "It was one of my big ambitions. I suppose it still is! We must have been celebrating our freedom. Our release. . . .

"*Gas*," he decided suddenly. "That's it. They must have used some new kind of psychochemical to knock everybody unconscious or confuse us. This is a side effect."

He studied the newspaper more carefully.

"Doesn't say a thing about gas. It says the police talked the gunmen out. I suppose you can muzzle the press a little . . . no, this was all too public. The story has to be true as written."

His telephone rang.

Hugh hurried naked into the next room to take the call.

Alison was sitting at the dressing table, concentrating on braiding her hair, when he returned. He noticed how she was trembling. His own body felt hollow and his skin was covered with goose bumps, though the air was warm.

"That was Don. He . . . he reacted very rationally, for a clown. He's in the same fix we are. After Don hung up, I tried to phone Martha. But I can't get through. All the lines are jammed. I tried to phone the police. I even tried to call . . . I tried to call the goddamn talking clock. Can't get it either. Everybody is phoning to find out what the bloody time is! It isn't just us, Alison. It's got nothing specifically to do with the Petrushka. It's everybody."

"Where's your radio? Switch it on."

"Kitchen."

Hugh fled, still naked, and she followed his bouncing rump.

A punk rock band was singing:

> . . . they'll bomb yer boobs!
> they'll bomb yer brains!
> they'll bomb yer bums!

The song faded.

The deejay said, "You've just heard the latest track from The Weasels. Hot stuff, eh? Like, *radio*-active . . . and that's what a radio's supposed to be: active. So I'm carrying straight on, even if you're all as confused as I am. That's right, loyal listeners, none of us here in the studio has any idea how we got here today. Or how it *got* to be today. But if you're all feeling the way I'm feeling, I've got this word of advice for you: stay cool, and carry on doing what you're doing. Keep on trucking that truck. Keep the traffic moving. Cook the lunch, Ma Jones, and don't set fire to the pan— the kids'll be soon home. And now to help you all, here comes a track from an old group, Traffic. It's called 'In a Chinese Noodle Factory.' . . ."

Hugh turned across the dial. One station had simply gone off the air; on others only music was being broadcast.

"Try short-wave," urged Alison. "Abroad."

When he picked up a gabbled French-language broadcast from Cairo, he realized that whatever had happened, had maybe happened world-wide.

Before the end of June, and during July and August, the effect repeated itself a dozen times. None of the subsequent "breaks" lasted as long as the first one had. Some swallowed up two or three days, and others only a few hours. But there was no sign that they were winding down.

Nor was there any conceivable explanation.

Nor could people get used to having their lives repeatedly broken at random.

For this was not simply like fainting or falling asleep. When awareness resumed—and who could promise that it would, next time? —all the world's activities were found to have flowed on as usual. Airplanes had jetted to and fro between London and New York. Contracts had been signed, and babies born. Newspapers had been printed—and the newsdealers' cry of "Read all about it!" was now an imperative, for how else could anyone find out in detail what had happened? A woman would find herself locked in a jail cell, but the police would have to consult their records before they could break the news to her that she had murdered, say, her husband— which raised strange new questions about guilt and innocence. . . .

Distressing it was, indeed, to find oneself suddenly at the controls of a jumbo jet heading in to land at an unexpected airport, or lying in a hospital bed after a mysterious operation, or running down a street . . . for what reason?

"What if we find ourselves in the middle of a nuclear war, with all the sirens wailing?" asked Alison. "I can't stand it. It's driving me mad." She poured herself another glass of gin.

"It's driving everybody mad," said Don. They were in Hugh's flat. "It's like that old Chinese torture."

"Which, the water dripping down on your skull till it wears a hole in it?"

"No, I mean the Death of a Thousand Cuts. I always wondered if the poor victims died from loss of blood. But it must have been from the accumulated shock. One painful shock after another. One, you could survive. A dozen, you could survive. But a thousand? Never! That's what'll destroy the human race. This is the Life of a Thousand Cuts."

"Good heavens," said Hugh, "you've got it." He rubbed his hands briskly. "*Cuts!* That's brilliant."

"It means we're like robots," Don went on, ignoring him. "We don't *need* consciousness. We don't need to be aware. A bird isn't aware. But that doesn't stop it from courting and raising young and migrating. Actually, it helps. No swallow with self-awareness would bother flying all the way to the tip of South Africa and back every year."

"Do you mean we've evolved too much self-awareness, and it's a dead end?" asked Alison.

"And now we're going to become robots again, and the world will run a lot more smoothly. But we won't know it. Any more than a sparrow or a mouse knows. They just *are*. Martha, you mentioned nuclear war. But have you realized how smoothly the Arms Limitation Talks are going all of a sudden?"

"That's because both sides are more scared of an accident than they've ever been."

"No, it isn't. I've been checking back. All the significant advances have occurred during breaks." Don chuckled softly. "Breakthroughs, during breaks! And remember, too, that the Petrushka siege ended peacefully— during a break."

"During a cut," Hugh corrected him.

"The Petrushka thing could so easily have ended in a bloody shoot-out, with the restaurant being stormed. But it didn't happen that way. . . ."

Don was driving his red Metro along the elevated section of the motorway into Central London, in fast heavy traffic. Some distance behind, a Volkswagen failed to overtake a large tractor-trailer. The tractor-trailer rammed it, skidding and jackknifing. As following traffic slammed into the wreckage, a ball of flame rose up.

"Bloody hell!" Don glanced at the calendar watch he had thought to equip himself with in the aftermath of the first break, before stocks ran out. "Two days, this time."

Alison was sitting next to him. Hugh was in the back seat. No sign of Martha. He hoped she was still alive.

"For Christ's sake, get us *off* here!" begged Alison. "It's a death trap."

"More like a bloody buffalo stampede! Why don't the idiots slow down?"

Somehow, Don reached the next exit ramp safely. The ramp was crowded with vehicles descending. Horns blared. Fenders and bumpers scraped and banged.

"Mustn't forget what we were talking about," Hugh reminded him, over his shoulder. "The life of a Thousand Cuts."

"There'll be a thousand cuts in the paintwork of this baby. . . ."

"Stop at the nearest pub, Don. We have to talk before we lose the continuity."

"About cuts," said Hugh, cradling a double Scotch.

The bar of the Duke of Kent was packed, but remarkably hushed as people waited for the filler music on the landlord's radio to stop, and the first hastily assembled news to take its place. Many people were not drinking at all, but merely waiting.

"You mentioned the Death of a Thousand Cuts, and of course, those were cuts in the flesh with a knife. But what do *we* mean by cuts?"

"A film," said Alison. "Editing. Switching scenes."

"Good girl!"

"I'm not a girl. Girls are twelve years old or less."

"Okay, *sorry.*"

"That's why I wouldn't ever go to bed with you."

"Okay, okay. I prostrate myself. Now, that's it exactly, the editing of a film—the cutting from one scene to the next. You don't need to see your characters drive all the way from A to B. They just leave, then they arrive. Otherwise a film would last as long as real life. Or the director would be Andy Warhol."

"As long as real life *used* to last. . . ."

"Quite. And what if reality itself is really a sort of film? A millennia-long Warhol movie with a cast of billions? Suppose, as holography is to flat photography, so to holography is . . . *solidography.* Suppose the world is being projected. It's a solid movie made of matter, not of light. We're an entry in the Film Festival of the Universe. *But.* . . ." He paused emphatically.

". . . Are we the completed masterpiece? Or are we the rushes on the cutting room floor . . . of reality? Because suddenly we've lost our own sense of continuity. Two days drop out. Three days drop out."

The music on the radio stopped.

"Shush!" hissed a roomful of snakes.

"This is the BBC Emergency Service and I am Robin Johnson. The date is September the first. The time is one-twenty-five in the afternoon. The most recent break measured approximately fifty hours. At the Helsinki disarmament talks, preliminary agreement has been reached on the reduction of. . . ."

"Come on, we can read all that stuff later."

Don had not yet started the engine of the Metro. "Wouldn't it spoil the natural flow of this film of yours if all the characters suddenly became aware that their lives are just a fiction?" he asked. "Maybe this is a very subtle, artistic touch. Maybe the director has suddenly gone into experimental cinema. He was making a realistic film before. But now he's into New Wave techniques—*meta*-film—like a French director. I still say we're all really living robots. But we never knew it before. Now we do," Don concluded.

"But that isn't a decline of awareness," Alison pointed out. "That's an increase in awareness."

"It's a bloody decline in our sense of control over what happens in the world. The important things are all happening offstage. They're happening off everybody's stage. Look at this progress in arms control . . . you heard Robin on the news."

"Maybe," said Alison, "God has decided to cut reality, and reedit it. Because it wasn't working out. Or it didn't work out the first time. It bombed out, literally. We're in a remake of the film of the world."

Hugh teased her, saying, "Maybe these breaks are for advertisements. Only, we can't see them any more than the characters in a film can see the commercials!"

"Rubbish. When you have a commercial," said Alison, "the film just stops. Then it starts up again from the same moment."

"In that case, you're right. Something *must* be editing reality," Hugh acknowledged.

"How can I possibly agree with that? But I can't disagree, either. Lord knows, reality *needs* editing."

An ambulance wailed by, bearing someone from the motorway pile-up. A police car raced the other way, blue light flashing on its roof.

"It's the Thousand Cuts," said Don. "And it'll drive us mad with stress. Like rats in an electrified maze. We'll go catatonic. We'll become a planet of zombies—a world on autopilot. Like the birds and the bees."

He started the engine. Driving out of the car park of the Duke of Kent, he turned left because it was easier to do so, before remembering that he had no idea where they had been heading. He slowed to let another ambulance race by.

Hugh suddenly began to laugh.

"I've just got it! Don't you see, we've got a way to test my idea. We may even have a way to communicate with the director himself! Listen, we'll do a special show. We'll do a show about editing reality. We'll make a film within The Film—a film *about* that Film. I'll package this as a great morale booster, which indeed it might well be! We'll get the whole country laughing at what's happening. It'll help keep people sane during the Thousand Cuts."

Alison clapped her hands.

"Thank you."

"Just so long as we aren't cut off," said Don. "You know, 'Normal transmission resumes as soon as the show is over.'"

"If we are cut off, we'll still be going full steam ahead. We can watch it all on videotape afterward. . . . Swing us around, Don. We're going back to my flat to get the whole thing set up. And we'll need to get hold of Martha. If somebody's editing reality, I'm joining in. We'll call the show 'The Making of *Reality, the Motion Picture*'!"

"Don't you mean 'Remaking'?"

"Yes, I do. Quite right, love. 'The Remaking of *Reality, the Motion Picture*'—that's it. I stand corrected." He slouched back in the seat of the Metro.

"So do we all, Hugh, if you're right. So do we all."

"Do what?"

"Stand corrected. . . ."

Two weeks later, Hugh cradled a phone and turned to his friends.

"Well, I don't know exactly what I've been *doing* the past four days. But I must have been busting my ass, as our American friends so colorfully put it. Our show's been given the green light for October the fourth, right after the nine o'clock news. Seven European countries are hooking up, using subtitles—and two major networks in the States are running us the same evening, with Australia and Japan following suit the next day. Even *Russia* is going to screen the show—subject, that is, to content analysis."

Martha sneezed. She had caught a cold. "Shouldn't be a problem," she sniffled. "Soviets have always laughed at God."

"Okay, so where were we, Don?" asked Alison.

"I've been going through this heap of notes. I'll get them knocked into shape with Martha, then we can start rehearsing on videotape, Thursday. See what runs, and what doesn't run."

"Could we please switch the radio on for a moment?" asked Alison.

"Why? Oh, to check out what's been happening in the"—Hugh grinned broadly—"*real* world? Why not? We might harvest some more ideas."

Fetching the radio, she set it on the bar.

"*. . . Helsinki. This agreement represents a major advance in the lessening of international tension. . . .*"

"How on Earth can an advance lessen something?" Martha asked.

"You should meet my publisher," quipped Don.

"*. . . first genuine reduction in weapons systems, with inspection and verification by neutral observers from the Third World. The actual dismantling and downgrading of. . . .*"

"It seems even God can't manage miracles overnight," Hugh remarked.

"Blah to that," said Alison. "They're all scared of what could happen during one of the zombie intervals. Or just after one, when everyone's confused."

"*. . . reported casualty figures following the most recent break are already in the thousands. The worst disaster occurred at Heathrow Airport, where. . . .*"

"See? It just takes one poor jerk to jab his finger at the wrong button. And *poof*. If this is an example of divine intervention, it's the most ham-fisted miracle I've ever come across," Alison said.

"When you're cutting film, love," said Hugh, "you waste a lot of good material for the sake of the picture as a whole."

"You sound as if you sneakingly admire what's going on," protested Don. "All this bloody cutting of our lives."

Hugh poured himself a brandy, and squirted some soda into the glass.

"No, it's ludicrous, and dangerous, and it's soul-destroying. But you've got to laugh at it, to get it in the right perspective—and yes, to keep our dignity and free will. It's a mad universe—and it's just turned out to be even madder than anybody could have imagined. Well, in my humble opinion the highest human art isn't tragedy. It's satire. And," here he nodded derisively toward the ceiling, "speaking as one trickster to another, I want whoever or whatever is directing this big show, Life, to notice that *I've* spotted what's going on. I've found out that reality is just a movie—and I can stay home and even laugh."

"*. . . have been inundated with requests for Librium and Valium. . . .*"

"I laugh, therefore I am. Birds don't laugh. Cows don't laugh. There's the difference. Now let's get on with it. Let's make everyone kill themselves laughing. They deserve it."

"The Remaking of *Reality, the Motion Picture*" was prerecorded during the afternoons of October the first and second—with Hugh Carpenter in the role of Cosmic Director and the lovely Alison as his continuity person—and it was edited into shape on the third.

It was, in the opinion of all concerned, just about the sharpest and funniest half-hour of TV in the history of the world.

Hugh turned from the video monitor to wave back to the technicians. Peter Rolfe, who had produced the show, pumped Hugh's hand and slapped him on the back, then embraced Alison and kissed her. After a moment's hesitation, he kissed Martha too. Though the show was prerecorded, the whole team had decided to be present for the transmission.

Hugh popped open one of the champagne bottles he had brought along.

"Out she flies, out she flies! To Manchester and Munich, to Tulsa and Tel Aviv! To Alpha Centauri and all points in the universe, if there's anybody out there! Cheers!"

Before long, Rolfe's telephone was flashing for his attention.

"Yes? Really? Oh superb!" he enthused. "Hugh! The switchboard is absolutely *jammed*. The viewers are just bubbling over. You've stopped them from throwing themselves under a bus tomorrow. You've stopped them from overdosing tonight. You've made the first real sense out of his ghastly mess. You've made the world *fun* again!"

"What, no negative reactions at all?" interrupted Don.

"Oh, there's a teeny little bit from the blasphemy brigade. But, my dear fellow, you can expect that."

"I do. I look forward to it. The negative reactions are so comical."

"Not this time, old son. It's heartfelt gratitude all round. The country's laughing its collective head off."

"Do you realize," asked Rolfe, as he hosted the celebration party at his Hampstead house the next evening, "this has been a new high for TV? In the last twenty-four hours, you must have clocked up viewing figures of half a billion people? Give or take the Soviets, who don't believe in ratings, mean beasts."

The carpet was strewn with telegrams. Kicking his way among them, Rolfe pressed another whiskey and water on Alison and kissed her again.

"You've probably outdone Armstrong stepping onto the moon," he called to Hugh.

Tipsy people sprawled on the floor, watching a rerun of the show, chortling and whinnying at the high points. It was almost all high points.

"*Salud!*" Rolfe toasted. "The whole world must be laughing tonight. . . ."

"Damn!" swore Don. He glanced at the passing road sign. "Petworth, half a mile. . . . We must be heading down to the cottage."

Hugh was hunched tensely on Don's left, with Martha and Alison behind. Martha was wearing an orange headscarf tied tightly around her black curls—which was remarkably impromptu of her, for a weekend with friends.

The fuel gauge was showing empty, though Don always kept the tank well filled.

Slowing—and really, he had been speeding, doing nearly sixty along this country lane—he relaxed and admired the trees in the reddening sunset of their foliage.

Hugh loosened up too. "You've got to laugh, haven't you?" he asked reflectively.

And then Don looked at his watch. It wasn't the weekend at all; it was midweek.

"Good God, it's October the twentieth. That's the longest break yet. We're at Peter's place in Hampstead, on the fifth—I mean, we *were*. That's a cut of two whole weeks."

"I've got the radio here," said Sarah.

The filler music was Beethoven's. It played jubilantly on and on.

"There's a lot to catch up on," remarked Hugh idly.

Finally the music died away.

"*. . . and I am Robin Johnson. The date is. . . .*"

"We'll be at the cottage in another ten minutes," Don said. "I've got a couple of spare gallons I keep there."

"*. . . news will come as a grave shock to you all. Briefly, the Helsinki disarmament talks collapsed in ruins on the eleventh of October. Yugoslavia was invaded by Warsaw Pact forces on the eighteenth, two days ago. Currently, Soviet armor is massing on the West German border. The NATO Alliance is on full alert, but so far. . . . Wait! . . . I've just received an unconfirmed report that several tactical nuclear weapons have exploded inside West Germany. This report is as yet unconfirmed. . . .*"

"But," said Hugh lamely.

"So that's why we're all trying to get down to the cottage on an empty tank. . . . We're trying to be the lucky ones."

The engine missed several times, coughed, then quietly gave out. The Metro coasted to a halt.

"It seems," said Alison quietly, "that we *did* kill ourselves laughing, after all."

"Do you mean," whispered Martha, "'God—or something—is not mocked'?"

"I don't know about 'God—or something,'" said Don bitterly. "But I suppose we have to describe this as, well, a negative reaction. And somehow it doesn't seem comical. The movie's been axed."

"Post-holocaust scenes now, I presume," grumbled Hugh. "No damn sense of continuity. . . ."

He wound the window down.

"Cut!" he screamed at the sky. "Cut! Cut!"

But the sky in the north brightened intolerably for a few seconds. Not long after, a fierce hot wind tore the red and gold leaves from the trees.

OCCAM'S DUCKS
Howard Waldrop

Producers Releasing Corporation Executive: Bill, you're forty-five minutes behind your shooting schedule.

Beaudine: You mean someone's waiting to see this crap??
                                   —William "One Shot" Beaudine

For a week, late in the year 1919, some of the most famous people in the world seemed to have dropped off its surface.

The Griffith Company, filming the motion picture *The Idol Dancer*, with the palm trees and beaches of Florida standing in for the South Seas, took a shooting break.

The mayor of Fort Lauderdale invited them for a twelve-hour cruise aboard his yacht, the *Gray Duck*. They sailed out of harbor on a beautiful November morning. Just after noon a late-season hurricane slammed out of the Caribbean.

There was no word of the movie people, the mayor, his yacht, or the crew for five days. The Coast Guard and the Navy sent out every available ship. Two seaplanes flew over shipping lanes as the storm abated.

Richard Barthelmess came down to Florida at first news of the disappearance, while the hurricane still raged. He went out with the crew of the Great War U-boat chaser, the *Berry Islands*. The seas were so rough the captain ordered them back in after six hours.

The days stretched on: three, four. The Hearst newspapers put out extras, speculating on the fate of Griffith, Gish, the other actors, the mayor. The weather cleared and calm returned. There were no sightings of debris or oil slicks. Reporters did stories on the *Marie Celeste* mystery. Hearst himself called in spiritualists in an attempt to contact the presumed dead director and stars.

On the morning of the sixth day, the happy yachting party sailed back in to harbor.

First there were sighs of relief.

Then the reception soured. Someone in Hollywood pointed out that Griffith's next picture, to be released nationwide in three weeks, was called *The Greatest Question* and was about life after death, and the attempts of mediums to contact the dead.

W. R. Hearst was not amused, and he told the editors not to be amused either.

Griffith shrugged his shoulders for the newsmen. "A storm came up. The captain put in at the nearest island. We rode out the cyclone. We had plenty to eat and drink, and when it was over, we came back."

The island was called Whale Cay. They had been buffeted by the heavy seas and torrential rains the first day and night, but made do by lantern light and electric torches, and the dancing fire of the lightning in the bay around them. They slept stacked like cordwood in the crowded belowdecks.

They had breakfasted in the sunny eye of the hurricane late next morning up on deck. Many of the movie people had had strange dreams, which they related as the far-wall clouds of the back half of the hurricane moved lazily toward them.

Nell Hamilton, the matinee idol who had posed for paintings on the cover of the *Saturday Evening Post* during the Great War, told his dream. He was in a long valley with high cliffs surrounding him. On every side, as far as he could see, the ground, the arroyos were covered with the bones and tusks of elephants. Their cyclopean skulls were tumbled at all angles. There were millions and millions of them, as if every pachyderm that had ever lived had died there. It was near dark, the sky overhead paling, the jumbled bones around him becoming purple and indistinct.

Over the narrow valley, against the early stars a strange light appeared. It came from a searchlight somewhere beyond the cliffs, and projected onto a high bank of noctilucent cirrus was a winged black shape. From somewhere behind him a telephone rang with a sense of urgency. Then he'd awakened with a start.

Lillian Gish, who'd only arrived at the dock the morning they left, going directly from the *Florida Special* to the yacht, had spent the whole week before at the new studio at Mamaroneck, New York, overseeing its completion and directing her sister in a comedy feature. On the tossing, pitching yacht, she'd had a terrible time getting to sleep. She had dreamed, she said, of being an old woman, or being dressed like one, and carrying a Browning semiautomatic shotgun. She was being stalked through a swamp by a crazed man with words tattooed on his fists, who sang hymns as he followed her. She was very frightened in her nightmare, she said, not by being pursued, but by the idea of being old. Everyone laughed at that.

They asked David Wark Griffith what he'd dreamed of. "Nothing in particular," he said. But he *had* dreamed: There was a land of fire and eruptions, where men and women clad in animal skins fought against giant crocodiles and lizards, much like in his film of ten years before, *Man's Genesis*. Hal Roach, the upstart competing producer, was there, too, looking older, but he seemed to be telling Griffith what to do. D. W. couldn't imagine such a thing. Griffith attributed the dream to the rolling of the ship, and to an especially fine bowl of turtle soup he'd eaten that morning aboard the *Gray Duck*, before the storm hit.

Another person didn't tell of his dreams. He saw no reason to. He was the stubby steward who kept them all rocking with laughter through the storm with his antics and jokes. He said nothing to the film people, because he had a dream so very puzzling to him, a dream unlike any other he'd ever had.

He had been somewhere: a stage, a room. He wore some kind of livery: a doorman's or a chauffeur's outfit. There was a big Swede standing right in front of him, and the Swedish guy was made up like a Japanese or a Chinaman. He had a big mustache like Dr. Fu Manchu on the book jackets, and he wore a tropical planter's suit and hat. Then this young

Filipino guy had run into the room yelling a mile a minute, and the Swede asked, "Why number-three son making noise like motorboat?" and the Filipino yelled something else and ran to a closet door and opened it, and a white feller fell out of it with a knife in his back.

Then a voice behind the steward said, "Cut!" and then said, "Let's do it again," and the guy with the knife in his back got up and went back into the closet, and the Filipino guy went back out the door, and the big Swede took two puffs on a Camel and handed it to someone and then just stood there, and the voice behind the steward said to him, "Okay," and then, "This time, Mantan, bug your eyes out a little more." The dream made no sense at all.

After their return on the yacht, the steward had performed at the wrap party for the productions. An Elk saw him, and they hired him to do their next initiation follies. Then he won a couple of amateur nights, and played theaters in a couple of nearby towns. He fetched and carried around at the mayor's house in the daytime, and rolled audiences in the aisles at night.

One day early in 1920, he looked in his monthly pay envelope and found it was about a quarter of what he'd earned in the theater the last week.

He gave notice, hit the boards running, and never looked back.

So it was that two years later, on April 12, 1922, Mantan Brown found himself, at eight in the morning, in front of a large building in Fort Lee, New Jersey. He had seen the place the year before, when he had been playing a theater down the street. Before the Great War, it had been part of Nestor or Centaur, or maybe the Thantouser Film Company. The Navy had taken it over for a year to make toothbrushing and trench-foot movies to show new recruits, and films for the public on how to spot the Kaiser in case he was working in disguise on your block.

It was a commercial studio again, but now for rent by the day or week. Most film production had moved out to the Western Coast, but there were still a few—in Jersey, out on Astoria, in Manhattan itself—doing some kind of business in the East.

Mantan had ferried over before sunup, taken a streetcar, and checked in to the nearby hotel, one that let Negroes stay there as long as they paid in advance.

He went inside, past a desk and a yawning guard who waved him on, and found a guy in coveralls with a broom, which, Mantan had learned in two years in the business, was where you went to find out stuff.

"I'm looking for The Man with the Shoes," he said.

"You and everybody else," said the handyman. He squinted. "I seen you somewhere before."

"Not unless you pay to get in places I wouldn't," said Mantan.

"Bessie Smith?" said the workman. "I mean, you're not Bessie Smith. But why I think of her when I see you?"

Mantan smiled. "Toured with her and Ma Rainey last year. I tried to tell jokes, and people threw bricks and things at me till they came back on and sang. Theater Owners' Booking Agency. The TOBA circuit."

The guy smiled. "Tough On Black Asses, huh?"

"You got that right."

"Well, I thought you were pretty good. Caught you somewhere in the City. Went there for the jazz."

"Thank you—"

"Willie." The janitor stuck out his hand, shook Mantan's.

"Thank you, Willie. Mantan Brown." He looked around. "Can you tell me what the hoodoo's going on here?"

"Beats me. I done the *strangest* things I ever done this past week. I work here—at the studio itself, fetchin' and carryin' and ridin' a mop. Guy rented it two weeks ago—guy with the shoes is named Mr. Meister, a real yegg. He must be makin' a race movie—the waiting room, second down the hall to the left—looks like Connie's Club on Saturday night after all the slummers left. The guy directing the thing—Meister's just the watch chain—name's Slavo, Marcel Slavo. Nice guy, real deliberate and intense—somethin's wrong with him, looks like a jakeleg or blizzard-bunny to me—he's got some great scheme or somethin'. I been painting scenery for it. Don't make sense. You'd think they were making another *Intolerance*, but they only got cameras coming in Thursday and Friday, shooting time for a two-reeler. Other than that, Mr. Brown, I don't know a thing more than you do."

"Thanks."

The waiting room wasn't like Connie's; it was like a TOBA tent-show alumnus reunion. There was lots of yelling and hooting when he came in.

"Mantan!"

"Why, Mr. Brown!"

"Looky who's here!"

As he shook hands he saw he was the only comedian there.

There was a pretty young woman, a high-yellow he hadn't seen before, sitting very quietly by herself. She had on a green wool dress and toque, and a weasel-trimmed wrap rested on the back of her chair.

"Somethin', huh?" asked Le Roi Chicken, a dancer from Harlem who'd been in revues with *both* Moran and Mack *and* Buck and Bubbles. "Her name's Pauline Christian."

"Hey, Mr. Brown," said someone across the room. "I thought you was just a caution in *Mantan of the Apes*!"

Mantan smiled, pleased. They'd made the film in three days, mostly in the Authentic African Gardens of a white guy's plantation house in Sea Island, Georgia, during the mornings and afternoons before his tent-shows at night. Somebody had called somebody who'd called somebody else to get him the job. He hadn't seen the film yet, but from what he remembered of making it, it was probably pretty funny.

"I'm here for the five dollars a day, just like all of you," he said.

"That's funny," said fifteen people in unison, "us all is getting *ten* dollars a day!"

While they were laughing, a door opened in the far corner. A tough white mug who looked like an icebox smoking a cigar came out, yelled for quiet, and read names off a list.

Mantan, Pauline Christian, and Lorenzo Fairweather were taken into an office.

"Welcome, welcome," said Mr. Meister, who was a shorter version of the guy who'd called off the names on the clipboard.

Marcel Slavo sat in a chair facing them. Willie had been right. Slavo had dark spots under his eyes and looked like he slept with his face on a waffle iron. He was pale as a slug, and smoking a Fatima in a holder.

"The others, the extras, will be fitted today, then sent home. They'll be back Thursday and Friday for the shooting. You three, plus Lafayette Monroe and Arkady Jackson, are the principals. Mr. Meister here"—Meister waved to them and Marcel continued—"has got money to shoot a two-reeler race picture. His friends would like to expand their movie investments. We'll go on to the script later, rehearse tomorrow and Wednesday, and shoot for two days. I know that's unusual, not the way you're all used to working, but this isn't the ordinary two-reeler. I want us all to be proud of it."

"And I—and my backers—want it in the can by Friday night," said Mr. Meister.

They laughed nervously.

"The two other principals will join us Wednesday. We can cover most of their shots Thursday afternoon," said Slavo.

He then talked with Lorenzo about the plays he'd been in, and with Mantan about his act. "*Mantan of the Apes* was why I wanted you," he said. "And Pauline," he turned to her, "you've got great potential. I saw you in *Upholding the Race* last week. A small part, but you brought something to it. I think we can make a funny satire here, one people will remember." He seemed tired. He stopped a moment.

"And—?" said Meister.

"And I want to thank you. There's a movie out there right now. It's the apotheosis of screen art—"

"What?" asked Lorenzo.

"The bee's knees," said Mantan.

"Thank you, Mr. Brown. It's the epitome of moviemaking. It's in trouble because it was made in Germany; veterans' groups picketing outside, all that stuff everywhere it plays. There's never been anything like it, not in America, France, or Italy. And it's just a bunch of bohunks keeping people away from it. Well, it's art, and they can't stop it."

"And," said Meister conspiratorially, "they can't keep us from sending it up, making a comedy of it, and making some bucks."

"Now," said Slavo, all business. "I'd like you to make yourselves comfortable, while I read through what we've got for you. Some of the titles are just roughs, you'll get the idea though, so bear with me. We'll have a title writer go over it after we finish the shooting and cutting. Here's the scene: We open on a shot of cotton fields in Alabama, usual stuff; then we come in on a sign: COUNTY FAIR SEPTEMBER 15–22. Then we come down on a shot of the side-show booths, the midway, big posters, etcetera."

And so it was that Mantan Brown found himself in the production of *The Medicine Cabinet of Dr. Killpatient*.

Mantan was on the set, watching them paint scenery.

Slavo was rehearsing Lafayette Monroe and Arkady Jackson, who'd come in that morning. They were still in their street clothes. Monroe must have been seven feet three inches tall.

"Here we go," said Slavo, "try these." What he'd given Lafayette were two halves of Ping-Pong balls with black dots drawn on them. The giant placed them over his eyes.

"Man, man," said Arkady.

Slavo was back ten feet, holding both arms and hands out, one inverted, forming a square with his thumbs and index fingers.

"Perfect!" he said. "Mantan?"

"Yes, Mr. Slavo?"

"Let's try the scene where you back around the corner and bump into him."

"Okay," said Brown.

They ran through it. Mantan backed into Lafayette, did a freeze, reached back, turned, did a double take, and was gone.

Arkady was rolling on the floor. The Ping-Pong balls popped off Lafayette's face as he exploded with laughter.

"Okay," said Slavo, catching his breath. "Okay. This time, Lafayette, just as he touches you, turn your head down a little and toward him. Slowly, but just so *you're* looking at him when he's looking at you."

"I can't see a thing, Mr. Slavo."

"There'll be holes in the pupils when we do it. And remember, a line of smoke's going to come up from the floor where Mr. Brown *was* when we get finished with the film."

"I'm afraid I'll bust out laughing," said Lafayette.

"Just think about money," said Slavo. "Let's go through it one more time. Only this time, Mantan. . . ."

"Yes, sir?"

"This time, Mantan, bug your eyes out a little bit more."

The hair stood up on his neck.

"Yes sir, Mr. Slavo."

The circles under Slavo's eyes seemed to have darkened as the day wore on.

"I would have liked to have gone out to the West Coast with everyone else," he said, as they took a break during the run-throughs. "Then I realized this was a wide-open field, the race pictures. I make exactly the movies I want. They go out to 600 theaters in the North, and 850 in the South. They make money. Some go into state's rights distribution. I'm happy. Guys like Mr. Meister are happy—" He looked up to the catwalk overhead where Meister usually watched from. "The people who see the films are happy."

He put another cigarette in his holder. "I live like I want," he said. Then, "Let's get back to work, people."

"You tell her in this scene," said Slavo, "that as long as you're heeled, she has nothing to fear from the somnam—from what Lorenzo refers to as the Sleepy Guy."

He handed Mantan a slim straight razor.

"Yes, Mr. Brown?" asked Slavo.

"Well, Mr. Slavo," he said. "This film's going out to every Negro theater in the U.S. of A., isn't it?"

"Yes."

"Well, you'll have everybody laughing *at* it, but not *with* it."

"What do you mean?"

"This is the kind of razor cadets use to trim their mustaches before they go down to the dockyards to wait for the newest batch of Irish women for the sporting houses."

"Well, that's the incongruity, Mr. Brown."

"Willie? Willie?"

The workman appeared. "Willie, get $2.50 from Mr. Meister, and run down to the drugstore and get a Double Duck Number 2 for me to use."

"What the hell?" asked Meister, who'd been watching. "A tree's a tree. A rock's a rock. A razor's a razor. Use that one."

"It won't be right, Mr. Meister. Mainly, it won't be as funny as it *can* be."

"It's a tiny razor," said Meister. "It's funny, if you *think* it can defend both of you."

Slavo watched and waited.

"Have you seen the films of Mr. Mack Sennett?" asked Brown.

"Who hasn't? But he can't get work now either," said Meister.

"I mean his earlier stuff. Kops. Custard. Women in bathing suits."

"Of course."

"Well, Mr. Sennett once said, 'If you bend it, it's funny. If you break it, it isn't.'"

"Now a darkie is telling me about the Aristophanic roots of comedy!" said Meister, throwing up his hands. "What about this theory of Sennett's?"

"If I use the little razor," said Mantan, "it breaks."

Meister looked at him a moment, then reached in his pocket and pulled three big greenbacks off a roll and handed them to Willie. Willie left.

"I want to see this," said Meister. He crossed his arms. "Good thing you're not getting paid by the hour."

Willie was back in five minutes with a rectangular box. Inside was a cold stainless steel thing, mother-of-pearl handled with a gold thumb-stop, half the size of a meat cleaver. It could have been used to dry-shave the mane off one of Mack Sennett's lions in fifteen seconds flat.

"Let's see you bend *that*!" said Meister.

They rehearsed the scene, Mantan and Pauline. When Brown flourished the razor, opening it with a quick look, a shift of his eyes each way, three guys who'd stopped painting scenery to watch fell down in the corner. Meister left.

Slavo said, "For the next scene. . . ."

It was easy to see Slavo wasn't getting whatever it was that was keeping him going.

The first morning of filming was a nightmare. Slavo was irritable. They shot sequentially for the most part (with a couple of major scenes held back for the next day). All the takes with the extras at the carnival were done early that morning, and some of them let go, with enough remaining to cover the inserts with the principals.

The set itself was disorienting. The painted shadows and reflections were so convincing Mantan found himself squinting when moving away from a painted wall because he expected bright light to be in his eyes there. There was no real light on the set except that which came in from the old overhead glass roof of the studio, and a few arc lights used for fill.

The walls were painted at odd angles; the merry-go-round was only two feet tall, with people standing around it. The Ferris wheel was an ellipsoid of neon, with one car with people (two Negro midgets) in it, the others diminishingly smaller, then larger around the circumference. The tents looked like something out of a Jamaica ginger-extract addict's nightmare.

Then they filmed the scene of Dr. Killpatient at his sideshow, opening his giant medicine cabinet. The front was a mirror, like in a hotel bathroom. There was a crowd of extras standing in front of it, but what was reflected was a distant, windswept mountain (and in Alabama, too). Mantan watched them do the scene. As the cabinet opened, the mountain disappeared; the image revealed was of Mantan, Pauline, Lorenzo, and the extras.

"How'd you do that, Mr. Slavo?" asked one of the extras.

"Fort Lee magic," said Meister from his position on the catwalk above.

At last the morning was over. As they broke for lunch they heard loud voices coming from Meister's office. They all went to the drugstore across the street.

"I hear it's snow," said Arkady.

"Jake."

"Morphine."

"He's kicking the gong around," said another extra.

One guy who had read a lot of books said, "He's got a surfeit of the twentieth century."

"Whatever, this film's gonna scare the bejeezus out of Georgia, funny or not."

Mantan said nothing. He chewed at his sandwich slowly and drank his cup of coffee, looking out the window toward the cold façade of the studio. It looked just like any other warehouse building.

Slavo was a different man when they returned. He moved very slowly, taking his time setting things up.

"Okay . . . let's . . . do this right. And all the extras can go home early. Lafayette," he said to the black giant, who was putting in his Ping-Pong ball eyes, "carry . . . Pauline across to left. Out of sight around the pyramid. Then, extras. Come on, jump around a lot. Shake your torches. Then off left. Simple. Easy. Places. Camera. Action! That's right, that's right. Keep moving, Lafe, slow but steady. Kick some more, Pauline. Good. Now. Show some disgust, people. You're indignant. He's got your choir soloist from the A.M.E. church. That's it. Take—"

"Stop it! Stop the camera thing. Cut!" yelled Meister from the catwalk.

"What?!" yelled Slavo.

"You there! *You!*" yelled Meister. "Are you blind?"

An extra wearing sunglasses pointed to himself. "Me?"

"If you ain't blind, what're you doing with sunglasses on? It's night!"

"How the hell would anybody know?" asked the extra, looking around at the painted square moon in the sky. "This is the most fucked-up thing I ever been involved with in all my life."

"You can say that again," said someone else.

"You," said Meister to the first extra. "You're fired. Get out. You only get paid through lunch." He climbed down as the man started to leave, throwing his torch with the papier-mâché flames on the floor. "Give me your hat," said Meister. He took it from the man. He jammed it on his head and walked over with the rest of the extras, who had moved back off camera. "I'll do the damn scene myself."

Slavo doubled up with laughter in his chair.

"What? What is it?" asked Meister.

"If . . . if they're going to notice a guy . . . with sunglasses," laughed Slavo, "they're . . . damn sure gonna notice a white man!"

Meister stood fuming.

"Here go," said Mantan, walking over to the producer. He took the hat from him, pulled it down over his eyes, took off his coat. He got in the middle of the extras and picked up an unused pitchfork. "Nobody'll notice one more darkie," he said.

"Let's do it, then," said Slavo. "Pauline? Lafayette?"

"Meister," said a voice behind them. Three white guys in dark suits and shirts stood there. How long they had been watching no one knew. "Meister, let's go talk," said one of them.

You could hear loud noises through the walls of Meister's office. Meister came out in the middle of a take, calling for Slavo.

"Goddamnit to hell!" said Slavo. "Cut!" He charged into Meister's office. There was more yelling. Then it was quiet. Then only Meister was heard.

Lafayette Monroe took up most of the floor, sprawled out, drinking water from a quart jug. He wore a black body suit, and had one of the Ping-Pong balls out of his eye socket. Arkady had on his doctor's costume—frock coat, hair like a screech owl, big round glasses, gloves with dark lines drawn on the backs of them. A big wobbly crooked cane rested across his knees.

Pauline fanned herself with the hem of her long white nightgown.

"I smell trouble," said Lorenzo. "Big trouble."

The guys with the dark suits came out and went past them without a look.

Meister came out. He took his usual place, clambering up the ladder to the walkway above the set. He leaned on a light railing, saying nothing.

After a while, a shaken-looking Marcel Slavo came out.

"Ladies and gentlemen," he said. "Let's finish this scene, then set up the next one. By that time, there'll be another gentleman here to finish up today, and to direct you tomorrow. I am off this film after the next scene . . . so let's make this take a good one, okay?"

They finished the chase setup, and the pursuit. Slavo came and shook their hands, and hugged Pauline. "Thank you all," he said, and walked out the door.

Ten minutes later another guy came in, taking off his coat. He looked up at Meister, at the actors, and said, "Another coon pitcher, huh? Gimme five minutes with the script." He went into Meister's office.

Five minutes later he was out again. "What a load of hooey," he said. "Okay," he said to Mantan and the other actors, "Who's who?"

When they were through the next afternoon, Meister peeled bills off a roll, gave each of the principals an extra five dollars, and said, "Keep in touch."

Mantan took his friend Freemore up to the place they told him Marcel Slavo lived.

They knocked three times before there was a muffled answer.

"Oh, Mr. Brown," said Slavo, as he opened the door. "Who's this?"

"This is Joe Freemore. We're just heading out on the 'chitlin circuit' again."

"Well, I can't do anything for you," said Slavo. "I'm through. Haven't you heard? I'm all washed up."

"We wanted to show you our act."

"Why me?"

"Because you're an impartial audience," said Mantan.

Slavo went back in, sat in a chair at the table. Mantan saw that along with bootleg liquor bottles and ashtrays full of Fatima and Spud butts, the two razors from the movie lay on the table. Slavo followed his gaze.

"Souvenirs," he said. "Something to remind me of all my work. I remember what you said, Mr. Brown. It has been a great lesson to me."

"Comfortable, Mr. Slavo?" asked Freemore.

"Okay. Rollick me."

"Empty stage," said Mantan. "Joe and I meet."

"Why, hello!" said Joe.

"Golly, hi," said Mantan, pumping his hand. "I ain't seen you since—"

"—it was longer ago than that. You had just—"

"—that's right. And I hadn't been married for more than—"

"—seemed a lot longer than that. Say, did you hear about—"

"—you don't say! Why, I saw her not more than—"

"—it's the truth! And the cops say she looked—"

"—that bad, huh? Who'd have thought it of her? Why she used to look—"

"—speaking of her, did you hear that her husband—"

"—what? How could he have done that? He always—"

"—yeah, but not this time. I tell you he—"

"—that's impossible! Why, they told me he'd—"

"—that long, huh? Well, got to go. Give my best to—"

"—I sure will. Good-bye."

"Good-bye."

They turned to Slavo.

"They'll love it down in Mississippi," he said.

It was two weeks later, and the South Carolina weather was the crummiest, said the locals, in half a century. It had been raining—a steady, continuous, monotonous thrumming—for three days.

Mantan stopped under the hotel marquee, looking out toward a gray two-by-four excuse for a city park, where a couple of ducks and a goose were kicking up their feet and enjoying life to its fullest.

He went inside and borrowed a Columbia newspaper from the catatonic day manager. He went up the four flights to his semiluxury room, took off his sopping raincoat and threw it over the three-dollar Louis Quatorze knock-off chair, and spread the paper out on the bed.

He was reading the national news page when he came across the story from New Jersey.

The police said that, according to witnesses, during the whole time of the attack, the razor-wielding maniac had kept repeating, "Bend, d–n it, don't break! Bend, d–n it, don't break!"

The names of the victims were unknown to Mantan, but the attacker's name was Meister.

Twenty years later, while he was filming *Mr. Pilgrim Progresses*, a lady brought him a War Bond certificate, and a lobby card for him to autograph.

The card was from *The Medicine Cabinet of Dr. Killpatient, Breezy Laff Riot*. There were no credits on it, but there on the card were Mantan, Pauline Christian, and Lorenzo Fairweather, and behind them the giant Lafayette Monroe in his medicine cabinet.

Mantan signed it with a great flourish with one of those huge pencils you get at county fairs when you knock down the Arkansas kitty.

He had never seen the film, never knew till now that it had been released.

As the lady walked away, he wondered if the film had been any good at all.

—For Mr. Moreland, and for Icky Twerp

Afterword

I'm glad Oscar Micheaux and other filmmakers of the separate "race," or black cinema of the teens through the '50s, are getting their due. They made films, sometimes on less than nothing, sometimes with a budget that would approach one for a regular-movie short subject, to be shown in theaters in black neighborhoods in the North, and at segregated showings throughout the South (where the black audience all sat in the balconies, even though they were the *only* ones there; it was the same place they sat when a regular Hollywood film was shown). Sometimes Micheaux would get some actors, shoot some photos for stills and lobby cards, and take them around the South, saying to theater owners, "This is knocking 'em dead in Harlem and Chicago, but I only have three prints. Give me twenty dollars and I'll guarantee you'll get it first when I get the new prints." With the money he and his coworkers got that way, he'd go and make the movies, sometimes with different actors than had appeared in the stills . . . (Roberts Townsend and Rodriguez didn't *invent* credit-card filmmaking—it was just that credit cards weren't around back then; if they had been, Micheaux could have saved lots of shoe leather . . .).

Starring in these race pictures (usually the entire cast was black, with a token Honky or two) were black entertainers from vaudeville, theater, the *real* movies (these were the only times they'd ever have leads in films and be top-billed), plus people who seem to *only* have acted in race movies (and who probably had day jobs). The films were comedies, dramas, horror movies, gangster films, backstage musicals, even Westerns (*Harlem on the Prairie, The Bronze Buckaroo*). In other words, the same stuff as Hollywood, only different—all the actors were black and they weren't under the Production Code, the *bête noire* of regular filmmaking from 1934 through the late '50s.

Black actors hopped back and forth from playing comedy relief, singing convicts, elevator operators, musicians, and back-lot natives in real movies to these films.

This story is dedicated to two people; the one to Mr. Moreland is self-explanatory after you've read the story. I needed someone about five years older for my purposes, but I'm not making up much. Mantan Moreland's filmography is about as eclectic a one as you'll find, outside Andy Devine's, Lionel Stander's, and Kate Freeman's. He was everywhere, he did everything; this was besides vaudeville and service-station openings too, I assume. And unlike them, he was in a couple of dozen race movies besides.

The other dedicatee takes a little explaining. Icky Twerp was Bill Camfield, who worked for KTVT Channel 11 in Ft. Worth in the '50s and '60s. In the afternoons and on Saturday mornings, he was Icky Twerp, with a pinhead cowboy hat, big glasses, and some truly Bad Hair; he showed the Stooges on *Slam-Bang Theater*, with the help of gorilla stagehands named Ajax and Delphinium, on a pedal-powered projector he mounted like a bicycle, from which sparks shot out. That's six days a week of live TV: But wait! There's more!—Saturday nights he was Gorgon, the host of *Horror Chiller Shocker Theater* (which ran the *Shock Theater* package of Universal classics plus some dreck). Unlike Count Floyd, he was *good*: Not only that, he did stuff with videotape, then in its infancy, that matched some of what Kovacs was doing. Since it *looked* real, kids would scream and yell, "How'd he do that?"

I think his real job, the one he'd been hired for, was as announcer and newsman. Besides all that, when Cap'n Swabbie (another newsman) had had too much spinach the night before, Camfield filled in for him on *Popeye Theater*, on just before *Slam-Bang*. . . .

What does that have to do with race pictures? Not much. But Camfield and Moreland are what it's all about; work where, when, and how you can. And be funnier than hell, which both of them were. They're both gone. I miss them.

Twist the dial on your WABAC Machine to just after WWI. . . .

DEAD IMAGE
David Morrell

"**Y**ou know who he looks like, don't you?"

Watching the scene, I just shrugged.

"Really, the resemblance is amazing," Jill said.

"Mmm."

We were in the studio's screening room, watching yesterday's dailies. The director—and I use the term loosely—had been having troubles with the leading actor, if acting's what you could say that good-looking bozo does. Hell, he used to be a male model. He doesn't act. He poses. It wasn't enough that he wanted eight million bucks and fifteen upfront points to do the picture. It wasn't enough that he changed my scene so the dialogue sounded as if a moron had written it. No, he had to keep dashing to his trailer, snorting more coke (for "creative inspiration," he said), then sniffling after every sentence in the big speech of the picture. If this scene didn't work, the audience wouldn't understand his motivation for leaving his girlfriend after she became a famous singer, and believe me, nothing's more unforgiving than an audience when it gets confused. The word-of-mouth would kill us.

"Come on, you big dumb son of a bitch," I muttered. "You make me want to blow my nose just listening to you."

The director had wasted three days doing retakes, and the dailies from yesterday were worse than the ones from the two days before. Sliding down in my seat, I groaned. The director's idea of fixing the scene was to have a team of editors work all night patching in reaction shots from the girl and the guys in the country-western band she sang with. Every time Mr. Wonderful sniffled . . . cut, we saw somebody staring at him as if he were Jesus.

"Jesus," I moaned to Jill. "Those cuts distract from the speech. It's supposed to be one continuous shot."

"Of course, this is rough, you understand," the director told everyone from where he sat in the back row of seats. Near the door. To make a quick getaway, if he had any sense. "We haven't worked on the dubbing yet. That sniffling won't be on the release print."

"I hope to God not," I muttered.

"Really. Just like him," Jill said next to me.

"Huh? Who?" I turned to her. "What are you talking about?"

"The guitar player. The kid behind the girl. Haven't you been listening?" She kept her voice low enough that no one else could have heard her.

That's why I blinked when the studio VP asked from somewhere in the dark to my left, "Who's the kid behind the girl?"

Jill whispered, "Watch the way he holds that beer can."

"There. The one with the beer can," the VP said.

Except for the lummox sniffling on the screen, the room was silent.

The VP spoke louder. "I said who's the—"

"I don't know." Behind us, the director cleared his throat.

"He must have told you his name."

"I never met him."

"How the hell, if you. . . ."

"All the concert scenes were shot by the second-unit director."

"What about these reaction shots?"

"Same thing. The kid only had a few lines. He did his bit and went home. Hey, I had my hands full making Mr. Nose Candy feel like the genius he thinks he is."

"There's the kid again," Jill said.

I was beginning to see what she meant now. The kid looked a lot like—

"James Deacon," the VP said. "Yeah, that's who he reminds me of."

Mr. Muscle Bound had managed to struggle through the speech. I'd recognized only half of it—partly because the lines he'd added made no sense, mostly because he mumbled. At the end, we had a close-up of his girlfriend, the singer, crying. She'd been so heartless clawing her way to the top that she'd lost the one thing that mattered—the man who'd loved her. In theory, the audience was supposed to feel so sorry for her that they were crying along with her. If you ask me, they'd be in tears all right, from rolling around in the aisles with laughter. On the screen, Mr. Beefcake turned and trudged from the rehearsal hall, as if his underwear was too tight. He had his eyes narrowed manfully, ready to pick up his Oscar.

The screen went dark. The director cleared his throat again. He sounded nervous. "Well?"

The room was silent.

The director sounded more nervous. "Uh . . . so what do you think?"

The lights came on, but they weren't the reason I suddenly had a headache.

Everybody turned toward the VP, waiting for the word of God.

"What I think," the VP said and nodded wisely, "is we need a rewrite."

"This fucking town." I gobbled Di-Gel as Jill drove us home. The Santa Monica freeway was jammed as usual. We had the top down on the Porsche so we got a really good dose of car exhaust.

"They won't blame the star. After all, he charged eight million bucks, and next time he'll charge more if the studio pisses him off." I winced from heartburn. "They'd never think to blame the director. He's a god-damned artist, as he keeps telling everybody. So who does that leave? The underpaid schmuck who wrote what everybody changed."

"Take it easy. You'll raise your blood pressure." Jill turned off the freeway.

"Raise my blood pressure? Raise my— It's already raised! Any higher, I'll have a stroke!"

"I don't know what you're so surprised about. This happens on every picture. We've been out here fifteen years. You ought to be used to how they treat writers."

"Whipping boys. That's the only reason they keep us around. Every director, producer, and actor in town is a better writer. Just ask them, they'll tell you. The only problem is they can't read, let alone write, and they just don't seem to have the time to sit down and put all their wonderful thoughts on paper."

"But that's how the system works, hon. There's no way to win, so either you love this business or leave it."

I scowled. "About the only way to make a decent picture is to direct as well as write it. Hell, I'd star in it too if I wasn't losing my hair from pulling it out."

"And twenty million bucks," Jill said.

"Yeah, that would help too—so I wouldn't have to grovel in front of those studio heads. But hell, if I had twenty million bucks to finance a picture, what would I need to be a writer for?"

"You know you'd keep writing, even if you had a hundred million."

"You're right. I must be nuts."

"Wes Crane," Jill said.

I sat at the word processor, grumbling as I did the rewrite. The studio VP had decided that Mr. Biceps wasn't going to leave his girlfriend. Instead, his girlfriend was going to realize how much she'd been ignoring him and give up her career for love. "There's an audience out there dying for a movie against women's lib," he said. It was all I could do not to throw up.

"Wes what?" I kept typing on the keyboard.

"Crane. The kid in the dailies."

I turned to where she stood at the open door to my study. I must have blinked stupidly because she got that patient look on her face.

"The one who looks like James Deacon. I got curious. So for the hell of it, I phoned the casting office at the studio."

"All right, so you found out his name. So what's the point?"

"Just a hunch."

"I still don't get it."

"Your script about mercenary soldiers."

I shrugged. "It still needs a polish. Anyway, it's strictly on spec. When the studio decides we've ruined this picture sufficiently, I have to do that Napoleon miniseries for ABC."

"You wrote that script on spec because you believed in the story, right? It's something you really wanted to do."

"The subject's important. Soldiers of fortune employed by the CIA. Unofficially, America's involved in a lot of foreign wars."

"Then fuck the miniseries. I think the kid would be wonderful as the young mercenary who gets so disgusted that he finally shoots the dictator who hired him."

I stared. "You know, that's not a bad idea."

"When we were driving home, didn't you tell me the only way to film something decent was to direct the thing yourself?"

"And star in it." I raised my eyebrows. "Yeah, that's me. But I was just making a joke."

"Well, lover, I know you couldn't direct any worse than that asshole who ruined your stuff this morning. I've got the hots for you, but you're not good-looking enough for even a character part. That kid is, though. And the man who discovers him. . . ."

". . . can write his own ticket. If he puts the package together properly."

"You've had fifteen years of learning the politics."

"But if I back out on ABC. . . ."

"Half the writers in town wanted that assignment. They'll sign someone else in an hour."

"But they offered a lot of dough."

"You just made four hundred thousand on a story the studio ruined. Take a flyer, why don't you? This one's for your self-respect."

"I think I love you," I said.

"When you're sure, come down to the bedroom."

She turned and left. I watched the doorway for a while, then swung my chair to face the picture window and thought about mercenaries. We live on a bluff in Pacific Palisades. You can see the ocean forever. But what I saw in my head was the kid in the dailies. How he held that beer can.

Just like James Deacon.

Deacon. If you're a film buff, you know who I'm talking about. The farm boy from Oklahoma. Back in the middle fifties. At the start a juvenile delinquent, almost went to reform school for stealing cars. But a teacher managed to get him interested in high-school plays. Deacon never graduated. Instead, he borrowed a hundred bucks and hitchhiked to New York, where he camped on Lee Strasberg's doorstep till Strasberg agreed to give him a chance in the Actors Studio. A lot of brilliant actors came out of that school: Brando, Newman, Clift, Gazzara, McQueen. But some say Deacon was the best of the lot. A bit part on Broadway. A talent scout in the audience. A screen test. The rest, as they say, is history. The part of the younger brother in *The Prodigal Son*. The juvenile delinquent in *Revolt on Thirty-Second Street*. Then the wildcat oil driller in *Birthright*, where he upstaged half a dozen major stars. There was something about him. Intensity, sure. You could sense the pressure building in him, swelling inside his skin, wanting out. And authenticity. God knows, you could tell how much he believed the parts he was playing. He actually was those characters.

But mostly the camera simply loved him. That's the way they explain a star out here. Some good-looking guys come across as plain on the screen. And some plain ones look gorgeous. It's a question of taking a three-dimensional face and making it one-dimensional for the screen. What's distinctive in real life gets muted, and vice versa. There's no way to figure if the camera will like you. It either does or doesn't. And it sure liked Deacon.

What's fascinating is that he also looked as gorgeous in real life. A walking movie. Or so they say. I never met him, of course. He's before my time. But the word in the industry was that he couldn't do anything wrong. That's even before his three movies were released. A guaranteed superstar.

And then?

Cars. If you think of his life as a tragedy, cars were the flaw. He loved to race them. I'm told his body had practically disintegrated when he hit the pickup truck at a hundred miles an hour on his way to drive his modified Corvette at a racetrack in northern California. Maybe you heard the legend. That he didn't die but was so disfigured that he's in a rest home somewhere to spare his fans the disgust of how he looks. But don't believe it. Oh, he died, all right. Just like a shooting star, he exploded. And the irony is that, since his three pictures hadn't been released by then, he never knew how famous he became.

But what I was thinking was, if a star could shine once, maybe it could shine again.

"I'm looking for Wes. Is he around?"

I'd phoned the Screen Actors Guild to get his address. For the sake of privacy, sometimes all the Guild gives out is the name and phone number of an actor's agent, and what I had in mind was so tentative that I didn't want the hassle of dealing with an agent right then.

But I got lucky. The Guild gave me an address.

The place was in a canyon north of the Valley. A dusty, winding road led up to an unpainted house with a sundeck supported on stilts and a half dozen junky cars in front along with a dune buggy and a motorcycle. Seeing those clunkers, I felt self-conscious in the Porsche.

Two guys and a girl were sitting on the steps. The girl had a butch cut. The guys had hair to their shoulders. They wore sandals, shorts, and that's all. The girl's breasts were as brown as nutmeg.

The three of them stared right through me. Their eyes looked big and strange.

I opened my mouth to repeat the question.

But the girl beat me to it. "Wes?" She sounded groggy. "I think out back."

"Hey, thanks." But I made sure I had the Porsche's keys in my pocket before I plodded through sand past sagebrush around the house.

The back had a sundeck too, and as I turned the corner, I saw him up there, leaning against the rail, squinting toward the foothills.

I tried not to show surprise. In person, Wes looked even more like Deacon. Lean, intense, hypnotic. Around twenty-one, the same age Deacon had been when he made his first movie. Sensitive, brooding, as if he suffered secret tortures. But tough-looking too, projecting the image of someone who'd been emotionally savaged once and wouldn't allow it to happen again. He wasn't tall, and he sure was thin, but he radiated such energy that he made you think he was big and powerful. Even his clothes reminded me of Deacon. Boots, faded jeans, a denim shirt with the sleeves rolled up and a pack of cigarettes tucked in the fold. And a battered Stetson with the rims curved up to meet the sides.

Actors love to pose, of course. I'm convinced that they don't even go to the bathroom without giving an imaginary camera their best profile. And the way this kid leaned against the rail, staring moodily toward the foothills, was certainly photogenic.

But I had the feeling it wasn't a pose. His clothes didn't seem a deliberate imitation of Deacon. He wore them too comfortably. And his brooding silhouette didn't seem calculated, either. I've been in the business long enough to know. He dressed and leaned that way naturally. That's the word they use for a winner in this business. He was a natural.

"Wes Crane?" I asked.

He turned and looked down at me. At last, he grinned. "Why not?" He had a vague country-boy accent. Like Deacon.

"I'm David Sloane."

He nodded.

"Then you recognize the name?"

He shrugged. "Sounds awful familiar."

"I'm a screenwriter. I did *Broken Promises*, the picture you just finished working on."

"I remember the name now. On the script."

"I'd like to talk to you."

"About?"

"Another script." I held it up. "There's a part in it that I think might interest you."

"So you're a producer, too?"

I shook my head no.

"Then why come to me? Even if I like the part, it won't do us any good."

I thought about how to explain. "I'll be honest. It's a big mistake as far as negotiating goes, but I'm tired of bullshit."

"Cheers." He raised a beer can to his lips.

"I saw you in the dailies this morning. I liked what I saw. A lot. What

I want you to do is read this script and tell me if you want the part. With your commitment and me as director, I'd like to approach a studio for financing. But that's the package. You don't do it if I don't direct. And I don't do it unless you're the star."

"So what makes you think they'd accept me?"

"My wife's got a hunch."

He laughed. "Hey, I'm out of work. Anybody offers me a job, I take it. Why should I care who directs? Who are you to me?"

My heart sank.

He opened another beer can. "Guess what, though? I don't like bullshit, either." His eyes looked mischievous. "Sure, what have I got to lose? Leave the script."

My number was on the front of it. The next afternoon, he called.

"This script of yours? I'll tell you the same thing you said to me about my acting. I liked it. A lot."

"It still needs a polish."

"Only where the guy's best friend gets killed. The hero wouldn't talk so much about what he feels. The fact is, he wouldn't say anything. No tears. No outburst. This is a guy who holds himself in. All you need is a close-up on his eyes. That says it all. He stares down at his buddy. He picks up his M16. He turns toward the palace. The audience'll start to cheer. They'll know he's set to kick ass."

Most times when an actor offers suggestions, my stomach cramps. They get so involved in their part, they forget about the story's logic. They want more lines. They want to emphasize their role till everybody else in the picture looks weak. Now here was an actor who wanted his largest speech cut out. He was thinking story, not ego. And he was right. That speech had always bothered me. I'd written it ten different ways and still hadn't figured out what was wrong.

Till now.

"The speech is out," I said. "It won't take fifteen minutes to redo the scene."

"And then?"

"I'll go to the studio."

"You're really not kidding me? You think there's a chance I can get the part?"

"As much chance as I have to direct it. Remember the arrangement. We're a package. Both of us, or none."

"And you don't want me to sign some kind of promise?"

"It's called a binder. And you're right. You don't have to sign a thing."

"Let me get this straight. If they don't want you to direct but they offer me the part, I'm supposed to turn them down. Because I promised you?"

"Sounds crazy, doesn't it?" The truth was, even if I had his promise in writing, the studio's lawyers could have it nullified if Wes claimed he'd been misled. This town wouldn't function if people kept their word.

"Yeah, crazy," Wes said. "You've got a deal."

In the casting office at the studio, I asked a thirtyish thin-faced woman behind a counter, "Have you got any film on an actor named Crane? Wes Crane?"

She looked at me strangely. Frowning, she opened a filing cabinet and sorted through some folders. She nodded, relieved. "I knew that name was familiar. Sure, we've got a screen test on him."

"What? Who authorized it?"

She studied a page. "Doesn't say."

And I never found out, and that's one of many things that bother me. "Do you know who's seen the test?"

"Oh, sure, we have to keep a record." She studied another page. "But I'm the only one who looked at it."

"You?"

"He came in one day to fill out some forms. We got to kidding around. It's hard to describe. There's something about him. So I thought I'd take a look at his test."

"And?"

"What can I say? I recommended him for that bit part in *Broken Promises*."

"If I want to see that test, do you have to check with anybody?"

She thought about it. "You're still on the payroll for *Broken Promises*, aren't you?"

"Right."

"And Crane's in the movie. It seems a legitimate request." She checked a schedule. "Use screening room four. In thirty minutes. I'll send down a projectionist with the reel."

So I sat in the dark and watched the test and first felt the shiver that I'd soon know well. When the reel was over, I didn't move for quite a while.

The projectionist came out. "Are you all right, Mr. Sloane? I mean, you're not sick or anything?"

"No. Thanks. I'm. . . ."

"What?"

"Just thinking."

I took a deep breath and went back to the casting office.

"There's been a mistake. That wasn't Crane's test."

The thin-faced woman shook her head. "There's no mistake."

"But that was a scene from *The Prodigal Son*. James Deacon's movie. There's been a switch."

"No, that was Wes Crane. It's the scene he wanted to do. The set department used something that looked like the hayloft in the original."

"Wes. . . ."

"Crane," she said. "Not Deacon."

We stared.

"And you liked it?" I asked.

"Well, I thought he was ballsy to choose that scene—and pull it off. One wrong move, he'd have looked like an idiot. Yeah, I liked it."

"You want to help the kid along?"

"Depends. Will it get me in trouble?"

"Exactly the opposite. You'll earn brownie points."

"How?"

"Just phone the studio VP. Tell him I was down here asking to watch a screen test. Tell him you didn't let me because I didn't have authorization.

But I acted upset, so now you've had second thoughts, and you're calling him to make sure you did the right thing. You don't want to lose your job."

"So what will that accomplish?"

"He'll get curious. He'll ask whose test it was. Just tell him the truth. But use these words: 'The kid who looks like James Deacon.'"

"I still don't see. . . ."

"You will." I grinned.

I called my agent and told him to plant an item in *Daily Variety* and *Hollywood Reporter*. "Oscar-winning scribe David Sloane, currently prepping his first behind-the-lens chore on *Mercenaries*, toplining James Deacon lookalike Wes Crane."

"What's going on? Is somebody else representing you? I don't know from chicken livers about *Mercenaries*."

"Lou, trust me."

"Who's the studio?"

"All in good time."

"You son of a bitch, if you expect me to work for you when somebody else is getting the commission—"

"Believe me, you'll get your ten percent. But if anybody calls, tell them they have to talk to me. You're not allowed to discuss the project."

"Discuss it? How the hell can I discuss it when I don't know a thing about it?"

"There. You see how easy it'll be?"

Then I drove to a video store and bought a tape of *The Prodigal Son*.

I hadn't seen the movie in years. That evening, Jill and I watched it fifteen times. Or at least a part of it that often. Every time the hayloft scene was over, I rewound the tape to the start of the scene.

"For God's sake, what are you doing? Don't you want to see the whole movie?"

"It's the same." I stared in astonishment.

"What do you mean, the same? Have you been drinking?"

"The hayloft scene. It's the same as in Wes Crane's screen test."

"Well, of course. You told me the set department tried to imitate the original scene."

"I don't mean the hayloft." I tingled again. "See, here in *The Prodigal Son*, Deacon does most of the scene sprawled on the floor of the loft. He has the side of his face pressed against those bits of straw. I can almost smell the dust and the chaff. He's talking more to the floor than he is to his father behind him."

"I see it. So what are you getting at?"

"That's identical in Wes Crane's test. One continuous shot with the camera at the floor. Crane has his cheek against the wood. He sounds the same as Deacon. Every movement, every pause, even that choking noise right here as if the character's about to start sobbing—they're identical."

"But what's the mystery about it? Crane must have studied this section before he decided to use it in his test."

I rewound the tape.

"No, not again," Jill said.

The next afternoon, the studio VP phoned. "I'm disappointed in you, David."

"Don't tell me you didn't like the rewrite on *Broken Promises*."

"The rewrite? The . . . oh, yes, the rewrite. Great, David, great. They're shooting it now. Of course, you understand I had to make a few extra changes. Don't worry, though. I won't ask to share the writing credit with you." He chuckled.

I chuckled right back. "Well, that's a relief."

"What I'm calling about are the trades today. Since when have you become a director?"

"I was afraid of this. I'm not allowed to talk about it."

"I asked your agent. He says he didn't handle the deal."

"Well, yeah, it's something I set up on my own."

"Where?"

"Walt, really, I can't talk about it. Those items in the trades surprised the hell out of me. They might screw up the deal. I haven't finished the negotiations yet."

"With this kid who looks like James Deacon."

"Honestly, I've said as much as I can, Walt."

"I'll tell you flat out. I don't think it's right for you to try to sneak him away from us. I'm the one who discovered him, remember. I had a look at his screen test yesterday. He's got the makings of a star."

I knew when he'd screened that test. Right after the woman in the casting department phoned him to ask if I had a right to see the test. One thing you can count on in this business. Everybody's so paranoid they want to know what everybody else is doing. If they think a trend is developing, they'll stampede to follow it.

"Walt, I'm not exactly trying to sneak him away from you. You don't have him under contract, do you?"

"And what's this project called *Mercenaries*? What's that all about?"

"It's a script I did on spec. I got the idea when I heard about the ads at the back of *Soldier of Fortune* magazine."

"*Soldier of* . . . David, I thought we had a good working relationship."

"Sure. That's what I thought too."

"Then why didn't you talk to me about this story? Hey, we're friends, after all. Chances are you wouldn't have had to write it on spec. I could have given you some development money."

And after you'd finished mucking with it, you'd have turned it into a musical, I thought. "Well, I guess I figured it wasn't for you. Since I wanted to direct and use an unknown in the lead."

Another thing you can count on in this business. Tell a producer that a project isn't for him, and he'll feel so left out he'll want to see it. That doesn't mean he'll buy it. But at least he'll have the satisfaction of knowing that he didn't miss out on a chance for a hit.

"Directing, David? You're a writer. What do you know about directing? I'd have to draw the line on that. But using the kid as a lead. I considered that yesterday after I saw his test."

Like hell you did, I thought. The test only made you curious. The items in the trades today are what gave you the idea.

"You see what I mean?" I asked. "I figured you wouldn't like the package. That's why I didn't take it to you."

"Well, the problem's hypothetical. I just sent the head of our legal department out to see him. We're offering the kid a long-term option."

"In other words, you want to fix it so no one else can use him, but you're not committing yourself to star him in a picture, and you're paying him a fraction of what you think he might be worth."

"Hey, ten thousand bucks isn't pickled herring. Not from his point of view. So maybe we'll go to fifteen."

"Against?"

"A hundred and fifty thousand if we use him in a picture."

"His agent won't go for it."

"He doesn't have one."

That explained why the Screen Actors Guild had given me Wes's home address and phone number instead of an agent's.

"I get it now," I said. "You're doing all this just to spite me."

"There's nothing personal in this, David. It's business. I tell you what. Show me the script. Maybe we can put a deal together."

"But you won't accept me as a director."

"Hey, with budgets as high as they are, the only way I can justify our risk with an unknown actor is by paying him next to nothing. If the picture's a hit, he'll screw us next time anyhow. But I won't risk the money I'm saving by using an inexperienced director who'd probably run the budget into the stratosphere. I see this picture coming in at fifteen million tops."

"But you haven't even read the script. It's got several big action scenes. Explosions. Helicopters. Expensive special effects. Twenty-five million minimum."

"That's just my point. You're so close to the concept that you wouldn't want to compromise on the special effects. You're not directing."

"Well, as you said before, it's hypothetical. I've taken the package to somebody else."

"Not if we put him under option. David, don't fight me on this. Remember, we're friends."

Paramount phoned an hour later. Trade gossip travels fast. They'd heard I was having troubles with my studio and wondered if we could take a meeting to discuss the project they'd been reading about.

I said I'd get back to them. But now I had what I wanted—I could truthfully say that Paramount had been in touch with me. I could play the studios off against each other.

Walt phoned back that evening. "What did you do with the kid? Hide him in your closet?"

"Couldn't find him, huh?"

"The head of our legal department says the kid lives with a bunch of freaks way the hell out in the middle of nowhere. The freaks don't communicate too well. The kid isn't there, and they don't know where he went."

"I'm meeting him tomorrow."

"Where?"

"Can't say, Walt. Paramount's been in touch."

Wes met me at a taco stand he liked in Burbank. He'd been racing his motorcycle in a meet, and when he pulled up in his boots and jeans, his T-shirt and leather jacket, I shivered from déjà vu. He looked exactly as Deacon had looked in *Revolt on Thirty-Second Street*.

"Did you win?"

He grinned and raised his thumb. "Yourself?"

"Some interesting developments."

He barely had time to park his bike before two men in suits came over. I wondered if they were cops, but their suits were too expensive. Then I realized. The studio. I'd been followed from my house.

"Mr. Hepner would like you to look at this," the blue suit told Wes. He set a document on the roadside table.

"What is it?"

"An option for your services. Mr. Hepner feels that the figure will interest you."

Wes shoved it over to me. "What's it mean?"

I read it quickly. The studio had raised the fee. They were offering fifty thousand now against a quarter million.

I told him the truth. "In your position, it's a lot of cash. I think that at this point you need an agent."

"You know a good one?"

"My own. But that might be too chummy."

"So what do you think I should do?"

"The truth? How much did you make last year? Fifty grand's a serious offer."

"Is there a catch?"

I nodded. "Chances are you'll be put in *Mercs*."

"And?"

"I don't direct."

Wes squinted at me. This would be the moment I'd always cherish. "You're willing to let me do it?" he asked.

"I told you I can't hold you to our bargain. In your place, I'd be tempted. It's a good career move."

"Listen to him," the gray suit said.

"But do you *want* to direct?"

I nodded. Until now, all the moves had been predictable. But Wes himself was not. Most unknown actors would grab at the chance for stardom. They wouldn't care what private agreements they ignored. Everything depended on whether Wes had a character similar to Deacon's.

"And no hard feelings if I go with the studio?" he asked.

I shrugged. "What we talked about was fantasy. This is real."

He kept squinting at me. All at once, he turned to the suits and slid the option toward them. "Tell Mr. Hepner my friend here has to direct."

"You're making a big mistake," the blue suit said.

"Yeah, well, here today, gone tomorrow. Tell Mr. Hepner I trust my friend to make me look good."

I exhaled slowly. The suits looked grim.

I'll skip the month of negotiations. There were times when I sensed that Wes and I had both thrown away our careers. The key was that Walt had taken a stand, and pride wouldn't let him budge. But when I offered to direct for union scale (and let the studio have the screenplay for the minimum the Writers Guild would allow, and Wes agreed to the Actors Guild minimum), Walt had a deal that he couldn't refuse. Greed budged him in our favor. He bragged about how he'd outmaneuvered us.

We didn't care. I was making a picture I believed in, and Wes was on the verge of being a star.

I did my homework. I brought the picture in for twelve million. These days, that's a bargain. The rule of thumb says that you multiply the picture's cost by three (to account for studio overhead, bank interest, promotion, this and that), and you've got the break-even point.

So we were aiming for thirty-six million in ticket sales. Worldwide, we did a hundred and twenty million. Now a lot of that went to the distributors, the folks that sell you popcorn. And a lot of that went into some mysterious black hole of theater owners who don't report all the tickets they sold and foreign chains that suddenly go bankrupt. But after the sale to HBO and CBS, after the income from tapes and discs and showings on airlines, the studio had a solid forty million profit in the bank. And that, believe me, qualifies as a hit.

We were golden. The studio wanted another Wes Crane picture yesterday. The reviews were glowing. Both Wes and I were nominated for—but didn't receive—Oscars. "Next time," I told Wes.

And now that we were hot, we demanded fees that were large enough to compensate for the pennies we'd been paid on the first one.

Then the trouble started.

You remember that Deacon never knew he was a star. He died with three pictures in the can and a legacy that he never knew would make him immortal. But what you probably don't know is that Deacon became more difficult as he went from picture to picture. The theory is that he sensed the power he was going to have, and he couldn't handle it. Because he was making up for his troubled youth. He was showing people that he wasn't the fuckup his foster parents and his teachers (with one exception) said he was. But Deacon was so intense—and so insecure—that he started reverting. Secretly he felt that he didn't deserve his predicted success. So he did become a fuckup as predicted.

On his next-to-last picture, he started showing up three hours late for the scenes he was supposed to be in. He played expensive pranks on the set, the worst of which was lacing the crew's lunch with a laxative that shut down production for the rest of the day. His insistence on racing cars forced the studio to pay exorbitant premiums to the insurance company that covered him during shooting. On his last picture, he was drunk more often than not, swilling beer and tequila on the set. Just before he died in the car crash, he looked twenty-two going on sixty. Most of his visuals had been completed, just a few close-ups remaining, but since a good deal of *Birthright* was shot on location in the Texas oil fields, his dialogue needed rerecording to eliminate background noises on the soundtrack. A friend of his who'd learned to imitate Deacon's voice was hired to dub several key speeches. The audience loved the finished print, but they didn't realize how much of the film depended on careful editing, emphasizing other characters in scenes where Deacon looked so wasted that his footage couldn't be used.

So naturally I wondered—if Wes Crane looked like Deacon and sounded like Deacon, dressed like Deacon and had Deacon's style, would he start to behave like Deacon? What would happen when I came to Wes with a second project?

I wasn't the only one offering stories. The scripts came pouring in to him.

I learned this from the trades. I hadn't seen him since Oscar night in March. Whenever I called his place, either I didn't get an answer or a spaced-out woman's voice told me Wes wasn't home. In truth, I'd expected him to have moved from that dingy house near the desert. The gang that lived there reminded me of the Manson clan. But then I remembered that he hadn't come into big money yet. The second project would be the gold mine. And I wondered if he was going to stake the claim only for himself.

His motorcycle was parked outside our house when Jill and I came back from a Writers Guild screening of a new Clint Eastwood movie. This was at sunset with sailboats silhouetted against a crimson ocean. Wes was sitting on the steps that wound up through a rose garden to our house. He held a beer can. He was wearing jeans and a T-shirt again, and the white of that T-shirt contrasted beautifully with his tan. But his cheeks looked gaunter than when I'd last seen him.

Our exchange had become a ritual.

"Did you win?"

He grinned and raised a thumb. "Yourself?"

I grinned right back. "I've been trying to get in touch with you."

He shrugged. "Well, yeah, I've been racing. I needed some downtime. All that publicity, and. . . . Jill, how are you?"

"Fine, Wes. You?"

"The second go-around's the hardest."

I thought I understood. Trying for another hit. But now I wonder.

"Stay for supper?" Jill asked.

"I'd like to, but. . . ."

"Please, do. It won't be any trouble."

"Are you sure?"

"The chili's been cooking in the Crock-Pot all day. Tortillas and salad."

Wes nodded. "Yeah, my mom used to like making chili. That's before my dad went away and she got to drinking."

Jill's eyebrows narrowed. Wes didn't notice, staring at his beer can.

"Then she didn't do much cooking at all," he said. "When she went to the hospital . . . this was back in Oklahoma. Well, the cancer ate her up. And the city put me in a foster home. I guess that's when I started running wild." Brooding, he drained his beer can and blinked at us as if remembering we were there. "A home-cooked meal would go good."

"It's coming up," Jill said.

But she still looked bothered, and I almost asked her what was wrong. She went inside.

Wes reached in a paper sack beneath a rose bush. "Anyway, buddy." He handed me a beer can. "You want to make another movie?"

"The trades say you're much in demand." I sat beside him, stared at the ocean, and popped the tab on the beer can.

"Yeah, but aren't we supposed to be a team? You direct and write. I act. Both of us, or none." He nudged my knee. "Isn't that the bargain?"

"It is if you say so. Right now, you've got the clout to do anything you want."

"Well, what I want is a friend. Someone I trust to tell me when I'm fucking up. Those other guys, they'll let you do anything if they think they can make a buck, even if you ruin yourself. I've learned my lesson. Believe me, this time I'm doing things right."

"In that case," I said, vaguely puzzled.

"Let's hear it."

"I've been working on something. We start with several givens. The audience likes you in an action role. But you've got to be rebellious, antiestablishment. And the issue has to be controversial. What about a bodyguard—he's young, he's tough—who's supposed to protect a famous movie actress? Someone who reminds us of Marilyn Monroe. Secretly he's in love with her, but he can't bring himself to tell her. And she dies from an overdose of sleeping pills. The cops say it's suicide. The newspapers go along. But the bodyguard can't believe she killed herself. He discovers evidence that it was murder. He gets pissed at the cover-up. From grief, he investigates further. A hit team nearly kills him. Now he's twice as pissed. And what he learns is that the man who ordered the murder—it's an election year, the actress was writing a tell-it-all about her famous lovers—is the president of the United States."

"I think"—he sipped his beer—"it would play in Oklahoma."

"And Chicago and New York. It's a backlash about big government. With a sympathetic hero."

He chuckled. "When do we start?"

And that's how we made the deal on *Grievance*.

I felt excited all evening, but later—after we'd had a pleasant supper and Wes had driven off on his motorcycle—Jill stuck a pin in my swollen optimism.

"What he said about Oklahoma, about his father running away, his mother becoming a drunk and dying from cancer, about his going to a foster home. . . ."

"I noticed it bothered you."

"You bet. You're so busy staring at your keyboard you don't keep up on the handouts about your star."

I put a bowl in the dishwasher. "So?"

"Wes comes from Indiana. He's a foundling, raised in an orphanage. The background he gave you isn't his."

"Then whose. . . ."

Jill stared at me.

"My God, not Deacon's."

So there it was, like a hideous face popping out of a box to leer at me. Wes's physical resemblance to Deacon was accidental, an act of fate that turned out to be a godsend for him. But the rest—the mannerisms, the clothes, the voice—was truly deliberate. I know what you're thinking— I'm contradicting myself. When I first met him, I thought his style was too natural to be a conscious imitation. And when I realized that his screen test was identical in every respect to Deacon's hayloft scene in *The Prodigal Son*, I didn't believe that Wes had callously reproduced the scene. The screen test felt too natural to be an imitation. It was a homage.

But now I knew better. Wes was imitating, all right. But chillingly, what he had done went beyond conventional imitation. He'd accomplished the ultimate goal of every Method actor. He wasn't playing a part. He wasn't pretending to be Deacon. He actually *was* his model. He'd so immersed himself in a role which at the start was no doubt consciously performed that now he *was* the role. Wes Crane existed only in name. His background, his thoughts, his very identity, weren't his own anymore. They belonged to a dead man.

"What the hell is this?" I asked. "*The Three Faces of Eve*? *Sybil*?"

Jill looked at me nervously. "As long as it isn't *Psycho*."

What was I to do? Tell Wes he needed help? Have a heart-to-heart and try to talk him out of his delusion? All we had was the one conversation to back up our theory, and anyway he wasn't dangerous. The opposite. His manners were impeccable. He always spoke softly, with humor. Besides, actors use all kinds of ways to psych themselves up. By nature, they're eccentric. The best thing to do, I thought, was wait and see. With another picture about to start, there wasn't any sense in making trouble. If his delusion became destructive. . . .

But he certainly wasn't difficult on the set. He showed up a half hour early for his scenes. He knew his lines. He spent several evenings and weekends—no charge—rehearsing with the other actors. Even the studio VP admitted that the dailies looked wonderful.

About the only sign of trouble was his mania for racing cars and motorcycles. The VP had a fit about the insurance premiums.

"Hey, he needs to let off steam," I said. "There's a lot of pressure on him."

And on me, I'll admit. I had a budget of twenty-five million this time, and I wasn't going to ruin things by making my star self-conscious.

Halfway through the shooting schedule, Wes came over. "See, no pranks. I'm being good this time."

"Hey, I appreciate it." What the fuck did he mean by "this time"?

You're probably thinking that I could have stopped what happened if I'd cared more about him than I did for the picture. But I did care—as you'll see. And it didn't matter. What happened was as inevitable as tragedy.

Grievance became a bigger success than *Mercenaries*. A worldwide two-hundred-million gross. *Variety* predicted an even bigger gross for the next one. Sure, the next one—number three. But at the back of my head, a nasty voice was telling me that for Deacon three had been the unlucky number.

I left a conference at the studio, walking toward my new Ferrari in the executive parking lot, when someone shouted my name. Turning, I peered through the Burbank smog at a long-haired bearded man wearing beads, a serape, and sandals, running over to me. I wondered what he wore, if anything, beneath the dangling serape.

I recognized him—Donald Porter, the friend of Deacon who'd played a bit part in *Birthright* and imitated Deacon's voice on some of the sound-track after Deacon had died. Porter had to be in his forties now, but he dressed as if the sixties had never ended and hippies still existed. He'd starred in and directed a hit youth film twenty years ago—a lot of drugs and rock and sex. For a while, he'd tried to start his own studio in Santa Fe, but the second picture he directed was a flop, and after fading from the business for a while, he'd made a comeback as a character actor. The way he was dressed, I didn't understand how he'd passed the security guard at the gate. And because we knew each other—I'd once done a rewrite on a television show he was featured in—I had the terrible feeling he was going to ask me for a job.

"I heard you were on the lot. I've been waiting for you," Porter said.

I stared at his skinny bare legs beneath his serape.

"This, man?" He gestured comically at himself. "I'm in the new TV movie they're shooting here. *The Electric Kool-Aid Acid Test.*"

I nodded. "Tom Wolfe's book. Ken Kesey. Don't tell me you're playing—"

"No. Too old for Kesey. I'm Neal Cassady. After he split from Kerouac, he joined up with Kesey, driving the bus for the Merry Pranksters. You know, it's all a load of crap, man. Cassady never dressed like this. He dressed like Deacon. Or Deacon dressed like him."

"Well, good. Hey, great. I'm glad things are going well for you." I turned toward my car.

"Just a second, man. That's not what I wanted to talk to you about. Wes Crane. You know?"

"No, I. . . ."

"Deacon, man. Come on. Don't tell me you haven't noticed. Shit, man. I dubbed Deacon's voice. I knew him. I was his friend. Nobody else knew him better. Crane sounds more like Deacon than I did."

"So?"

"It isn't possible."

"Because he's better?"

"Cruel, man. Really. Beneath you. I have to tell you something. I don't want you thinking I'm on drugs again. I swear I'm clean. A little grass. That's it." His eyes looked as bright as a nova. "I'm into horoscopes. Astrology. The stars. That's a good thing for a movie actor, don't you think? The stars. There's a lot of truth in the stars."

"Whatever turns you on."

"You think so, man? Well, listen to this. I wanted to see for myself, so I found out where he lives, but I didn't go out there. Want to know why?" He didn't let me answer. "I didn't have to. 'Cause I recognized the address. I've been there a hundred times. When Deacon lived there."

I flinched. "You're changing the subject. What's that got to do with horoscopes and astrology?"

"Crane's birth date."

"Well?"

"It's the same as the day Deacon died."

I realized I'd stopped breathing. "So what?"

"More shit, man. Don't pretend it's coincidence. It's in the stars. You know what's coming. Crane's your bread and butter. But the gravy train'll end four months from now."

I didn't ask.

"Crane's birthday's coming up. The anniversary of Deacon's death."

And when I looked into it, there were other parallels. Wes would be twenty-three—Deacon's age when he died. And Wes would be close to the end of his third movie—about the same place in Deacon's third movie when he. . . .

We were doing a script I'd written, *Rampage*, about a young man from a tough neighborhood who comes back to teach there. A local street gang harasses him and his wife until the only way he can survive is by reverting to the violent life (he once led his own gang) that he ran away from.

It was Wes's idea to have the character renew his fascination with motorcycles. I have to admit that the notion had commercial value, given Wes's well-known passion for motorcycle racing. But I also felt apprehensive, especially when he insisted on doing his own stunts.

I couldn't talk him out of it. As if his model behavior on the first two pictures had been too great a strain on him, he snapped to the opposite extreme—showing up late, drinking on the set, playing expensive pranks. One joke involving firecrackers started a blaze in the costume trailer.

It all had the makings of a death wish. His absolute identification with Deacon was leading him to the ultimate parallel.

And just like Deacon in his final picture, Wes began to look wasted. Hollow-cheeked, squinty, stooped from lack of food and sleep. His dailies were shameful.

"How the hell are we supposed to ask an audience to pay to see this shit?" the studio VP asked.

"I'll have to shoot around him. Cut to reaction shots from the characters he's talking to." My heart lurched.

"That sounds familiar," Jill said beside me. I knew what she meant. I'd become the director I'd criticized on *Broken Promises*.

"Well, can't you control him?" the VP asked.

"It's hard. He's not quite himself these days."

"Damn it, if you can't, maybe another director can. This garbage is costing us forty million bucks."

The threat made me seethe. I almost told him to take his forty million bucks and. . . .

Abruptly I understood the leverage he'd given me. I straightened. "Relax. Just let me have a week. If he hasn't improved by then, I'll back out gladly."

"Witnesses heard you say it. One week, pal, or else."

In the morning, I waited for Wes in his trailer, when as usual he showed up late for his first shot.

At the open trailer door, he had trouble focusing on me. "If it isn't teach." He shook his head. "No, wrong. It's me who's supposed to play the teach in—what's the name of this garbage we're making?"

"Wes, I want to talk to you."

"Hey, funny thing. The same goes for me with you. Just give me a chance to grab a beer, okay?" Fumbling, he shut the trailer door behind him and lurched through shadows toward the miniature fridge.

"Try to keep your head clear. This is important," I said.

"Right. Sure." He popped the tab on a beer can and left the fridge door open while he drank. He wiped his mouth. "But first I want a favor."

"That depends."

"I don't have to ask, you know. I can just go ahead and do it. I'm trying to be polite."

"What is it?"

"Monday's my birthday. I want the day off. There's a motorcycle race near Sonora. I want to make a long weekend out of it." He drank more beer.

"We had an agreement once."

He scowled. Beer dribbled down his chin.

"I write and direct. You star. Both of us, or none."

"Yeah. So? I've kept the bargain."

"The studio's given me a week. To shape you up. If not, I'm out of the project."

He sneered. "I'll tell them I don't work if you don't."

"Not that simple, Wes. At the moment, they're not that eager to do what you want. You're losing your clout. Remember why you liked us as a team?"

He wavered blearily.

"Because you wanted a friend. To keep you from making what you called the same mistakes again. To keep you from fucking up. Well, Wes, that's what you're doing. Fucking up."

He finished his beer and crumpled the can. He curled his lips, angry. "Because I want a day off on my birthday?"

"No, because you're getting your roles confused. You're not James Deacon. But you've convinced yourself that you are, and Monday you'll die in a crash."

He blinked. Then he sneered. "So what are you, a fortune-teller now?"

"A half-baked psychiatrist. Unconsciously you want to complete the legend. The way you've been acting, the parallel's too exact."

"I told you the first time we met—I don't like bullshit!"

"Then prove it. Monday, you don't go near a motorcycle, a car, hell, even a go-kart. You come to the studio sober. You do your work as well as you know how. I drive you over to my place. We have a private party. You and me and Jill. She promises to make your favorite meal: T-bones, baked beans, steamed corn. Homemade birthday cake. Chocolate. Again, your favorite. The works. You stay the night. In the morning, we put James Deacon behind us and. . . ."

"Yeah? What?"

"You achieve the career Deacon never had."

His eyes looked uncertain.

"Or you go to the race and destroy yourself and break the promise you made. You and me together. A team. Don't back out of our bargain."

He shuddered as if he were going to crack.

In a movie, that would have been the climax—how he didn't race on his birthday, how we had the private party and he hardly said a word and went to sleep in our guest room.

And survived.

But this is what happened. On the Tuesday after his birthday, he couldn't remember his lines. He couldn't play to the camera. He couldn't control his voice. Wednesday was worse.

But I'll say this. On his birthday, the anniversary of Deacon's death, when Wes showed up sober and treated our bargain with honor, he did the most brilliant acting of his career. A zenith of tradecraft. I often watch the video of those scenes with profound respect.

And the dailies were so truly brilliant that the studio VP let me finish the picture.

But the VP never knew how I faked the rest of it. Overnight, Wes had totally lost his technique. I had enough in the can to deliver a print—with a lot of fancy editing and some uncredited but very expensive help from Donald Porter. He dubbed most of Wes's final dialogue.

"I told you. Horoscopes. Astrology," Donald said.

I didn't believe him until I took four scenes to an audio expert I know. He specializes in putting voices through a computer and making visual graphs of them.

He spread the charts in front of me. "Somebody played a joke on you. Or else you're playing one on me."

I felt so unsteady that I had to press my hands on his desk when I asked him, "How?"

"Using this first film, Deacon's scene from *The Prodigal Son* as the standard, this second film is close. But this third one doesn't have any resemblance."

"So where's the joke?"

"In the fourth. It matches perfectly. Who's kidding who?"

Deacon had been the voice on the first. Donald Porter had been the voice on the second. Close to Deacon's, dubbing for Wes in *Rampage*. Wes himself had been the voice on the third—the dialogue in *Rampage* that I couldn't use because Wes's technique had gone to hell.

And the fourth clip? The voice that was identical to Deacon's, authenticated, verifiable. Wes again. His screen test. The imitated scene from *The Prodigal Son*.

Wes dropped out of sight. For sure, his technique had collapsed so badly he would never again be a shining star. I kept phoning him, but I never got an answer. So, for what turned out to be the second-to-last time, I drove out to his dingy place near the desert. The Manson lookalikes were gone. Only one motorcycle stood outside. I climbed the steps to the sunporch, knocked, received no answer, and opened the door.

The blinds were closed. The place was in shadow. I went down a hall and heard strained breathing. Turned to the right. And entered a room.

The breathing was louder, more strident and forced.

"Wes?"

"Don't turn on the lights."

"I've been worried about you, friend."

"Don't. . . ."

But I did. And what I saw made me swallow vomit. He was slumped in a chair. Seeping into it would be more accurate. Rotting. Decomposing. His cheeks had holes that showed his teeth. A pool that stank of decaying vegetables spread on the floor around him.

"I should have gone racing on my birthday, huh?" His voice whistled through the gaping flesh in his throat.

"Oh, shit, friend." I started to cry. "Jesus Christ, I should have let you."

"Do me a favor, huh? Turn off the light now. Let me finish this in peace."

I had so much to say to him. But I couldn't. My heart broke.

"And buddy," he said, "I think we'd better forget about our bargain. We won't be working together anymore."

"What can I do to help? There must be something I can—"

"Yeah, let me end this the way I need to."

"Listen, I—"

"Leave," Wes said. "It hurts me too much to have you here, to listen to the pity in your voice."

"But I care about you. I'm your friend. I—"

"That's why I know you'll do what I ask"—the hole in his throat made another whistling sound—"and leave."

I stood in the darkness, listening to other sounds he made: liquid rotting sounds. "A doctor. There must be something a doctor can—"

"Been there. Done that. What's wrong with me no doctor's going to cure. Now if you don't mind. . . ."

"What?"

"You weren't invited. Get out."

I waited another long moment. ". . . Sure."

"Love you, man," he said.

". . . Love you."

Dazed, I stumbled outside. Down the steps. Across the sand. Blinded by the sun, unable to clear my nostrils of the stench in that room, I threw up beside the car.

The next day, I drove out again. The last time. Jill went with me. He'd moved. I never learned where.

And this is how it ended, the final dregs of his career. His talent was gone, but how his determination lingered.

Movies. Immortality. See, special effects are expensive. Studios will grasp at any means to cut the cost.

He'd told me, "Forget about our bargain." I later discovered what he meant—he worked without me in one final feature. He wasn't listed in the credits, though. *Zombies from Hell.* Remember how awful Bela Lugosi looked in his last exploitation movie before they buried him in his Dracula cape?

Bela looked great compared to Wes. I saw the zombie movie in an eight-plex out in the Valley. It did great business. Jill and I almost didn't get a seat.

Jill wept as I did.

This fucking town. Nobody cares how it's done, as long as it packs them in.

The audience cheered when Wes stalked toward the leading lady. And his jaw fell off.

THE CONSTANTINOPLE ARCHIVES
Robert Shearman

i

We can speculate, and we can speculate, but the probability is that few of the silent movies made during the siege of Constantinople in 1453 were very good. And there are clear reasons for this, both political and cultural.

On the one hand, we have to bear in mind the extremely trying circumstances under which the movies were being filmed. In attacking Constantinople, the Ottoman Turks were also attacking the last bastion of the Roman Empire (if only in symbolic form), a direct line of power that stretched back some two thousand years. It was also the seat of the Orthodox Christian Church, a force equal and opposite to the Catholic Church in Rome. Expansionist wars were two a penny in the fifteenth century, but this was no run-of-the-mill example, it was already rife with meaning, and no doubt the Byzantines under threat would have been only too aware of that. Besides which, on a purely practical level, the constant cannoning of the city walls must surely have been a distraction. Even making silent movies, surely, some peace and quiet is required for concentration's sake.

On the other hand, and perhaps more pertinently, Byzantine art had always defined itself by a certain flat austerity. Their mosaics and paintings that we can study today are colourful, but there's a grim functionality to all that colour; the lines are severely drawn and make the characters depicted seem two-dimensional and undramatic. It would be foolish to expect that in the creation of an entire new art form that several centuries of engrained Byzantine culture would be abandoned overnight. It is unfair to imagine that the clowns who pratfalled and danced and poked each other in the eyes in Constantinople cinema were other Chaplins, or Keatons, even other Fatty Arbuckles. The conditions were wrong. Their genius could not have flowered.

And yet, of course, we remain fascinated by those movies from the Byzantine age. And again, partly this will be because they were the pioneers, the history of cinema begins here with these shadowy figures by the Bosporus doomed to be killed or enslaved by the Muslim potentate. But I hope our fascination is not purely academic. That we honour not merely the historical significance of what was invented, but that, with care and study, and an open mind, we try to appreciate the art on its own terms.

ii

No entire print of a Byzantine movie survives, and that is to be expected. When the sultan Mahomet II appealed to the Byzantines to surrender, with the promise that their lives would be spared, his terms were rejected. The Byzantine emperor, Constantine XI Palaiologos, said that the city could not be yielded, for it was no single man's possession to yield. And with these brave words he sealed the fate of the fifty thousand inhabitants of Constantinople, and, more importantly, the fate of those few precious cans of film kept within. The Turks had besieged Constantinople for fifty-five days. They were tired and angry. When they broke the defences, as was the custom, the soldiers had permission to ransack and pillage the city for three whole days, taking plunder, razing buildings to the ground, and raping and slaughtering the populace. These were not conditions in which a fledgling film industry was ever likely to prosper.

And yet, we are lucky. In spite of all, some sequences of film are extant. They are fragments only, most no more than a few seconds long, but they still afford us a tantalising impression of early cinematography, and what those Byzantine audiences must have enjoyed. One man tries to sit down upon a stool, and a second pulls it away, so he falls to the ground with his legs splayed in the air. A farmer waters his crops with a bucket of water, but a prankster holds it upright; when the farmer pours the bucket over his head to see what's wrong, he gets soaked. It is not sophisticated comedy, granted, but there is a spirit of mocking fun to it; yes, it plays upon the weak and the vulnerable, but no one gets hurt, no one gets savaged, and certainly no one experiences the sort of carnage that is awaiting them at the end of the siege. Some historians have tried to read a political subtext into the extracts, but I think that can be exaggerated. One of the more (justly) admired sequences is of a beggar, or tramp, who at dinner sticks a knife into two vegetables and proceeds to do a puppet dance with them. In siege times food was scarce, and this flagrant disregard for its value can be seen as something deliberately provocative, a renunciation of the very crisis that would have caused the food shortage in the first place, and thus a renunciation of war. But what attracts us to the film is not its message, but its simple beauty; there is such elegance to the dance, and to the comic conceit of it, and for the duration the tramp smiles out at the viewer in childlike innocence.

One might have expected that there would have been a pronounced propagandist element to the films. But the Ottoman Turks are never referenced, and instead what is offered to us is cheap comedy and heightened melodrama. The longest extant extract—and, sadly, one of the most tedious—is a case in point. A moustachioed villain, sniggering silently to camera, ties a damsel in distress to a set of railway tracks. The damsel is left there for no fewer than six minutes of static inaction, as we wait in vain for a train to come and flatten her; however, since we are many centuries shy of the invention of a locomotive engine, it is unclear how much jeopardy the girl can really be in. The tracks are not the important part; it is the villain. Wearing a gabardine common in fashion at the time, he looks like an everyday Byzantine. He's not given a turban, or a Muslim beard, or shifty Oriental eyes. It's the ideal opportunity for the filmmaker to identify and feed off a common threat to the audience, but it refuses to do so; even in its monsters, Byzantine cinema remains stubbornly domestic.

Many eyewitnesses recorded the siege of Constantinople for posterity, and the most celebrated is George Sphrantzes. Sphrantzes recounts the conflict from a mostly militaristic perspective and pays depressingly little heed to the day-to-day to and fro of the thriving visual arts scene. Nevertheless, he does record in his diary how, one evening, shortly after the siege had been raised, he was ushered into a big hall, alongside some other hundreds of citizens. There he took a seat, and the windows were covered with sacks, and the room was cast into darkness. He describes an expectation in the audience, something apprehensive, like fear, but more pleasurable than fear. And then, at the end of the room, facing them all, a large piece of white cloth was illuminated. He writes: "At first I thought there was a stain upon it, and then the stain enlarged, as if by magick." It was no stain; it was the image of a horse and cart, and its approach towards the camera. George Sphrantzes describes the awe and wonder as the "moving painting" flickered upon the makeshift screen—and then the rising panic as it became clear that the horse and cart were coming directly at them. People rose from their seats; they stumbled towards the exit; they fell over in the darkness—if they didn't escape, within *minutes* the cart would reach them and there might be an irritating bump. Sphrantzes records how the authorities arrested the man in charge of the exhibition for disturbing the peace.

No name of any actor has survived the fall of Constantinople. But the name of that man *has* survived, and he must be regarded as the first maverick genius of cinema. His name was Matthew Tozer.

iii

It is all too easy to be seduced by images of the Byzantine Empire as a thing of great glory. That was true at its zenith, but its zenith was centuries past. By the time the Ottoman Turks lay siege to Constantinople, the empire had shrunk to little more than a city-state, and the population within were a random ragtag of different nationalities from different backgrounds. Matthew Tozer (or Toza, or Tusa) was probably a Greek Cypriot, but his name is peculiar, and no one can say for sure. There is no physical description of the man. There is no record of his beliefs, or anything he stood for—save his obvious love for the cinematic medium.

It is not even clear what Tozer's part in the craze was, merely that he was at the very centre of it. Had he invented the principle of moving photography himself? Was he instead the director of the films, exploiting someone else's discoveries? It is possible that he merely ran the cinema in which the movies were shown. Scientist, artist, entrepreneur—scholars argue which of them he may have been. Maybe there is no single Matthew Tozer. This essay does not purport to take any great interest in specious biography. For simplicity's sake we shall assume Tozer is all three rolled into one; not so much a man, but a personification of a new art form; we can never know Tozer the individual, let us instead study Tozer the wave of revolution.

The earliest account we have of Tozer is what we now refer to as the Horse and Cart Debacle. Punishment in the Middle Ages was typically severe, especially in times of military crisis. But within days Tozer has been freed and, moreover, is showing new films, we can only suppose with the blessing of the authorities. Sphrantzes writes again, after a turgid account of a day setting up the city's defences and his concerns of a maritime engagement with the Turkish fleet: "And, in the evening, to the picture house, there to see a comedic play about three men and a mule. Silly stuff. Amiable."

Sphrantzes might dismiss it as silly stuff, but it is clear that Tozer was doing something right. He set up a cinema just a stone's throw from the Hagia Sophia, and there he'd show the latest movie releases—and the people of Constantinople began to flock to them in droves. It is important to remember what siege conditions were like in the fifteenth century. They were frightening, yes, and they were desperate, and they were hungry; but mostly they were very *boring*. With the Ottoman Turks on one side, and a naval blockade upon the other, there was really very little for the Byzantine folk to go and do in the evenings. However silly the movies on offer may have been, the distractions they provided were hugely popular, and tickets became highly prized; one anonymous commentator writes that to get in to see one particular blockbuster, a family bartered a week's supply of precious bread. Tozer was forced to put on more and more screenings, sometimes letting his cinema run all night until dawn. He employed janissary bands to accompany the films with the music of harp, lyre, and zither; he employed young girls to serve sweet snacks in the intervals.

And what Tozer was accomplishing was not merely artistic, but also sociological. Because if these citizens of a dying empire were merely desperate stragglers with no real identity, here, at least, they could find something that unified them. They could sit in the dark together and laugh and cry as one collective. Is it too much to hope that at last they discovered that they had more in common with their fellow man than they had realised—that the same stunts thrilled them, the same custard-pie fights kept them amused? Is this the irony of the end of the Byzantines, that only in their final days they became a proper people?

As for Tozer, he appears to have worked tirelessly. With almost superhuman energy he released several new movies a week, filming them during the day and presenting the results on screen once the sun went down. To satisfy the appetite of a citizenry starved of entertainment, he produced an oeuvre that makes Steven Spielberg look like some dilettante hobbyist. And with the introduction of a new art form, inevitably the people are inspired; they are no longer content to be mere spectators, they want to take part in the art form too. Sphrantzes complains, but when does Sphrantzes not complain? He writes that the most pressing concern the Byzantine population faced was the Muslim hordes outside the gates, and that work should be done repairing those gates, building new walls, training all able-bodied men to fight. Instead everybody wanted to be an actor, to star in the movies, to see themselves flicker on the white cloth screens, to be famous, to be adored.

The greatest tragedy of the fall of Constantinople is that not one frame of Matthew Tozer's masterpiece, *The Ten Commandments*, survives. A true epic, it ran for nearly six hours and used over a thousand extras. It was a gamble on Tozer's part; to find time to make it he had to close the cinema for three full days, and there was civil unrest and small-scale rioting whilst the people were left starved of their fix. But the gamble paid off. It is a testament not only to Tozer's vaulting ambition but to his commercial canniness—even if you weren't in the movie yourself you knew someone who was, and if you saw only one movie that season it had to be *The Ten Commandments*! The sets, by all reports, were sumptuous. The cast were on peak form. And the special effects were remarkable: to achieve the parting of the Red Sea, Tozer had used up a half of the besieged city's water supply.

It was Tozer's greatest achievement. Emperor Constantine XI Palaiologos took time off being the champion of the Orthodox Church to attend the premiere, and had even taken a cameo role as a burning bush. Could Tozer have suspected that it was all downhill from here? And that all that ambition would prove his undoing?

iv

On 29th May 1453, the Ottoman Turks broke through the walls of Constantinople. Their troops numbered some one hundred thousand to the Byzantines' seven thousand. The Turkish flag was flown from the battlements, and many of the Christian defenders lost heart. Emperor Constantine XI Palaiologos himself declared, "The city is fallen and I am still alive," and he tore off his purple cloak of majesty and entered the fray as a common soldier. His body was never found. The Byzantine people fought bravely, but with a certain dispassion perhaps, a certain defeatism.

The talkie movies had not been a success.

Matthew Tozer had been experimenting with sound for a little while now. He would have the orchestra time their drum beats to the exact moment an explosion appeared on screen, to give the impression that the bang had come from the movie itself. It was witty, but it was a gimmick, and the audience enjoyed it as a gimmick. When at the end of May Tozer announced the premiere of the first proper talking picture, with full dialogue and a prerecorded score, the people were incredulous, then doubtful, then baffled.

Some extracts survive. As film historians it is impossible not to appreciate what Tozer is attempting. But in practice, as casual viewers, we would have to judge it doesn't work. Tozer has not found a way to make the sound sync accurately to the image; it is rarely more than a second or two out, but that jarring second makes everything seem imprecise and unreal, even eerie. And the voices of the actors are not what we might expect. We see the tramp again. In the silent movies he demonstrates a charm that is both winning and humane. In the sound rushes, he reveals he has a high-pitched voice like a strangled dolphin. The charm is gone. So, too, is the illusion.

As the Turks invade, so Tozer's picture house is burned to the ground. It is not clear whether the Turks or the Byzantines are to blame.

V

Matthew Tozer's fate is unknown. Many people fled the city, and there is every chance that he too might have escaped. But if he did, there is no record of his attempting to make any more films. Either Tozer becomes like Emperor Constantine, one of those anonymous casualties who were lost in the battle—or he survives, in exile, disillusioned, thinking himself a failure and his art form a failure, rejecting his talents and never returning to them for as long as he lives.

Is it wrong to hope that he was butchered by Turks? Is it wrong to wish for him that one little mercy?

Historical opinion has turned against Tozer in recent years. The argument is that without his interference the population would not have been distracted, and would have been better prepared to repel the Ottoman conquest. Professor Kettering has even published his theories that Tozer was a Turkish spy, deliberately undermining the morale of the Byzantines from within with his dreadful movies; it is a theory that I find at once both absurd and heinous, though nothing Kettering says any more should surprise me.

What is harder to dispute is Tozer's legacy. Sadly, it is negligible. The footage of Tozer's movies was only discovered in a basement in Ankara in the 1920s. By the time Tozer's advances came to light, the motion picture industry was already in full swing. The great filmmakers of the 1890s, Lumière, Michon, Méliès, all reinvented cinema without ever realising Matthew Tozer had been there first. Mack Sennett produced his movies without Tozer's influence; David O. Selznick, head of production at RKO Pictures, famously viewed the recovered prints of Tozer's films, shrugged, and asked what all the fuss was about: "It's already been done."

And yet surely we cannot write off Matthew Tozer as a failure. We must not.

When we see the history of the world put before us, it's easy to think it's just a catalogue of wars and genocidal atrocities. Of peoples conquering peoples, and then getting conquered in turn. That the development of mankind has been nothing more than an exercise in studying new acts of brutality to be turned against still larger sizes of population. That, in effect, all Mankind's inspirations are directed towards evil.

But what then of Matthew Tozer? What then of that spark to *create*, to produce art for art's sake, if only because it wasn't in existence before? To take a population and want not to decimate it or enslave it, but instead crowd it together, into one room, into the dark, and make it laugh? And maybe with Matthew Tozer the spark didn't die. Maybe the spark lasted out the centuries, just waiting for the right conditions in which to take fire. Maybe, in spite of all, Matthew Tozer and the better impulse will win out.

We can speculate. And, oh, we can speculate, we can imagine, we can dream. Sometimes I think that's the true gift Matthew Tozer left us.

each thing i show you is a piece of my death
Gemma Files and Stephen J. Barringer

"There is nothing either good or bad, but thinking makes it so."
—*The Tragedy of Hamlet, Prince of Denmark*, William Shakespeare

From a journal found in a New Jersey storage unit, entry date unknown:

Somewhere, out beyond the too-often-unmapped intersection of known and forgotten, there's a hole through which the dead crawl back up to this world: A crack, a crevasse, a deep, dark cave. It splits the earth's crust like a canker, sore lips thrust wide to divulge some even sorer mouth beneath—tongueless, toothless, depthless.

The hole gapes, always open. It has no proper sense of proportion. It is rude and rough, rank and raw. When it breathes out it exhales nothing but poison, pure decay, so bad that people can smell it for miles around, even in their dreams.

Especially there.

Through this hole, the dead come out face-first and -down, crawling like worms. They grind their mouths into cold dirt, forcing a lifetime's unsaid words back inside again. As though the one thing their long, arduous journey home has taught them is that they have nothing left worth saying, after all.

Because the dead come up naked, they are always cold. Because they come up empty, they are always hungry. Because they come up lost, they are always angry. Because they come up blind, eyes shut tight against the light that hurts them so, they are difficult to see, unless sought by those who—for one reason, or another—already have a fairly good idea where to start looking.

To do so is a mistake, though, always—no matter how "good" our reasons, or intentions. It never leads to anything worth having. The dead are not meant to be seen or found, spoken with, or for. The dead are meant to be buried and forgotten, and everybody knows it—or should, if they think about it for more than a minute. If they're not some sort of Holy Fool marked from birth for sacrifice for the greater good of all around them, fore-doomed to grease entropy's wheels with their happy, clueless hearts' blood.

Everybody should, so everybody does, though nobody ever talks about it. Nobody. Everybody. Everybody . . .

. . . but them.

(The dead)

July 26/2009
FEATURE ARTICLE: COMING SOON TO A DVD NEAR YOU?
"BACKGROUND MAN" JUMPS FROM 'NET TO . . . EVERYWHERE
By Guillaume Lescroat, strangerthings.net/media

Moviegoers worldwide are still in an uproar over *Mother of Serpents*, Angelina Jolie's latest blockbuster, being pulled from theatres after only four days in wide release due to "unspecified technical problems." According to confidential studio sources, however, the real problem isn't "unspecified" at all—this megabudget Hollywood flick has apparently become the Internet-spawned "Background Man" hoax's latest victim.

For over a year now, urban legend has claimed that, with the aid of careful frame-by-frame searches, an unclothed Caucasian male (often said to be wearing a red necklace) can be spotted in the background of crowd scenes in various obscure films, usually partially concealed by distance, picture blur, or the body parts of other extras. Despite a proliferation of websites dedicated to tracking Background Man (over thirty at last count), most serious film buffs dismissed the legend as a snipe-hunt joke for newbies, or a challenge for bored and talented Photoshoppers.

But all that changed when the Living Rejects video "Plastic Heart" hit MTV in September last year, only to be yanked from the airwaves in a storm of FCC charges after thousands of viewers confirmed a "full-frontally naked" man "wearing a red necklace" was clearly visible in the concert audience . . . a man that everybody, from the band members to the director, would later testify under oath hadn't been there when the video was shot.

"You know the worst thing about looking for Background Man? While you're waiting for him, you gotta sit through the crappiest movies on the planet! C'mon, guy, pick an Oscar contender for once, wouldja?!"
   —Conan O'Brien, *Late Night with Conan O'Brien*, November 18, 2008

Background Man has since appeared in supporting web material for several TV shows (*House*, *Friday Night Lights*, and *The Bill Engvall Show* have all been victims) and has been found in a number of direct-to-DVD releases as well, prompting even Conan O'Brien to work him into a monologue (see above). *Mother of Serpents* may not be the first major theatrical release to be affected, either; at least three other films this summer have pushed back their release dates already, though their studios remain cagey about the reasons. The current consensus is that Background Man is a prank by a gifted, highly placed team of post-production professionals.

This theory, however, has problems, as producer Kevin Weir attests. "Anybody involved who got caught, their career, their entire life would be wrecked," says Weir. "Besides the fines and the criminal charges, it's just totally f–ing unprofessional—nobody I know who could do this would do it; it's like pissing all over your colleagues." Film editor Samantha Perry agrees, and notes another problem: "I've reviewed at least three different appearances, and I couldn't figure out how any of them were done, short of taking apart the raw footage. These guys have got tricks or machines I've never heard of."

Hoax or hysteria, the Background Man shows no signs of disappearing. However, our own investigation may have yielded some insights into the mysterious figure's origin—an origin intimately connected with the collapse last year of the Toronto-based "Wall of Love" film collective's *Kerato-Oblation/Cadavre Exquis* project, brainchild of experimental film-makers Soraya Mousch and Max Holborn. . . .

From: Soraya Mousch sor16muse@walloflove.ca
Date: Friday, June 20, 2008, 7:08 PM
To: Max Holborn mhb@ca.inter.net
Subject: FUNDRAISING PITCH DOC: "KERATO-OBLATION" (DRAFT 1)

To Whom it May Concern—

My name is Soraya Mousch, and I am an experimental filmmaker. Since 1999, when Max Holborn and I founded Toronto's Wall of Love Experimental Film Collective, it has been my very great pleasure both to collaborate on and present a series of not-for-profit projects specifically designed to push—or even, potentially, demolish—the accepted boundaries of visual storytelling as art.

Unfortunately, given that film remains the single most expensive artistic medium, this sort of thing continues to cost money . . . indeed, with each year we practice it, it seems to cost more and more. Thus the necessity, once government grants and personal finances run out, of fundraising.

- - - - - - -

(mhb): <yeah, say it exactly like that, thatll get us some money [/ sarcasm]>

- - - - - - -

To this end, Mr Holborn and I have registered an internet domain and website (kerato-oblation.org), through which we intend to compile, edit and host our next collaborative project, with the help of filmmakers from every country which currently has ISP access (ie, all of them). The structure of this project will be an exquisite corpse game applied to the web-based cultural scene as a whole, one that anybody can play (and every participant will "win").

WHY KERATO-OBLATION?
Kerato-oblation: Physical reshaping of the cornea via scraping or cutting.

With our own version—the aforementioned domain—how we plan to "reshape" our audience's perspectives would be by applying the exquisite corpse game to an experimental feature film assembled from entries filed over the internet, with absolutely no boundaries set as to content or intent.

WHAT IS AN EXQUISITE CORPSE?
An exquisite corpse (cadavre exquis, in French) is a method by which a collection of words or images are assembled by many different people working at once alone, and in tandem. Each collaborator adds to a composition in sequence, either by following a rule (e.g. "The adjective noun adverb verb the adjective noun") or by being allowed to see, and either elaborate on or depart from, the end of what the previous person contributed. The technique was invented by Surrealists in 1925; the name is derived from a phrase that resulted when the game was first played ("Le cadavre exquis boira le vin nouveau."/"The exquisite corpse will drink the new wine."). It is similar to an old parlour game called Consequences in which players write in turn on a sheet of paper, fold it to conceal part of the writing, then pass it to the next player for a further contribution.

Later, the game was adapted to drawing and collage, producing a result similar to classic "mix-and-match" children's books whose pages are cut into thirds, allowing children to assemble new chimeras from a selection of tripartite animals. It has also been played by mailing a drawing or collage— in progressive stages of completion—from one player to the next; this variation is known as "mail art." Other applications of the game have since included computer graphics, theatrical performance, musical composition, object assembly, even architectural design.

- - - - - - -

(mhb): <dont know if we need all this history, or the whole exquisite corpse thing—just call it "spontaneous collaboration" or something? keep it short>

- - - - - - -

Earlier experiments in applying the exquisite corpse to film include Mysterious Object at Noon, *an experimental 2000 Thai feature directed by Apichatpong Weerasethakul which was shot on 16 mm over three years in various locations, and* Cadavre Exquis, Première Edition, *done for the*

2006 Montreal World Film Festival, in which a group of ten film directors, scriptwriters and professional musicians fused filmmaking and song-writing to produce a musical based loosely on the legend of Faust.

- - - - - - -

(mhb): <the montreal things good, people might actually have seen that one—one more example?>

- - - - - - -

For your convenience, we've attached a PDF form outlining several support options, with recommended donation levels included. Standard non-profit release waivers ensure that all contributors consent to submit their material for credit only, not financial recompense. By funnelling profits in excess of industry-standard salaries for ourselves back into the festival, we qualify for various tax deductions under current Canadian law and can provide charitable receipts for any and all financial donations made. Copies of the relevant paperwork are also attached, as a separate PDF.

For more information, or to discuss other ways of getting involved, either reply to this e-mail or contact us directly at (416)-[REDACTED]. We look forward to discussing mutual opportunities.

With best regards,
Soraya Mousch and Maxim Holborn
The Wall of Love Toronto Film Collective

- - - - - - -

(mhb): <for crissakes soraya DONT SIGN ME AS MAXIM–if i have to be there at all its just max, k?>

8/23/08 1847HRS
TRANSCRIPT SUSPECT INTERVIEW 51 DIVISION CASEFILE #332
PRESIDING OFFICERS D. SUSAN CORREA 156232, D. ERIC VALENS 324820
SUBJECT MAXIM HOLBORN

D. VALENS: All right. So you had this footage for what, better than six weeks—footage apparently showing somebody committing suicide—and you didn't ever think that maybe you should let the police know?

HOLBORN: People send us stuff like this all the time, man! The collective's been going since '98. . . . Most of it's fake, half of it has a fake ID and half of the rest doesn't have any ID at all.

D.VALENS: Yeah, that's awful lucky for you, isn't it?

D.CORREA: Eric, any chance you could get us some coffee?

HOLBORN: I don't want coffee.

(D.VALENS LEFT INTERROGATION ROOM AT 1852 HRS)

D.CORREA: Max, I'm only telling you this because I really do think you don't know shit about this, but you need to do one of two things right now. You need to get yourself a lawyer, or you need to talk to us.

HOLBORN: What the fuck am I going to tell a lawyer that I didn't already tell you guys? What else do you want me to say?

D.CORREA: Max, you're our only connection to a dead body. This is not a good place to be. And your lawyer's going to tell you the same thing: the more you work with us, the better this is going to turn out for everyone.

HOLBORN: Yeah. Because that's an option.

From: 11235813@gmail.com
Date: Wednesday, June 25, 2008, 3:13 AM
To: submissions@kerato-oblation.org
Subject: Re: KERATO-OBLATION FILM PROJECT

To Whom It May Concern—
Please accept my apologies for not fully completing your submission form. I think the attached file is suitable enough for your purposes that you will find the missing information unnecessary, and feel comfortable including it in your exhibition nevertheless. I realize this will render it ineligible for competition, but I hope you can show it as part of your line-up all the same.

Thank you.

THE CUTTING ROOM

<- Rue Morgue Party | Main | Rumblings on the Turnpike ->

July 23, 2008
"Wall of Love" Big Ten Launch Party

Got to hang out with two of my favourite people from the Scene last night at the Bovine Sex Club: Soraya Mousch and Max Holborn, the head honchos behind the Wall of Love collective. The dedication these guys've put into keeping their festivals going is nothing short of awesome, and last night's launch party for the next one was actually their tenth anniversary. Most marriages I know don't last that long these days. (Doubly weird, given Max and Soraya are that rarest of things, totally platonic best opposite-sex straight friends.)

For those who've been under a rock re the local artsy-fart scene over each and every one of those ten years, meanwhile, here's a thumbnail sketch of the Odd Couple. First off, Soraya. Armenian, born in Beirut, World Vision supermodel-type glamorous. Does music videos to pay the bills, but her heart belongs to experimentalism. Thing to remember about Soraya is, she's not real big on rules: When a York film professor told her she'd have to shift mediums for her final assignment, she ended up shooting it all on her favorite anyways (8mm), then gluing it to 16mm stock for the screening. This is about as crazy as Stan Brakhage gluing actual dead-ass moths to the emulsion of his film *Mothlight* . . . and if you don't know what that is either, man, just go screw. I despair of ya.

Then there's Max: White as a sack of sheets, Canadian as a beaver made out of maple sugar. Meticulous and meta, uber-interpretive. Assembles narratives from found footage, laying in voiceovers to make it all make (a sort of) sense. Also a little OCD in the hands-on department, this dude tie-dyes his own films by swishing them around in food-color while they're still developing, then "bakes" them by running them through a low-heat dryer cycle, letting the emulsion blister and fragment. The result: Some pretty trippy shit, even if you're not watching it stoned.

Anyways. With fest season coming up fast, M. and S. are in the middle of assembling this huge film collage made from snippets people posted chain-letter-style. You might think this sounds like kind of a dog's breakfast, and with any other self-proclaimed indie genius you'd be right. But S. took me in the back and showed me some of the files they hadn't got to yet, and man, there's some damn raw footage in there, if ya know what I mean; even freaked her out. So if you're looking for something a little less *Saw* and a little more *Un Chien Andalou*, check it out: October 10, the Speed of Pain. . . .

From: Soraya Mousch sor16muse@walloflove.ca
Date: Wednesday, June 25, 3:22 PM
To: Max Holborn mhb@ca.inter.net
Subject: Check this file out!

Max–

Sorry about the size of this file, I'd normally send it to your edit suite but it's got some kind of weird formatting - missing some of the normal protocols - I don't have time to dick around with your firewalls. Anyway, YOU NEED TO SEE THIS. Get back in touch with me once you have!

From: Soraya Mousch sor16muse@walloflove.ca
Date: Wednesday, June 25, 3:24 PM
To: Max Holborn mhb@ca.inter.net
Subject: Apology followup

Max: Realized I might've come off a little bitchy in that last message, wanted to apologize. I know you've got a lot of shit on your plate with Liat (how'd the CAT-scan go, BTW?); last thing I want to do is make your life harder. You know how it goes when the deadline's coming down.

Seriously, though, the sooner we can turn this one around, like ASAP, the better—I think this one could really break us wide open. If you could get back to me by five with something, anything, I'd be really grateful. Thanks in advance.

See you Sunday, either way,
Soraya.

From: Max Holborn mhb@ca.inter.net
Date: Wednesday, June 25, 4:10 PM
To: Soraya Mousch sor16muse@walloflove.ca
Subject: Re: Apology followup

s.—

cat-scan wasn't so great, tell you bout it later. got your file, i'm about to review. i'll im you when it's done.

m.

TRANSCRIPT CHAT LOG
06/25/08 1626-1633

<max_hdb>: soraya? u there?
<sor16muse>: so whatd you think?
<max_hdb>: jesus soraya, w?t?f? who sent THIS in? even legal to show?
<max_hdb>: i didnt get into this to go to jail
<sor16muse>: message came in from a numbered gmail account, no sig – check out the file specs?
<sor16muse>: relax max – we didnt make it, no way anybody cn prove we did, got to be digital dupe of a tape loop
<max_hdb>: yeah, i lkd at specs – these guys know tricks i dont. u can mask creation datestamp in properties to make it LOOK blank, bt not supposed to be any way to actually wipe that data out without disabling file
<sor16muse>: my guess is the originals at least 50 yrs old
<sor16muse>: max, we cant NOT show this
<max_hdb>: gotta gt somebody to lk/@ it first – im not hanging my ass out in th/wind
<sor16muse>: why dont we meet @ laszlos? he can run it through his shit, see what pops
<max_hdb>: dont like him. his house smells like toilet mold, hes a freak

<sor16muse>: whatever, hes got the best film-to-flash download system in the city doesnt cost $500 daily rental, so just grow a fucking pair

<max_hdb>: you know he tapes every conversation goes on in there, right? wtf w/that?

<sor16muse>: (User sor16muse has disconnected)

<max_hdb>: and btw, next time you wanna show me shit like that try thinking about liat first

<max_hdb>: (User max_hdb has disconnected)

July 26/2009
"BACKGROUND MAN," Lescroat, strangerthings.net/media (cont'd)

"That original clip? Hands down, some of the scariest amateur shit I've ever seen in my life," says local indie critic/promoter Alec Christian, self-proclaimed popularizer of the "Toronto Weird" low-budget horror culture movement. "A little bit of *Blair Witch* to it, obviously, but a lot more of early Nine Inch Nails videos, Jorg Buttgereit and Elias Merhige. That moment when you realize the guy's body is rotting in front of you? Pure *Der Todesking* reference, and you don't get those a lot, 'cause most of the people doing real-time horror are total self-taught illiterates about their own history."

Asked if there's any way the clip might be genuine, rather than staged, Christian laughs almost wistfully. "There are still people who think *Blair Witch* was real; that doesn't make it so," he points out. "Anyway, think about how hard it would be to shoot this using World War One technology and logistics, at the latest, which is what we'd be looking at if it was real—and if it was filmed later but aged to look older, then everything else could have been engineered as well. Sometimes you just have to go with common sense."

TRANSCRIPT EVIDENCE EXHIBIT #3 51 DIVISION CASEFILE #332
RECOVERY LOCATION 42 TRINITY STREET BSMT DATE 8/20/2008

Item: 89.2 MB .MPG file retrieved from hard drive of laptop SONY VAIO X372 s/n 10352835A, prop. M. Holborn, duration 15m07s.

0:00 – (All images recorded in black-and-white monochrome.) Caucasian male subject (Subject A), 40s, est. 6'1", 165 lbs, dark hair, wearing black or brown suit appearing to be 1920s cut, shown sitting in upright wooden chair looking directly at camera. Room is a single chamber, est. 8' x 10', hardwood floor, one window behind subject, one door in right-hand wall at rear. No painting or other decoration visible on walls. Angle of light from window suggests filming began early morning; light traverses screen in right-to-left direction, suggesting southward facing of window and room. Unknown subject has no discernible expression.

0:01 – 4:55 – Subject A rises and removes clothes, beginning with detachable celluloid collar. Each garment removed separately, folded, and placed on floor. Care and pacing of garment removal suggests ritual purpose. Subject is shown to be uncircumcised. Subject continues no discernible facial expression.

4:55 – 5:19 – Subject A resumes seat and looks straight into camera without movement or speech. Enhanced magnification and review of subject's right hand reveals indeterminate object, most likely taken from clothing during removal.

5:20 – 5:23 – Subject A opens object in hand, demonstrating it to be a straight razor. Subject cuts own throat in two angular incisions, transverse to one another. Strength and immediacy of blood flow indicates both carotid and jugular cut. Evenness and control of movement suggests anesthesia or psychosis. Review by F/X technicians confirms cuts too deep to have been staged without use of puppets or animatronics. Subject maintains lack of facial expression.

5:23 – 6:08 – Subject A's self-exsanguination continues until consciousness appears lost. Subject collapses in chair, head draped over back.

6:09 – Estimated time of death for Subject A.

6:11 – Razor released from subject's fingers, drops to floor.

6:12 – 13:34 – Clip switches from real-time pacing to timelapse speed, shown by rapidity of daylight movement and day-night transitions.

Reconstruction analysis specifies 87 24-hour periods elapse during this segment. Subject's body shown decomposing at accelerated pace.

7:22 – Primary liquefaction complete; desiccation begins. Clothes left on floor have developed mold.

10:41 – Desiccation largely complete. Rust visible on blade of razor. Fungal infestation on clothes has spread to floorboards.

13:10 – Subject's cranium detaches and falls to floor.

13:17 – Subject's right hand detaches and falls to floor.

13:25 – Subject's left arm detaches and falls to floor. Imbalance in weight causes remains of subject's body to fall off chair.

13:34 – Decomposition process complete. Footage resumes normal real-time pacing.

14:41 – Subject B walks into frame from behind camera P.O.V. Subject B's appearance 100% consistent in identity with initial Subject A, including lack of circumcision and identifiable body marks. Remains of Subject A still visible behind Subject B.

15:01 – Subject B bends down in front of camera and looks into it. Subject B shows no discernible facial expression.

15:06 – Subject B reaches above and behind camera viewpoint.

15:07 – CLIP ENDS

TRANSCRIPT EVIDENCE EXHIBIT #2 51 DIVISION CASEFILE #332 RECOVERY LOCATION 532 OSSINGTON AVENUE BSMT RESIDENCE LASZLO P HURT DATE 8/19/2008 AUDIOTAPE PROPERTY OF LASZLO P HURT

(IDENTIFICATION RETROACTIVELY ASSIGNED TO VOICES FOLLOWING CONFIRMATION FROM M HOLBORN AND S MOUSCH OF CONTENT)

V1 (MOUSCH): (LOUD) . . . see, here it is. Never see it if you weren't looking for it.

V2 (HOLBORN): (LOUD) Shit. He really does have his own place bugged. What's this for? Legal protection?

V1 (MOUSCH): (VOL. DECREASING) Maybe, but I think it's really just because he wants to. Like his whole life is a big cumulative perfomance art piece. Sort of like in that Robin Williams movie, where people have cameras in their heads, and Robin has to cut a little film together when they die to sum up fifty years of experience?

V2 (HOLBORN): Yeah. That really sucked.

V1 (MOUSCH): I know. Just . . . keep it in mind, that's all I'm saying.

(BG NOISE: TOILET FLUSH)

V3 (HURT): Sorry about that. I haven't got new filters put in on the tap-water yet.

V2 (HOLBORN): That's . . . okay, Laszlo.

V3 (HURT): Yeah, you want some helpful input? Try not patronizing me.

V1 (MOUSCH): Laz, come on.

V3 (HURT): Yeah, okay, okay. So I reviewed your file.

V2 (HOLBORN): And?

V3 (HURT): First thing comes to mind is a story I heard through the post grapevine, one of those boojum-type obscurities the really crazy collectors go nuts trying to find. Though this can't be that, obviously, the clip would be way older, not digitized—

V1 (MOUSCH): People digitize old stuff all the time!

V3 (HURT): Really? Yeah, Soraya, I get that, actually; do it for a living, right? Look, the upshot is that you do have some deliberate image degradation going on here, so—

V2 (HOLBORN): I knew it, I knew it was a fake. Thank Christ.

V3 (HURT): I'm not finished. There is image degradation, but it wasn't done through any of the major editing programs; I've run your file through all of them and tested for the relevant coding, and this thing's about as raw as digicam gets. I'm betting whoever sent this to you digitized it the old brute-force way, like a movie pirate: Physically projected the thing, recorded it with a digital camera, saved it as your .mpeg, and sent it to you as is. Whatever the distortions are, they're either from that projection, or they were in the source clip all along.

V1 (MOUSCH): So . . . this could be a direct copy of that original clip you were talking about. The "urban legend boojum."

V3 (HURT): Yeah, if you wanna buy into that shit.

V2 (HOLBORN): And when Laszlo Hurt tells you something's too weird to believe. . . .

V1 (MOUSCH): Max, don't be a dick; Laz's doing us a favour. Right?

V2 (HOLBORN): Yeah, okay. Sorry.

V3 (HURT): (PAUSE) Way I heard, it goes back to this turn-of-the-century murderess called Tess Jacopo. . . .

8/23/08 1902HRS

TRANSCRIPT SUSPECT INTERVIEW 51 DIVISION CASEFILE #332

PRESIDING OFFICERS D. SUSAN CORREA 156232, D. ERIC VALENS 324820

SUBJECT MAXIM HOLBORN

D.VALENS: Jacopo. That was in Boston, in the 1900s—she was a Belle Gunness–type den mother killer, right? The female H.H. Holmes.

HOLBORN: Why am I not surprised you know this?

D.CORREA: Mr. Holborn, please. Go on.

HOLBORN: The story isn't really about Jacopo herself. What happened was, this guy who'd been corresponding with Jacopo in prison, her stalker I guess he was, he managed to bribe a journalist who was on-site at her execution into stealing a copy of the official death-photo and selling it to him. Guess he wanted something to whack off with after she was gone. Anyway, a couple weeks later this guy's found in his flat, dead and swollen up, the Jacopo photo on his chest.

D.CORREA: How did he die?

HOLBORN: I don't think it matters. The point is, somebody there took a photo of the photo, and that became one of the biggest murder memorabilia items of the 20th century. You know these guys, right—kinda weirdos who buy John Wayne Gacy's clown pictures, shell out thousands to get Black Dahlia screen-test footage, 'cause they think they'll unearth some lost snuff movie they can show all their friends. . . .

D.VALENS: I'm not seeing what this has to do with your film clip, Mr. Holborn.

HOLBORN: Okay. This is where the urban legend kicks in. See, Jacopo's mask slipped a bit during the hanging, so you can just barely see a sliver of her eyeball, and the story says if you blow up and enhance the photo like a hundred times original size, you're supposed to be able to see in the eyeball the reflection of what she was looking at when she died. Like an asphyx.

D.VALENS: Ass-what?

HOLBORN: It's the word the Greeks used for the last image that gets burned on a murdered person's retina, like a last little fragment of their soul or life-force getting trapped there.

D.CORREA: And under sufficient magnification, you're supposed to be able to see this?

HOLBORN: "Supposed to," yeah. Thing is, everyone who ever tried this, who actually tried blowing up their copy of the Jacopo photo? Went nuts or died. Unless they burned their photo before things got too bad. That's supposed to be why it's impossible to find any copies.

D.CORREA: Why? What did they see?

HOLBORN: How the fuck should I know? It's a spook story. Maybe they saw themselves looking back at themselves, whatever. The point is . . . it's not about what those people saw, or didn't. It's about the kind of voyeuristic obsession you need to go that deep into this shit. And Laszlo said that was what the clip reminded him of. Somebody trying to make some kind of, of—"mind-bomb", was the term. An image that'd scar you so badly, the mere act of passing it on would be enough to always keep its power alive.

D.CORREA: Uh . . . why?

HOLBORN: Excellent question. Isn't it?

From: Liat Holborn liath@ca.inter.net
Date: Thursday, July 3, 10:25 AM
To: Soraya Mousch sor16muse@walloflove.ca
Subject: Max and me

Dear Soraya,

I was talking to Max last night about how we're going to try to handle the next few months, and it came out that for whatever reason, Max still hadn't filled you in completely on our situation. I think he finds it pretty tough to talk about, even to you. Upshot is, the last CAT-scan showed I have an advanced cranial tumour, and Dr. Lalwani thinks there's a very good chance it could be gliomal, which (skipping all the medicobabble) is about the least good news we could get. Apparently, it's too deep for surgery, so the only option we have is for me to go into a majorly heavy chemo program ASAP. So I'm going to be spending a lot of time in St. Michael's, starting real soon now.

My folks've volunteered to foot a lot of the bill, which is great, but poor Max is feeling kind of humiliated at needing the help—and of course he totally can't complain about it, which just makes it gall him even more. The reason I'm telling you all this is because (a) I want the pressure of keeping this a secret to be off Max, and (b) I know how much you depend on Max this time of year, and I don't want you to think he's bailing on you if he has to take time out for me, or that he's finally gotten fed up with you, the Wall of Love, or your work.

(Actually, I'm pretty sure the festival's the only thing that's kept him stable this past little while. I hope you know how much I appreciate the support you give him.)

Could you show this e-mail to Max when you get a chance, and apologize to him for me when he blows his top at my big mouth? :) He doesn't feel he can shout at me any more about anything, obviously. But I really think things'll be easier once all the cards are on the table.

Thanks so much for your help, Soraya. Come by and see me soon—I want you to get some photos of me before I have to ditch the hair.

Much love and God bless,

Liat

P.S.: BTW, I'm also totally fine with accidentally seeing that thing you sent Max, that file or whatever, so tell him that, okay? Impress it on him. He seems to think it "injured" me somehow—on top of everything else. Which is just ridiculous.

I have more than enough real things to worry about right now, you know?

—L.

8/23/08 1928HRS
TRANSCRIPT SUSPECT INTERVIEW 51 DIVISION CASEFILE #332
PRESIDING OFFICERS D. SUSAN CORREA 156232, D. ERIC VALENS
324820
SUBJECT MAXIM HOLBORN

HOLBORN: We were on about the third or fourth draft of the final mix when we started splicing in the clip—

D.VALENS: Splicing? I thought you said this was purely electronic.

HOLBORN: It is, it's just the standard term for—look, do you want me to explain or not?

D.CORREA: We do. Please. Go on.

HOLBORN: We broke the clip up into segments and spliced it in among the rest of the film in chunks; we were even going to try showing some shots on just the edge of subliminal, like three or four frames out of twenty-four. This was a few weeks ago, beginning of August. And then it started happening.

D.CORREA: What started, Max?

HOLBORN: The guy. From the clip. He started . . . appearing . . . in other parts of the film.

D.VALENS: Somebody spliced in more footage? Repeats?

HOLBORN: No, goddammit, he started popping up in pieces of footage that were already in the film! Stuff we'd gotten like weeks before, from people who never even saw the clip or knew about it. Like that performance art piece in Hyde Park? Guy walks by in the background a minute into the clip. Or the subway zombie ride, you look right at the far end of the car, there he is sitting down, and you know it's him 'cause he's the only one not wearing any clothes. This was stuff nobody ever shot, man! Changing in front of our fucking eyes! Christ, I saw him show up in one segment—I ran it to make sure it was clear, ran it again right away and he was just fucking there, like he'd always been in the frame. The extras were fucking walking around him. . . .

(FIVE SECOND PAUSE)

D.CORREA: Could it have been some kind of computer virus? Something that came in with your original video file and reprogrammed the files it was spliced into?

HOLBORN: Are you shitting me?!

D.VALENS: Dial it back, Holborn. Right—now.

HOLBORN: Okay, sorry, but—no. CGI like that takes hours to render on a system ten times the size of mine, and that's for every single appearance. A virus carrying that kinda programming would be fifty times bigger than the file it rode in on and wouldn't run on my system anyway.

Besides, it kept getting worse. He didn't just show up in new segments, he'd take more and more prominent places in segments he'd already, corrupted, I guess? Goes from five seconds in the background to two minutes in the medium frame. I'd get people to resend me their submissions, I'd splice 'em in to replace the old ones and inside of a minute he's back in the action. It was like the faster we tried to cut him out the harder he worked at—I don't know—entrenching himself.

ERROR MESSAGE
404 Not Found

The webpage you were trying to access ("http://www.kerato-oblation.org/cadavrexquis") is no longer available. It may have been removed by the user or suspended by administrators for terms-of-use violation. Contact your ISP for more information.

TRANSCRIPT CHAT LOG
08/07/08 0344-0346

   <sor16muse>: max, wtf
   <sor16muse>: the sites gone. like GONE
   <sor16muse>: did u do that? ur only other one w/password

<sor16muse>: wtf max, were supposed 2 b live tomorrow WHY

<sor16muse>: u there?

<sor16muse>: max, u there? need 2 talk.

<sor16muse>: laz sez he maybe has an idea who sent the file, and why. need 2

<max_hdb>: im not going 2 b here, back

<max_hdb>: don't know when.

<max_hdb>: liat had episode. bad. in hosp. st mikes.

<max_hdb>: u ever want 2 talk in person, that's where ill b.

<max_hdb>: (User max_hdb has disconnected)

<sor16muse>: (User sor16muse has disconnected)

8/23/08 1937HRS

TRANSCRIPT SUSPECT INTERVIEW 51 DIVISION CASEFILE #332

PRESIDING OFFICERS D. SUSAN CORREA 156232, D. ERIC VALENS 324820

SUBJECT MAXIM HOLBORN

D.VALENS: So who was that guy? In the film?

HOLBORN: No idea. It's not like he—

D.CORREA: And what's it got to do with Tess Jacopo?

HOLBORN: Nothing, directly. But it's like Internet memes, man; Laszlo understood that. Stuff gets around. Maybe this guy heard about the thing with the photo, and thought: Oh hey, wonder how that'd work with a moving picture. Maybe he just stumbled across the concept all on his lonesome, or by accident: I don't know. But . . . he did it.

D.VALENS: Did WHAT, Holborn?

HOLBORN: He put himself in there. Made himself an asphyx.

D.CORREA: So he could live forever.

HOLBORN: Yeah. Maybe. Or maybe just . . . so he could . . . not die. Maybe—

(TEN SECOND PAUSE)

HOLBORN: Maybe he was sick. Like, really sick. Or sick in the head. Or both.

Maybe it just seemed like a good idea, given the alternative.

At the time.

D.CORREA: So what did happen to the Wall of Love mainframe, Max?

HOLBORN: I crashed it. (BEAT) I mean—I told people there was a big Avid crash and the whole server got wiped . . . actually, I used a magnet. Like Dean Winchester in that "Ghostfacers!" SUPERNATURAL episode.

D.VALENS: What?

HOLBORN: Doesn't matter. Ask me why.

D.CORREA: . . . why?

HOLBORN: Because I thought maybe I could trap him there, like he must have trapped himself inside that loop. Because he probably didn't think about that, right? When he was doing it. How it wasn't likely anybody was really going to watch that sort of shit, once they figured out what it was, let alone show it in public. How probably it would just end up left in the can, passed from collector to collector, never really watched at all, except by one person at a time. One . . . very disturbed . . . other person.

I thought I could stop him from going any further, so I crashed my own mainframe, without telling Soraya. But. . . .

D.VALENS: . . . it didn't work.

HOLBORN: Well. Would I even be here, if it did?

CYBER-CRIME OFFICE, TORONTO POLICE SERVICE 51 DIVISION
EXCERPTED REPORT
DETECTIVE LEWIS McMASTER (CYBERCRIME) SUPERVISING
DETECTIVES ERIC VALENS, SUSAN CORREA (HOMICIDE) CON-
TRIBUTING
Casefile #332: Notes

INITIAL CONTACT:
Aug 14 2008 – CyberCrime received anonymous email sent from Hotmail account created that morning, with copy of "suicide guy" .mpg attached. Flagged as "harmful matter." Email noted .mpg was sent to kerato-oblation.org as experimental film clip submission; identified source of original message, webmail address 11235813@gmail.com.

[Hotmail account eventually traced through Internet café to Laszlo Hurt, known member of local Toronto "collector" circuit; Hurt now missing, presumed deceased. –EV, SC]

INVESTIGATION:

August 15 – Flagged file screened and sent for forensic analysis, results inconclusive. Source of original submission email traced to Google-owned server in Newark, New Jersey, United States of America.

August 16 – Established contact with Detective Herschel Gohan of Newark CyberCrime Unit, who persuaded server admins to cooperate with investigation; message back-tracked and triangulated to establish physical location and address of originator machine. Address is confirmed as unit #B325 of E-Z-SHELF storage locker facility, 1400 South Woodward Lane, Newark. Facility manager, Mr. Silvio Galbi, provides name of renter ("John Smith"), confirms unit prepaid for six months with cash. Mr. Galbi refuses to cooperate with search request without a warrant.

August 18 – Warrant issued for search and seizure operation at 1400 South Woodward, Unit #B325, by Judge Harriet Lindstrom. Operation executed under supervision of Detective Gohan. Contents of unit as follows:

– Unclothed body of unidentified male, Caucasian, est. premortem age mid-20s, seated on floor in pool of waste.

– One (1) empty film canister.

– One (1) 35mm film projector, set up to project upon unit interior wall.

– One (1) 35mm film reel mounted in projector, est. 15 minutes in length, confirmed on-site to be original of transmitted .mpg file.

– One (1) white cotton sheet at base of same interior wall; tape on corners indicates sheet was hung on wall.

– One (1) SONY video camera, with tripod, set up focused on same interior wall.

– One (1) TV monitor, with built-in VCR and DVD player.

– One (1) DELL laptop computer, with built-in wi-fi modem.

– One (1) Coleman oil lantern, fuel supply depleted.

– Pile of empty water bottles.

– One (1) Black & Decker emergency brand power generator.

– Fifty (50) gallon gasoline containers, empty.

– Two (2) six-socket power bar outlets.

– One (1) tube-gun of industrial caulking sealant.

Galbi confirms he accepted illegal payment to lock unit on "Smith's" written instructions without confirming contents, in violation of state safety and insurance regulations. Galbi arrested and cited.

FORENSICS:

Examination of laptop hard drive reveals series of webcam captures which suggest basic chronology of events as follows:

– Unidentified male (UM) arrives in unit roughly two weeks before email sent to kerato-oblation.org.

– UM uses video camera to record digital copy of original film reel from wall projection (distortion visible in .mpg file caused by loose fabric in sheet).

– UM uses laptop to program recorded file into continuous video loop on DVD.

– UM arranges laptop and webcam to face DVD monitor, setting DVD on continuous play and webcam on indefinite record.

– UM remains seated in front of monitor for majority of remaining time, urinating and defecating in place. Time-signatures confirm he created .mpg file, wrote submission email, then waited until death was imminent to send it, on date above.

– Final action of UM on morning of death was to use sealant gun to caulk up door, rendering unit virtually airtight. This prevented odors from escaping unit, and retarded decomposition by hindering evaporation of fluids from the body.

AUTOPSY:

Body shows no sign of struggle or restraint. Autopsy reveals primary cause of death as oxygen deprivation, aggravated by starvation and dehydration. Probable date of death on or around June 25 2008 (date on which .mpg file was sent to kerato-oblation.org). Corneas of victim preserved by airtight environment, and found to be deformed on both exterior and interior surfaces, damage suggesting both physical and heat trauma to tissue. Computer reconstruction of deformation suggests artificial origin, as pattern appears to portray a fixed image: the face of suicide victim in original film, in close-up still frame. Pathologists unable to establish cause or method of corneal deformation.

RECOMMENDATIONS:
Unidentified male's selection of Holborn/Mousch as recipients suggests foreknowledge, possible contact. Recommend either Holborn or Mousch be brought in for further questioning.

> From: Det. Herschel Gohan hgohan@newarkpolice.gov
> Date: Thursday, August 21, 7:20 AM
> To: Det. Lewis McMaster lewis.mcmaster@torpolservices.net
> Subject: Notification: Evidence compromise

Lewis –
Bad news. We had a fire in our station evidence locker last night; looks like some meth really past its sell-by date may have spontaneously cooked off. Nobody hurt, but we lost some critical evidence on a number of cases, including, sorry to say, your film-nut-in-the-storage-unit material. The film reel's melted, the laptop motherboard is gone, and most of the other equipment's unusable now. I've attached .jpgs to document the losses; I'm hoping this'll be enough for your dept. to maintain provenance on your own stuff.

Sorry again; call me if you need to know anything not covered by the pictures.
—Herschel

8/23/08 1928HRS
TRANSCRIPT SUSPECT INTERVIEW 51 DIVISION CASEFILE #332
PRESIDING OFFICERS D. SUSAN CORREA 156232, D. ERIC VALENS 324820

SUBJECT MAXIM HOLBORN

HOLBORN: So I went home after crashing the mainframe, and I didn't go upstairs, because I thought my wife was asleep. And I wanted to let her sleep, because . . . she'd been in pretty bad shape, you know? She'd only just finished her chemo, she hadn't gotten a lot of . . . sleep. . . . But then I turned on TCM, to relax, and they were playing Richard Burton's adaptation of 'Dr. Faustus,' which was made the year before I was born, and—in the scene in the Vatican? Where Faustus is throwing pies at the Pope? I saw him. That guy.

Stuck around, kept watching; the next film was from 1944, an RKO gangster film, and he was in it too. In the background, until—it was like—he notices me watching him. Turns and smiles at me, raises his eyebrow, starts—coming closer.

I swear to God, I jumped back, physically. All by myself, in my apartment. Because I felt like if Cagney hadn't been in the way, then maybe the guy standing behind him would've come right out of the TV at me.

And then it was Silent Sunday, some all-night Chaplin retrospective, and . . . yeah. There, too.

Everywhere.

So. . . .

D.VALENS: Obviously, it didn't work. What you did to trap him.

HOLBORN: Obviously not.

(TEN SECOND PAUSE)

HOLBORN: My wife wasn't asleep, either, by the way. Just in case you were wondering.

D.VALENS: Aw, what the fuck—

D.CORREA: Shut up, Eric. [To HOLBORN] Look, you can't be serious, that's all. Are we supposed to believe—

HOLBORN: I don't give a fuck what you believe. Seriously.

D.CORREA: Okay. So what about the disappearance of Laszlo Hurt?

(FIFTEEN SECOND PAUSE)

HOLBORN: I don't know anything about that.

D.VALENS: And again: We should believe you on this . . . why?

[FIFTEEN SECOND PAUSE]

D.CORREA: Mister Holborn?

HOLBORN: . . . you know, I don't know if you guys know this or not, but . . . my wife? Just died. So, in the immortal words of every LAW AND ORDER episode ever filmed—charge me with something, or let me go. Or fuck the fuck off.

From: qmail@ca.geocities.mail.com
Date: Saturday, August 16, 9:45 PM
To: Soraya Mousch sor16muse@walloflove.ca
Subject: RE: LASZLO ANSWER ME

Hi. This is the administrator at qmail@geocities.com (00:15:32:A3)
Delivery of your message to {lazhurt@geocities.com} failed after <15> attempts. Address not recognized by system.
This is a permanent error; I've given up.

>Laszlo, it's Soraya, would you CALL ME PLEASE? I've left
>about twenty messages on your voicemail, Max and I have a big
>problem and we need your HELP! Where the fuck are you?
>Call me!
>S.

From: help@geocities.com
Date: Monday, August 18, 8:55 AM
To: Soraya Mousch sor16muse@walloflove.ca
Subject: RE: Account Tracking Request

Dear Ms. Mousch,

Sorry it took us so long to get back to you; we get a lot of backlog on weekends. I'm afraid I have to admit we're stumped on this one. I personally went through our server records day by day over the registration period you specified, and as far as I can tell, we have no record whatsoever of a "Laszlo Hurt" on our roster. I've checked under the "lazhurt," "laszloslabyrinth," and "hurtmedia" addresses and their variants, as well as with our billing department, and there's just no indication that this Mr. Hurt was ever a Geocities user.

I realize this may be an unwelcome explanation, but it sounds to me like you may have been a victim of an attempted phishing scam using dummy-mask addresses. I'd get your computer checked for viruses and malware right away.

Again, I'm sorry we couldn't be more help.

Best regards,

Jamil Chandrasekhar

Geocities.com Tech Support

From: Soraya Mousch sor16muse@walloflove.ca
Date: Saturday, August 23, 11:01 PM
To: Max Holborn mhb@ca.inter.net
Subject: Blank

Max, I'm just so sorry.

—S.

YOUR COMFORT SOUGHT
IN THIS TIME OF GRIEF

With sorrow we announce the passing of Liat Allyson Meester-Holborn on August 23, 2008, beloved daughter of Aaron and Rachel Meester and wife of Maxim Holborn.

Funeral service to be held at St. Mary's Star of the Sea Catholic Church, 8 Elizabeth Avenue, Port Credit, Mississauga
Tuesday August 26, 11:00 A.M.
Commemorative reception to be held at the Meester residence,
1132 Walden Road #744, 3:00 P.M.
Confirmations only

From: Max Holborn mhb@ca.inter.net
Date: Tuesday, September 2, 2:31 AM
To: Soraya Mousch sor16muse@walloflove.ca
Subject: look closer

s.-

hospital released the file on liat to me today. was going over it. couldn't sleep. found something.

the attached .jpg's a scan of the last x-ray they took, just before she crashed out. look at the upper right quarter, just up and right of where ribs meet breastbone. then do a b-w negative reverse on the image in your photoshop, and look again.

it's not a glitch. it's not me fucking with you. look at it. call me.

- m.

SURVEILLANCE TRANSCRIPT 14952, CASEFILE #332
9/19/08 2259H-2302H 416-[REDACTED] TO 416-[REDACTED]
WARRANT AUTHORIZED HON. R. BORCHERT 9/9/08

(CONNECTION INITIATED)
MOUSCH: Hello?
HOLBORN: You never answered my e-mail.
MOUSCH: What did you want me to say? I read it, I looked at the scans you sent. That . . . could be anything, Max. A glitch in the machine, some lab tech sticking his hand on the negative—
HOLBORN: Soraya—
MOUSCH: —and even if it's not, what's it matter? What difference can it make? (PAUSE) I'm sorry, Max. I didn't—I'm sorry.
HOLBORN: Uh huh.
(PAUSE)
HOLBORN: So . . . I hear you put your stuff up on eBay. Going Luddite?

MOUSCH: Well, uh . . . no, I'm just switching disciplines. Going non-visual. Film's . . . all played out, y'know? I mean, you've noticed that.

HOLBORN: Yup. Good luck, I guess. (BEAT) Everything just back to normal, huh?

MOUSCH: . . . hardly . . .

HOLBORN: You really think any of this is gonna help? Dropping anything with a lens like it's hot, cocooning?

MOUSCH: I don't. . . .

HOLBORN: You remember what I told you, at the hospital?

(FIVE SECOND PAUSE)

MOUSCH: . . . I remember.

HOLBORN: That guy killed my wife, Soraya. Just because she SAW him—over my shoulder, right? When she didn't even know what she was looking at. She's fucking dead.

MOUSCH: Liat's dead because she had a tumor, Max. Nothing we did made Liat die.

HOLBORN: What do you think he's going to end up doing to US, Soraya? After he's fucking well done with everybody else?

MOUSCH: Look . . . look, Max, Christ. Liat, Laszlo, that crazy fucking moron dude who made the clip in the first place, let alone sent it to us. . . . (BEAT) And why would he even do that, anyway? To, what . . . ?

HOLBORN: I don't know. Spread the disease, maybe. Like he got tired of watching it himself, thought everybody else should have a crack at it, too. . . .

(FIVE SECOND PAUSE)

MOUSCH: I mean . . . it's not our fault, right? Any of it. We didn't ask for—

HOLBORN: —uh, no, Soraya. We did. Literally. We asked, threw it out into the ether: Send us your shit. Show us something. We asked . . . and he answered.

MOUSCH: Who, "he"? Clip-making dude?

HOLBORN: You know that's not who I'm talking about.

(TEN SECOND PAUSE)

HOLBORN: So, anyhow, 'bye. You're going dark, and I'm dropping off the map. I'd say "see you," but—

MOUSCH: Oh, Max, goddamn. . . .
HOLBORN: —I'm really hoping . . . not.
(CONNECTION TERMINATED)

OFFICE OF FORENSICS, TORONTO POLICE SERVICE 51 DIVISION
EXCERPTED REPORT

Casefile #332

Final analysis of X-ray images taken of Liat Holborn (dcsd) shows no known cause of observed photographic anomaly. Hand-digit comparison was conducted on all possible candidates, including Maxim Holborn, attending physician Dr. Raj Lalwani, attending nurse Yvonne Delacoeur, and X-ray technician John Li Cheng: no match found. Dr. Lalwani maintains statement that cause of death for Liat Holborn was gliomal tumour. Conclusion: Photographic anomaly is spontaneous malfunction, resemblance to intact human hand coincidental.

Following lack of forensic connection between Maxim Holborn and Site of Death 1, and failure to establish viable suspect, this office recommends suspension of Case #332 from active investigation at this time, pending further evidence.

July 26/2009
"BACKGROUND MAN," Lescroat, strangerthings.net/media (cont'd)

One year later, the crash which brought kerato-oblation.org/cadavrexquis down—melting the server and destroying a seventy-four minute installation cobbled together from random .mpg snippets mailed in from contributors all over the world—has yet to be fully explained, by either Wall of Love founder. While Mousch cited simple overcrowding and editing program fatigue for the project's collapse, Holborn—already under stress when Kerato-Oblation got underway, due to his wife's battle with brain cancer—has been quoted as blaming a slightly more supernatural issue: a mysterious figure who appeared first in an anonymously submitted piece of digital footage, then eventually began popping up in the backgrounds of other . . . completely unrelated . . . sections. Background Man? Impossible to confirm or deny, without Holborn's help.

Still, sightings of a naked man wearing "red" around his neck wandering through the fore-, back-, and midground of perfectly mainstream movies, TV shows, and music videos continue to abound. Recent internet surveys chart at least five major recent blockbusters (besides *Mother of Serpents*) and three primetime television series rumored to have inadvertently showcased the figure.

At the moment, the (highly unlikely) possibility of pan-studio collaboration on a vast alternate-reality game remains unresolved, while at least three genuine missing persons reports are rumored to be connected with a purported Background Man personal encounter IRL. The meme, if meme it is, continues to spread.

Neither Mousch nor Holborn could be reached for comment.

And up they come—
(the dead)
Crawling through the hole with their pale hands bloody from digging, their blind eyes tight-shut and their wide-open mouths full of mud: Nameless, faceless, groping for anything that happens across their path. With no easy end to their numbers. . . .

For once such a door is opened, who will shut it again? Who is there—
—alive—
—that can?

No end to their numbers, or their need: The dead, who are never satisfied. The dead, who cannot be assuaged.

The dead, who only want but no longer know what, or from whom, or why. Or just how much, over just how long—here in their hole, which goes on and down forever, where time itself slows so much it no longer has any real value—
—can ever be enough.

CINDER IMAGES
Gary McMahon

Fade in. Beethoven's *Pastoral Symphony Number 6*, slow and sweet. No title bar or opening credits.

It starts with a little girl, running.

She is young—perhaps eight or nine years old—and she is pumping her arms and her legs as she runs along a dirt road. Behind her, fire burns a line along the horizon. Around her, there is scorched and blackened earth and the burnt-out ruins of red brick buildings. The girl is partially naked; her upper body is bare, her lower body is clad in torn rags. Her face is dirty, her cheeks are burnt. Flaps of ruined skin hang off her arms and legs, revealing pale pink patches beneath.

This could be Vietnam, it could be Cambodia; it might be Serbia, Afghanistan, or the West Bank. It could be anywhere, at any time.

But it is England.

It is now.

The girl keeps on running even though the soles of her feet are worn away and bleeding. She feels no pain; she is beyond simple feelings. Her mother and father are dead. Her brothers and sisters have been blown apart by the bombs and bullets of an unknown enemy.

A single gunshot rings out and a bullet takes her down. The hair at the right side of her head puffs out, blood and brain and bone spatters in a vivid arc, spraying the grey ground red.

She falls, limp.

Dead.

The audience leans forward, trying to catch the girl; or they are just desperate to get a better view, a closer look at the blood and the carnage?

The music on the soundtrack soars, triumphant.

You try to close your eyes but you cannot. You have to see—you *need* to see this. There are things that must be endured, sights that cannot be ignored. You owe it to the girl; her lonely death must not go unwitnessed. So you sit there with your eyes forced open, taking it all in.

The screen goes dark. The lights come up.

"And that, ladies and gentlemen," says a low, cultured voice through a hidden speaker, "is our little war project."

A ripple of polite applause.

You grit your teeth.

When you glance down, at your hands, you see that you are clapping too, but you don't know why, or for whom the applause is intended. The lights turn red and it looks like blood on your hands. You start to rub them together, but the stains remain.

When the lights flicker a signal for the end of the performance and the rest of the audience members start to leave, you pick up your bag from underneath your seat, stand, and walk out with them. You feel numb. Your skin is cold.

Out in the foyer a fat man in a black suit and John Lennon spectacles is shaking people's hands, answering questions, and posing to have his photograph taken. He is the director, the creative mind behind the brief decontextualised images you have just seen.

"Thank you, thank you," he says, soaking up the kudos, filling up with misplaced pride.

"When will the finished film be available to screen in full?" A local reporter jabs a digital tape recorder into the director's fat face.

"Soon," says the director. "Very soon."

"What will it be called?"

The director opens his arms, lifts his head. *"Cinder Images,"* he says in a loud voice, making sure that everyone can hear. His eyes are bright behind the lenses of his glasses.

You consider approaching him to ask why you were invited to the screening, but then think better of such a rash move. It might draw attention to your discomfort. They might stare at you and see the fear that lies beneath your shell.

So you walk outside, into the cold night air, and try to breathe again. The glassed-in posters on the multiplex walls advertise action movies, romantic comedies, films about comic-book superheroes. There is no mention of the teaser footage you have just seen; this was a private show, for members of the press and a few lucky winners of competitions. You got hold of your ticket at the underground station, when a publicity man in a fake hazmat suit pushed it into your hand, smiling and nodding his pale, bald head.

"Free show," he'd whispered, as if it were a secret. "Just for you. It must be your lucky day."

Curiosity brought you here, and disgust sends you away. It was not your kind of film. Those images were not something you like to see. Or were they? The film has summoned questions about yourself that you'd rather not answer, not right now.

"How was the movie?"

You turn to see a woman leaning against the boot of a red car. She is smoking a cigarette. Her tiny hands move quickly through the air; her face is delicate, like that of an exquisite china doll.

"Excuse me?" You stop walking but wish you hadn't. You should have just carried on out of the car park.

"The film. Any good? I tried to get in but they wouldn't let me. I didn't have a ticket."

"If I'd have known, you could have had mine."

"That bad, eh?" She blows out smoke. It hangs in a small white cloud before her small dark eyes.

"Just . . . disturbing."

"Yes, he's known for that—the director. It's his specialty."

You shrug and begin to move away, unable to think of anything else to say.

"Hang on a minute." She stubs out her cigarette on the car bumper and follows you. Her long, dark coat hangs open to reveal a tight-fitting midnight-blue blouse; she has on either leggings or skin-tight jeans and a pair of ankle boots with long, spiked heels. She looks alternative; not your type at all.

"It's dark," she says, as if that explains everything. "I'm cold."

Somehow you end up going for a drink in a pub near the cinema. It's busy but not packed; the customers all seem in good cheer. You order a pint of beer for yourself and vodka for the woman. She hasn't told you her name and you don't feel much like asking. She's attractive, but you sense trouble. Maybe even outright danger.

"Thanks," she says, accepting the drink. She takes off her coat and grabs a table just as a group of people get up to leave. Once you are both seated, she undoes the top two buttons of her blouse. The skin on her breastbone is red, livid. Her fingernails are painted black.

"Cheers," you say, lifting your glass to your mouth.

She smiles. Takes a tiny sip of vodka, and brushes her foot against your leg under the table. Just when you convince yourself that it was accidental, she does it again.

You feel your cheeks go hot. You start to blink uncontrollably.

"Don't be shy," she says. "I do this all the time."

You have no idea what she means. Or you do and you are unwilling to admit it.

Several drinks later and you're both sitting in the back of a taxi heading out of town, to her place. She licks the side of your neck and her hand strays into your lap. This is not the kind of thing that ever happens to you—you're either lucky or have walked head-first into some kind of disaster. Only time will tell.

She lives in a ground-floor flat opposite a row of shops and an Italian restaurant. The restaurant is empty; most of the shops are boarded up. You have no idea where you are. The streets are unfamiliar and you were too caught up in the moment to look out of the window and follow the route.

The skin on the side of your neck is still damp from her tongue.

She grabs your hand and pulls you out of the car. She waits at the kerb while you pay the fare. The taxi driver doesn't even look up at you as he accepts the money. Then he drives away without thanking you for the tip.

Upstairs, her flat is like a showroom: minimal furniture, zero clutter, no photos, no pictures on the white walls. There is not even a stereo or a television to keep her company.

"I live alone," she whispers. "I don't like to keep a lot of stuff around me."

She pours two glasses of whisky without asking and smiles as you swallow yours in one mouthful. She tops up the glasses and smiles again. There's something different about her; on her own turf, she seems less aggressive, more passive.

"I don't usually do this . . . it's not my style."

"Don't worry," she says. "I've had a lot of practice." She slips off her blouse and takes off her bra. Then she unpeels the leggings and stands there in just her panties, sipping her drink and watching you, waiting to see what you will do.

She has a lot of tattoos. Thin black lines curl around her upper arms, purple flowers erupt on her stomach, and a thick dragon is wrapped around her right thigh.

"You're beautiful." Your voice sounds strange, as if it's a struggle to speak.

"I know," she says. "That's why I got the role."

She turns away and walks lightly across the carpet. You stare at the stylised tattoos of thick black medical stitches down her spine, her tight little backside, the back of her well-toned legs. You finish your second whisky and start to feel drunk. Not just on the alcohol—but on the situation, too. Years ago, you might have dreamed of this moment, but now it is actually happening you are unsure of how to act.

She opens a door, stops, glances over her bare shoulder. Her smile is as wide as the heavens. It's obvious what she wants you to do.

You wait until the door closes behind her before following her across the room. You don't want to seem too keen in case she changes her mind. The thought makes you smile; the fear drops away.

You approach the door and stop, reaching out to touch the handle. You play your fingers across the brass knob, teasing yourself with the proximity of her body on the other side. Then, feeling silly, you turn the handle and open the door.

When you enter the room she is face down on the bed. She is naked. Her panties are balled up on the floor at the foot of the bed. She is lying on her stomach, with her backside raised up in the air. She turns her head and stares at you. Her eyes are dark; her skin is pale; her teeth are bright.

"Why me?" You have wanted to ask the question since she first approached you.

"Why not?" she says, and gives you one of her self-satisfied smiles.

You move slowly across the room and stand at the side of the bed, realising that you should be taking off your clothes and climbing onto the mattress beside her. But something is holding you back—images from the film clip you saw earlier are stirring inside your head.

"That's right," she says. "Just let it come." Her legs tremble. She clenches her fists and raises her arms above her head, grabbing the headboard. The muscles in her forearms tense, becoming rigid. She is preparing for something.

You realise that there is somebody else in the room with you. When you turn your head to the side, you see the little girl from the film. She is crouching down in the corner of the room, large flaps of skin hanging like a ruined flag around her shoulders, and she's covering her face with her battered hands. She is crying but there is no sound.

"Shall I turn it up?" The woman on the bed sits up and turns around. She grabs a remote control handset from a cabinet at the side of the bed and points it at the girl. The sound leaks gradually into the room, the volume rising steadily. The girl's sobs are heartbreaking, and underscored with a soft classical music score. You wonder if she knows that you are there and that you can hear her weeping.

You can do nothing but stand and stare, and after a short while it becomes uncomfortable. You experience the same feelings of shame and sadness as you did while watching the film, but this time the emotions are real. They have context.

"What is this?" You take a step forward and then stop, unable to continue. "What's happening here?"

"This is the footage you never got to see." Her voice is like a song; it holds a tune, but one you can barely recognise. "This is what happens when the cameras are turned off and the film crew go home. This is what's left behind, the outtakes."

The girl is still crying. Her shoulders are hitching up and down; she is pulling at her hair with her small, dirty hands. She lowers her arms and looks up, staring right at you, right through you.

Where her eyes should be, there are only burnt and blackened holes, the edges crisped. Deep inside the holes that take up most of the upper part of her face, you can see flickering yellow flames. There's a fire inside the girl, but you aren't sure if it's one that was started by the things she has seen or if it was already there, smouldering quietly.

"What did you think this was—a seduction?" The woman on the bed begins to laugh. The girl joins in, and when she opens her mouth there are no teeth in her gums. Flames curl out of her mouth, between her lips and down across her chin. Her cheeks bulge outwards, the skin turning red and almost transparent.

The woman stands up and walks away from the bed. Her tattoos are moving, creating new pictures across the canvas of her body. Each one is a replica of the running girl from the film—the same girl who is now on fire in the corner, blazing away silently. Like an old-fashioned flicker frame, the thin, black figures run on the spot, never really going anywhere, just stuck to the woman's flesh.

The girl is now nothing but a blackened husk, a charcoal shell. The intensity of the blaze has painted the outline of her form on the white wall behind her; a cinder image, a memory that will never be erased.

You turn away and approach the door. Behind you, the woman is laughing again; she begins to speak in tongues, calling you names in a variety of languages you cannot understand.

You open the door.

Outside the room is a blasted landscape. Blackened ruins, a long dirt road, a wavering thread of fire along the horizon. You spin around and the door, along with the room beyond it, has vanished. All you can see for miles is more of the same empty, smoking landscape. In the distance, a vehicle approaches you at speed. As it gets closer, you see that it is an army jeep, but you don't recognise the decals and markings on the bodywork.

The man in the passenger seat of the jeep is holding a gun, aiming it in your direction. At this distance he might miss, but if they come any closer he'll hit you for certain.

These are trained soldiers, possibly even paid mercenaries belonging to no official army. They were taught to kill. No longer individuals, they are now part of a larger project: war as installation art; indiscriminate killing as a means of making an artistic statement.

These are not men; they are symbols, ciphers.

Meat is murder. . . .

War is hell. . . .

Born to kill. . . .

Once the jeep is close enough that you can see the men are smiling and laughing, you turn around and start to run. You try to pretend that you didn't see the severed head stuck to the front of the car, impaled on a spoke of the shattered radiator grille.

When you glance down at the ground, you see that you are wearing heavy army-issue boots. Your legs are clad in baggy camouflage cargo pants, and you are wearing a green shirt and combat jacket. You do not have a weapon, but there are bullets in a pouch on your belt.

A sudden burst of flames peels first the shirt and jacket and then the skin from your back. You clench your tattered fists and pump your arms and legs, trying to outrun the war—any war; whatever damned war is raging endlessly behind you.

You feel small. Tiny. Defenceless.

Up ahead of you is a naked little girl. She is running, too, and screaming. You grab her arm as you move to overtake her, pulling her up into a tight embrace. You recognise her face as she looks into your eyes, still screaming. The last time you saw her, she was ashes. You keep on going, not letting your stride falter. You need to get away; you have to save her this time.

Her screams drown out your thoughts. All you can think of is that you have to get away and protect the girl.

But there is nowhere for you to run; there is no hiding place for either of you out here, in the war zone, chased by an enemy you do not even know.

You are gripped by a terrible feeling of *déjà vu*:

This could be Vietnam, it could be Cambodia; it might be Serbia, Afghanistan, or the West Bank. It could be anywhere.

It could be anywhere at all. Any time at all.

But it is England.

It is now.

And it is happening to you.

Just as you hear the first gunshot, you see a flash of white light from a mound of rubble at the side of the road—the sun flaring off a camera lens, winking conspiratorially as you finally enter the scene and hit your mark.

A second shot rips the air apart close to your right ear. The impact ruffles your hair, shoves you sideways. You stumble, losing your grip on the girl, and feel your heart drop all the way through your body to your knees. A cry escapes your lips as you realise that you will fail her. You have already failed her.

Then all you know is explosive pain and the sense that an audience is waiting to catch you when you fall.

It ends with a man and a girl. They are no longer able to run. No music. No closing credits. Slow fade to black.

And then it starts all over again.

THE PIED PIPER OF HAMMERSMITH
Nicholas Royle

If you've ever sat alone at night in one of those houses or flats that back on to the overground sections of the Hammersmith & City line, then you will know—as Michael did—that the trains that go by, with images and light shining out of oblong frames, are not trains at all, but movies.

After the many hours he spent as a child watching them day after day, night after night, year after year, Michael knew he was destined for a life in movies. But it didn't work out the way he might have planned it.

Michael had never set eyes on his mother, a first-reel casualty. His father lived in a world of his own, its dimensions those of his house in Shepherd's Bush. Michael rented a Hammersmith bedsit. Uncomfortably close to his father, it's true, but the old man could have had no idea—or even care—that Michael was even still alive, never mind living under a mile away.

Michael worked for one of the big production companies. In Dispatch. In a Great Titchfield Street basement, cans of film stacked up high on the shelves. Videocassette Canary Wharves—U-matic, Betacam, VHS. Michael signed them in and signed them out. A life in movies. The only time he ever saw a piece of film was if a dispatch rider dropped a can and the lid fell off.

"What's all this about shift work?" his manager asked him.

"Movie commitments," Michael replied, quick as a flash. "Film work."

The guy gave him a funny look, but it was true enough and it got Michael the late shifts he was after. All so that when he went home on the overground sections of the Hammersmith & City line, it was nighttime on the other side of the screen.

"Now it's dark," Michael muttered in deliberate echo of Dennis Hopper's Frank Booth every time he boarded at Great Portland Street. "Now it's dark."

Darkness was the first prerequisite for film projection. Just as matinée shows weren't proper screenings, so too the trains that ran during daylight were not real movies. The Hammersmith & City line was genuine cinema. They may have only been short films, curtain-raisers, appetite-whetters, but Michael gave it all he had. Every ride home in the dark was a fresh performance, another stab at the part.

He hadn't satisfied himself that he knew where these films came from or who made them or why they were different from the ones on his shelves at work or indeed, in video format, on his shelves at home. But he took them seriously—as seriously as if the Oscar were up for grabs every night of the week.

As the carriages trundled between Great Portland Street and Baker Street, this was the leader edge of the first reel, black celluloid, no images to project. Sometimes the film would get stuck in the gate of the projector between Baker Street and Edgware Road. The actor-passengers around Michael would cluck with impatience, improvising frenetically as they watch-checked, mobile-phoned.

Michael remained calm. Sooner or later the driver-projectionist would right the film and, once they were out of Edgware Road, the movie proper began. An illuminated strip of celluloid shooting out into the night, its audience the rear mansion flats of Gloucester Terrace, the boxy council apartments of Westbourne Park, the Edwardian owner-occupieds of Shepherd's Bush—one of them Michael's father's place, the portion of the audience Michael kept especially in mind as he worked on his performance night after night. Just as day after pitiless day, Michael had lain in his cot watching, from behind its bars, as the trains went by. Twenty-four hours a day—his father working obsessively on his own doomed projects, his painstaking documentaries of animal life and reproductive cycles.

Michael's room was at the back of the house. He lay in his cot and he sat in his pram and watched the trains. Lucky if he got fed once a day. He cried and yelled and watched the trains through his tears.

Michael had noticed the blind people at Great Portland Street. Who hadn't—apart from the blind people themselves? The station saw a lot of white-stick merchants passing through its gates, their reactions to normal acts of kindness—offers of assistance out of the station, across the road—ranging from genuine pleasure to unmasked irritation. Michael liked to help. Liked being thanked, disliked having charity thrown back in his face.

In Dispatch, Michael was ticking off the days. A can of film had sat on the bottom shelf, the bottom shelf at the back, for just under six months, having appeared one day before the start of his shift and never been picked up. Never even appeared on the worksheet.

He gave himself six months. Long enough for a mistake to be rectified. If no one came to pick up the can in six months, not only did Michael feel he could legitimately sneak it home himself, but he could assume it had been put there for him—and he had passed some kind of test by not taking it before.

He hadn't even opened the can. It could be empty. But something told him it wasn't. He didn't even need to check—as long as he left it undisturbed for six months it would turn out to contain film for his eyes only.

He became jaunty with the dispatch riders, cocky with the company runners.

For the final week of the six-month wait, Michael brought a hold-all to work and took it home again at the end of his shift. Hefted it conspicuously whenever an opportunity arose.

On the last day, he slipped the can into the hold-all, zipped it up. Left as if everything were normal. Just another day at the office. Another ride on the tube.

A couple of pavement-shufflers were waiting at Great Portland Street. Michael watched them on the bank of closed-circuit monitors at the same end of the platform where he stood every night. The end which would leave him farthest from the exit at Hammersmith—he didn't like people coming up behind him on the platform. He still hadn't figured out the obstacle-dodgers' significance in the nightly movie show, though the irony wasn't entirely lost on him—that of these sightless characters appearing in a visual medium to be enjoyed by an audience of west Londoners with eyes in their heads but no love in their hearts.

Michael's father's place backed on to the line between Shepherd's Bush and Goldhawk Road, only the market separating back yard from railway. Michael lived between Goldhawk Road and Hammersmith; his room offered a similar view to the one he'd *not* enjoyed throughout his cheerless childhood. When looking for a place, he hadn't really considered any alternative to the view he knew.

Michael directed himself all the way home, zooming in on the hold-all—the occasional whip-pan to frame either of the blind passengers. Pretending not to know each other, they were travelling at opposite ends of the carriage.

The only thing Michael had taken with him when he left his father's house was one of the old man's collection of 16mm movie projectors. He, too, would have preferred for his life in movies to have been different to the way it turned out, but his later seven-hour natural-history epics fell between two stools, hitting the right note with neither BBC nor ICA. His entry in the record books was for having amassed the world's largest collection of 16mm projectors owned by an individual.

He didn't even possess the imagination to switch them on and have them all running at the same time showing different movies, or even the same movie, which *might* have appealed to the ICA.

Michael had never used the projector he'd nicked from his old man. He switched it on now and again to check the bulb, projecting a white square onto the bare wall, but had always been waiting for the right film to come along. In the meantime he'd watched videos. His bedsit contained a rickety unit crammed with cassettes—*Jacob's Ladder*, *Eraserhead*, *Halloween*, *Blue Velvet*, etc. A decent-sized TV and his director's chair completed the picture.

Heading home, the film in his bag, Michael did nothing to embellish his performance, to mark it out as different from normal. All he ever did was sit or stand, depending on the time at which he'd boarded, until the terminus. He'd vary the door at which he got off, but he hardly overdid it.

This time, he disembarked at the far end.

In the morning it mattered less where he sat, what he did. Morning trains were rehearsals.

He didn't need to rehearse. He needed only to get to work and pretend this was just another day. Another autumn day.

The film he'd watched the night before had shown him not only the significance of the eye-test rejects but also where the short films of the Hammersmith & City line came from.

Unlikely perhaps that one short piece of film should have answered both questions, but the answers were the same. Michael knew he heard voices—he'd admitted as much to the people at Charing Cross Hospital—so he'd watched the film a second time to make sure he wasn't being taken for a ride.

Lying in bed watching the late movies outside his rain-streaked window, he'd realised what he had to do, and, scanning the calendar on his wall, he'd worked out when he would do it.

That very week. Friday. Halloween.

Every evening, walking to the tube, Michael passed the RNIB in Great Portland Street. But, wilfully or not, he contrived not to see it, and the presence of so many blind passengers in the tube station continued to be a mystery—now solved.

Since watching his father's film, he had all the answers. The film in the can had been his father's work.

On the Friday evening—Halloween—Michael picked up two blind stragglers on the way, an elbow in each hand. He helped them through the barriers, down to the platform.

Down to the far end they went, away from the few other passengers. "It's busy tonight. You don't want to get knocked onto the track." The indicator board showed that the first train to arrive would be a Hammersmith service, but he told his two unseeing charges that it was a semi-fast Watford train and that he just had to go somewhere for a minute and they should wait for him. He would be back to help them get to where they were going. So saying, he tracked back up the platform. Picking out a couple more blind folk.

"Can I help?" Innocence itself. "Which train are you waiting for?" The Hammersmith train wooshed into the station, doors glided open, none of the blind commuters got on.

Anyone who has ever used the Hammersmith & City line will know there can be substantial gaps between trains bound for Hammersmith. By the time the next one appeared, Michael had assembled eight blind passengers and one guide dog at his end of the platform, having deflected a number of complaints about the delay. Michael watched himself and his flock in the rack of CCTV monitors. He stuck his chin out, punched hands into pockets, struck poses.

The Hammersmith train rumbled in, rattled to a halt. Doors slid open. POV switched to a camera hung in the ceiling arch of the station. The tops of nine heads moved on to the train, disappearing from view. Only the soundtrack records the closing of the doors. The train starts to move.

NEW ANGLE

Train leaving Great Portland Street station. Blurred figures still getting settled in last carriage.

EXT. NIGHT. ROYAL OAK.

Train doors sliding shut on platform. Inside last carriage Michael stands, surveys nine passengers seated around him, one with guide dog—all are blind except Michael. Michael draws a long-bladed knife from inside coat pocket. Flash of light on blade—

DISSOLVE TO—

Shower of sparks from train wheels.

NEW ANGLE. LONG SHOT.

View of train leaving Royal Oak station from rear of flats lining Westbourne Park Villas. Michael playing with knife in front of his fellow passengers. Guide dog begins to bark.

EXT. OUTSIDE TRAIN. WESTWAY. MEDIUM SHOT.

Last carriage from other side. Shot from car passing on Westway near Ladbroke Grove, motorway and railway side by side. Michael mock-ballet-dancing around carriage, swinging from pole to pole.

INT. INSIDE MOVING TRAIN. MEDIUM SHOT.

Michael bending down, up close to the face of one of the passengers, staring into his filmy, opaque eyes.

PASSENGER (agitated)

What is it?

MICHAEL (looking dreamy, whispering)

I know your secret. I know all about you.

PASSENGER (moving head from side to side)

What's going on?

MICHAEL (still whispering)

The Ozark cavefish in the subterranean limestone quarries of Missouri. ... (voice trails off). I saw this film. Last night. One of these natural history films. Never exposed to the light of day, they evolved without eyes. Blind cavefish. Just like you.

EXT. ESTABLISHING SHOT. BBC TV CENTRE.

Long shot across tube line of huge satellite dishes at BBC TV Centre. Train sweeps into foreground.

PAN—

to follow train and take up position on the line showing the cab at the end of the last carriage as train heads into Shepherd's Bush station, where it stops, no one alighting, then resumes its journey.

NEW ANGLE. EXTREME CLOSE UP. MICHAEL (whispering).

Celluloid miners. That's what you are. Celluloid miners. You quarry these films from beneath London. Deprived of light you have become blind. Blind celluloid miners enslaved to the monster you created.

EXT. LONG SHOT OF MOVING TRAIN FROM INSIDE HOUSE.

To the accompaniment of a childlike tune from a musical box. From behind the bars of MICHAEL's cot in his *old* house, his *father's* house, we see the train trundle by. Yellow light pours out of the train windows, oblong like individual frames on celluloid. The tinkle from the musical box grows louder. The intensity and brightness of the light increase.

(MICHAEL—WHISPERED VOICEOVER)

You seek emancipation. I will give it to you. I am your saviour.

EXT. MOVING SHOT OF TRAIN FROM INSIDE HOUSE.

Camera moves out from between bars of cot toward window. As the last carriage passes the house, more and more light pours out of the train. We are allowed a quick glimpse of the interior of the last carriage—a blurry confusion of flashing knife blade and bright red gouts of blood splashing against train windows. Musical box crescendo. The light increases further in intensity, diluting the red then obliterating it completely.

WHITE OUT

MUSIC FADES

ROLL CREDITS

FILMING THE MAKING OF THE FILM OF THE MAKING OF *FITZCARRALDO*
Garry Kilworth

He told me his name was Cartier and we arranged a meeting at once, in a café on the Boulevard St. Augustin. He was a small, thickset man with dark features and an Eskimo's eyes. He claimed to be a Canadian and spoke a form of French that I had to translate mentally into the purity of my own tongue. His story essentially involved three people—himself, a man called McArthur, and McArthur's niece, a twenty-year-old called Denise. Somehow—this was never fully explained—Cartier got wind of the filmmaker Werner Herzog's decision to make the movie *Fitzcarraldo* and the three of them followed Herzog and his crew to the South American jungles, determined, clandestinely, to film the German at work.

I ordered cognacs, before Cartier got too involved with his story, and we waited for a few moments, watching the Parisian passersby, until the drinks were on the table. I then signalled for Cartier to continue.

"We pooled our money—all we had—and set off in pursuit of Herzog's crew. It might seem, now, that taking Denise with us was a bad decision, but she absolutely worshipped McArthur and unfortunately most of the money came from her. Anyway, McArthur had always been strong on family, you know. He wasn't married and his parents were dead. His sister, to whom he had always been close, was working somewhere in Asia. So he felt it was his duty to include his niece, her daughter, in the expedition, if that's what she wanted."

It was with intense annoyance (a mild word, I should have thought) that Cartier and McArthur realised an official movie of the making of the film was already in progress. In fact it was this second crew that he and McArthur had to shoot, since this party remained a barrier between Herzog's main crew and Cartier's secret camera.

"Denise stayed well behind at this stage, in a second canoe, but McArthur and I disguised ourselves as Indians and followed at a distance as they went upriver. McArthur had the camera in the nose of our canoe, camouflaged with reeds. In any case, we were quite a way behind and *we* had our Indians, who waved to those in front. We hoped they *would* just think us curious natives."

The Cartier-McArthur camp was established a little downriver from the other two crews, and on the opposite bank, their movements hidden by the thick foliage of the rainforest.

"The Indians helped us to make some huts out of the broad-leafed plants. They weren't much, but they provided shelter from the tropical rain. McArthur was like a schoolboy at first. Everything excited him— the jungle life, especially. He had a new single-reflex stills camera—with a close-up lens—and he photographed anything that buzzed, croaked, or hissed. The place was teeming with life. It got into all the equipment and our clothes. The only things McArthur wasn't too fond of were the snakes and spiders. His phobias were very suburban.

"Denise, on the other hand, was contemptuous of everything in the rain forest. She showed neither interest in any creature, nor fear. I personally believe she was utterly incapable of being fascinated. That is, she saw no magic in this quite extraordinary world, only squalor. To her there were only two kinds of creature, in myriad shapes—'slimes' and 'crawlers.' Oh, she knew the names for them all right, but she just wasn't going to waste her time finding the right word. That would have meant giving *them* a specific identity, acknowledging that they were even of minor importance to her, personally.

"All Denise was interested in was getting the job done. She didn't like *me* very much either. I think I was a 'crawler.' And she was forever pestering me. One morning I had the camera in pieces—the spare wasn't working either.

"'Can I help?' she asked, but wearing one of those wooden expressions that I hated. She had several facial masks which were designed to keep me at a distance and in my place.

"'Yeah—you can scratch my insect bites,' I told her. 'They're killing me.' I lifted my shirt to show her three or four large red lumps on my stomach.

"She didn't even say, 'You're disgusting,' or anything like that. She merely looked at me blankly and remarked, 'I mean with the camera.'

"'No, I'll have it fixed soon.'

"'What about the spare?'

"'I'll work on that next. You're in my light.'

"McArthur was busy cooking something and he said, 'Get out of his way, Denise. Let him see the light.'

"She laughed at that. I didn't think it was very funny, but they did. She went over to one of the Indians then, who was painting his body. He had a cut, which was infected, over the part of his face on which he was applying the ochre. She started remonstrating with him, quietly, though he couldn't understand a word she was saying.

"'Don't mother him,' I told her. 'He knows what he's doing.'

"Sure enough, when she tried to interfere, he slapped her hand away. She went very red, glanced at me as if it were my fault, and looked as though she were going to cry.

"McArthur had seen the incident—a small one you might think, but when all expectations are met with frustrations, and the rain forest is sending its squadrons of insects to harass you day and night, *no* incident is minor or too trivial—everything that happens is of a magnitude that threatens sanity.

"He put his arm around her and she nestled in his shoulder for a moment. I watched them out of the corner of my eye. 'All right?' he asked her, and she nodded, still flushed, before getting up and going into her hut.

"The trouble with Denise was she wanted to be doing things, all the time, to help—and there really wasn't that much to do. I didn't see it then, though I do in retrospect. God, she was so eager to help it was stretching her nerves to tight wires. I think if a maniac had run into the camp, waving a gun, she would have looked around eagerly for someone to throw herself in front of, in order to take the bullet. She wanted to make her mark on the project—sacrifice herself—to give it every chance of success, so that afterwards she couldn't be accused of being just a passenger. If I had given her the onions to peel, and said, 'You know, Denise, we couldn't have made it without you,' she'd have been my friend for life.

"The funny thing was, it was her presence that kept us going, only she didn't realise it. She thought she had to give something physically, or intellectually, or it wasn't worth anything. Her strength of will—the spiritual pressure she applied—was powerful enough to keep us there, working away with almost no material.

"Nothing was stated, you understand. McArthur and I didn't say to each other, 'Let's go home,' and then, 'No, we can't, because Denise will be disappointed in us.' The fact that she was there prevented even this much admittance of failure. I just know, in myself, that had she not been with us, we would have gone home after just a few days.

"However, because it was one of those buried truths, *she* didn't know it, and she still sought some way, any way, of proving that her presence was necessary to the project.

"If only I had given her some acknowledgement of the very real part she was playing . . . but I didn't. All I could do was grumble that she was in my way. So we carried on as we were, stumbling around in the dark, and with Denise fluttering around us like some giant moth, ready to throw herself into the candle flame if it would provide us with more light."

Cartier paused here. There was a tenseness to him which the brandy seemed to exacerbate, rather than relieve. He was gripping the glass as if to crush it.

"It was McArthur who thought of the idea," he said, placing the glass carefully on the table, "because nothing, absolutely nothing of interest was happening—not for us. All we could do was shoot that damn boat from a distance and watch the crews working and eating—not the stuff of exciting cinema.

"McArthur had noticed a certain antagonism evident between our own Indians and those in Herzog's camp. Something to do with territorial areas I expect. He said it wouldn't be a bad thing—for us—if something developed.

"'Like what?' I asked him.

"'Well, if one of our Indians should meet, face to face, with one of theirs, we wouldn't be responsible, would we?'

"Denise understood him instantly—they had a strange kind of mental rapport that needed few spoken words. It was only when he said, 'I suppose it should be me,' did I get the idea. I'm not saying I didn't approve the scheme, because I did. I was as anxious as the other two to go home with something of worth on film. But I was scared. Not only was it unethical, even criminal, it carried a very dangerous undercurrent. We might start something we wouldn't be able to stop.

"So I did endorse the plan, and we made certain preparations. McArthur had volunteered himself because he believed himself to be an archer. He was the obvious choice. I was as dark as he, and my disguise was convincing, but the man behind the bow had to be good. We didn't want a death on our hands: just a little action for the film. You understand. I could blame the heat, the insects, the rain forest— you know we had to wipe everything, each day, to get rid of the mould that grew on our possessions overnight—the humidity was unbelievable. We had begun to bicker continually amongst ourselves, fighting over silly things that meant nothing—nothing at all—even McArthur, whose initial wonder in the place had since dissipated. There was an indefinable sickness amongst us, that we battled with medication and had a hard time holding down.

"It was another world—a kind of heavy, drug-dream place. A place in which we felt we had a right to make our own rules. We had come a long way from civilisation—used all our resources to get there—and we had to go back with *something*. Oh, I could blame a thousand things—the excuses proliferate, even as I talk to you now.

"So—we did it. The next time we saw a fisherman leave Herzog's camp in his canoe, we followed on foot, keeping pace with it along the bank. McArthur had borrowed bow and arrows from one of our Indians and when the man stepped ashore, he shot him, aiming for his leg.

"Now, I'm not saying that McArthur's expertise with the weapon he normally used was wanting—he was probably very good with a precision-made longbow—but the Indians use much longer arrows and smaller bows. McArthur fired two arrows, I think, or maybe it was three—I can't remember exactly. The idea was to wound the fisherman, have him running back to his people, and provoke some sort of reaction from them. We had a naive vision of flights of arrows whizzing across the river and nobody actually getting hurt—badly, that is—so that some attention would be focused on our side of the water. We wanted a skirmish to film.

"Anyway, it was a disaster. The last of McArthur's arrows caught the fisherman in the throat. There was a kind of gagging sound and the man went down, disappearing into the foliage. I've got it all here, on the film. You'll be able to see exactly what happened when I show it to you. Even now I have difficulty in remembering the details. You know, when you're working, you're too involved with the business of filming to register a conscious blow-by-blow description of the scene in your own mind—the director's supposed to do that, and my director was one of the actors in this particular scene.

"I know I cried, 'My God, you've killed him!' when the next thing I realised was that McArthur was on the ground himself. He was staring stupidly at an arrow protruding from his thigh, as if it had just grown there—you know, like a bamboo branch had sprung from his flesh. I'm still not sure where that shaft came from, but I guess the fisherman must have fired back, from a prone position. The angle seemed to indicate something of that nature."

Cartier must have seen a look of enquiry on my face because he added, "They fish with bow and arrows, there.

"Anyway, I dragged McArthur away with me and we headed back to camp, he using me as a prop while he limped along. He was as white as fish belly, I can tell you, and he was vomiting the whole way."

I interrupted the story here. "I remember seeing a wounded Indian in the film of the making of *Fitzcarraldo*—was that the same man?"

"I think so. He lived, thank God. Or thanks to the doctor that their crews had taken with them.

"I got McArthur back to our camp and we put him in one of the huts. Denise was absolutely distraught—McArthur was babbling by this time, delirious, and Denise kept shouting about poison on the tip of the arrow.

How she got that idea I don't know. I thought it was just shock—there was no obvious discoloration around the wound. No dark red lines going up into his groin.

"She wanted to get the doctor from the other camp, but after what we'd done I thought we'd be in for a nasty reception from the wounded fisherman's tribe. I was absolutely against it. I convinced her that the arrow, which we had left behind, was a fishing arrow and would not be poisoned. Finally, she agreed, and decided to nurse him herself. She went into that hut and, well, I have my own ideas about the events that followed, bizarre as they might seem to you now, in the light of a Parisian day. Things were different there. It was all a little surreal. *Our* light, filtered by the roof of the rain forest, was of a sickly, greenish hue, and shadows moved back and forth through it, like phantoms. There were the constant murmur of insects and sudden confrontations with amphibians and reptiles, which seemed to appear on trees, in the grass, as if by magic. The whole place had a sense of the fantastic about it.

"Perhaps the arrowhead *had* been tipped with some kind of substance? Anyway, McArthur went into a state of fever. I heard him yelling occasionally, between bouts of absolute silence. Most of his complaints were concerned with being too hot, or too cold, but I also heard him shouting about the 'snake' and the 'river'—and following these cries, the low, soft voice of Denise, telling him it was all right, she would protect him. I didn't go into the hut. They had no need of me.

"Of course, fever can bring on hallucinations during bouts of delirium, but I believe it was more than that—something quite extraordinary was happening to McArthur. The mind is a delicate mechanism—if that's the right analogy—and once you tamper with its intricacy, its balance, it can respond in strange ways, playing havoc with reality. As I said before, I have my own ideas—ideas about memories and self-protection.

"The mind is like a camera, recording memories, which are never projected. Short films, locked away and only replayed internally, so there is never any doubt of their unreality. I say *never*, but I think in McArthur's case, there was.

"When McArthur was yelling about the snake, I think he was talking about the anaconda we had seen basking on the river bank a few days earlier. From the canoe we had watched it uncoil its enormous length, as thick as a man's thigh in places, and slip into the river. McArthur had been petrified. He thought the creature might come towards the canoe and he was shaking so much there was a danger of the canoe overturning.

"It didn't. It swam away, upriver—slow, sinuous movements through the brown water, its blunt head showing just above the surface.

"I think that McArthur's mind was replaying this encounter, projecting it and superimposing it on the actual scene—the interior of the hut. A sort of double-exposure effect, which had him believing that the snake was *in* there with him and as real as everything else around him."

Cartier paused as a waiter passed our table, as if he did not want any eavesdroppers to hear what he had to say next. Once the man was out of earshot, he continued.

"He was projecting, not just memories of the snake, though, but longer, deeper memories, which he had buried to keep from the light. These too began to emerge, to superimpose themselves on the dim scene within the hut. Memories evoke not only recognition of their familiarity, but emotions. Just as the snake stirred some primal fear within him, those older memories aroused a forbidden desire, a passion indulged during earlier years. McArthur's past was with him in that hut, and he could not separate real from unreal. Combined with this was his need to be protected from that terrible serpent, and Denise was there to provide that protection. She wanted to *help* him, you understand? She saw it as essential to herself to do what she could for him, at the same time, making her contribution to the expedition."

Cartier took a swallow of his cognac. I sensed that the revelation was about to emerge and tried not to make any movement that might distract him. He seemed on the verge of abandoning the tale altogether. So I sat, quietly, waiting for him to continue.

"They were in that hut three days," he said. "I sent in food and drink, of course, but I didn't enter the place myself, not until I heard McArthur talking in more rational tones. I couldn't hear exactly what was being said—there was an intense quality to the speech—but the long periods of silence, punctuated by irregular sessions of screaming, had ceased.

"I went in, then. I'm afraid I interrupted them. I was expecting to see—well, I don't know what I was expecting, but it wasn't two naked bodies locked together. I left immediately, but though Denise hadn't seen me, McArthur had."

I groaned inwardly, expecting now that I would get a sob story about how much he, Cartier, had been in love with Denise, and that he had never suspected that her uncle would take advantage of her hero worship.

"So—it was incest," I said, hoping to ward off his outpourings. "A fairly mild form though. Both adults—and the relationship not as close as it could have been."

He stared at me, his dark eyes holding mine, something troubling their depths.

"Yes. That's what I thought—and no doubt Denise. She didn't know either, you see."

"Know what?"

It was the first time since we had met that I saw anything like real discomfort registering in Cartier's features.

He said, "She didn't know McArthur was her father."

My thoughts did a few acrobatics and I said, instinctively, "But Denise was his sister's daughter." Then I stopped. I had the whole picture. He had fathered his sister's child and had now taken that daughter to bed. What a mess! The whole thing was revolting: incest in layers.

"He told you this?" I asked.

"Shortly afterwards. We pieced together the theory of memory projection from it. You can see how it relates to the film."

"And you want me to distribute this movie?"

I stared out of the café window, waiting for his reply, watching people hurrying along the boulevard. My distaste for this project almost made me jump to my feet and join them, but I decided to see the thing out.

"Yes—we all do. We thought you should have some background to the movie—it might help to create a little publicity, don't you think?"

Cartier's face was devoid of expression. I tried to imagine what was going on in his mind. It wasn't easy.

"Let me take the film away with me. I'll contact you tomorrow."

He agreed and we went outside and transferred the movie from his car to mine. I did not shake hands with him. I just climbed into my car and said, "Tomorrow then."

I had noticed, when we left the café, that he was limping.

As I drove home I thought about my own predicament. The bills were mounting up and I still had not found the successful movie that would get me out of the rut. My recent decisions might have been sound ones, based on my experience in the business, except that no one can predict certain success in the movie world.

That evening I watched the film in my private studio. It was a boring collage of river and forest scenes. The Herzog boat was there, the area around busy with people, but it could have been an amateur movie, taken by a camp follower, or, more likely, it had been put together from stolen discarded cuttings of *Fitzcarraldo* itself, and the film of the film, to form a bastardised child of both. The whole effort folded in on itself, until nothing made sense because it was too internalised. It exposed too much of its inner self, which in the revelation showed nothing but a confusion of scenes and snatches of close-ups. It revealed everything, yet it revealed nothing, because at any core, whether it is human emotion or something more substantial, there is no truth that can be grasped and understood. Everything becomes a cluttered wash of incomprehensible colour tones, weakened further by the continual rinsing of the thing in itself, until all you have is a faded copy of a copy, recurring.

When the film reached the scene where the arrows were exchanged, I paid particular attention, but even here I was disappointed. The light was all wrong, either too weak or too strong. There were figures in the gloom of the forest, and action certainly took place, but, bright and dark, what came out of it was a flurry of furtive movements, glimpsed through curtains of leaves and fences of tree trunks. There was a close-up of the wound in McArthur's leg, which looked genuine enough, as did the agony on his face, but it had been done better, by Charlton Heston in *El Cid*. McArthur, on film, was of course the spitting image of the man I met in the restaurant, calling himself Cartier.

There was also a single scene of the niece, or daughter, or both, half hidden behind smoke from a campfire. Either the shot was overexposed or she was thin and pale, almost translucent, with red-rimmed eyelids. The sort of will-o'-the-wisp female who gets cast as a fairy extra in *A Midsummer Night's Dream*.

What it amounted to was an unholy tangle. Of course, if the story were true, there were enough vultures in the world to make the film a success in terms of sales at the box office. Artistically, it stank, but some cinemagoers would be curious about this trio and their incestuous goings-on in the South American jungle. If it were released to the media, the gutter press would provide all the publicity needed.

However, I doubted very much that the story *was* true and I had my integrity to consider.

I met Cartier, or McArthur, at the same café the next day.

I gave him the standard rejection.

"It's not good cinema," I said.

He seemed very disappointed, leaving me his card and saying I was to call him if I changed my mind. I replied that there was little chance of that. Once I had made a decision, I told him, I usually stuck with it.

His eyes went to a corner of the café, where there was a door with a small window set in it. I thought I caught a flash of something behind the glass of that window and turned back to him. He had a dejected expression on his face.

"Who's behind the door?" I said.

He seemed about to argue, then must have changed his mind. I suppose that, since I had rejected his offer, he saw nothing to gain by denial.

"A friend of mine—cameraman. He's filming us. I thought it would make a good postscript to the movie—you and I meeting, discussing the project."

I looked him straight in the eyes.

"*You're* McArthur, aren't you? Who's that behind the door? Cartier?"

Before he could reply, I saw his eyes widen as he looked up, over my left shoulder. Then a tremendous explosion filled my head. I felt the heat of a blast on my cheek, and smelt the acrid odour of cordite. My head rang with the noise and for a few seconds I could not see, let alone hear anything. If any sensible thought at all crossed my mind, it was that the café had been bombed by some terrorist organisation.

When I was able to register a conscious understanding of what was happening, I realised that McArthur was sprawled on the floor, where he had gone flying backwards. There was blood in his hair, on his collar. What I had heard was the sound of a revolver being fired close to my ear.

As I turned around, still groggy and shocked, she was just putting the barrel of the gun beneath her chin. There was another explosion, not so loud as the first, since it was muffled by soft flesh. The body struck my shoulder as it fell and I think I screamed.

The next thing I knew I was being helped to my feet and led away towards the bar. My legs were shaking violently and someone forced a brandy down my throat. I couldn't even hold the glass, my hands were trembling so much. There was a lot of shouting, which I could hear above the ringing in my ears. I remember glancing back at the woman's corpse, once. But it was impossible to tell whether the face—now covered in gore—belonged to the girl I had seen in the movie the previous evening. It crossed my mind that it might even be McArthur's sister, the mother of their daughter.

An unholy tangle. The police came and took me into another room at the back. I can't recall what I told them, but I must have just recounted what had passed over the last two days, between the man on the floor and myself. I found out later that they had secretly videoed my statement. Finally, I remembered about the cameraman, behind the window in the door, and started to tell them when one of them pointed towards the corner of the room. There was another man there, talking to more policemen. He glanced across at me and I recognised him.

There was a movie camera, on the table, between him and his interviewers. He gave me a look, as he nodded at his recording device. It was difficult not to interpret that gesture into a language I knew well, that said:

"I've got it all here on film, if you want to use it."

That was just before the TV crews arrived, and I believe you saw what followed, for yourselves, on the six o'clock news.

Alain d'Ivry, the talk-show compere, offers me a glass of water, and with the cameras still working, I take a long drink.

"Are we still on?" I say.

He nods. "But don't worry—we'll edit this out later. Let's get back to the café scene. You say you didn't recognise the woman's face after she turned the gun on herself, but now of course. . . ."

ONLOOKERS
Gary A. Braunbeck

". . . all those bodies which compose the mighty frame of the world have not any subsistence without a mind—that their being is to be perceived or known."

—George Berkeley (1685–1753)

"It is a simple equation: take me, subtract film, and the solution is zero."

—Akira Kurosawa

They are filming something on the street, in front of our house, very close to the front door.

Even though he can't see them when he pulls up his blinds or pushes aside one of the curtains, my six-year-old son Brian senses that someone is watching. After dismissing his claims as ". . . an overactive imagination," Dianne, my wife, finally admitted to feeling the same way, though with the nervous, slightly embarrassed, "Maybe-I'm-Just-Full-Of-Shit-Today" laugh she always uses whenever she can't put her finger on what's bothering her. So far neither of them have directly asked me what I think, how I feel, do I believe them or not.

I think this is exactly what the Onlookers want, for you to convince yourself that it's just your imagination playing tricks on you; it'll make the work easier for them, and perhaps less terrifying and painful for the rest of us, if and when we cumulatively figure out what's happening; after all, isn't perception both perceiving *and being* perceived? If the Onlookers are edging us toward a state of non-being without our knowing it, then what can we do to stop it, to re-balance the equation, to perceive while being perceived?

My wife and son are fading before my eyes, you see; and more than once in the last few days, both have asked me if I've been losing weight, which means I am lessening in their perception, as well.

All around, the colors of our life are become paler. There is a dogwood tree in our back yard, and the red spots on all the leaves have turned to the same foggy gray as an old black-and-white film; as have many of the leaves on the other trees; as has much of the grass.

Dianne and Brian say I'm too pale lately. (Dianne called it "looking a bit gray around the gills.")

I can't bring myself to tell them they look the same to me.

They are filming something on the street, in front of our house, very close to the front door.

Something tells me they're going to want their interior shots soon, before they lose the light.

I don't think there's any way I can stop them.

I first saw the Onlookers when I was a child, but had no idea what they were, what they wanted, or of what they were capable.

In the summer of 1964, when I was five, my father—who sold medical supplies—took my mother and me along on a business trip to New York. Spending nearly a third of every year on the road, Dad always felt bad because we'd never had a "proper" family vacation; rightly thinking that Mom and I got sick of spending every summer stuck in Cedar Hill, he hoped this ". . . madcap excursion in the wilds" (as he called it, like it was going to be some Great Adventure worthy of Jules Verne) would suffice.

We had a wonderful time, as I recall (being only five, my memories are divided into two categories: the bus, taxi, or subway ride *to* someplace in the city, and the *cool* stuff I got to do once we arrived).

Dad was meeting with some doctors whose offices were on the Upper

West Side in the 140s, near the Hudson River, and for a few hours Mom and I were left to our own devices—which meant sightseeing and shopping.

We'd just left a restaurant where I'd had the best ice-cream sundae in the history of ice-cream sundaes (that I ate way too quickly; it would later come back to haunt me with a stomachache) and were heading for some boring old antique store when we rounded the corner and walked right into a movie—or, rather, the movie walked into us, in the form of a hunched, roundish man in a dark coat that was far too heavy for the summer weather. His head was down so that his face was buried behind the high upturned collar of the coat; all I could see of him was that coat and the gray, flattened hat he wore (which Dad later told me was called a "Porkpie" hat).

The man bumped into Mom, almost knocking her over (he was walking *very* fast and seemed to be trying to get away from something), then veered left and plowed straight into me.

I spun around, arms pinwheeling, trying to catch my balance, tripped over my own feet, fell backward against one of the sawhorses, went over, tried to twist around so I didn't crack my skull on the pavement, and landed on the other side on my butt. I immediately began crying; everything hurts more when you're five years old, and it *especially* hurts more when it happens in a big, strange, scary city that seems like it could eat visitors from Ohio for breakfast and still want a second helping.

I looked up, hoping to see Mom's face lowering toward me; instead she stood frozen, having just seen the face of the man in the coat and Porkpie hat.

And that's when I saw my first Onlooker.

My head and vision were still swimming from the tumble—everyone and everything around me seemed to be spiraling—so it took a moment for me to realize that one of the people in the crowd had a camera for a head; to my momentarily skewed five-year-old's perception, that's what it looked like: instead of a human head, one of those old-fashioned oversized box cameras sat atop their shoulders, and on either side of the box, like the eyes of a horse, a half-sphere of metal blinked opened and closed with a soft metallic *shnick!* (no, I couldn't actually hear them, but I imagined that to be the sound these "eyes" made when they blinked). For a moment all I could do was stare at this weird but wonderful thing in the back of the crowd, then the pain from my fall fully registered and the world was lost under a heavy wash of tears that blurred everything into one shimmering mass; I pulled in a deep breath, wiped my eyes on my shirt sleeve, and looked up to see that the scary man in the dark coat was now on one knee and reaching for me.

"Hey there, little fellah," he said in a deep, croaky voice that sounded like it belonged to some old monster frog. "Took a little tumble there, did you? I'm sorry—didn't see you. But if you don't mind me saying, you can take a fall with the best of them!"

Mom laughed when he said that, and I cried all the harder because here she was, laughing at something this scary man in the dark coat said when she ought to be down here giving me hugs and telling me it was all right and promising me another ice-cream sundae if I was brave. I looked around to see if Camera-Head was still nearby—the memory of it made me want to laugh and I figured if I saw it again I'd laugh and everything would be all right—then I saw the kneeling man's face and screamed.

I'd never actually seen someone with an eye patch in person; sure, there had been all those pirate movies, people *always* wore eye patches in those, but that was just pretend; the scary man in the porkpie hat had one for real and it was *so* scary. I tried backing away from him like a crab but then hit the curb behind me and almost did a somersault into the street.

Mom and the scary, one-eyed man applauded.

I stopped crying; my butt and back still hurt, but now I was just pissed, so I scowled at both of them.

"That's quite the little tumbler you got there," said One-Eye Porkpie, turning toward my mother, who introduced herself and shook his hand like she was meeting President Johnson or Elvis.

One-Eye Porkpie removed his hat and waved to a bunch of people with cameras and microphones and lights who were behind him (Camera-Head wasn't among them, either, and I wondered: had he been trying to run away from these people?), and that's when I realized that I'd landed on something that looked like a train track, and that one of the cameras that had been following One-Eye Porkpie was setting in a wagon of some sort that was attached to the tracks. I was suddenly terrified that the camera wagon was going to roll right over and cut me in half, but it stopped moving when One-Eye Porkpie waved. I thought it was weird that he'd been running *away* from the camera, because it seemed to me it hadn't been going all *that* fast.

Mom looked down at me and smiled. "It's all right, hon, he's not going to hurt you."

"Wouldn't hurt a fly," said One-Eye Porkpie in his froggy voice, helping me up.

Mom dug into her massive shoulder bag and removed the Cine-Kodak 8 Model 90 home movie camera that Dad had insisted she carry ". . . in case you see any movie or TV stars." She'd never been able to operate it properly, and as she chatted with One-Eye Porkpie she fumbled around with it until he took it from her and got it going.

"Wanna be in a movie with me, little fellah?" he asked me.

"My name's Patrick," I said, trying to sound grown-up.

"Is it now? Well, mine's Joseph," he replied, offering his hand. "Pleased to meet you."

Mom spent the next ten minutes filming him clowning around with me; at one point he made a big show of shaking out his hands and reaching behind my left ear to remove a shiny silver dollar, then did the same with my right ear. (He let me keep them, and that made him less scary, though it didn't help my butt from being any less sore,)

As we were getting ready to leave (a man Mom said was ". . . the director" told everyone they needed to get moving because they had a schedule to keep), Porkpie called over a sweet-faced woman he introduced as ". . . my wife and official handler, Eleanor," and asked her to take some pictures of him and me. At one point, he removed his hat and put it on my head.

"Say there, little fell—'scuse me, *Patrick*—that hat looks right at home on your noggin." He looked at his wife. "Don't you think it looks right at home?'

She and Mom both agreed that it did. I thought it felt like it was going to drop down and eat my face, it was so big.

"You okay there, Patrick?" One-Eye Porkpie asked.

To which I responded, with all the tact of a child: "What happened to your eye?"

He laughed, then flipped up the patch to show me his other eye was still there. "Nothing. They just wanted me to wear it in this movie."

"How come?"

He leaned forward, whispering: "Heck, I have *no idea*. I guess they think it makes me look creepy or tragic or something. But it's want they wanted, and they're paying me to act, not think or ask questions, so I go along with it."

"Just pretend, huh?"

He nodded. "Just pretend, that's right."

Porkpie knelt down beside me for a few more pictures. He smelled like cigarettes and medicine. "I think you ought to keep that hat, is what I think, Patrick."

"But it's your only one."

Everyone around us laughed.

"I bet maybe I got a couple more around here someplace," he said, winking at me. "Besides, it ought to belong to a little buster like yourself."

"What's a buster?"

Another laugh. "That's a nickname Harry Houdini gave me when I was born. It means some little fellah like you that can take a tumble with the best of them." Then he winked, like he was letting me in on some Big Secret. "That hat's got a lot of miles on it. A *lot* of miles. You keep it safe for me, and if I ever lose the other ones, well . . . you'd let me borrow it back wouldn't you?"

"I sure would."

"That's all a fellah can ask for, then."

He called over someone else—a tall, skinny, hawk-nosed man with round wire-framed glasses and a shock of spiky white hair on his head—and said, "Sam, I want you to meet Patrick. Patrick here is a first-class tumbler."

"It's a honor to meet you, little sir," said Hawk-Nose. He had a rich, musical accent that reminded me of Father Fitzgibbon from that Bing Crosby movie *Going My Way* that Mom always watched whenever it was on TV. Porkpie insisted that Hawk-Nose be in a picture with us, and even though it seemed like the guy felt awkward about it, he knelt down on the other side of me so Eleanor could get us all in. Mom kept filming with the Kodak.

"*Esse est percipi*," said Hawk-Nose.

"Huh?" I said.

Porkpie shook his head. "It don't mean nothing, little fellah." He leaned forward so as to look past me at the other man. "Sam, I'm warnin' you, don't go starting in with all that malarkey about perception and non-being and the flight from extraneous perception breaking down in the inescapability of self-perception and . . . whatever in the hell else it is that this picture's supposed to be about. Brother—I just gave myself a headache *talking* about it."

Hawk-Nose smiled; I got the feeling the two of them argued like this all the time, and that both of them enjoyed it. "A thousand pardons, Joseph."

"I still say what this picture needs is a couple of good sight gags."

"Anything more would distress your director," Hawk-Nose replied.

Porkpie shook his head. "And you wanted *me* to be in *Godot*. Half the time this Existentialist stuff makes me want to jump out a window."

I laughed at the way he said it—"win-duh," his froggy voice cracking—and he gave me a hug while his wife took some more pictures.

"You take good care of that this," he said, placing a hand on top of the hat on my head as Mom and I were leaving. "This's one of my magic ones, and I might need it back some day."

"I will, sir, I promise."

Hawk-Nose smiled at me, then touched his index finger between my eyes and said, "*Esse est percipi*."

"Thank you very much for the pictures, sir." Still having no idea what he'd said.

It wasn't until fifteen years later—when we were studying Absurdist Cinema in my college film class—that I figured out Porkpie had been Buster Keaton and that Hawk-Nose had been Samuel Beckett.

The course instructor had managed to track down a copy of *Film*, a 22-minute short black-and-white movie written by Beckett and starring Keaton. It was a little past the midway point of the movie that I began recognizing some of buildings from the Upper West Side, and was so stunned by the realization that I missed most of what happened for the rest of the movie.

Afterward the instructor was bemoaning how no filmed record of the production itself existed, and how ". . . invaluable to film history" such a record might have been; I was about to raise my hand and say, "You're not going to believe this, but . . ." when it occurred to me that I had never seen the home movie Mom had shot that day. Until that moment, I'd all but forgotten about it.

By then both Keaton and my dad were over a decade in their graves (Dad from a heart attack, Keaton from lung cancer), and while the college-me thought it was kind of cool in a for-shits-and-giggles way, it would be another ten years before I genuinely understood just what an honor it had been to meet the Great Stone Face in person—not only that, but have myself on film with him.

Somewhere, at any rate.

Still, actually having that film in my possession might do wonders for my final grade in Film class, so I went back to my dorm room that night and called Mom in Florida (where she'd been living for the past six years).

As soon as she was on the phone, Mom said: "I did it. I went wild and bought myself a Betamax. A Sony SLC9. I even bought a couple of movies, too. I got you *Apocalypse Now*—you liked that one, right?"

I admitted that, yes, I might have liked it, considering I saw it nine times in the theater.

"Does this mean you'll come down here and visit me on Spring Break?"

"I'll skip out a week early."

"You'll do no such thing. I already bought your plane ticket. You'll skip out *two days* early. Yes, I know, I'm the greatest mom in the history of moms."

"You sure are."

"Flattery will get you everywhere. Now—what's going on?"

"Why does anything have to be going on? Why can't I just call my mom to see how she's doing and chat?"

Mom sighed. "Because, *hon*, you're not a phone-chatter. If you call someone, me included, it's because you've got a specific reason. You're just like your dad in that way. So what is it?"

I told her about what happened in Film class, and asked her if she still had the home movie she'd taken that day.

"Not only do I still have it," she said, "but I just had *all* our home movies transferred onto videotape so we can watch them on my spiffy new Beta-max—did I mention that I bought myself one?"

"Rub it in." At the time, the C9 was *the* state-of-the-art machine. I was so envious I could have bitten the receiver in half.

"You can play with it all you want while you're visiting."

And you bet I did just that.

Three days before Spring Break ended, Mom and I were watching the transferred home movies in her condo (part of a retirement community in South Florida, a really nice place, actually) when she popped in the videotape of that day in New York. I'd forgotten that the Cine-Kodak had sound recording capabilities, and it was amazing to both see and hear the five-year-old me, as well Keaton and Beckett.

"I tried reading some of that Beckett's plays," said Mom. "Either I'm dumber than a mud fence or he doesn't know how to write."

She started going on about *Waiting for Godot*, how all that happened during the entire play was that two bums sat by the side of the road waiting for some guy who never showed up.

I was only half-listening, having just spotted something in the back-ground that was there only long enough to attract my attention and then vanish. I picked up the remote control, re-wound the tape, let it play, then pushed the "Pause" button.

Mom leaned forward. "What is it, hon?"

"Do you see that, to the left?"

"See what?"

"*On the left*. Look at Beckett's right shoulder, then look past it."

"I don't see any—oh, wait a second. Do you mean that guy with the big camera?"

I nodded, saying nothing, because it was most definitely there: half-sphere metal horse-eyes on each side of its square head, and a jutting lens from the front that from this angle looked like some kind of beak.

I leaned closer for a better look, slowly advancing the tape frame by frame.

"You're not supposed to do that," said Mom. "The instructions said you could break the tape, doing that too much."

I pushed "Play" and let it run. I'd seen what I was looking for; the camera was exactly in the place where a head should have been; I distinctly saw a human neck connecting the camera-thing to the body.

Of course it made sense *now*; *Film* was a piece of Absurdist Cinema, so it wasn't any great suspension of disbelief that in an Absurdist film written by Samuel Beckett, there'd be some extra in the background wearing a camera for a head—albeit one that was deliberately constructed to resemble that of a living thing, a horse or maybe bird.

"Can I take this tape back with me?" I asked.

"You sure can. After your call, I figured you'd ask me, so I had an extra copy made."

I looked at her and smiled. "You really are the best mom in the history of moms."

"Nice of you to notice, *finally*."

I watched Buster Keaton put his porkpie hat on my head, then turned to Mom and said, "Whatever happened to that hat?"

"I put it plastic-wrap and stored it in one of my old hatboxes."

"Can I take that back with me, too? My Film professor would get a big kick out of seeing it."

"The man gave it to *you*, it's yours. But you'd better take good care of it. That's a real piece of movie history."

"I promised him I would."

"Then how come I was the one who found it on the floor in your bedroom when you were seven?"

"Because I was *seven*."

"Good point."

I turned back to the television and watched as Keaton and Beckett, dwindling into the background as Mom and I walked away, stood waving good-bye. "I thought the Kodak took color film."

She nodded. "It did." She nodded toward the screen. "Colors look fine to me."

The movie was in black-and-white . . . except for the extra wearing the camera-head costume; admittedly, it was far into the background by now, but I could have sworn that its half-sphere eyes were bright gold and its lens-beak a shiny silver. I dismissed this as the result of an old 8mm home movie having faded over the years.

Around ten p.m., after Mom had gone to bed, I popped open a bottle of Coke and went outside the lounge under the stars. I thought about how much I missed Dad, and how lucky both Mom and I were that he'd had such great insurance, and how grateful I was that she'd gotten such a good price on the house. She was a thoughtful woman, Mom was; half of the insurance settlement and the house-sale money was in a trust fund that I had barely touched since turning twenty-one. One more year and I'd be out of school, my Journalism degree qualifying me to flip burgers somewhere until (or if) I decided to enter a graduate program. I considered it money that both Mom and Dad had spent their lives working for, and I was damned if I was going to spend it frivolously. I figured—

—*shnick!*

I sat up, looking around, trying to see what—

—*shnick!*

I knew that sound . . . or *thought* I did, anyway.

I stood up and scanned the nearby trees and bushes, and once thought I caught a glitter of moonlight reflected off of something old, then—

—*shnick! Shnick! Shnick-nick-nick-nick-nick!*

I figured one of the neighbors must be taking pictures of the moon; despite how bright it was outside, the trees and bushes surrounding the condo building created deep, elongated shadows all around the back area of the condo, so if they were behind me, I wouldn't have been able to spot them.

"I hope they turn out," I said, gesturing toward the moon. "It *is* a helluva sight to see, isn't it?"

As if to answer me in the affirmative, a last *shnick!* echoed from the shadows. I toasted the moonlight, then went back inside.

Film is a strange and difficult movie. Shot in black-and-white, it has no sound (with the sole exception of one character delivering a sibilant "*Shhh!*" early on). In it, Keaton plays a character called "O" (as in Object) whose face is never seen until the final moments of the movie. "O" is moving through the streets, sometimes walking very fast, other times running, always hunched down so that all we see of him is the back of his coat and the top of his porkpie hat (and for much of the 22-minute running time, that hat is the only indication that it's Buster Keaton we're watching). It's obvious that he's being pursued, but by what or whom we don't know.

"O" passes several people during his flight; sometimes these people look at his face, sometimes they look past him, but in every encounter, these people end up shrinking away in horror. The more this happens, the more the viewer comes to understand that what "O" is running from—and the thing that elicits such horror from passersby—is the second main character, named "E" (as in Eye, as in Camera-Eye): "O" is running away from the camera; he does not want to be seen.

Upon entering his cramped apartment, "O" immediately shoos his cat and dog out into the hallway, closes the door, and begins ripping apart every family photograph in the room—he doesn't even wish to be seen by the faces in the pictures.

Once this is done, once he has isolated himself from all things that could perceive him or be perceived *by* him, only then does "O" turn around to reveal his face.

He has only one eye, the other covered by a heavy black patch.

"O" sees that all of his efforts have been for nothing, because "E" is right there in the room with him, and the movie ends with "O" releasing a silent scream and anguish and horror. The expression on Keaton's face when he turns to face the camera is right out of a nightmare: the look of unparalleled horror will sear itself into your memory.

Beckett's explanation (according to his published journals) is that he has sundered his main character in two: the character "O" who is pursued by the subject "E." As long as "E" stays behind "O," "O" will avoid being perceived. The camera is designated, in Beckett's phrase, an ". . . angle of immunity" of 45 degrees, which it must not exceed at the risk of causing "O" to experience the ". . . anguish of perceivedness."

My Film professor argued that the reason "O" has only one eye is because "E" is the other one, thus keeping the equation of perception continually split—"Because in order for 'O' to have full perception, he must also possess *depth-perception*; since he does not, full perception cannot be achieved." It is *the film's audience* that causes the final coalescing of the separate perceptions into one; it's not the presence of "E" that causes "O" to scream in horror, it's the presence of the audience (whom "O" can theoretically see when he turns around); by watching both "O" and "E," they force full perception to occur: the cinematic equivalent of the Observer Effect.

When asked during an interview what he thought *Film* was about, Keaton answered, "What I think it means is that a man can keep away from everybody, but he can't get away from himself."

The day after I returned from Florida, I arranged to meet my Film professor in the Media Center, where I showed her the porkpie hat, told her about my encounter with Keaton and Beckett, then showed her the home movie. While she was watching the tape, I asked her if I could screen *Film* because I wanted to see if I could figure out where in the story they'd been when Mom and I collided with Keaton.

I set up the projector, checked out the movie, threaded everything into place, and watched it.

Nowhere in the movie is there an extra wearing a camera-head costume. I knew from class that nothing had been cut from *Film*—the director, Alan Schneider (who came from the Theatre, specializing in Absurdist plays), was working in film for the first time, and had planned out every shot in almost fanatical detail so that everything would be used (his arguably humorless approach leading to numerous on-set disagreements with Keaton).

I watched *Film*, all the time thinking: *What the hell was that guy doing hanging around with that thing on his head?*

I answered the question almost at once: *Easy; he was a street crazy, or maybe someone who'd hoped to get into the movie by standing out.*

Only he hadn't stood out. As I remembered it, he seemed to be trying to stay in the background the whole time, trying to hide as much as "O" was trying to run away.

I decided to write it off as one of those passing oddities that sometimes make interesting conversational tidbits.

My Film professor was suitably impressed, as were my classmates, and for one day I was a Hot Topic; then the videotape and Keaton's hat went back into storage boxes, I graduated college, flipping burgers for only three months before I landed a job as a Feature writer at *The Cedar Hill Ally*, eventually meeting a young doctor named Dianne who lost her mind and agreed to marry me and a year later gave birth to our son.

Every so often I would hear a faint *shnick!* somewhere nearby, but never thought much about it (working at a newspaper, you get used to hearing the sound of a shutter-click); every once in a while the sound would be accompanied by a glint of gold or silver in my peripheral vision, but I never gave it much thought: Camera-Head was only a dim, distant, dusty memory, emerging every few years just long enough for me to decide it was too silly to bother with before retreating into the shadows where we keep all those things that no longer belong in our lives.

Then came the afternoon that Brian attended a matinee at the Auditorium Theatre with one of his friends and his friend's parents, and came home to tell me all about the ". . . funny old man who did magic tricks when no one else was around."

"What do you mean, honey?" Dianne asked him, giving me a quick but seriously concerned look.

"Well," said Brian, "Jimmy had to go pee, so his dad took him, and Jimmy's mom, she asked me if I wanted some more popcorn—Jimmy and me ate all of it before the movie even started, and they got *real good* popcorn there—and I said yeah, that would be great, so she told me to stay right there in my seat and I *did*, I was good, I never moved, and then when I was all alone, this old man behind me reached around and pulled something from my ear." Brian reached into his pocket and removed a shiny silver dollar.

I took it from him and looked at the date: 1964.

"Did he tell you his name?"

"Nope."

"So it wasn't any of Daddy's friends that you've already met?"

"Nope."

"Brian, buddy," I said, "what exactly *did* this old guy say to you?"

My son became as bright and animated as I'd ever seen him. "He told me about the card tricks he knew, and then he told a couple of jokes, and then he pulled two more silver dollars out from my ears. He had *real weird* breath. It wasn't stinky. It kinda smelled like that cough medicine Mom makes me take when I'm sick. Oh, yeah—he told me to tell you that he needed his hat back, please."

The silver dollar slipped from my fingers and clattered to the floor.

"Did Jimmy's mom and dad see him?" asked Dianne.

"Nope. He was all gone before they got back."

Dianne saw something in my expression. "What is it? What's going on?"

I shook my head, telling her it was nothing, then—after telling Brian it was not a good idea to talk to strangers (something we re-emphasized from time to time, Brian being a particularly open, trusting, and friendly child)—went upstairs to my office and pulled Mom's hatbox from its place in the back of the closet. Unwrapping Keaton's hat, I heard the echo of his voice saying, *You take good care of that this, this's one of my magic ones, and I might need it back some day.*

Silently, I added: *And you promised.*

I realized there was probably a rational explanation for it, that one of my friends who knew the story had spotted Brian at the movies and decided to play a joke on me, but as soon as I'd seen the date on the silver dollar, I knew something wasn't quite right: my friends *might* have gone to those lengths to play a joke on me, but I doubted it; and none of them would have approached Brian without first telling him who they were, especially if they'd not met him before.

I slipped the hat into my briefcase, told Dianne there was some background material for an article I'd forgotten at *The Ally*, and drove downtown.

Parking on the square, I walked past the soon-to-be renovated Midland Theatre and crossed the street to the soon-to-be-closed Auditorium Theatre. Paying no attention to what movie was showing, I bought a ticket for the showing that was already twenty minutes in and headed for the balcony (Brian and Jimmy always sit in the balcony).

The only other person up there was a small, roundish man sitting in the middle of the third row of the loge. Even from behind, I recognized him.

Making my way down toward him, I opened the briefcase and removed the hat.

"I thought for sure you'd have lost that thing years ago," he said in the same croaky voice I'd always remembered.

"I keep my promises," I said.

And took my seat next to Buster Keaton—not the fit, trim, athletic Keaton of his triumphant silent film days, but the pot-bellied, slightly droopy, cancer-ridden Keaton of *Film*, *A Funny Thing Happened on the Way to the Forum*, and *War, Italian Style*.

"What's going on?" I asked, handing over the porkpie.

"I'll be—you sure took good care of it." He straightened the brim, flattened down the top a little more, and set it on his head. Had I not been so frightened, I would have been in absolute awe. "Still fits. Thank you."

"You're welcome," I replied. "What the hell is happening?"

"It's the Onlookers," he answered, then turned to face me. "Them camera-head fellahs you spotted way back when?"

I nodded.

"Well, turns out there was something to Sam's malarkey, after all. That old Irish son-of-a-bitch, he hit on something with that picture he wasn't supposed to—kind of like when Pasteur made his big discovery by accident. Only with Sam and *Film*, the process he discovered ain't quite so helpful in the long run."

"What process?"

Keaton pointed his index finger at me, just like Beckett had done, and touched me right between my eyes. "Perception, young fellah. How it ain't just a two-way thing, but a *three-way* thing. You, the camera, and the audience."

"The audience being the Onlookers?"

"No—they're the camera. The Onlookers, they're the ones perceiving everything *through* the camera." He shrugged, then winked at me; I know he meant it to be reassuring, but there was something infinitely sad in the gesture.

"I don't really know what, exactly, the Onlookers are; only that they've been watching us for a long, long time. See, the way I understand it, is that as long as none of us were aware they were watching, everything was okay. It was like me running from that camera in the picture; as long as I didn't turn around to see it, I wouldn't know the audience was watching me through the blasted thing. But once I turned around and saw the camera, well . . . that made the audience part of it, because then we were all aware. It was like a chain reaction. Do you get what I'm saying? I sure as hell'd hate to have to try explaining this a second time."

"I think so," I said. "By making that movie, you guys somehow . . . somehow . . ."

". . . somehow lifted a barrier between them and us that nobody knew was there until Old Sam hit on the idea. But that's all it took—one guy hitting on the idea, then making others aware of it. Image, camera, audience— *wham!* The three ingredients needed to pull off that extra level of perception and let some of us start seeing the things the Onlookers *see us* with."

"So . . . what happens now?"

Before Keaton could answer me, a rapid series of shutter-clicks—*shnick-nick-nick-nick-nick-nick!*—echoed from the seats below. I rose up, peering over the edge, and saw that a full one-fourth of the audience below had square heads, golden half-sphere eyes, and silver lens-beaks.

No one else seemed to hear or see them.

One by one, the Camera-Eyes turned to look up toward the balcony. I jumped back from the railing and hunkered as far down into my seat as I could.

"Hate to be the one to say it," said Keaton, "but I think they seen ya."

"Is this supposed to be how 'O' felt?"

Keaton parted his hands in front of him. "Damned if I know."

"What's going to happen now?"

He gave me a long, silent look of pity. "You know how at the end of *Film* the camera freezes on my face and then it all just goes to black? Old Sam told me that the idea there was that, once 'O' and 'E' and the audience make that three-way connection, then a state of . . . what'd he call it? . . . oh, yeah, *non-being* followed." He snapped his fingers. "Everything just stops, ceases to be. It's like the way all colors together form black; all perceptions together create . . ." He made his hand into a fist, brought the side of the fist up to his mouth, then blew into it while opening his hand.

I didn't need words; the meaning was clear enough.

"Isn't there any way to stop them?" I asked.

"The Onlookers? Huh-uh. They've always been and always will be. Now if you're asking me, is there any way to stop them things down there from seeing you, the only idea I got is for you to not see them. *Un*-see 'em."

"How the hell do I *un*-see something?"

He placed the tip of his index finger between my eyes. "'To perceive is to be perceived.' That's what Sam said to you . . . course he had to say it French 'cause he was kind of an intellectual snob, but he was an okay fellah, once you got to know him." He rolled his eyes upward, saw something wrong with the angle of his hat, and adjusted the brim once more.

"Why do you need the hat back?" I asked.

"If you're expecting a complicated Sam Beckett answer, you're gonna be disappointed. This particular hat was my favorite . . . I just didn't realize it until after you'd gone. Eleanor, God love her, forgot to get your names and address from your mother. Took a while to track you down."

"Why here? Why this old movie house?"

"Because this old movie house used to be a damn nice theatre in the days of Vaudeville. My family and me played here quite a few times when I was just a kid. There's a wall underneath that stage that all the companies used to sign as they came through. You'd shit a brick if you knew some of the names on that wall. But I ain't gonna bore you with nostalgia; you got a family to get back to."

He started to rise; I reached up and grabbed his arm. "How can I un-see them?"

He shook his head. "Just between us, I don't think it can be done. I wouldn't worry too much, I was you. How fast the process takes depends on how perceptive you really are. You'll start noticing things, like colors changing or fading away. Not all at once, but gradually. After that, other things'll fade, little by little. That's just the slow road perception takes to non-being." He pulled from my grip, then gently patted my shoulder. "But it'll be okay, young fellah. I'll be waiting over there to show you around, and—oh, what have we here?"

In two quick, smooth, fluid movements, he reached behind my ear and removed a shiny silver dollar. I took it from him, looked at it and smiled, and when I looked back up he was all gone.

I left the theatre and walked toward my car, hearing the endless chattering shutter-clicks of *shnick-nick-nick-nick-nick-nick!* following me. I became frightened, started running, but the Camera-Eyes were never far behind; even though I never once turned around to look for (or at) them, I knew they were there.

I darted down alleys, around the square, through an abandoned lot, and back around to where I'd parked my car, all in an effort to lose them.

It did no good.

I finally got in my car and drove home, taking several detours and side streets along the way.

When I came inside, I all but slammed the door behind me, then leaned against it, gulping air.

Dianne called from the kitchen: "Did you find what you were looking for?"

I almost said: *No, but it found me.* "Everything's good," I said, lying.

And felt someone watching.

That was less than a week ago.

Since then, the dogwoods' red spots have turned gray; as have many of the leaves on the trees in our back yard; as has most of the grass. The blue of the sky is fading. The colors of our life are going away. My wife and son are lessening in my perception, as I am in theirs.

How fast the process takes depends on how perceptive you really are, Keaton had told me.

Well, so much for being proud of having a perceptive family.

I keep wondering who or what the Onlookers really are, but I suppose their true nature and form won't be revealed to me until I—like "O"—turn to fully face the Camera-Eye.

How do you un-see something?

Tonight, after Dianne and Brian had gone to bed, I dug around and found my wife's medical bag. I rummaged through it. She has hypodermics, vials of morphine, sutures, bandages . . . and a scalpel.

I keep thinking about the final image of *Film* and my professor's explanation for the patch worn by "O."

Shnick! Shnick-nick-nick-nick-nick!

They are filming something on the street, in front of our house, very close to the front door.

I remember the patch, and the perception equation, and my Film professor's explanation, and as I turn the scalpel from side to side so it reflects the light, I think of my family, and how much I love them, and whisper to myself: it will be only *one* eye. . . .

RECREATION
Lucy A. Snyder

We would be two larks winging
our way through the Master's
best, you said. I'd be your Grace
Kelly, your Audrey. Your eager eye
documenting our recreation, old-style
eight millimeter, hand-cranked.

I don't remember Grant getting naked
as he fled the marauding sky, flat
fields, drab motels, but a true auteur
is no script-slave. Spellbound, I shed
my retro dress, hit the marks you ordered,
amateur heart fluttering in its dark cage.

But you've stopped wearing your tie,
your ring. You've switched to digital
video, the cost of the darkroom too dear.
The trunk of your old green Ford is filled:
coils of rope and plastic sheets. The shower
scene is tomorrow, you smile. I'm silent,
skull-rehearsing my own altered script
as I lie beside you in the feather bed.

BRIGHT LIGHTS, BIG ZOMBIE
Douglas E. Winter

"When I started using dynamite, I believed in many things. . . .
Finally, I believe only in dynamite."
—Sergio Leone, *Giu la testa*

IT'S 6 A.M.
DO YOU KNOW
WHERE YOUR BRAINS ARE?

You are not the kind of zombie who would be at a place like this at this time of the morning. You are not a zombie at all: not yet. But here you are, and you cannot say that the videotape is entirely unfamiliar, although it is a copy of a copy and the details are fuzzy. You are at an after-hours club near SoHo, watching a frantic young gentleman named Bob as the grooved and swiftly spinning point of a power drill chews its way through the left side of his skull. The film is known alternatively as *City of the Living Dead* and *The Gates of Hell*, and you're not certain whether this version is missing anything or not. All might come clear if you could actually hear the soundtrack. Then again, it might not. The one the other night was in Swedish or Danish or Dutch, and a small voice inside you insists that this epidemic lack of clarity is a result of too much of this stuff already. The night has turned on that imperceptible pivot where 2 a.m. changes to 6 a.m. Somewhere back there you could have cut your losses, but you rode past that moment on a comet trail of bullet-blown heads and gobbled intestines, and now you are trying to hang onto the rush. Your brain at this moment is somewhere else, spread in grey-smeared stains on the pavement or coughed up in bright patterns against a concrete wall. There is a hole at the top of your skull wider than the path that could be cork-screwed by a power drill, and it hungers to be filled. It needs to be fed. It needs more blood.

THE DEPARTMENT
OF VICTUAL
FALSIFICATION

Morning arrives on schedule. You sleepwalk through the subway stations from Canal Street to Union Square, then switch to the Number 6 Local on the Lexington Avenue Line. You come up from the Thirty-third Street Exit, blinking. Waiting for a light at Thirty-second, you scope the headline of the *Daily News*: STILL DEAD. There is a blurred photograph of something that looks vaguely like a hospital room. You think about those four unmoving bodies, locked somewhere inside the Centers for Disease Control in Atlanta. You think about your mother. You think about Miranda. But the light has changed. You're late for work again, and you've worn out the line about the delays at the checkpoints. There is no time for new lies.

Your boss, Tony Kettle, runs the Department of Victual Falsification like a pocket calculator, and lately your twos and twos have not added up to fours. If Kettledrum had his way, you would have been subtracted from the staff long ago, but the magazine has been shorthanded since Black Wednesday, and sooner or later you manage to get your work done. And let's face it, you know splatter films better than almost anyone left alive.

The offices of the magazine cover a single floor. Once there were several journals published here, from sci-fi to soft porn to professional wrestling. Now there is only the magazine, a subtenant called Engel

Enterprises, and quiet desperation. You navigate the water-stained carpet to the Department of Victual Falsification. Directly across the hall is Tony's office, and you stagger past with the hope that he's not there.

"Good morning, gorehounds," you say as you enter the department. There are six desks, but only three of them are occupied. Brooks is reading the back of his cigarette package: Camel Lights. Elaine shakes her head and puts her blue pencil through line after line of typescript. Stan, who has been bowdlerizing an old Jess Franco retrospective for weeks, shuffles a stack of stills and whistles an Oingo Boingo tune. J. Peter and Olivia are dead.

What once was your desk is now a prop stand for a mad maze of paper. An autographed photo of David Warbeck is pinned to the wall and looks out over old issues of *Film Comment*, *Video Watchdog*, *Ecco*, *Eyeball*, the *Daily News*. Here are the curled and coffee-stained manuscripts, and there the rows of reference volumes, from *Grey's Anatomy* to Hardy's *Encyclopedia of Horror Film*. Somewhere in the shuffle are two lonely pages of printout, the copy you managed to eke out yesterday from the press kit for John Woo's latest bullet ballet, smuggled through Customs between the pages of a Bible.

Atop it all is a pink message slip with today's date: Ruggero Deodato called. Don't forget about tonight. "And hey," Brooks says, finally lighting up a cigarette. "We had another visit from the Brain Police." You are given a look that is meant to be serious and significant.

You have spent the last five years of your life presenting images of horror, full color and in close-up, to a readership—perhaps you should say viewership—of what you suspected were mostly lonely, adolescent, and alienated males who loved these kinds of films. The bloodier the better. Special effects—the tearing of latex flesh, the splash of stage crimson, the eating of rubber entrails—were the magazine's focus, and in better days, after a particularly vivid drunk that followed a screening of the latest *Night of the Living Dead* rip-off, you and J. Peter and Tony came to call yourself the Department of Victual Falsification.

That was then, and this is now. The dead came back, not for a night but for forever. Your mother. Black Wednesday. Miranda. Cannibals in the streets. The bonfires in Union Square. Law and order. Congressional hearings. Peace, complete with special ID cards and checkpoints and military censors.

You remember, just before the Gulf War, reading newspaper articles about high school students who paged through magazines that were to be sent to the troops in Saudi Arabia, coloring over bras and bare chests, skirts that were too short, cigarettes caught up in dangling hands. You thought that this was supremely funny. Now each month you do something much the same. The magazine publishes the latest additions to the lists, recounts the seizures from the shelves of the warehouses and rental stores. At first the banished titles were the inevitable ones, the old Xs and the newer NC-17s and, of course, anything to do with the living dead. In recent months, the lists have expanded into the Rs and a few of the PG-13s.

You are detectives of the dying commodity called horror, and there are fewer places where the magazine is sold, and fewer things that you can say, and fewer photos for you to run and, of course, there are fewer people left alive, fewer still who care.

THE FUTILITY
OF FICTION

You see yourself as the kind of zombie who would appreciate a quiet night at home with a good book. You watch TV instead. Tonight there is the Local News, followed by the National News, and then, of course, the game shows begin and will continue on until the Local News, followed by the National News, and then, of course, the game shows again. There are 106 other channels on your television set, but all of them are awash in a sea of speckled grey and have been for nearly a year.

The path that awaits you is clear. You reach into the back of your bookcase, behind the wall of unread Literary Guild Alternate Selections, to slip out tonight's first videotape, a pristine copy, recorded on TDK Pro High Grade at SP, of the Japanese laser disc of Ruggero Deodato's *Cannibal Holocaust*. You waited months for your dealer to get this one, and now you wait patiently for the first real moment of truth, that glimpse of the tribesmen as they tear off and eat the flesh of their prey. Although you tell yourself that this is what you want, that this is really what you want, this is not what you get. There is a cornfield on your forty-inch television monitor. It is late summer, nearly the harvest, and there in the tall stalks is Miranda, walking with racehorse grace in her bleached jeans and turtleneck sweater, hair in golden braids and face shining with the sun. You turn your back on the monitor and you listen. For some time after Miranda died, you knocked on the door of the apartment before you entered. You would turn the key slowly in the lock and then pause here in the living room in the hope that you would hear her in the bedroom, that she had returned, that she was waiting for you, that none of this had happened, that none of this was real. The video plays on. "How could you explain what a movie is?" A voice calls to you from the screen: "They're all dead, aren't they?" You look back and the cannibals at last are feasting. You watch, and you wish. Nothing seems to be what you want to do until you consider horror. A random sampling of the titles hidden at the back of the bookcase induces a delicious expectancy: *Anthropophagus. Eaten Alive. Trap Them and Kill Them.* Little wonder that the Gore Commission should have found so many of these films so wanting. The covers of the video boxes are themselves a kind of foreplay, wet and bright with colors, most of them red. *Make Them Die Slowly.* Here the label reads: "Banned in thirty-one countries." Make that thirty-two. You know so much about these motion pictures, about the stories that they have to tell. You feel that if only they had given you the camera back then in the eighties, back when such things could be, you could have given shape to this uncertain passion that nightly inhabits your gut.

You have always wanted to make films. Getting the job at the magazine was only the first step toward cinematic celebrity. You never stopped thinking of yourself as a writer and director of horror films, biding his time in the Department of Victual Falsification. But between the job and the life, there wasn't much time for the screenplays or even the short experimental films. That first, and only, Christmas, Miranda had given you the video camera. For a few weeks afterward, you would shoot Miranda as she walked around the apartment, Miranda with shampoo in her hair, Miranda and the new kitten, Miranda at the stove, Miranda at the fireplace,

Miranda and Miranda and Miranda. Then, what with the zombies and everything, life started getting more interesting and complicated. You worked for the magazine and you had once met George A. Romero and you had your collection of videos, so chic now that the lists were out and the tapes were gone from the rental shelves. People were happy to meet you and to invite you to their parties. Then things got worse, and then came Black Wednesday and the bodies in the streets and the soldiers and the fires in Union Square.

You pull your video camera from its hiding place beneath the floorboards of the closet and set it up on its tripod. You have no blank videotape, of course. You take the cassette from the VCR and push it into the camera. You decide to start immediately with the film you have in mind. You aim the camera at the far wall of the apartment, bare and white. The autofocus blurs, then holds. Through the viewfinder you see exactly what you want.

You press the start button. You tape nothing.

A TOMB
WITH A VIEW

You dream about the Still Dead. You sneak down the corridors of the Center for Disease Control. Nobody can see you. A door with a plaque reading *C'EST LA MORT* opens into the Department of Victual Falsification. Miranda is spread-eagled across the top of your desk, her wrists and ankles bound with strips of celluloid, the censored seconds from the first reel of Deodato's *Inferno in diretta*. Around her in white hospital beds, like the four points on a compass, are the Still Dead. You approach and discover that she isn't moving. You touch her. She is cold. Quiet. One of them. Still dead. But then she opens her eyes and looks at you. You make a sound like a scream, but it is the telephone ringing. The receiver is hot and wet in your hand.

"I'm sick." You expect the caller to be Elaine or, worse yet, the Kettledrum himself. Ta-dum, ta-dee, ta. . . .

"I knew that from the day I met you." The voice is unmistakable. In his prime, he made the covers of *New York* and *Interview* and *Spy*. Now no one cares; but you never know, perhaps they will again. Sunlight is in your eyes. The clock says 10. You listen to Jay's latest proposition. A duplication center somewhere in the Bronx. Edit onto one-inch tape, copies to VHS. Sales in back rooms, some bars, the private clubs, on the street. Money to be made. Fame. And, most important, screen credits. "Your name in lights."

In this new world, there is no longer a place for dreams. Yet you have no doubt that he can do these things. It is the catch that troubles you, but only for a moment. You know you can be had. Jay says *ciao*, and he's gone.

You're not dressed and out of the apartment until 11. The uptown train pulls away just as you make the platform. Clutched beneath your elbow, the *Daily News* is screaming: BRIDGE BLOWN. This time it was the George Washington. You wonder whether the dead are being kept out or the living kept in. Now if you want to get to New Jersey, you swim. The Still Dead are buried on page five. No new developments: "Still Dead." The CDC will issue another statement on Sunday. Billy Graham will lead a candlelight prayer vigil. The president has expressed cautious optimism.

It's 11:30 when you reach Park Avenue South, 11:40 by the time you get a cup of coffee and an elevator. Kettledrum is waiting, and he holds his glasses in his hand. A bad sign. You consider saying something. An excuse, an apology. Just offering a smile. It is all a joke. The glasses start to twirl. You know you are in trouble.

Tony does not waste words. The magazine has had visitors again. The military censor took a hard look at the new issue and found not one, but two, discussions of the contents of listed videos in your article on Umberto Lenzi.

"What about the First Amendment?" Tony looks at you. You look at Tony. Tony is the first to laugh. You decide to nod your head and join in when you see the photo in Tony's hands. Black and white and red all over. It's Miranda. Her legs are spread wide, left hand fondling the rope of raw intestine that dangles provocatively between them, dripping wet blots of blood onto the headless body on the floor. You look again and it is not Miranda. Of course not. It is some actress from a splatter film, and this is a publicity photo. A still. Still life.

LES YEUX SANS VISAGE

You met her in one of those Midwestern towns where the sunsets were gold and not impaled by tall buildings. You had gone from NYU Film School to waiting for jobs to waiting tables at the Salvador Deli, and when the magazine asked, you answered. Soon after you had written the expected fanboy froth about Troma and Incarnate and the rest of the local scene, you were sent into the heartland to write the set report on the latest annual installment in the film life of a hockey-masked hooligan. At night you would stand around for hours while thirty-year-olds trying to act like teenagers were taped up with rubber tubes that would, for the few seconds of a take, spout out a mixture of Karo Syrup and melted chocolate that looked something like blood. In the mornings you would sleep and then, in the afternoons, write a few pandering paragraphs of the usual nonsense before taking a walk around the town, the reporter from the big city, and stop by the Rexall and the Kroger and the Payless Shoe Store and on the third day, after boredom had set in soundly, you found her in a place called Kenny's. You remember that she was drinking a Nehi, leaning easily against a wall, one blue-jeaned leg crossed over the other. She was wearing black Keds. Her eyes were closed, and she was listening to a song on the jukebox, something by Public Image Limited, the two of them so out of place there in Hicksville that you thought you had walked into a dream. You wanted to shoot her, just to shoot her right then and there, and you wished that you had a camera. You told her she should be in movies, and, of course, this is what she wanted to hear.

Within the week, she had moved in with you. She talked about the day your movie would go into production. All your plans were aimed at Hollywood. She wanted to live in The Malibu, and you wished to join the film life of El Lay. You watched videocassettes of Lang and Franju, Bava and Pasolini, and bullshitted her with beginning film theory until you both had enough to drink and then you went to bed. It wasn't long before you decided you would marry her.

You returned to New York with the question of what Miranda was going to do. She had talked about college, talked about modeling, talked about children. She wasn't sure what she wanted to do. People were always telling Miranda that she should be in movies. At dinners you would talk about directors and their actress wives: Bardot and Vadim, Russell and Roeg, Rossellini and Lynch. About how only you could direct her. About how only you could show the world Miranda. And then, of course, she died.

STILL DEAD

No one is kind. Their jobs are on the line. You have been inclined of late to underestimate the value of the dollar. Now you wonder what you would do if the magazine were gone.

You wander down the hall to the archives and browse through back issues. That first appearance of the magazine, way back in 1979, wore Godzilla on the cover and promised a photo preview of *Alien*. It seems like a century ago. No one in this country had heard of Deodato or Lenzi or Fulci; certainly no one cared. You flip through the years, and the bright-blooded covers, and you wonder at everything that has changed.

Later you find an empty office and make the call. You take a deep breath and dial the number of Jay's loft. You don't recognize the voice at the other end. "Tell him I'll do it." The voice asks you to identify yourself. "Tell him that Dario Argento called, and that he'll do it." The voice says that she has no idea what you are talking about, but that if you would leave your number, Jay would call right back. You hang up the phone and wonder whether it could have been traced. In your mind are images of men in blue suits with badges.

You escape the building without incident. It is a cold, snowy morning. Fall or winter. Miranda died in October. They called it Black Wednesday, but the day was bright and clear. There were leaves on the ground the morning she died, a blanket of green and gold that turned wet and red by noon and then grey with ash by night. It was mid-afternoon before the National Guardsmen had secured the apartment building. It was two weeks until the barricades were complete and the city was safe again. Each morning you would awaken to the smell of Miranda on your pillow, and then the other smell, the smell of the corpses burning in the midnight heaps at Union Square.

You slip into a bar near Penn Station. On the large-screen TV is a repeat of the Morning News. The daily CDC press conference is uninformative. As is that from Central Command. Protests continue outside the White House. The bartender rolls his eyes and says, "Fucking hippies." No one trusts a man who will not wear a flag on his lapel or tie a yellow ribbon to the antenna of his car. You nod and drink your beer.

It's late when you leave the bar, your footsteps uncertain, the sidewalk slick with ice. You haven't seen a taxi in months. Ahead is a checkpoint and you brush your pockets, trying to remember if you're holding. You imagine a pat down, the sound of a gloved hand on a plastic case. A copy of Fulci's *Zombie* in your coat could get you six months, maybe a year with the right judge; don't even think about the contents of your apartment. You're next at the gate. The soldier shines a flashlight into your eyes and you say, "Jack Valenti." No smile. "Forty-fifth president of the United States." He doesn't appreciate the joke, just waves you through, and you can't help but feel that you have escaped something.

At your apartment, you discover an envelope with the logo of Jay's former employer, a comic book company, stuck beneath the door. Inside there is a note: SOON.

CANNIBALS, QUESTI, AND GUINEA PIGS

Your interest in film doesn't normally take you beyond the racks marked HORROR and SUSPENSE, but at the moment there seems to be a shortage of inventory in both departments. This morning you are standing on the second floor of RKO Video on Broadway, where a patron is complaining to the cashier about the quality of her copy of *Pretty Woman*. You are looking for something, anything, with the word "dead" in its title. Nothing is to be found. You start looking instead for the word "living."

He walks past you, blood-brown Armani coat flapping like wounded wings. "Mister. . . ."

"Fulci," you say, slipping a copy of *Heaven Can Wait* from the shelf in front of you.

He nods and smiles and follows you back to the checkout counter. The woman there looks like she would rather be at the dentist's. It could be a mistake to rent this tape and leave some sort of record of where you were and when. You excuse your way to the front of the line and announce in a loud but tempered voice that you would like to special order *Faces of Death*, all three installments, and by the time that the kid has hold of you, pulling you back, people are talking and the woman at the counter has a telephone in her hand.

You run for the doorway, and the lights suddenly are bright. A security guard looms in front of you; he doesn't like what he sees. You toss him the video and his hands react. A perfect catch. You feel the kid pushing, and you look back over your shoulder as you reach the exit. You are laughing a little too hard.

Outside you take opposite sides of Broadway, and when you watch the kid wander into an alley off Fifty-seventh, you step in after him and try on a smile.

"Got it, dude." Now he is smiling, too. "All yours. Uncut *Django Kill*. From Argentina. *Se habla? No más, mi muchacho. Ingles*, my man, with subtitles."

"How much?"

"Hundred dollar."

"Get lost."

"Pure stuff. Uncut. Got the scalping scene."

"Right. Twenty-five."

"I ain't giving the stuff away."

"I can't do more than fifty."

"It's a steal. Fifty. You're robbing me."

You can't believe you're doing this. Finally you follow the kid farther down the alley. "I want a look."

"Shit," he says. "Who do you think you are, Siskel and Ebert? This is a steal, man. I'm telling you it's good."

You give him the fifty and then there is nothing to do but hustle it back to your apartment and give it a try. The tape is unmarked but for a torn handwritten label that reads GIULIO QUESTI. You want to believe that this means something. Images of dust and blood and molten gold are burning in your mind. You watch a few seconds of noise, and then a faded color spectrum appears. Finally you see a picture, so grainy that you need to squint. It's not *Django Kill*, oh no, not at all. You think you can see something happening, something with a Japanese girl tied to a dingy bed, and there is man in a samurai helmet standing over her, the lights turned blue and a long-handled knife that dips down into her torso and comes up wet. He cuts away her right hand, throws blood onto the walls. You seem to think that this video is called *Guinea Pig*. There is no story to it, just the girl kidnapped, bound, and slowly cut into pieces. Finally the psycho eats her eyeballs. You want to feel something, do something, say something, but it's only 11:30 in the morning, and everyone else in the world is dead or has a job.

NO CULTURE

Over coffee and toast, you read the *Daily News*. Miami is gone, carpet-bombed back into swampland. The president is regretful but unshaken in his resolve. Food riots in Boston and Providence. A news team in Palm Springs got footage of what looks like a zombied Tom Cruise, his buttocks chewed away but otherwise intact. And there is another entry in the Still Dead. This makes five of them. Five who have died only once. Five who have not returned. They wait in that white room at the CDC, and the whole world waits for them.

At dawn you woke like a man accustomed to the hour, your vision clear and in focus. You are committed to the task that awaits you. You wanted to call Jay again, maybe tell him you see the storyboards, you see frame by frame, you see and see and see.

It is Saturday, and your apartment is a dungeon from which you must escape. You decide to go to the movies. The only remaining theaters are in Times Square, but the Times Square you remember is gone. A Holiday

Inn has supplanted the Pussycat Empire on Broadway. What was the Peppermint Lounge is now Tower 45. You pass the Marriott Marquis and walk onto Forty-second Street. The Urban Development Corporation has done its work so very well. Ghosts of grindhouses past fade in and out like distant television signals. The Adonis, the XXXtasy Video Center, Peepland: all gone. Even the Funny Store has vanished beneath the weight of another office tower. Progress is our most important product, and progress has taken them, one by one.

The new theaters on Forty-second Street are sedate and shadowless waiting rooms, places of pleasant dreams, not nightmares. The first is showing Disney cartoons, the next *Jesus of Nazareth*. You wonder what they will do about Lazarus. There is no choice but the third one, which does not admit children. You are hopeful, but there is no doubting the fear.

With two cans of beer hidden in your coat, you move away from the ticket booth and find a seat in the middle of the theater. The lights dim. An animated usherette tells you not to smoke and to use the trash receptacles as you exit. The following preview has been approved for all audiences by the Motion Picture Association of America. *The Absent-Minded Professor.* Your knees are shaky. You sip at the first beer. You stand and walk back up the aisle. This will not work.

Finally the previews are at an end. You sneak another drink of beer and take a seat on the aisle, just in case. The following motion picture has been rated PG-13 by the Motion Picture Association of America. This is a London Film Production. There is a clock tower, Big Ben; the time is 11. The music is so very strange, plucking strings, a zither. The film is called *The Third Man*. Written by Graham Greene. Directed by Carol Reed. It is set in Vienna, after the Second World War. Some man named Holly Martins, a writer, comes to visit his friend Harry Lime, but Harry Lime is dead. There is no color. The faces look out at you in black-and-white. Nothing is happening. The actors are just talking and talking, walking and walking.

You clutch at the armrests and wait for the next surge to hit you. It comes just as you begin to understand. Harry Lime is back from the dead. He was never dead, not really. It was a joke of some kind. "We should have dug deeper than a grave." As the audience murmurs, you stand up, knowing that Harry Lime is alive, yes alive, even to the very end, when the bullets find him. You think about the squibs that could explode from beneath his clothing, sending clots of blood across the grey walls of the sewers, and you hear yourself groan with the knowledge of what is missing, what is gone, what was never there.

People are turning in their seats to look at you. They are saying *Sit down!* and *What does he want?* An usher in a suit is hurrying down the aisle. At least he is in color. Another usher is coming from the other side. You move along the row of seats, bumping knees and outstretched hands. The beer falls onto the carpet, another unseen stain. You do not resist as one of the ushers takes your arm.

In the lobby you see nothing but the poster for the film, and then the night waiting outside. There, in black-and-white, is the knowledge of the way that we have chosen to be entertained, like a book read once too often, leaving a trail of images and emotions so familiar that there is nothing left to see or feel. You know the future, and it is now; it always will be now.

BLOOD AND SYMPATHY

Later you return to the scene of your crimes. You wonder at the silence, whether it is absolute or only the hour. There are no signs that the magazine has been closed down. Still you feel strange stepping out of the elevator and into an unlit corridor. That the hour is past midnight doesn't help.

Tony's door is closed and dark. There's a light on in the Department of Victual Falsification. Elaine is at her desk. She looks up when you come in, but she does not seem surprised. You tell her that you've come to get your things. "Don't bother," she tells you. Then: "I've been waiting here all day for you." Waiting for what? "You could have called." That is when you notice that your desk is clear. The photo on the wall looks down on nothing. You don't need to look to know that the drawers are empty.

"We had more trouble here this morning," Elaine says. "A search warrant." Now you realize that she is holding a pistol in her left hand. "Tony says it's over. Done. Finished." The pistol looks like it might be loaded.

"What do you think?"

You want to tell her the truth. Instead you say: "I think it's only just begun."

She's smiling. The pistol is back in her purse. "I thought you might want these." Four plastic cases. "My secret stash."

You hold up the first of the videos, factory fresh and labeled: *Revenge of the Dead*. It is Pupi Avati's *Zeder*. You deep-breathe and feel your nostrils go like ice.

"Elaine." She raises her eyebrows. Now you are committed. In the elevator, you ask her where she wants to go.

"How about your place?"

You walk and walk and at Fifth Avenue, just past the Flatiron Building, Elaine takes your hand and leads you into a Chinese carryout, where she orders dim sum for you both. From the restaurant you walk toward Union Square. Each step takes you closer to your apartment, to the place where Miranda lived. Where Miranda died. This was your neighborhood. That boarded-up storefront was your grocer, the next your video store. Now the vista has gone upside down, and nothing will ever be the same.

"Best bonfire in the city," Elaine says, pointing to Union Square. A trio of National Guardsmen in urban camouflage huddle with their cigarettes. They watch over a graveyard of concrete and ash, circled with rolls of barbed wire. The fragrance reminds you of the mornings after Black Wednesday, when you woke to the smell of the corpses burning, the perfumed ghost of Miranda sleeping beside you. It seems a lifetime ago, but still you can see her sleeping, the flicker of flames across the face that wasn't there.

Soon Elaine is lying next to you in that same room, her dark hair a shadow on the pillow. The only light is from the small bedside television. After *Zeder* you watch the uncut *Apocalypse Domani*, and after that she opens your shirt, her hand against your chest. You watch the TV screen go black, then grey, and in the moments before you try, but fail, to make love, she says: "When there are no more films, we'll have to make our own."

SOMETIMES
A VOGUE
NATION

You wake up with a severed head on your chest. Its lips are moving, but you can't hear the words. After a few seconds you realize that the head isn't talking—it is chewing. A hand rises into view, clutching a fistful of entrails. The clock on the VCR blinks a continuous 12:00. That would be noon, judging by the sunlight that zigzags through the blinds. The last thing you remember was that Elaine was sleeping while you watched the final moments of Deodato's *L'ultima cannibali*. The tribesmen had split Mei Mei Lay open from groin to breastbone, dug out her organs, and sewn her back up for cooking. You have the feeling that you may have missed something good.

You remove the little television from your chest just as Doctor Butcher begins to rev up his band saw. The shot is static, almost matter-of-fact. The stage blood, when it comes, is orange-ish, surreal. You would have given the scene depth, momentum—not simply shock, but true anguish. There is a note on the nightstand, a few lines in black ink; you read it and smile a thank you to Elaine. You are on your second cup of coffee and the final moments of *Doctor Butcher, M.D.* when the telephone rings. It's Joe D'Amato. He wants to take you sightseeing, probably tonight or tomorrow, sometime after 10. He'll call again. You tell him you'll be waiting.

Then you hit the streets, in search of a sandwich and today's *Daily News*. You wonder what Jay will do for lighting and whether you will need your tripod. At your favorite Greek diner, you order chicken salad and more coffee. When you spread the newspaper across the counter, you learn that the first of the Still Dead, a thirty-three-year-old black male from suburban Chicago, otherwise unidentified, came back last night and was trepanned with a surgical power saw. Life is still imitating art. Doctor Butcher would have been proud.

Across a few more streets and down an alley is the backdoor to Forbidden Planet. You keep your head down, feel like you look guilty, and shove your hands deep into your pockets. Money talks and bullshit walks.

You need an extra battery for your camera, and maybe somebody at the Planet will be selling.

"Got what you want," someone says, though it's hard to hear over the noise of a boom box, an incessant orgy of doom thrash metal. The kids lean into the walls and don't look at you. They wear their biker jackets, black t-shirts, and jeans like uniforms.

"Say man." A skin-headed nymphet in torn fishnets twists down the volume, raises her paste-white face to you. "You know where we could get some stuff?"

"Stuff?" You want to keep walking, get this over with as quickly as you can. Who knows who might be watching.

"You know." Her eyes, black circles scored at their far corners with silver, dart around, mock fugitive. She sucks at her cigarette, blows back smoke and the word of the hour. "Some good G O R E?"

"No can do." Your hands seem caught in your pockets. These are your readers. Your public. They sent you letters, sometimes. But you never thought of them when you wrote, not really. You thought about something else, something. . . .

"Like *New York Ripper*?"

"No." But you can't walk away. You are. . . .

"*Eaten Alive*, maybe? *Man from Deep River*? Some cannibal. . . ."

"Listen, I. . . ."

"I do," she says, and for the first time she is alive, truly alive. She bites at her purple lips, finally works up a smile. "Like, we know where we can score something, but we don't got the dollars. You wanna go in with us, maybe?"

You look at them, and they look back at you, expectant—a line of lost moviegoers, waiting for what you can show them. You tell yourself that you are not this desperate. You are looking for a battery. That's all. At last you shrug and start to walk away. She turns the music back up, and now that rotten Johnny Lydon is ranting away:

This is what you want
This is what you get
This is what you want
This is what you get. . . .

You feel them pulling at you, pulling you back. But it's not them, not really. You want so desperately to see. You came here in search of something, something you thought you wanted, but now you aren't sure. You wonder if you ever were sure. You want to give in to it, let it take you away again to that place where you never need to be sure.

Whether you want to or not, you think about Miranda. You try to remember the way she was before Black Wednesday, before the night she died, before the dead came back and the apartment walls went red with blood. And before everything was whitewashed back into this thing they call reality.

THE NIGHT
SHIFTS

You are hungry and you are thirsty; you need to see something, but you're not sure what. Nothing hidden on your bookshelf is enough anymore.

You walk down into SoHo, past all the empty restaurants and art galleries, a showplace of spray paint and shattered glass. When you cross Prince Street, a walkie-talkie crackles at you from the darkness. A cough and clipped voices. Soldiers are on the street corners. All of the city seems armed and ready. Like the morning after Black Wednesday.

At first you could not believe that Miranda was dead. Now you find it hard to believe that she was ever really alive. That you were married. Shared wine and loud music and laughter. That there ever was anything but this.

You decided long ago not to think about that day. It was months after the first reports came in from the Pennsylvania countryside. About the dead that came back to life. The dead that walked. The dead that ate the living. You had your doubts about the stories, even when it was Dan Rather who told them. After all, this was the stuff of horror movies.

Before it happened, you had never thought about Miranda's death. You were too young, too happy, to think about it. You spent no time in anticipation of it, because death was something that would not happen, could not happen, at least until you yourself were old and tired and ready.

Helicopters flutter overhead. Their searchlights bite holes in the darkness. At Houston you find a market that is still open, buy a carton of beer, and head back to the apartment.

"Do you love her?" your mother had asked that first, and last, time the two of you visited. You didn't know what to say. Of course you loved her. You had married her, hadn't you?

You thought you would faint when you came home that night, in those long lost moments of shadow and flame. Miranda had been beautiful. That was the way you wanted to remember her. Like in the photographs her parents had sent, now on the mantle of the apartment, taken when she was younger than you had ever known her.

You could have given her life eternal through the lens of your camera. Video. Film. Pictures. You could have loved her forever. How could you explain the feeling of being misplaced, of always standing to one side of the world, of watching the world as if it existed only when recorded and replayed on tape, and wondering if this was how everyone felt. You always believed that other people could see more directly, could actually see and understand the world through their own eyes, and didn't worry quite so much about why. You could see it only through a lens, through what you could record and edit and assemble into a tangible, meaningful whole, locked safely and securely within the four walls of a picture. Then, and only then, could you see and understand . . . and yes, love.

You drink more than one beer on your trek back to the apartment, and once there you drink more than one more. You slip another video into the deck. Deodato again. *Camping del terrore*, although for once you prefer the English title: *Body Count*. More beer and another video, and then another and another, and after a time the images blur and bleed into a single color.

Sooner or later the telephone rings. It is time.

GONE

The barricades are back up at the major intersections, and the city has become very small. Your head is hollow, cracked and scooped out like an oyster on the half shell. You followed the flicker of red video across the television screen in pursuit of some kind of answer. Then the tapes ran out; as you watched the last line of credits, superimposed on a staggering horde of zombies as they crossed the Brooklyn Bridge, you suddenly saw yourself in hideous close-up, gape-mouthed in worship before a forty-inch altar of flickering light.

You caught the telephone on the second ring. Through the noise and a distant sound that sooner or later you realized was gunfire, you heard that it was Jay, that he wanted you to meet him at Patchin Place. This is not a test. Your presence, and your video camera, are required. You told him you'd be there in minutes, and now you're there, camera in hand, and you can feel it about to happen.

The alleyway is awash in the yellow spray of flares and flashlights. Elaine stands in the shadows, her pistol pointed into the night sky; at her side is some black guy with a shotgun. Jay is watchful, waiting, waiting. Finally he looks at you.

"Do it," he says and then gestures grandly to the others. "Lights." Shadows twist over a gas generator; a ratcheting, a cough, and a spray of white cuts the alley into an urban dreamscape, the stuff of Lang and Reed.

"Something's happening, uptown and down. . . ." He wears a joker's grin, a shotgun in his black-gloved hand. "Could be Black Wednesday all over again." You hear a shout, footsteps racing on wet concrete. He shrugs and nods into the darkness. "Someone has to shoot the picture." His hand busses your shoulder. "So do it," he says again. "Sound," he announces; and, as he walks away, "Speed." Then you're alone, with your finger on the trigger.

Through the viewfinder, you see the world, your world, the world made flesh on the grey-silver screen. Mad shadows chase one of Jay's nerdy protégés into view, and he dances before you, arms in flight, and mugs breathlessly for the camera. Finally he leans in at you and cries: "They're heeeeer!"

Then he is gone, and your world is the world of the dead. The first one is an old-timer, work shirt and spotted trousers, shuffling around the corner in vague pursuit. The left side of his face is gone, eaten. You can see the teeth marks as you smash zoom in on him. From somewhere to your left comes the bullroar of the black guy's shotgun. The top of the old-timer's head lifts away. You watch him fall and see your take replayed endlessly on the monitors of an editing bay. Perfect. Picture perfect. He collapses to the sidewalk in an unceremonious and uncinematic heap.

You slide the camera over the corpse and up the wall, where the shadow of the next one spiderwebs nicely into POV. "Got him," you hear Elaine call. This one is a kid, your random Puerto Rican street punk, and he looks fairly fresh. You hit him with a medium close-up just in time to catch the jagged line of bullet holes that Elaine punches into his chest. Craters erupt—grey skin, blood, and squirming maggots—and you zoom into one then out just in time to catch the headshot as the black guy steps in stage right, swings his shotgun up, and lets both barrels go. The body cartwheels back, out of the light, and you've lost it to the black beyond.

"Take . . . it . . . easy." Jay sounds anxious and upset. "Not . . . so . . . fast." But there are sirens in the distance and the sound, you think, of radios and marching feet. White noise and distant voices. Order is about to be restored. You don't have much time.

You peek over the viewfinder, and there is another shadow climbing the wall. Elaine is twisting a speedloader from her belt. Shell casings ping-pong down the alley. You look in again and see shadow turn to skin. It's a woman. Tall. Long blonde hair. Pale skin. As you squint and let the focus go, ready for a soft fade-in, you hear her footsteps stumble forward. Your finger finds the autofocus as you let the lens sweep the pavement slowly to her feet. Black Keds. Then up. Bleached jeans. Slowly. White blouse, half-unbuttoned, a tiny pearl necklace at her throat, and pale, pale skin. Slowly up to her face. Her beautiful face. A small clicking sound is coming from your throat. The picture shivers once, twice, then dims. Finally you hear your voice: "Mir-an-da!"

You pull the shot away from her and left. Elaine kneels, stiff-arms the handgun. You hear sounds like belches and swing your eyes, the camera, back. Miranda's left forearm angles impossibly, then breaks, strands of flesh stretching, then snapping, hand clutching at empty air as it spins and floats away. You see the shot in slow motion, a mad Peckinpah pirouette, suddenly shattered in mid-turn as the force of a shotgun blast kicks out her legs. You fall to your knees with her, losing your balance, nearly dropping the camera; still you hold onto the shot. You have her now. She can't escape you. You feel the urge for a close-up, but you cannot risk moving from the medium shot as Miranda rears back into frame. Another roar, and the top of her right shoulder explodes. A great brown geyser of blood erupts. Grey flesh and bone graffiti the alley wall.

Somehow she stands, keeps walking. Her head jerks to the right as the black guy chunks in another round; the shotgun kicks again, a miss that showers a sudden snow of brick and dust. You swing the camera down then up from her bullet-blown knees in time to catch Elaine's next volley, three shots that spit through Miranda's chest and neck and crease her cheek. Her mouth opens wide in response. You don't know if it is a laugh or a scream.

Still she is coming, past the black guy, past Elaine, who looks at you with angry fear. They can't fire now, not back at you and Jay and the rest of the crew. Your shot is steady, sure, a reverse zoom that frames her just so, the alley seeming to widen behind her as she approaches. Now your back is against the wall and the lens is open wide; she walks on and gives you your close-up. She is yours, all yours.

A flash of movement cuts the picture; the camera is nearly lost from your arms as she skitters backward. Then you see the muzzle and hard-wood butt of the shotgun, and Jay's gloved right hand as he hits her again, and you hold the shot as she falls and you're down on the ground with her, the camera looking up across her body into a night sky punctured by distant stars. You can see her tongue through the open left side of her face. One of her eyes is blinking, out of control; the other one is gone. You know she has never been more beautiful than now. She is yours, and will be yours forever.

You watch as Jay joins you at her side. He lowers the shotgun; the barrel slides along her stomach, her chest, her neck, to the tip of her chin. Finally its hot and smoking mouth kisses hers. And as you hold her in lingering close-up, he shoves the barrel down. You hear the crack of teeth and bone and then the shotgun kicks and there is a shriek and you are caught in a warm wet rain that washes over the lens until you can see nothing, nothing, nothing at all but red.

You hear laughter, and you know that it is your own. You can no longer see, but you can run, and you drop the camera, hear the shatter of glass and plastic, the whir of the eject as you grab at the tape and you run, you run and run into the darkness, into the night until at last you can see a distant light, and you run in its direction. You hold on to your tape and run.

Finally you see the sanitation trucks lined before you on this side of Union Square. You watch as body bags are carried out by men in gas masks and white camouflaged parkas and dumped onto the fire, sending smoke, and the smell, over you. No matter how far you run, the smell will follow you. It recalls you to another morning. You arrived home from the magazine after drinking most of the night; Miranda had called just before midnight, wondering where you were. When you arrived, the apartment was steeped in this same aroma. The soldiers stood warming themselves around the flames. Miranda was gone. You could count the bullet holes across the lobby, the stairway, and the walls of the apartment itself; you could count the bodies sprawled in the streets, fuel for the flames. You had seen it all before; you had seen it all, but you had never believed in it. It wasn't real; it could never be real. But it was. The films, the videos, were just the coming attractions, a sneak preview of the epic now playing around the clock in the world outside.

You approach the last of the trucks. A sanitation worker hefts another body bag from its wide belly, drops the heavy plastic cocoon unceremoniously to the pavement.

"Dead." This is what you say to him, although you meant to say something more.

"What was your first clue?" He turns and walks toward the Square. The fire rages high, a false dawn. The workers, and the soldiers who guard them, look at the flames, and not at you.

You get down on your knees and tear open the body bag. The smell of the corpse envelops you. When you touch it, your hands find something soft and wet. The first bite sticks in your throat and when you try to swallow, you almost gag.

You will have to go very slowly.

You will have to forget most everything you have ever learned.

for Stephen R. Bissette

SHE DRIVES THE MEN TO CRIMES OF PASSION!
Genevieve Valentine

The scene was this: Cocoanut Grove, Saturday night, packed so tight you had to hold your drink practically in your armpit, and the band loud enough that you gave up on conversation and nodded whenever you heard a voice just in case someone was talking to you.

You never went to the Grove on the weekends if you had any kind of self-respect at all—by 1934 all the stars had turned their backs on the Grove and fled to the Sidewalk Café, where they could drink themselves onto the floor without any prying eyes. The reporters had given up trying, and now they came to the Grove to dig up dirt on the third-rate bit players.

It was fine for the bit players, but I had some prospects.

Well, one picture. It hadn't done well. I knew they were talking about putting me on pity duty with the melodramas that shot in four days on the same set. No extras, no stars; nothing to do but come to the Cocoanut Grove and look around at the bit players you were going to be stuck with for the rest of your life.

"You need a friend in the studio, fast," said Lewis. "Come down to the Grove with me. There's bound to be someone."

I nursed my Scotch and grimaced at the crowd for an hour, looking for a studio man I could talk to.

None. Damn Sidewalk Café.

I was on my way across the floor to leave when the music ended, and the dance floor opened, and I saw Eva.

She'd been dancing—strands of her dark hair stuck to her shining brown skin, a spiderweb across her forehead. If she'd been wearing lipstick it was gone, but her lids were still dusted with sparkly shadow in bright green and white that shone in the dark like a second pair of eyes.

I saw her coming and held my breath. I could already see her at the end of the lens—turning to look over her shoulder at the hero, giving him a smile, tempting him to do terrible things.

"You should be in pictures," I said, and it sounded like a totally different line when you meant it.

Her audition alone got me into Capital Films for a feature with her. I knew it would.

There was no point in making her into an ingénue (exotic and ingénue did not mix), so we went right to the vamp. I made her a fortune-teller in *On the Wild Heath*. She captivated the lord of the manor, put a curse on him when he scorned her, and got shot just before she could lay hands on the lady of the house.

The Hollywood Reporter called her "Exotic Eva" in the blurb—couldn't have planned it better—and went on for a paragraph about the passion in her Spanish eyes. They wrapped with, "We suspect we haven't seen the last of this sultry siren."

Capital signed me for another flick, and started making us reservations at the Sidewalk Café.

Eva wore green satin that matched her eyes, and as we danced under the dim lights there were shimmers of color across her skin.

"I think I love you," I said.

She said, "You would."

It sounded ungrateful, but I let it go. There was time for all that; right now, our stars were rising.

Capital didn't want her being a heroine yet. ("Keep her mysterious," they said. "The fan magazines can't even tell if she's really Mexican or if it's just makeup. It's perfect.")

I made her a flamenco dancer next, in *Stage Loves*.

The lead, Jack Stone, was nothing much—I was doing the studio a favor just having him—but at least he looked properly stunned whenever she was in the frame.

Originally Stone's theatre patron was going to seduce her and leave the virginal heiress for a life with the variety show, but word came down that Capital was going to start getting strict about the Production Code, so the hero sinning was right out.

So instead Eva seduced the patron, and got strangled by the jealous stage manager in the last reel.

(The poster featured her bottom left, with a banner: "Eva Loba is Elisa the Spanish Temptress—She drives the men to crimes of passion!")

The new script must have worked just as well; the studio asked for two more movies as soon as the film was in.

After the Sidewalk Café one Sunday I drove her home, to some bank of stucco apartments in a no-man's-land north of the city.

"We have to get you a better place if you're going to be worth photographing," I said. "I'll talk to the studio."

"You shouldn't," she said. "I like it here."

"But the cameras don't," I said, and cut the engine.

I helped her out of the car. Her skin was shining in the light, and her sharp green eyes were captivating, and I felt like some poor sucker lord of the manor for letting her get to me like this. I should know better. My head was swimming; I wanted her, I needed her.

Before she was steady on her feet, I pulled her roughly against me.

She took a breath. Then for an instant she was in two dimensions, flat enough for the streetlight to bleed through her like a stained glass window, and before I could even really understand what I was seeing the world had snapped back into place, and there was a flurry of jewel-colored bodies and sharp green wings.

They scattered, and I was left with a satin dress in my hands, blinking at the startling-white impressions of two hundred vanished birds.

My first thought was, *Something terrifying has just happened.*

My second was, *The girl knows how to make an exit.*

Eva was set to play Ruby, the sultry Latin dancer in the musical of the month (*Down Mexico Way*, maybe, or *You're Lovely Tonight*, musicals all look the same to me). I wasn't directing, but it was common knowledge that I was bringing her up the ranks, and if she didn't show, it wouldn't look good for me.

But when I got to the set the next morning she was already there and in costume, practicing the steps on the nightclub set with her partner.

I didn't dare push it with him right there, so I watched quietly from behind the camera all morning, until the director called lunch and the crew scattered.

She stayed where she was, and for a moment I thought about how to keep the cameras rolling in case she did it again. (I couldn't help it; a director's always looking for the shot no one can top.)

"You look like you have something to say," she said, folded her arms.

I kept my distance. If it wasn't on film, there was no point in provoking her.

"Where did you learn to do that?"

She smiled thinly. "It can't be taught. It's just something you are."

"No, I didn't mean—where did you *come* from?"

"Nogales."

That wasn't what I meant, either. "But there had to be some reason you showed me and not anyone else," I went on.

She looked at me, frowning, like I was some kind of idiot instead of the guy who had built her career from the ground up.

"I'm here to be an actress," she said. "I'm not doing any of this for you."

I let it go. It wasn't the time to argue facts.

I said, "We could make a movie about it. I could build the whole plot around you, a leading part. Something from the Arabian Nights!" I paused, overcome with the image of a pasha's throne room and a storyteller who has a trick up her sleeve.

"Just think," I said, "we could show everyone what kind of star you can be."

"No."

That stung. You'd think she'd have taken a starring role from the guy who knew how to direct her. "But imagine it," I pleaded. "Forget the *Reporter*—this would be history! This town would never top it. We'd go down in the record books with the shot no one could ever figure out."

She narrowed her eyes. "No one would believe it."

Who cared what anyone believed so long as they paid to see it, I thought.

I said, "I can make people believe anything."

Then the crew was filing back in, and the director wanted to see her, so I let her go.

I stayed all afternoon to watch her backstage-at-the-contest scene (I was a better director than the music man), and to think how best to go about getting hold of that moment again.

She was too caught up in the thrill of it to remember who had given her the first shot; she didn't understand how I had built up her audience, that was all.

At least she didn't have much of a part in the musical. When she came back to me for her next contract, I thought, we'd have another talk about who makes a star.

The weekend the musical opened, the *Reporter* wrote her up as "Eva with the Ruby Throat" (I laughed—what were the odds?), and the studio sent her to the Trocadero alone, without telling me.

Turns out they had engineered a romance for Eva with Paul Maitland over at Atlas Pictures. He was marquee material—his last gig had been *Ivanhoe*, and they were talking about him for *Robin Hood* next. He was light in his loafers, though, so someone at Atlas had struck a deal with Capital to get curvy little Eva on his arm but quick.

They had arranged for Maitland to be waiting just under the canopy, so that when Eva slid her arm into his, an enterprising photographer could get a decent shot before they ducked inside.

And plenty did.

The *Reporter* ran two pictures of them on the front page: one of them arm in arm, and one of him kissing her goodnight at the curb, his arms around her. The gossip column squealed—"Sultry Spanish Siren Seduces Arch Aristocrat!"—and wondered when they'd have the pleasure of seeing them together on the screen.

She really was good at what she did. The way she looked at him in those pictures—if you didn't know, you'd think she'd loved Paul for years.

But now I knew better, and all I could do when I got the paper was stare at Maitland's arms around her waist and wonder what he was going to do when she turned into a flock of birds and vanished.

She didn't vanish.

The contract she signed for the Maitland affair must have been stellar, because her next two pictures went to other directors, and every time I picked up the *Reporter* there was a picture of her, her jewelry shimmering in the flashbulbs.

At first it was always with Maitland, and I didn't like it, but I could understand. There were terms in her contract she had to fulfill.

But sometimes she was alone. Those I hated, those snaps of her standing in the doorway of the Brown Derby or the Trocadero like she had sprung up there all by herself, like she knew something the world didn't know, like she had made this happen all on her own.

I knocked out two movies that year: a detective picture and a turn-of-the-century romance. The romance took off ("Starmaker Strikes Again!"), and soon I could get into the Trocadero no matter who I had on my arm.

I never went alone; when you had as many movies under your belt as I did, it wasn't hard to find a woman who would appreciate it.

(Eva rarely appeared where I was going. I suspected the studio had arranged things that way.)

I read up on the ruby-throated hummingbird, just on a whim. Turned out she wasn't lying; the Aztecs had used them as talismans because of their power. Maybe that really was just something you were.

I saw the scene unfold in front of me: an ancient stone temple, a hundred wailing warriors, a human sacrifice loved by the gods who exploded into glittering birds. I'd have to put in some explorers (for moral perspective, the Code was pretty clear on that), but it could be a spectacular movie if only she'd agree.

Capital called me in. They wanted a historical epic, and they wanted me.

Right there in the office, I pitched them *Lord of the Birds*. Exotic siren, cast of thousands, dancing girls and bloody battles and history coming to life.

"I have an effect no one's ever dreamed of," I said. "People will wonder about it for a hundred years."

They upped my budget on the spot, asked me who I wanted most.

"Eva," I said.

The office men loved it, of course. They knew who made a star.

Lewis called from Legal. He told me Eva had a competing contract offer from Atlas Films that she was willing to take rather than be in a movie of mine.

"We don't want to make waves," said Lewis. "You can find another leading lady—they're a dime a dozen, you know that."

Eva wasn't some leading lady, she was a star, but I didn't have to tell Lewis. They knew it. That's why they were cutting me to keep her.

I didn't tell him that she was the key to the whole movie. Best case: he'd think I was out of my mind. Worst case: he'd believe me, and pull my funding.

"I'll look around," I said. "Where should I go?"

I ended up at the Sidewalk Café, watching Eva dancing with a string of men, and hating her.

When she saw me she looked a little upset (I wasn't proud of how happy it made me, but I'd take anything I could get). She sat for three songs, and then she got a light from Maitland and vanished through the crowd.

I went outside after her.

When she saw me she shook her head, ground out her cigarette underfoot, and turned to leave.

"Just hear me out," I said. I hated her for making me beg. I was above begging.

"When I move to Atlas," she said, "you can tell your friends at Capital why."

"You have to understand," I told her. "I promised the studio a special effect like they've never seen. Without your hummingbird trick, the whole movie's a bust."

She raised her eyebrows nearly to her hairline. "My trick?"

"If you don't do it, the studio will make me a laughingstock!" I saw her face and added, "And you! If this doesn't happen, it's going to come back to you, you wait and see."

"I'll live," she said.

And then (just to spite me, I know it) she broke apart, flashes of green and red and the whir of birds disappearing into the dark, and nothing left of her but glimpses of white at the edges of my vision like a scattering of teeth.

A good director films a story that's set in front of him.

A great director can make a story out of nothing.

I stood in the dark outside the club, watching as a straggler fluttered up into the dark, and the rest of her story came to life in front of me.

The next morning I called Lewis and told him that I would find another leading lady.

"I saw Eva last night," I said. "She's not doing very well for herself, it looks like. Looking old. I was thinking we'd do Marie Antoinette instead of that Aztec crap. Everyone loves the French costumes, and then we don't have to worry about making the Code happy."

I was scrabbling, and I knew it, but the only way to get ahead in this town is to lie like you mean it, so I went on, "We can use that blonde instead—you know, the one who can sing?"

(Turned out there were several; that phone call took a while.)

Then I called the publicity office and told them I wanted to offer Eva a part in my new movie; did they know if she was meeting Maitland tonight?

When she left her house that night I was waiting for her, leaning against my car.

Eva was in white silk that looked nearly green in the moonlight, and now I couldn't look at her without looking for a flash of red near her throat.

I knew her so well; it stung that she wouldn't give me credit for it.

"You ruined my movie," I said, casually. "Without you I had to change the whole thing. If that doesn't work, Capital is out a lot of money, and I'm sunk."

"That's because you promised something that wasn't yours to give," she said.

"How do you think movies get made, Eva?"

Now she looked wary. God, her face was exquisite. I realized, too late, I should have brought a camera.

"Do you think this is still just for the movie?" she asked.

She was looking right at me, and I felt guiltier than I had in a long time.

"Someday you'll understand," I said.

Then I yanked the gun out of my jacket and pulled the trigger.

As a director, there were two problems with what happened next.

1) I was a pretty cheap shot—I'd just bought the gun, it's not as if I had practiced—so the recoil surprised me and the bullet went wild, which takes away the power of the moment.

2) When you tell someone "Someday you'll understand" right before you shoot, you're not absolving yourself so much as you are giving them a moment to prepare, and then what happens is that by the time your shot

285

goes wide you're already staring at the last of the hummingbirds disappearing into the trees.

Still, when I stopped worrying if I'd broken my thumb, I saw that there was a hummingbird hopping around on the dirt in front of me in a panic, one of its outstretched wings suddenly much shorter than the other.

The singed edges were still warm to the touch where the bullet had struck, I noticed, after I scooped it up and kissed it.

The birdcage is an antique, a gift from the studio. It's big enough that the hummingbird could fly around pretty comfortably, if it could still fly.

(I named it Polly for the present, because that was just the best name for a bird. Whenever people come over, they laugh themselves sick when I tell them, and then they try to call her over like it's actually a parrot and can answer to the name. I'm working on getting some more sophisticated people.)

I keep the cage just near enough to the window that when the others come looking they'll see Polly sitting there, and just far enough in that there's no stealing her out without coming all the way inside.

And they will come back; Eva can't become human without all of them, and there are only so many places you can hide two hundred hummingbirds.

("Rising Star Falls," cried the *Reporter*. "Exotic Eva Disappears—Have We Seen Her Last Film?")

I hope that's not the case. I'm not out to harm anyone. When she comes back to bargain, I'll be happy to bargain.

She knows who makes a star.

EVEN THE PAWN
Joel Lane

Early on a February morning in the city centre, two refuse collectors found a human body wrapped in double-strength bin liners. It had been dumped in one of the tall bins at the back of a Chinese restaurant, with no serious attempt at concealment. As if whoever put it there had wanted it to be found. The refuse collectors had chased a few crows away from the bin, and immediately seen what they had attacked. Before the rush hour, the body was in the city morgue next to the law courts.

Fortunately, the crows hadn't reached her face. Though what identification we managed was of limited value. She was aged eighteen or so, white, possibly Slavic. Her hair was cut short, spiked and bleached. She had complex injuries, external and internal, that pointed to sustained beating and sexual abuse. What made headlines was that she'd died after being left in the bin, though probably without regaining consciousness.

The photo that appeared in the papers showed her face after the mortician had toned down the bruising. It was a strong face with dark-blue eyes and good teeth, a few loose. She was somewhat overweight. When dumped, the body had been wearing a T-shirt and shorts that were too small for her, probably not hers. We failed to match her face, teeth, and DNA with anyone on record.

In the week following local press coverage of the death, we received three anonymous phone calls from men who claimed to know the dead girl. All of them said her name was Tania, and she'd worked in a massage parlour in the city. Two of them named a place in Small Heath, one a place in Yardley. Both parlours were owned by the Forrester brothers, two local businessmen whose affairs we weren't likely to be investigating soon. They had important friends in the force and the local council—by "friends" I mean people they owned. There are other kinds of friends, though it seemed that Tania hadn't had any kind.

The hostesses at both parlours told us the same thing: Tania had been sacked because she was unreliable. A colleague some distance up the food chain from myself had a word with the Forrester brothers, who claimed no knowledge of what had happened to her. We'd already established by default that Tania—which almost certainly was not her real name—had been trafficked from Eastern Europe, but since the Forresters were above reproach we had little to go on.

My involvement in the case started with something the hostess at the Kittens parlour in Yardley had said. There was a "regular" at Kittens who always phoned to ask if Tania was there. If she was busy when he arrived, he waited for her. Since most of the punters chose other girls, this fanboy had made quite a difference to Tania's confidence. Since her departure— the hostess claimed to be unsure whether the dead girl was really Tania— he hadn't been back.

Yardley being part of my regular patch, I was asked to monitor Kittens and try to track down this possible stalker of the dead girl. It was one of several parlours near the Swan Centre, a convenient stopping-point for sales reps and long-distance drivers. The hostess—"receptionist" was her official job title—was a tired-looking woman in her forties called Martina. She promised to call me on my mobile if Tania's former admirer turned up.

Before I left, Martina showed me the waiting area, where two girls were watching TV and drinking coffee. They were both wearing blue cat masks. I didn't stay, but the image bothered me for days afterwards. At least the sins you commit in your heart don't expose you to blackmail.

The call came a few weeks later, but not from Martina. The man on the phone said he sometimes visited Kittens, and had been friendly with Tania. He hadn't been there in a while. Today, when he'd turned up,

Martina had warned him the police were after him. "I thought I'd better contact you myself."

We interviewed the punter, whose name was Derek, for two three-hour sessions. He was aged nearly forty and lived alone. It soon emerged that he was an alcoholic. The interviews were very dull. He wanted to talk to us about Tania and his distress at her death. But he seemed to know nothing that could help us. The weekend of her death he'd been in Stafford, helping his parents move house. We checked the alibi and it held. He was harmless, ignorant, and about as interesting to listen to as woodlice in the loft.

"We were close," he said more than once. "Tania liked me, I could tell. The way she reacted when I touched her. Sometimes I'd make her cum. Sometimes we'd make love fast, then just sit together and talk until the time ran out. We didn't meet up outside the parlour, but we would have eventually. I could tell she didn't have a lover. Sometimes I know things without being told them."

His sensitivity didn't extend to knowing who had killed her. "I could tell something was wrong, that was all. She was frightened. I think she got sacked, then some pimp made her an offer she couldn't refuse. I wish she'd called me. I gave her my number, you know. Asked her to phone me if she was in trouble. Maybe she didn't get the chance."

The one unexpected thing he told us was near the end of the second session, when we pressed him for any hint she might have dropped regarding who she knew, how she'd got here. "She just wouldn't talk about that," he said. "I saw what happened. In a dream. Kept seeing it. Hearing her scream. The blows. It was driving me insane. All the men were wearing masks." For a moment his face looked much older. "I don't suppose that's evidence."

"Evidence of what?" my colleague Di Hargreave said wearily. She'd had about enough of Derek's inner life.

The last question I asked him was "Why have you started going back to Kittens?"

He looked at me, and there was no hint of self-dramatisation in his face. Only blank despair. "What else have I got?"

The investigation stalled. It was partly the block on anything that might inconvenience the Forresters, and partly our failure to trace anyone connected with the murdered girl. The name "Tania" was a mask. For us, the case was symptomatic of a wider pattern. Birmingham needed something to replace its rapidly collapsing industrial base, and the city's financiers had decided the answer was business conferences. That meant convention centres, mammoth hotels, expensive restaurants, and a blue-chip sex industry. Not girls on the streets, but girls in private clubs and parlours. Even without blackmail, the silence of the Council would have been guaranteed. It was business.

One question we spent some time looking at was why Tania had been dumped in the city centre. It was clearly a message to someone. Most probably to the girls working in the lap-dancing clubs, porn cinemas, and massage parlours scattered between Holloway Head and Snow Hill, the hinterland of Eastern European flesh kept behind closed doors and guarded by discreet pimps on the payroll of local businessmen. A simple message: *Don't get lazy.* The Chinese restaurant was two blocks away from an "executive gentlemen's club" owned by the Forresters. But Tania wouldn't have worked there: she wasn't the right physical type.

Within a year, we were given a solution to the case. But it wasn't one that would cut much ice with the CPS. A local filmmaker called Matt Black, backed by Skin City Productions, had made a film "reconstructing" Tania's life and death. A heavily cut version of *The Last Ride* was screened at the Electric Cinema in Birmingham, and a few other art cinemas across the country. A "director's cut" was sold to adults via the Internet, and screened privately a few times.

The police team investigating the murder, including me, watched the full version on DVD at the Steelhouse Lane station. It showed a girl called Katja working on the streets in Romania, then being trafficked to Birmingham and given a new name. Her pimps were an Arab gang, nothing like the Forresters. Another prostitute told her better money could be earned doing private parties for businessmen. She was given a number, but didn't call it until she lost her job at the parlour. The rest was violence.

It was a sleazy, brutal film. There were images that combined hardcore sex with prosthetic simulations of injury. Matt Black clearly thought himself a talented *auteur* with urban lowlife as his canvas. But the wooden acting and flat dialogue suggested that he saw the character of Tania only as a temporary barrier between the camera and her wounds. *The Last Ride* was as weak on external circumstances as it was strong on forensic detail.

Matt Black was interviewed for an arts review programme that went out on Central TV, late on Friday night. I watched it at home. He was about thirty, with a retro-style tailored suit and a nervous smile. The interviewer asked him what the main purpose of *The Last Ride* was. He said, "To deal with Tania as an icon. A media construct. We don't know who she really was, where she came from. The film explores how her identity was constructed through the same transformations that destroyed her as a person. It's also an examination of the Madonna-whore image in Western culture."

The interviewer nodded in a slightly bemused way, then asked why two versions were being released at the same time. "It's a statement against censorship," Black said at once. "There's a false distinction in our culture between art and pornography. *The Last Ride* deliberately blends the style codes of art cinema and gonzo porn. We're breaking down boundaries."

"That leads to another question people are asking. Why did you use hardcore porn techniques in a film about sexual violence and abuse? You're pushing not only what can be released, but what can legally be filmed at all."

Black smiled. "This film challenges the censors to admit the audience out there are really adults. They're saying you should not be allowed to *see these images*. Skin City is all about breaking boundaries. Including flesh boundaries." His smile momentarily became a grin. "The anal space has traditionally been taboo in all cinema except porn. We're saying, liberate the image. Open all the doors."

"Does the image have a life of its own, apart from the human reality?"

"You're asking the wrong question," Black said. "You should be asking, does the human reality have a life of its own apart from the image?"

The programme cut away from the interview there, just as I saw my hands reach out towards the TV with the intention of strangling it. I switched it off and went upstairs to bed. Elaine was already asleep.

Months went past. Our vague hope that *The Last Ride* might stimulate someone who knew the murdered girl to get in touch came to nothing. Other crimes and more accessible villains took our attention. It was November when I got a call from the Steelhouse Lane station to tell me that Matt Black had disappeared. My immediate reaction was "Have you tried looking up his arse?"

We assumed the filmmaker had gone on an unplanned trip somewhere, for research or recreation. But when Christmas came and went and no one had heard from him, Black was added to the list of missing persons. A film he'd been working on, about the dark side of Internet dating, was shelved indefinitely. His absence provoked a renewal of interest in *The Last Ride*, and there was speculation in the press that he'd been swallowed up by the world his films explored.

In late January, I phoned the Kittens parlour and had a chat with Martina. She'd already been made to realise that cooperating with us was sensible. The Forrester brothers might be safe from police action, but she wasn't. I asked her whether Derek had been in lately. "We saw him just before Christmas," she said. "He comes in every few weeks, sees a different girl every time. But you know what they told me? He won't put his hands on them. And while he does it, he keeps his eyes shut. They call him the sleepwalker."

Several days later, Martina called me in the evening. "He's here," she said. I was off duty, but I apologised to Elaine and left my dinner unfinished. I parked across the Coventry Road from the parlour and watched carefully from my car. When Derek emerged, I crossed over and followed him at a distance. He was walking slowly, his head tilted, as if drunk.

I caught up with him as he was passing the children's playground near the canal walkway. "Hi Derek. How's it going?" He didn't look surprised to see me. "Could we have a chat?" I asked. He nodded.

We crossed the canal bridge into the Ackers, a patch of semi-wasteland used regularly for cruising and shooting up in warmer weather. Just now it was deserted. The damp grass brushed the ankles of my jeans. Derek lit a cigarette, didn't offer me one. It was dark, but the moon was out and the lights of the Coventry Road weren't far away. "Do you get out much?" I asked. "Go to the cinema?"

"I bought it on DVD," he said. "Didn't think much of it. Is that what you wanted to know?" I didn't say anything. "It was empty," he said. "No truth. I don't mean facts. I mean it wasn't *her*. I don't blame the actress. But the bloke who made it. Smart little fucker. Mouthing off on TV like he knew it all. He knew *nothing*. What I could have told him . . ." He stopped and drew hard on his cigarette.

"He didn't know anything about Tania," I said. "Someone had to put him straight. Make him understand."

Derek stared into the murky distance. "You think I killed him, don't you? But I didn't. I don't know where he is now. Neither does he."

There was a long silence. I wasn't armed, and didn't look forward to arresting a desperate man. He turned slowly and looked at me. In the half-light his face was a mask with holes for eyes. "What did you do to him?" I asked.

"This," he said, and touched my face.

The scream that tore her mouth apart. A baby on fire in her womb. Everyone she had ever loved maimed, infected, destroyed. The men who used her four, five, six at once, making new holes when they ran out. The crows that pecked at her hands and feet. The city that broke into fragments, stone rats that scarred every child they could find. The pain that never stopped, spreading through the past and the future, the grey mist, the sea of blood, the cloud of sperm, the bone-faced men, the cries for help, the broken cat mask.

The next few days are a blur. I don't know exactly where I went. The images in my head were the only reality. I spent a night under a railway bridge, another night in a derelict house. I used the cash in my wallet to buy vodka from a few off-licences and heroin from someone I met on the streets. I smoked it under bridges in the dead of night. For a week or more I was trapped in someone else's memories. And the pain of those final hours never left me.

One frozen morning, I followed a misty thread of forgotten life into a police station. While I sat inert on a bench, they checked my wallet and contacted my department. I was diagnosed as having suffered an acute nervous breakdown. They gave me tranquillisers, silenced the terror, wrapped me in chemical bandages. I spent a month in hospital. Elaine visited me, and when I heard her voice a little of myself came back.

I assume Matt Black is still out there somewhere, numbing the pain with alcohol or narcotics, on the run from something he can't leave behind. I don't like to think about it. It took me a long time to recover, and not all of me got through. Years later, there are still words I can't stand to hear. And I don't like to have anything touch my face, not even rain.

TENDERIZER
Stephen Graham Jones

Brutal Is the Night: A Review

Remember *The Blair Witch Project*'s marketing campaign? It was an update of sorts on 1971's *The Last House on the Left*, except where Wes Craven would have us keep reminding ourselves that it's just a movie, it's just a movie, *Blair Witch* kept whispering that this was actual found footage. It's the same dynamic, though; it was tapping the same sensationalistic vein.

Writer/director Sean Mickles (*Abasement, Thirty-Nine*) knows this vein very well. And, for *Tenderizer*, he let it bleed.

As you probably recall, the first trailer was released as a "rough cut," with the media outlets quoting Mickles's grumbled objection that *Tenderizer* wasn't ready, that production difficulties were built into a project like this, weren't they?

Speculation was that he just wasn't ready to let it go, of course.

It wouldn't be the first time.

Whether actually released with his approval or not, that first trailer definitely had nerve. Just the title at lowest possible right in a "rough-cut" font, then ninety seconds of black screen, punctuated by shallow breathing, the kind that makes you hold your eyes a certain way, in sympathetic response. At the end of it there wasn't even any large-sized title branded on or swooping in—there were no closing frames. It was all closing frames. It was as if a minute and a half of our pre-movie attractions had been hijacked. Watching it, you had the feeling you could look up at the theater's tall back wall, see a prankster's face smiling down at you from the projection booth.

Except that breathing, it was supposed to be actual recorded breathing. From one of the twenty-four victims of the Woodrow High School Massacre.

Neither Mickles nor Aklai Studio ever suggested it, but in the press surrounding the trailer's release, Aklai did deny it, and not just in an oblique way, but in a way that felt coached. By a lawyer.

Mickles had no comment.

It was obvious he was part of this junket very much against his will.

Soon enough, another rumor found its way into circulation, from no source anybody could ever cite. But it was so terrible it had to be true. It was that that black screen, that nervous breathing, it was the last voicemail Mickles had received from his six-year-old daughter nearly ten years ago, when she was playing hide and seek with her nanny—when Mickles, according to the reports, assumed she was just carrying the cordless phone with her and had accidentally speed-dialed him.

Whether an intentional call or not, she still suffered the same fate: carbon monoxide in the garage, her new best hiding place.

The rumor about *Tenderizer*, then, was that Mickles was dealing with his own grief (or guilt) by exploring visuals that breathing could have been associated with, for a girl playing hide and seek on another ordinary day.

If either theory were true—the breathing was from a victim of the massacre, the breathing was from his own daughter's accidental death—then the studio should have stopped the project right there. Aklai would have lost a few dollars, sure, but it would have gained some public opinion points, which are finally worth more.

Film is intensely personal, yes, and it can be violently pornographic, but playing either the labored breathing of someone now dead or the last missive from a daughter to a father, that's combining the two in a way that shouldn't be flirted with, right? Shouldn't there be a line?

Apparently not.

Six months after that initial trailer, there was the soon-to-be-famous thirty-second spot—perhaps originally intended for network, for prime-time—that featured footage culled from on-the-scene news reports, complete with station identifications, license plates, and sports logos blurred over. No, not blurred: smeared over. Instead of scrubbing the pixels or smudging the print, Mickles was showcasing his art-house pedigree. The news footage was playing on a small television, and the legally necessary "blurring" was actually Vaseline dabbed onto the screen. Which is to say those thirty seconds were shot, cut, and piped into a television monitor, then paused and rewound continually to wipe and reapply the Vaseline, a process that would have taxed even a Claymation artist's patience. And for what effect, finally?

As with the rest of Sean Mickles's body of work since his daughter's accident, that's always the question, yes.

Of course, save for one telltale glare of the screen right at the end of those thirty seconds, it takes a trained eye to even clock that it's a television screen being filmed in the first place. Simply because of what that television is playing: thirty seconds of respondents and interviewees and witnesses to the Woodrow Massacre. Which of course we've all seen nearly to the point of memorization. Those easy, iconic moments weren't the one Mickles chose for this trailer, though.

Do people know about heads and tails anymore, as it applies to film? It's how you give a scene punch, how you cut run-time: snip as much off the front and back as you can, until only the absolutely vital remains. Because the modern audience doesn't have time for the rest. In the early days of film, heads and tails were often bought off editing-room floors and spliced into what they called 'shadow movies,' where you could tell the story was actually happening in the space just beside the screen. There was an audience for it in the early 1930s, and not just because the theaters those shadow movies played in were cheaper.

That audience never died, either. It just went to sleep for a couple of generations.

Sean Mickles shook it awake.

The moments he clipped for *Tenderizer*'s second trailer, they're the moments right before those witnesses' and parents' and emergency personnel's voices creak on, when they're looking past the camera, into some unclaimed middle distance. It evokes not so much a fly caught in a web, sensing some many-legged, inevitable shape taking form at the limits of its perception, but a human dreamer waking in that same web, about to offer an excuse to the spider. How this is all a big misunderstanding.

There were eight of these clips, of varying length, none longer than six seconds.

It left us all leaning forward, turning our heads sideways so as not to miss a breath. As if, from the shape those lips were about to take, we could get the word, too.

We wanted one of those people to have got it right, was the thing.

There was truth in them, you could see it in their eyes. They were there, after all. It was still raw, was still happening. Surely one of them was about to stumble into one of those magic utterances that define a generation, that epitomize a decade—a "What we have here is a failure to communicate" sort of thing.

Ich bin ein Berliner.

Go ahead, make my day.

I see dead people.

Except Mickles didn't let any of that happen.

Instead of closure, he raked the wound open all over again, refusing to let it heal over.

At which point the studio still didn't pull the plug, and the public didn't rally, or boycott, or even protest at all.

It was just a movie, right?

Art's how we process tragedy, isn't it? And art can't be right or wrong, it can just be good or bad. To allow it any kind of truth-valance would be admitting its importance, which in turn would make it hard to justify relegating it to the fringes of society.

Watch *Tenderizer*, though, and see if that argument still stands.

On the heels of that second trailer, then, Aklai (or somebody with Aklai) leaked the "behind the scenes" footage: those very respondents and interviewees and witnesses being interviewed on set, and talking about how many takes the ever-patient Sean Mickles had forced them through in order to elicit a performance he could actually print.

Remember?

We all nodded, almost glad to have been fooled, if it meant we could disregard the feelings the combination of those first two trailers had provoked.

Except then, of course, and as if by design, grainy cell-phone footage began to surface, confirming that those "actors" in the behind-the-scenes trailer, they'd actually been on scene for the Woodrow Massacre. Just background lurkers, none of them quite ever interviewed. But they'd been there.

I don't know about you, but that left a distinct hollow feeling in my chest, one it's hard to tease into words: indecency? transgression? grief? complicity?

And all because maybe these weren't actors.

Had Mickles found some way to leverage these grieving parents and shy officials and shell-shocked witnesses into playing along with his little film? If so, it was unconscionable. But, where did that leave us, right? Had he had some intimation of what was going to happen at Woodrow that day, and stationed extras in the background? Had he found his daughter at last, hiding in the best place ever, and had she whispered to him, about where to point his camera?

Impossible.

Even Sean Mickles would have called the authorities, had he known.

All that left then was that the real reason for *Tenderizer*'s delays wasn't Mickles playing Kubrick, trying to control every last detail, perfect every nuance, dot every visual *i*, it was simply the cost and the effort necessary for him to find lookalikes. Actors close enough in build and facial features to those "extras" in the background, actors with the craft to adopt this official's bureaucratic mannerisms, that witness's faltering delivery, this father's way of licking his lips like he's about to say something. Mickles's makeup team and Aklai's in-house digital effects could cover the rest.

And, if this was the case (as we hoped), was it then high art or poor taste? And what of us, compulsively rewinding, rewatching frame by frame, trying to wring the celluloid dry? Was it that we thought if we looked hard enough, our media savvy would let us see through to the artifice we so needed in order to distance ourselves from that day at Woodrow High?

But what if these weren't actors at all? That was the most effective conversation killer.

No more trailers were necessary after this. *Tenderizer's* marketing campaign had taken on a life of its own.

Lookalikes surfaced, digital manipulation was proven and disproven, legal action was vaguely threatened, petitions were signed, footage the news crews hadn't had use for was auctioned off then shown to be fake. More than that, *Tenderizer's* box office receipts were guaranteed beforehand, simply by the outrage levied against it. People were going to pay to be insulted by a studio capitalizing on their tragedy, and they were probably going to go back for seconds, just to be sure they'd been as offended as they thought they'd been.

To Mickles's credit, though, *Tenderizer* doesn't pander to the sensationalistic.

The easy route for the film to have taken would have been to "document" or re-dramatize the fateful events of that day—to create a visual bullet-point list of loosely verifiable scenes and already-legendary acts, and lock them together into a sequence that would, hopefully, serve as a sort of pressure-release valve for the nation's feelings regarding the massacre, and perhaps finally give the shooter or shooters the face and name we so needed, as then we could burrow into the backstory, explain the Woodrow Massacre away as bad parenting, as an example of how the system is built to fail, as a reminder that we should more closely monitor our children's activities.

Even if Mickles had them wear ski masks the whole time, and even if, after they'd herded their classmates into the front office, he'd stranded us out in the hall to await the explosion that would hide all the evidence, still, at least we'd be in the hall, right? Not forever out at the flapping yellow tape.

But what we really wanted, of course, was all the requisite heroes and last stands, the insistent prayers and secret-but-doomed love stories, all capped by the tearful, lingering, practically trademarked shots on the grand aftermath of violence.

None of which Mickles would ever even consider delivering.

Now, though, at the point where *Tenderizer* has only screened one time, to a roomful of survivors and parents and dignitaries, and one row of reviewers, there's evidently a series of images circulating that claim to be the original storyboards for *Tenderizer*. Not as it is now, but as Mickles had to package it to get funding: a Norman Rockwell'd sanitization of the Woodrow Massacre, complete with a slow list of names at the end.

If he'd shot that, it would have outsold every film of the season, and doubtless been an Oscar contender.

Except Sean Mickles has always calculated success differently, it would seem.

Take *Abasement*. It was box-office poison for good reason. Not that the premise is unsound: an accountant tells a joke at a dinner party one night and the joke slays, and this accountant starts to believe he might have been a comedian all along. *Abasement* is his slow, awkward awakening. At its heart, it's the sports story we all know: believe in yourself, insist that you can win, and you will, even if you lose the game. That was *Abasement*'s potential, anyway—remember the poster? "Laugh or Death"? It was all set up such that this accountant's wife could have been waiting just past the footlights, after his first big bomb. Or she could have been the one heckling him from the bar all along, prodding him to be better, to rise to the occasion, become the jokesmith she'd known he was all along.

Instead, Mickles takes us along for the accountant's fledgling attempts to tell jokes. To coworkers, deli attendants, whomever. And the jokes fail each time, worse and worse, such that, when the accountant starts to laugh at them himself, trying to prime the pump, as it were, his eyes open the whole time to watch, see if it's working, you want to leave the theater, please.

Abasement indeed.

Worse, it leaves those unformed jokes in your head in such a way that, when you try to sweep them out, they scuttle into an even darker corner.

It's not for the faint of heart.

It was a first attempt, though. That was the excuse. Mickles was showing promise, he just had a little bit of film school left to shake off. Let him be, he's coming along fine, so this wasn't *Duel* or *Eraserhead*, okay. It can at least be *THX-1138*, right? *Dark Star*?

Thirty-Nine, then, it was supposed to be a new direction, his second chance, where everybody could see the wings investors kept insisting he had.

And we of course know why it was called *Thirty-Nine*, right? Though Mickles had been charged by Unshelved Productions to re-imagine Hitchcock's *The Thirty-Nine Steps*, possibly by returning to Buchan's source material, the thriller he instead gave us (eight months late . . .) had the necessary MacGuffin, yes, but at the end of the very first sequence, he let us look into the case.

Teeth.

Thirty-nine of them.

The central mystery, what's supposed to supply the narrative tension, it comes not from some cinematic game of Clue, as Hitchcock perhaps would have done it, or even the three-card monte kind of shenanigans you expect to be surprised by in any good caper flick, but from an increasingly uncomfortable meditation on the source of those teeth, and whether or not our point-of-view character is inserting them into the gums of sleeping passengers. And whether they're even teeth at all.

In the famous final scene, when the teeth finally spill onto the floor of the train and wriggle for the shadows of insteps and the black caverns between luggage, that persistent rattle we've come to associate with them, it's not just missing, it actually leaves a sort of gaping cavity in the soundscape.

The result of that missing familiar sound is that it makes your tongue, completely independent of your instructions, check your own teeth.

And then you check them again.

It's this more than anything else that's responsible for *Thirty-Nine*'s brief theatrical stay—who wants to be in the dentist's chair?—and Mickles's contentment with that response, his refusal to explain or deny or do anything more than shrug and turn away, it's likely why the studio licensed him for the handle-with-care content of *Tenderizer*.

With *Abasement* and *Thirty-Nine* he had proven he didn't have it in him to flinch anymore, that that response had, perhaps, been burned out of him by finding his daughter in the garage on the fourth day. With *Abasement* and *Thirty-Nine*, he had proven that he was more concerned with art than receipts. That he had vision, and that he would insist on it at the cost of all else. To borrow from another era, Mickles had established that he didn't think the public deserved its spoonful of sugar.

Where many directors anesthetize us with spectacle, charm us with frivolity, Mickles is more interested in laying eggs in our subconscious. Or perhaps in squeezing them from a bloody cuticle, then rubbing his finger on the insides of our skulls.

And, of course, had his daughter not played that one game of hide-and-seek, what director would we have then? What set of movies?

We'll never know.

And now it's time to talk about what I just saw.

You already know the movie's premise, of course—no, the conceit, the logline: the Woodrow Massacre happened over the course of forty minutes between two and two-forty on the afternoon of March 9th. But what happened that morning?

This is *Tenderizer*.

You don't even need an epic-voiced announcer for it.

And, true to its promise, there's no violence whatsoever in the film's seventy-one minutes. Actually, had Aklai wanted, they could have petitioned the ratings board for a G, based solely on content.

All that happens for seventy-one torturous minutes is that an unnamed person has a handheld video camera, and is making a last circuit or tour of his or her house. As if taking stock. As if recording each item. Lingering on this chair, that painting, while a memory surfaces unseen, behind the camera.

Unseen but specifically felt.

It's an elegy is what it is. For a violation that's yet to take place. It's a suicide note without any words, it's a bitter apology, it's an explanation if we've got the eyes to see. One last look around before stepping into the fire.

Worse, there's a quality to it that suggests a sense of waiting. A distinct willingness to be convinced not to go through with it, like the day could have gone either way from here.

Except we've all already gone through that day.

Tenderizer never would have gotten that G. Were triple-X in fact a real rating, not a marketing ploy, *Tenderizer* likely would have required that mythical "fourth" X. It doesn't need NC-17, it needs an NC-300, because America isn't old enough to be seeing this yet. And by the time it is, it should know better.

What the two trailers had done was get us locked into considering options that were never really on the table at all.

This isn't Mickles's daughter's accidental last voice mail, and it isn't the digitally scrambled faces of the bottom-feeders of the acting world. And, all those production delays? They had to have been staged.

I'm saying this to keep you away. But I know it's not going to work like that.

We are what we are.

This is what I propose: somehow or another, in the months following Woodrow, Aklai Studio came into possession of the actual shooter's actual video recording from before the Massacre—likely it was mailed before lunch that day, perhaps with the title already in place—and, to insulate themselves from it, Aklai attached a controversial, difficult-but-capable director. A director known for leading the audience down suspicious paths, and then leaving them with the light failing.

Tenderizer is real, though. Even if it's not. And this isn't because of any chain of possession or documented provenance that surfaces. And it's not because of the padded envelope that probably showed up in Aklai's general delivery later that week, while we were all still watching them sift through the rubble on television.

Tenderizer is real because it's real.

Even without the shadow of the coming massacre draped over it, it would be just as haunting, just as cloying.

It's something about the actual succession of items, something both profane and instinctual—I can't articulate it any better than that, I'm sorry.

Maybe "succession" is the wrong word, though.

Progression? Order?

No: procession. Like for a funeral.

You know how in magic, in spells, words are supposed to have an innate, possibly occult power, and, when recited in certain orders, they can enact the user's will on the world?

Tenderizer has found the visual analog to that.

Mickles isn't the dreamer, this time out, but the weaver.

And he's hungry.

It gets to the point where you're in such lockstep with the film that it ceases to be a film altogether. Worse, you can almost guess what the next item is going to be, much in the same way you've been conditioned to know which note follows which in music. You may not be able to quite guess that a B-flat is coming up, but you do hear the slight clang when that B's sharped, don't you? Even if it's your first time through this piece of music.

It's the same with *Tenderizer*.

Thirty minutes in, you're dreading that fork, that lap blanket, that skate-board-scarred baseboard with such intensity that when the viewframe catches it at the edge of its demure green lines, then settles on it as if relieved to have remembered it, you can feel fingers lightly on your back, worms wriggling in your hair, something unnamable and blind rising in your throat.

If this isn't actual footage recorded by the shooter, then Mickles has seen that footage, anyway, and mocked-up the interior of a similar-enough house, planted the same items, crawled across them with a torturously slow camera.

As if that's not bad enough, then—I'm trying to inoculate you here, yes; I'm trying to protect you—the viewfinder drifts as it has to, to the promise of the foggy sliding door just off the dining room table.

Into the backyard.

Into the rest of this day.

No, you're saying, watching it. Shaking your head please.

You'll look through your fingers, though.

I did.

The film-school graduate in me of course catches the all-too-obvious edit as the camera passes across the threshold of this sliding door, and I fumble for the term, the technique, come up empty-handed. What it is, simply, is Mickles reminding us that this is a film we're watching. The jangly cut is visual shorthand for a clumsy splice—it is that clumsy splice.

In another film, it would break the spell.

In *Tenderizer*, it only deepens it.

Next, the film critic in me tries to interpret the meaning behind the sunny day over this backyard. The blue skies that weren't hovering over Woodrow on March 9th, or that whole week.

Is this heaven?

No.

Though we hear a dog, and expect a dog, what that green frame finally settles on is the lower legs of a little girl, in a swing.

Whether the recording actually stopped at the screen door, this playback now showing what the shooter had been recording over—another day, before all this—or whether this is actually Mickles's own daughter spliced in and memorialized, the way that girl's toes point at the ground, then catch it, it's so natural, so complete, so hollowing, so familiar that you might realize you've stopped breathing.

And then, in stark contrast to the contemplative quality of every other sequence in the film, the camera starts to flip around, panning across the side of the house—a house—catching the sky reflected in a bedroom window, a rake leaned up against brick, a patio set rusting at the welds, and comes to rest on what that little girl's seeing, on the person holding this camera, and then the shot stays there for maybe a second, a second and a half.

It's enough to see that no one's there. That no one's been there the whole time.

And what you see next, it's what you first saw of *Tenderizer* all those months ago: that famous "black" trailer that wasn't a trailer at all, but the last ninety seconds of the movie.

Except now the ragged breathing, it's yours and yours alone.

Welcome to the new world.

Welcome home.

ARDOR
Laird Barron

—Yukon-Kuskokwim Delta, February 9, 1975

What is it Pilot John says right before we drop from the sky?

Where is Molly's body? No, that's my own voice haunting me on account of someone else's ghost, someone else's guilt.

The pilot's head inclines to the left, slick as any disco floor pro. He gasps and takes the good Lord's name in vain. There's a quality of terror in the sharp inhalation that precedes this utterance. There's rapture in the utterance itself. His words are distorted by electronic interference through the headset. The snarl of a lynx wanting its fill of guts.

Obligingly, the world rolls over and shows its belly—

—I come to after the crash and call Conway's name the way I sometimes do upon surfacing from a nightmare. In this nightmare he is kissing me, but his left eye is gone and I can see daylight shining all the way through his skull. He says hot into my mouth, *This wound won't close.*

Now, I'm awake and alive. Hell of a surprise, the being alive part.

Snow trickles down through a hole in the fuselage and crystallizes in my lashes and beard. The last of the daylight trickles through the hole too and the world around me resolves into soft focus. Buckets of white light saturate everything until it's all ghostly and delicate. I'm strapped into the far back seat of the Beaver. I close my eyes again and recall low mountains rising on our left and the shadow of the plane descending toward an ice sheet that seems to stretch unto the end of creation.

Our particular jag of beach lies south of Quinhagak, not that that helps. In the summer, this is a vast circulatory system of bogs and streams on the edge of the Bering Sea. Ptarmigan and wolves, bears and fish dwell here, feast upon one another here. In the winter, it's one of God's abandoned drawing slates. The temperature is around negative thirty Fahrenheit. That's cold, my babies. The mercury will only keep dropping.

"Conway's in Seattle," Parker says. "He's safe. You're safe. Who's your favorite football team?" His breath is minty. He thinks I'm slipping away when I'm actually slipping *back* into the world. Sweet kid. Handsome, too. Life is gonna wreck him. That's funny and I chuckle. He grips my shoulder. His mittens are blue and white to match the stripes on the plane. "C'mon Sam, stay with me. Who'd you root for in the Super Bowl? The Vikings? I bet you're a Vikings man. My cousin met Fran Tarkenton, says he's a gem. Can't throw a spiral, but a hell of a quarterback anyhow."

"Cowboys fan." I'm remarkably calm, despite this instinctive urge to smack the condescension from him. He means well. His eyes are so blue. Conway's are green and green is my favorite color, so I'm safe as Parker keeps saying.

"The Cowboys! No kidding? Seattle doesn't have a club. One more year, right?"

"Dad is from Galveston." I haven't thought about my father in an age, much less acknowledged him aloud. Could be a concussion.

"Where's your accent? You don't have an accent."

"Dad does. Classic drawl." I hesitate. My tongue is dry. Goddamned climate. "How are the other guys?" The other guys being Pilot John, regional historian Maddox, and our wilderness guide extraordinaire Moses.

"Don't worry about them. Everybody's A-OK. Let's see if we can get you outta here. Gonna be dark any minute now. Moses thinks we need to be somewhere else before then."

His voice is too cheerful. I'm convinced he's lying about everyone being all right. Then I catch a glimpse of Pilot John slumped at the controls, his anorak splashed red. His posture is awkward, inanimate—he's a goner for certain. The engine has to be sitting on his legs. Snapped matchsticks, most definitely. The windshield blasted inward to cover him in rhinestones. I lack the strength to utter recriminations. Abrupt stabs of pain in my lower back suggest my body is coming out of shock. It isn't happy.

Parker strips free of a mitten and there are pills in the palm of his hand. He feeds me the pills.

I clear my throat and say, "Somebody will be along. The posse can't be far." Lord, the aspirin is bitter. A slug of lukewarm coffee from Parker's thermos helps. "John got a Mayday out, didn't he?" But what I recall is John with both hands on the wheel while the rest of us yell and pray. Nobody touches the radio in the eight or so seconds before it all goes black. "Sonofabitch. Tell me it's working." I know it's not working, though. The radio was smashed on impact along with Pilot John's body. That's how this tragedy is unfolding, isn't it? After making a career of fucking over others, finally we are the ones getting the screw job. O. Henry or Hitchcock should be on the case.

Parker says, "I wonder if you can walk."

While he struggles to extricate me from the ruins of the plane, I'm thinking not only is it a damned shame Pilot John failed to transmit a Mayday, he didn't even file a flight plan that accounts for our detour to this wasteland of tundra and ice. We're at least two hours southwest of the original destination. That potentially lethal blunder is on me. I'd gotten greedy and tried to squeeze in an unscheduled stop. Thanks to me we are all the way up shit creek.

A storm is moving in off the sea. Blizzard conditions will sock in search and rescue craft at Bethel. That means three, possibly four days of roughing it for us. If we're lucky. How lucky we are remains to be seen.

I cough on the raw taste of smoke.

"Heck." Parker glances over his shoulder. "Guess she's on fire."

Yes, Virginia, we're in trouble—

—Professor Gander invited me to lunch at the Swan Club in Ballard and laid it all on the table. Entrusted me with a withered valise stuffed with documents and old-timey photos. He endeavored to explain their significance through suggestion and innuendo. Two things I dislike unless we're talking romance, which we weren't. I disguised my fascination with a yawn.

He lighted a cigarette and set it in the ashtray without taking a drag first. "The papers were written by R. M. Bluefield, allegedly a mysterious Victorian fellow Stoker based the Renfield character upon. Bluefield was an avowed mystic, a fascination he acquired abroad in Eastern Europe and Asia. He possessed training in medicine, also from his world travels. He was obsessed with the concept of immortality, but then, so were many others of that era. His particular interest lay in the notion that it might be obtained through certain blood rites or the consumption of animal organs. Stoker, it is thought, perused the fellow's papers and mocked Mr. Bluefield's eccentricity.

"The journals changed hands, most recently belonging to an actor from the 1950s and '60s named Ralph Smyth. Where *he* acquired them is a matter of conjecture, although it's of scant consequence. For our purposes, we simply need to locate Smyth himself."

"Ah, the royal we. There's a booster, I presume. Got to love those guys. Richer than rich if he's going through you."

"Yes, Mr. Cope. I represent a patron. One with very deep pockets."

"God love 'em. And what does this patron want with Smyth?"

"You will locate him and ask a single question. Return with his answer, whatever that may be."

"A question?"

"One question. I'll even write it down for you." He produced a fancy pen and indeed did write it on a coaster. He also wrote his home address and a set of numbers that represented the payment on offer. A nice plump round figure, to be sure.

I lingered over the coaster and then put it in my pocket. "This is a little weird, professor. Not exactly my normal brief, so to speak. I take it this Smyth character is missing, or else you'd go ask him yourself."

"It is possible the fellow's dead, although we suspect he's very much alive. In hiding, we think. Took a powder into the Alaskan wilderness during the spring of 1967. There are more recent accounts, multiple sightings of a man matching Smyth's description."

"Seven years is a long time to be on the lam. The cops want him?"

"The authorities don't possess evidence to implicate him in any nefarious dealings, such as the disappearance of my patron's daughter. My patron suspects otherwise, naturally. That's where you come in."

"Maybe Smyth's got an aversion to overly aggressive film buffs." I smiled, but he didn't seem amused. "So, I'm going to put together a team and fly all over the ass end of Alaska, hunting for some guy basically nobody's ever heard of. . . ."

"Ralph Smyth, Ralph Smyth, surely you recall. . . ." Professor Gander buffed his signet ring and waited for the light to dawn in my presumably Neanderthal brain. Fucker wore a cardigan and rimless glasses. He'd gone prematurely white like Warhol.

"Surely I do not." I took a gulp of Redbreast. Glass number three. I'm not a heavy drinker, but suffering the good professor required extreme measures.

"A poor man's Lon Chaney who eked a career from getting violently offed in a dozen Hammer films. What he's famous for, however—"

"Nothing, apparently," I said, a teensy bit drunk already.

Gander bared his mismatched and silver-capped teeth. He wanted a taste of my blood, it could be assumed. He said, "Bravo, Cope. The man is famous for nothing. What he's *infamous* for is his final role in a French Canadian art film. *Ardor*. An exceedingly liberal interpretation of *Dracula*. Ten years ago this spring, *Ardor* premiered at a Quebec festival, then sank into obscurity. It is reviled by critics and forgotten by the public. Have you seen it? Amazing work."

"Oh, by art, you mean smut, eh? I dig."

"Yes, a pornographic movie. Rated triple-X for sex and violence. A notorious piece of cinema, even by genre standards. Banned in many countries. Only a few copies rumored to survive, et cetera, et cetera."

"I'm sorry I missed this one. A porno retelling of *Dracula*. What will they think of next?"

"The forces at work in the world are endlessly inventive. Artistic auto-coprophagy is here to stay."

I studied him through the haze of his untouched cigarette, preferring not to dignify his comment with a response. I made a mental note to look up autocoprophagy.

He said, "Why don't you come by my place tonight and I'll show you the film? I've got a bootleg reel. A few colleagues and some friends of the university will be in attendance. You can mingle, make new acquaintances.

311

A fellow in your line can always use new connections, and a better class of them, too."

"You and your cronies going to gather around the campfire to watch a stag flick, huh?" I said. "A banned stag flick. That's a relief. I prefer the company of miscreants."

"There's another item we'll need to discuss," he said. "The client is a dear friend of mine. That's why he's come to me in the wake of the law's failure to rectify his concerns. Nonetheless, I've reason to believe Smyth went to Alaska on a specific mission. He's a bibliophile and an antiquarian. His home, which he abandoned, was stuffed with extraordinary . . . items, shall we say? By all means extract the information my patron requires, but if you can bring home any significant papers or relics, or lacking that, photographic evidence of said, you'll be generously compensated."

"Well, in that case, here's another coaster."—

—I drove over to the professor's house around nine. Late enough that people would've settled in, but before any craziness had gotten started, or so I hoped. Gander struck me as a buttoned-down freak.

The address he'd scribbled on a coaster led me to an old mansion in the U-District, set back from the street. Parking is hell in the U, so I left the car in a likely spot and walked three blocks. The windows were dark and I wondered if it was the right place until Gander's housemaid answered the bell and greeted me by name. More of a gasped epithet, really. Her face was pale. She held a candle in an ornamental bowl.

The maid led me to a study eerily illuminated by a silver screen on the far wall. She fled. I got the impression of antique furniture and lots of bookcases. A throng of silhouettes was backlighted by the screen. I whiffed cherry pipe smoke and fancy cologne, a hint of marijuana.

A film played for this crowd of rustling shadows. Its frames jumped, were poorly spliced; the scenes were muddy and marred by frequent cigarette burns; the color flickered. Tiny subtitles and a strange, scratchy orchestral symphony accompanied the grunts and cries of the actors, all a half-beat offset from the action itself. Somebody was fucking somebody. Somebody was murdering somebody. Cocks everywhere, thrusting into every opening. A guillotine blade dropped through the neck of a devil clown. Gore splashed the thirteen dancing brides of Dracula and flecked the camera lens. Darkness flooded in. For an instant the gallery dissolved and I became dislocated, a bullet shot into the vacuum of deep space.

The lights came up while the film kept running. Someone said, "Jesus Christ!"

I beheld a congregation of the crème de la crème of UW faculty; fifteen or so middle-aged dudes in sweaters and slacks, drinks and smokes in hand, all of them sniffing in my direction like moles. The departments of anthropology, psychiatry, and literature were well represented.

Horror stretched Gander's face in all kinds of unpleasant directions. "What are you doing here?" he said. He gestured as if to ward away an evil spirit. "What are you doing here? You can't be here."

I wanted to tell him to piss off, he'd invited me, but I couldn't speak. There was too much blood in my mouth. I was naked and covered in blood. I extended my arms like the Vitruvian Man and the room rotated. Centrifugal force pinned me in place. On the screen, washed out, yet immense and wicked, naked Dracula embraced naked Renfield and crushed the life from him. The camera zoomed in on Renfield's glazed eye, penetrated the iris into the secondary universe, the anti-reality. It was snowing there, in hell. I was in there, in hell, in the snow, waving to myself.

A white glow ignited on my left where the doorway to the long hall should've hung. Instead, an ice field bloomed through a porthole. So bright, so beautiful, filling up my brain with fog—

—The team assembled at the Bull Moose Diner in downtown Bethel, Alaska, to plot a final sequence of site flyovers. Alaska is a big place. Nonetheless, we were running out of places to search for our quarry. If I couldn't find Smyth in the next few days, that might be curtains for the expedition.

Frankly, the frigid Alaskan winter wasn't doing my mood any favors. Relocating to western Washington for a vacation didn't sound half bad. I could take Conway to Lake Crescent for a romantic idyll, or hiking along Hurricane Ridge. Or maybe we'd hole up at my house and drink wine and watch the rain hit the windows.

Is retrieving the bones of a person treasure hunting? Or would you perhaps like to call it grave robbing? Conway posed this question with a smile—he could afford to smile because he didn't know the half of what I did for a living. That was the last time I'd seen him in the flesh. He'd spent the night at my place on Queen Anne Hill. The next morning would find me aboard a jet to Anchorage. He lived across town in North Gate; sold insurance to corporations. The job took him out of my life about as often as mine took me out of his. We'd been lovers for three years. I'm tallish and homely; he's shorter and handsome enough to model if he wanted. He's a man of his word and I'm shifty as they come. The arrangement worked, barely.

Grave robbing? Maybe Conway had it right. Over the past decade I'd flown thrice around the world in the service of numerous scholarly profiteers of the exact same mold as Professor Gander and his ilk. Missions frequently revolved around wresting artifacts of historical significance from the locals, or better yet, absconding with said relics before the locals even suspected chicanery was in the offing. Sometimes, this job being an example, I was sent to retrieve a real live person, or extract information from said. You just never knew. My chief talents? A willingness to follow orders and endure a not inconsiderable measure of privation and hardship along the way. I don't balk at getting my hands dirty. Runs in the family. Granddad shot people for the Irish mob back in the Roaring Twenties; made an art of it, or so the legends go. I'm not even close to being that kind of a hard case, just sufficiently mean to get matters across when it's called for.

The future would take care of itself. Meanwhile, here I sat in Bethel with a string to play out: four sites within striking distance of the village. Gold Rush mining camps abandoned since World War II, except for infrequent visits by tourists, researchers, and ne'er-do-wells. That last was us. My comrades were more inclined to the business of looting and pillaging native artifacts under the guise of academic inquiry.

"A sentient being isn't an artifact separate from the universe," said Moses as he counted out bills for the waiter. None of us had the first clue who he was speaking to. "Sentient beings are the sensors of the universe, its nerve endings. A colony of ants, a flock of geese, a city-state, are the places where enough sensors amass and the universe becomes self-aware." He paused with a scowl. "Somebody needs to kick in another two bucks."

That was doubtless Maddox who'd skimped on the tip. I tossed a five spot on the table to save time and frustration for all concerned. Prior to this assignment I'd not worked with any of them. I preferred the southwest states. My Alaska network was weak, forcing me to rely on a subcontractor in Juneau who'd made the initial referrals. Over the months I'd gotten to know this group, on a superficial level, at least. This line of work doesn't engender intimacy, it heightens eccentricities. A man becomes known by his foibles, his personality tics. Illusions of bonding or brotherhood are perfidious.

Pilot John was a boozy loser who'd washed out of life in Vermont. Maddox was a boozy loser who'd gotten dumped from the faculty at the University of Anchorage for a variety of sordid offenses. One too many coeds had dropped her panties for him, I gathered. Moses, our Yupik guide, was a boozy loser who'd blown his Western State degree and done five years in the pen for grand larceny. Nowadays he guided hunters and hikers and nefarious types such as me, even though his expertise lay somewhere in the area of philosophy and he didn't know an iota more about snow than anybody else schlepping around the Yukon Delta. Parker . . . him I couldn't figure. Didn't smoke, didn't drink, so what did he do? Clean as a whistle except for some domestic bullshit with a younger brother. His specialty was photography and he knew his way around the northern territories. The mystery was why a smart, clean-living guy like him couldn't get a reputable gig. Punching his brother in the kisser wasn't a satisfactory explanation for why he'd become persona non grata.

I hate mysteries, but the solution to this one had already suggested itself to me. What to do with my conclusions was the problem—

—I kicked in a lot of doors and looked under a lot of rocks to discover these five most pertinent facts of the Ralph Smyth case.

Fact One: He'd received training as a playwright and dramatic actor and it hadn't helped. His oeuvre mainly consisted of crappy black-and-white monster flicks that would've mildly entertained my twelve-year-old self. His schtick was playing second banana to the main villain. He chewed scenery as Igor or Renfield in at least half the movies and as an enforcer, arm-breaker, or button man in most of the others.

Fact Two: Smyth had had the reputation as a real sonofabitch. Small-time actor, yet connected behind the scenes. His father had owned majority interest in a lighting and set-making company. Money opened all the right doors. Ralphie baby was chummy with Karloff, Lugosi, and Cushing, and every two-bit producer that came down the pike. He enjoyed conning young, naïve starlet wannabes. He seduced them, screwed them, strung them out on dope, and then turned them over to one of the slimeball directors for further abuse and exploitation. Molly Lindstrom, so keen to escape the tyranny of daddy dearest, was just another fly in Smyth's web. She vanished six months after principal photography wrapped on *Ardor*. The authorities looked into it, Burt Lindstrom being important and such. Never came to anything.

Fact Three: The case went cold and Smyth dropped the acting gig and disappeared into the woodwork. His trail wound all over, from Juneau, to Anchorage, to Fairbanks, and west toward the bitter coast. He was a ghost with many aliases: George Renfro, Ogden Shoemaker, Bobby Stoker, and Gerald Bluefield were the popular ones. He had plenty of cash, and Alaska isn't the kind of place where people ask a lot of prying questions. There was a long line of secretive white men seeking some grand destiny in the wild.

I grudgingly admitted Gander was correct in his assessment that Smyth was on the trail of something big. He was a man of disconcerting depths. For example, our long-lost actor hadn't simply starred in the much-reviled *Ardor*, he'd written the script and sold it to the studio. Uncredited to boot. He'd allegedly gotten wasted at a cast party and told a grip that the Dracula legends were rooted in fact. *Yeah, Vlad the Impaler,* said the grip. Smyth laughed and said, *Not the Tepes horseshit. Think the Devil's Triangle. Think the sailing stones of Death Valley.*

Fact Four: Nine people had gone missing in the various regions of Alaska coinciding with Smyth's travels. Drunks, lost hunters, adventurers. Folks nobody would miss unless, like me, one paid attention to patterns. My man Smyth was a pervert and a cad of the worst sort. Sorting the old papers he'd lovingly collected on ritual cannibalism and human sacrifice, I wondered if he was also a murderer.

Fact Five: There are six quarts of blood in the body of a man and I'm low, very low. Now I know I should've stayed in Seattle with my true love—

—Sprung joints of the plane seethe smoke. Flames streak from the cowling that's half-nosed into the ice. The smoke is black and thick. The column rises several feet, and then spills down over the ground, pressed hard by the frigid temperature. Visages of devils float in the tide and shoot forth hot red tongues. The wind whips it until it boils. Concupiscent curds of death. Where oh where is my shirtless and muscular roller of big cigars? Call that bastard in here on the double! I have my second chuckle of the day in celebration of wit undimmed by the impingement of certain doom.

We've trudged a good distance inland. The plane is a toy. My glove blocks it easily. We are even farther from the brightening cold star fields. The blue-black horizon has enfolded the ocean like a curtain dropping onto a stage. Moses leads. Parker and Maddox drag me and our pitiable remnants of gear on a canvas tarp salvaged from the wreckage. My knee is sprained, my back is in spasms. I can but hope that's the worst of my injuries. We'll know tonight when the universe freezes and the aspirin supply disappears.

Pilot John screams way back there where we left him in his pyre. I can barely hear him over the rising wind and the crunch of boots in the snow. The men stop in their tracks and gaze back across the flats. Vapor wisps from their mouths. For a moment they resemble a lonely trio of caribou, separated from the main herd and bewildered at a sound foreign to their existence.

"Hey, he's not dead," Maddox says to Moses. His tone is reproachful.

Moses pulls down his hood. His face is broad and dark. His mustache is silver with frost. He frowns. No, he definitely doesn't look like a man who wants to believe what he's hearing. He stares wordlessly into the gathering darkness, into the coal at its heart.

"Oh, no. Moses, you said he was dead."

"That's the wind."

"No, it's him. God help us." Maddox crosses himself.

Parker glances from man to man. "What's happening?" He really doesn't get it. His hat has fur-lined earflaps; maybe that's why.

"Pilot John is frying," I say through gritted teeth. Nobody says anything for a minute or so. The screams have stopped. My hunch is the unlucky bastard woke up to his flesh popping like bacon, then promptly succumbed to smoke inhalation. Here's hoping. I can't help myself; I quote from the poetry of that long dead Yukon sage, Robert Service: *"The Northern Lights have seen queer sights, but the queerest they ever did see was the night on the marge of Lake Le Barge I cremated Sam McGee!"*

Moses raises his hood again. His coat is a really nice homemade one with a wolf ruff and more fur trim at the wrist and ankle openings. It'll take him a lot longer to freeze to death than it will for everybody else. He starts walking again, toward the foothills of the Kilbuck mountains. I can't help but imagine them as tombstones.

"Shouldn't we stay with the plane?" Parker says this for the third or fourth time. He managed to save his best camera and carries it on a lanyard around his neck.

"We'll die in the open." Moses doesn't glance backward. Shoulders squared, head lowered, he plods on.

"Gonna buy it either way," Maddox says, low and grumbly. Not a protest, it is an utterance of fact.

"Somebody might see the smoke," Parker says. His is the faint and fading voice of reason swallowed by the wilderness and the indifference of his comrades.

"C'mon," Maddox says. A bear of a man, red-eyed from lack of drink. He and Parker grasp the edges of the tarp and begin dragging me again.

According to the maps, long ago there was a village around here. I'd hoped to find Smyth or some clue regarding Smyth's whereabouts. The village has crumbled, or the ice has buried it. No trace of the fish camps or the mining camps either. A cruel wind blows, scouring the ice to dirt in spots and making brick ramps of the snow in others. The wind doesn't ever really stop in this place. It has, like Sandburg's grass, work to do erasing all signs of human habitation. The wind is the tongue of a ravening beast. It licks at our warmth, the feeble light of our miserly souls.

Our company founders and staggers and scrambles onward. It is dark when we tuck into the shelter of a rocky crevice. Nearby, the face of the mountain is glaciated. Water oozes and steams over ice stalactites and we lap at it. My lips are already cracking and it's only been a few hours. This kind of weather leaches a man, withers him to a husk.

By the beam of a heavy-duty flashlight, the men stretch the tarp as a windbreak. They shore and buffer the enclosure with hastily gathered alder branches and rocks. In the end, we basically cuddle into a hole and pull the lid over ourselves. I'm wedged between Parker and Moses. A rock digs into my spine. It is cold, concentrated cold, and numbs me with dreadful immediacy. The canvas molds over my face in a death masque, tightening, then slackening with the gusts. The wind roars in the absolute blackness. Farther off, a fluting note as ice shears free of its mooring and is dashed upon the rocks.

Tomorrow we'll find a better shelter, build a fire if we can, if we survive the night. I shiver uncontrollably. I am a particle adrift in a gulf. The horizontal fall is endless—

—"What's going on with you?" Conway says. He's got my cock in his hand, but not much is happening. "You're different these days." A not-good kind of different, apparently, because his voice is too flat to mean anything else.

I'm on my back on the bed, staring at the wall at the Walwal tapestry of a stigmatic Christ that I once appropriated from the estate of a wealthy geezer in Maryland. The image doesn't thrill me, nothing does. I am bereft and confused. I am still falling, have been since the night I went to Gander's house. When was that anyway? Before or after the year in Alaska? Before or after the crash?

"Sam?"

I turn my head and look him in the eye. I understand what he wants and choose to play dumb, which is a mistake. Despite his Ivy League degree, Conway's not the sharpest knife in the drawer, but he's far from dull. He's intuitive as the devil. Sometimes we're so synched it's as if he's in my head. Cue the persistent whisper in the back of my mind: *I came here to the coldest place I could find because it slows everything. The cold.* There is no way to explain my experience in Alaska to Conway any more than I could to the investigators or the shrink. Not in a truthful fashion. To the cops and officials I gave lies. With my beloved, I let my smile be the lie. Only, he isn't having it.

"Sam. Where are the others?"

I wish I knew. Except, I do know—

—The storm lasts thirty-nine hours, then there's a lull. Maddox crawls forth, reborn from the stone womb into a new Ice Age. The sun is a crimson blob low on the horizon, Polyphemus glaring through a hole in the clouds. The other two men follow him, creaking and cracking as they move. They are stick men, dry as tinder. It is so cold spit freezes on my lips. It is so cold my tongue is a clammy lump, separate from the rest of my flesh. Thirst gouges my throat. The others stand over me, black silhouettes seething. Maddox and Parker yank me from the hole like I'm a sack of feathers. Parker hands me a snowshoe to use as a crutch. I'm wobbly and in a lot of pain. On my feet and under my own power, however.

Moses says, "There's gonna be another blow." He's covered in a glittery coat of hoarfrost. He resembles a ghost. We all do. I'm thinking we're very close to it now. The abyss that men tumble into when they shuffle off the mortal coil is right here, always present in places such as this one. The bones of the earth are all around us.

We need a shelter, a fire, and water. Moses chops ice with a hatchet and stows it in a bag. We move against the flank of the mountains, searching for a cave or an abandoned cabin, any kind of habitation. The wind picks up again—

—There's a scene in *Ardor* that transcends the smut and the schlock. It is the scene wherein dutiful Renfield and the count repose after a murderous orgy. The count reveals that his body is an illusion, a projection of pure darkness given fleshly form. He isn't a sentient creature, merely the imitation of one, the echo of one. The consumption of blood is a metaphor, larger than sex, more terrible than repression. *There's a hole no man can fill,* says the count. *No amount of love or hate or heat poured into the pit. No amount of light. I am the voice of the abyss.*

The idea of Dracula as genius loci is, well, genius. Vampires as black holes, the dull and ravenous points of a behemoth's fangs. Out of place for a smut flick, I admit, yet brilliant. Too bad it didn't clue me in to my imminent peril. By a trick of the camera, Dracula implodes in slow motion, a star collapsing into itself, and for a moment the bed is rent with a slash of radiant blackness and bits of ash.

Then the film skips and it's back to fucking and sucking—

—I emerge from the bathroom and find Conway naked atop the covers. He's peering through a magnifying glass at the papers from the antique valise Professor Gander gave me.

Valise and contents are dated at approximately ninety years old. The leather is wrinkled, the documents crinkled and yellow as the piss I just took. These items, the curious circumstances of its last owner's flight from civilization, are supposed to convince me. Silly, wicked Gander. The only thing that convinces me is money.

Conway frowns. "Who wrote this? The fellow's penmanship was atrocious. From this passage all I can make out is, *My wound won't close.*"

I don't get a chance to answer because the next slide clicks into place and I'm shot forward in time and back to Alaska. Nobody knows the trouble I see, except my comrades, and none of them can do shit about it either.

Smyth emerges from the storm to deliver us from our predicament. His skull is stove in, as if by a hammer blow, so I can make out the ossified coils of his forebrain and I'm trying to remember if Dr. Seward trepanned Renfield in attempt to save his life. Smyth's appearance is more monstrous than any master makeup artist could hope to devise. He is an upright cadaver manipulated by strings of icy vapor.

His song is irresistible, although he explains it's not his, that he's merely a vessel. He speaks of cabbages and kings and how a combination of saline and cold will send a death spike into the depths of the sea, killing everything it touches. He describes a crack that runs through the dark of space and how it bends the light, how it wears faces, and how it wails. How it drinks heat. He is a madman. I've never seen a tongue so long or black.

Eventually, he lights a wooden pipe and passes it around the circle. Claims the hash is from a batch made by monks in 1756, so it's the good stuff. Calls it crypt dust, or something like that. Insists we fortify ourselves for the walk, and nobody argues. I don't taste much of anything, don't feel much of anything, and decide it's probably leaves and twigs. I change my tune a few minute later when the sun begins to contract and expand like an iris.

He leads us to a palace he's carved from ice and rock. Nothing lives anywhere around his home. The desiccated carcasses of bats lie strewn everywhere. Hundreds of them. A carpet of shrunken heads and brittle matchstick bones. Rocks for furniture, icicle stalactites for chandeliers, an irregular pit in the tilted floor. The pit is approximately four feet in diameter. It wheezes a foul, volcanic draft.

Smyth says coming down from the experience of starring in *Ardor* was nearly the death of him. In a fit of despair, he went to his dressing room and drank a fifth of bourbon and shot himself in the head. He wore hats everywhere after that incident.

I came here to the coldest place I could find because it slows everything. The cold. It keeps me. While he's talking, we're in a state of exultant exhaustion. We've taken a hit of the dragon and the world has the substance of a dream.

Parker asks about the hole.

"That's the crack that runs through everything," Smyth says. "I dug it myself." The sonofabitch doesn't even need to move fast, we're all dumb and stuck in our tracks as cows lowing on the ramp to the killing floor. He uses the hatchet that Moses brought along, two or three licks apiece. I'm lucky, it's only my thigh, and Parker's kind of lucky too.

The bodies of the unfortunate slough into the pit that's awaited us a million years—

—My parents are old as the dust that blows across Texas where they've retreated to for those golden years. I haven't spoken to them since Vietnam got cooking. Dad didn't take to his son turning out gay, honorable combat service or not, and Mom, well, as her husband went, so did she.

It's been a few months and I've slowed down on the pills and the booze and am sufficiently restored to humanity to report my true findings, the findings I haven't told anyone, not Gander, not the cops, not Conway.

Molly Lindstrom's parents remind me of mine, except a bunch richer. Their house is in a gated neighborhood amid carefully manicured forestland outside of Seattle. Burt Lindstrom made his dough in the engineering division of a certain well-known aerospace company. His is a precise and austere mind. Wouldn't know it from the décor. Antique hunting rifles, swords, and moose heads on the walls and nothing to do with aviation or aviators. He favors red-and-black-checked plaids, denim pants, and logging boots. Makes Lee Marvin seem soft and cuddly in comparison. His wife, Margaret, a former bathing beauty, has gone thick in the middle. She's in a dress, a blue one. Her eyes are cruel as a bird's.

Their guard, a goon named Larry, stands at the window. He's peering through binoculars back the way I drove in. "Brown sedan, last year's model. Just pulled a U-turn outside the gate. Two guys." He keeps on scanning with the binoculars. His lips move silently. He's got a gun slung under his ugly tweed jacket.

I'd seen the car on the highway, trying to blend with traffic and not quite making it.

"That'll be the feds," Mr. Lindstrom says to the goon while he stares at the brand-spanking-new scars on my cheeks where the frostbite laid its brand. "Got you on short leash, huh? They reckon you kilt that man of theirs. Left him on the ice. I gotta buck says you did. Kind of hombre you are."

Parker's white smile flickers in my mind. "I didn't kill him," I say with real weariness. It's the hundredth-and-first time I've said the words.

"And I don't give a shit," says Mr. Lindstrom.

"A drink?" Mrs. Lindstrom is already gliding toward the liquor cabinet. She's got the grace of a magician's assistant. Lickety-split, hubby and I are each clutching a Scotch and soda in front of the hearth. There's a fire in there. I'm sweating in the nice suit Conway made me wear, but frozen at the core. After Alaska, nothing will ever warm me up again.

She says to him, sweet as pie, "Civility, Burt. We agreed how you'd be." Those eyes again. I wouldn't want to be trapped on a lee shore with her and no supplies.

He smiles like you do when you get punched in the balls. "Sure, hon. How's the booze, Cope? Fix you another?"

"No, sir. I'm fine." I'm not fine. I'm minus a leg and I use a cane and I've gone from recreational drinker to hardened drunk.

"Gander says you have something for us. You met Smyth." Mr. Lindstrom's mouth twists and he visibly restrains himself, turns away, and says to the goon, "Get some air, Larry." The goon makes himself scarce.

Mrs. Lindstrom moves close to me. I doubt there's much contact between her and the husband, and she's starved. She smells bitter, like winter flowers. "He told you about my daughter?"

I nod and sip Scotch.

"You anglin' for more cash?" He gives a snort of contempt. "I'll write you a damned check on the spot. Out with it, man!"

"Easy, dear, easy," she says to her husband. Then to me, "We saw the film, Mr. Cope. There isn't anything you can say that will shock us. All we want is a little peace. Her marker is over an empty plot. I can't bear it anymore."

He drains his glass, seems poised to chuck it at the fire. "She had a bit part. Basically an extra, for Chrissake. Bride of Dracula Number Three. So what? Those rat bastard producers seduced her. Smyth sold her a bill of goods how he was gonna make her the next Monroe. Molly was a good girl. She mixed with bad people." He runs out of steam and stares dumbly into the distance.

"No argument here," I say. Bride of Dracula Number Three took it in the ass on screen, and did some other naughty stuff too. Not mine to judge. I steel myself. "Molly's dead, ma'am. She died ten years ago in Los Angeles. Remember when Mr. Lindstrom flew to L.A. to help the private dick he'd hired to search? Well, he and this lowlife named Brent Williams found her all right, shacked up with a hood from the projects, strung out on heroin and hooking for rent money. *Ardor* ruined her. Ruined her in every way you can imagine. There was an argument. Your husband killed her and the pimp in a twenty-dollar-a-night motel room. It was an accident, everything simply got out of hand. The dick got rid of the bodies himself." I stare at her, try to project compassion at her blank, shocked face. "It was you who hired me, isn't that right, ma'am? Your husband signed the check, but it was you, because you couldn't have known, and he went along, played the part of the grieving dad. And I guess maybe you *are* grieving, Mr. Lindstrom. Maybe you're sorry for what you've done."

Nobody says anything for a bit. Then Mrs. Lindstrom bursts into tears and flees the room, face buried in her hands.

"You bastard," Mr. Lindstrom says and shakes his head the way a confused bear might. "You come in here and make my wife cry? Bad mistake, son." He takes a knife from his pocket. A big one with a fixed blade that would've done nicely as a bayonet.

The guard confiscated my piece when I came onto the property. That's why I'm standing next to a pair of crossed cavalry sabers. I hope against hope they're sharp—

—Smyth wrote this in one of his abandoned journals: As a boy I started with bugs and small animals. I accidentally clipped the end of my index finger off at age sixteen while stacking chairs in the school gymnasium. It completely repaired itself within two and half years. Spontaneous regeneration. This was long before I discovered the Bluefield papers. Bluefield was a crank living in the wrong century. Still, his instincts were true. After my last film with Lewton, I visited Borneo on holiday and trekked into the brush, learning the old ways. I ate a fresh human heart. The hetman of a friendly tribe told me I'd inherit the strength and the vigor of the fallen warrior. It tasted sweet. There's no returning from that. Sadly, it's only part of the secret. The keyhole you peer through. The dark mystery itself is unapproachable.—

—Parker is still ticking, still got some fight in him. He's missing some pieces, so not *that* much fight. He says to me in a tired voice, "I suppose the fact your grandfather was a gangster makes us meeting like this sort of poetic."

"You say poetic, I say pathetic. Wait a second . . . You're a cop?" I mug at him, best as I am able. He chuckles, horribly. I'm groggy. Haven't had a sip of water in hours. Two days since I last ate. The tips of my fingers and toes are numb and my heart knocks too fast. I'm bruised, possibly concussed. My back is sprained. Worst of all, my left thigh is severely lacerated. None of this bodes well.

Beyond this litany of woes looms a bigger problem.

The others have bled out on the ice floor of the crystal cave. All that life coagulated into a crimson slick. The enormous cascade of blood is too hot to completely freeze. It oozes toward the hole in the floor. The pit that has awaited us for a million years.

Parker and I cling to a rough section a few feet upslope. We've linked arms and combined our waning strength. The ice is damp and slippery. Inch by inch our purchase loosens and we slide toward doom.

The man who once played Renfield on the silver screen throws back the hood of his bearskin parka and laughs. His hands are bare to the elements, fingernails blackened or gone. I try not to consider what he's done, what he's going to do.

He says, "The tragedy is that the Renfield figure wants what the master already has. Immortality. After all my searching, all my supplication, all my obeisance, I have found only a slower way of dying."

The walls of ice molt crimson. They seep and drip.

My grip fails. Parker groans and slides past me, down the bloody ice chute into the shaft that probably goes straight past hell to China. The groan is just a sound he's making. It doesn't touch his eyes. I'll never get to ask him if he'd gone undercover to bust me or to get a line on Smyth, that alleged murderer of starlets.

A moment later I'm gone too and Smyth whistles to mock my departure—

—And then I die—

—Maybe an eon passed in the void. How would I know? Mostly I spent the time falling like a stone into an abyss. There were interludes where I segued from falling into walking through a vast maze, a hedgerow of obsidian. The sky was also obsidian splintered by jags of white light. The light was so dim and so far away it might've been the inverse of itself. Figures moved in the distance. Moses and Maddox. I couldn't quite catch them to see for certain. Parker paced me by trudging backwards. A bit green around the gills and sickly pale. Breathing, though. I cried out to him and he smiled and drifted away.

Sometimes Smyth's disembodied voice echoed along the twists and turns: "I didn't travel into the wilderness to find the dark. I brought the dark with me. The seed is inside everybody, waiting for a chance."

Another occasion he said, "I went out there to be alone. You got what you wanted, you stupid twit?"

I realized I was probably talking to myself and in those moments of clarity the maze disintegrated and I'd be lying in that grave on the ice between my comrades, or plummeting from the sky in the plane, or kissing Conway at the Phoenix Theatre, or transfixed in a study while *Ardor* squelched and squealed on the wall and stodgy guests gawked at my apparition.

In every case the snow returns, and covers me—

—I wake in the summer to a good-morning blowjob, but the ruined nerves in my leg kill me and the vertigo unmans me and I scream and Conway has to hold me down until I stop. I lie there in a sweat and tell him the fog has lifted. I remember everything in Technicolor.

He cautions that I can't trust my recollections, claims I returned to Seattle a night before I ever left and then blinks and says he didn't say anything that crazy. He leaves red marker messages on the mirror: *Where's her body, Sam?* I confront him and he kisses my ear and says I didn't get eaten by the Ouroboros and shit out into an alternate universe. Take your meds and do your physical therapy, Sam. *Where's her body, Sam? Where's Parker's body? Where are they, Sam?*

If I didn't die, if this isn't hell, then what has actually transpired is worse. Always something worse. That first night in the storm does for Moses, his fabulous parka notwithstanding. Maddox may or may not have had life in him. Parker is only strong enough to tow one of us and despite my length, I don't weigh much. The good cop drags me back to the seashore and we await rescue near the plane's wreckage. Along the way a diamond-hard sliver of ice or a jagged rock has torn through my overalls and sliced my thigh to the bone. I don't feel it happen and the blood covers my legs like I've a lap full of rubies. We hunker for two days. Parker's face turns black and his eyes go milky blue. He stays with me a while, and then between buffets from the north wind he's gone.

The troopers are able to dig Pilot John's remains from the barbeque pit. They are mystified at the bullet hole in his skull. Bits of glass in there, so the bullet was fired from the ground as he banked the plane for a pass is what they conclude. Helicopter rides, hospital wards, a long white veil over the universe come next. Ice covers the Earth, then recedes and reveals the green. I'll never walk quite right again. I lose an ear, all my fingernails, my belief in the rational, my sanity.

Night after night I dream of *Ardor* and Renfield in his cell with worms, lice, and flies for sustenance. He gibbers and hoots until the count slips in and maims him, leaves him paralyzed in the shitty rags of his bedding. I follow the camera into his glazed eyeball and come out on the other side inside a cheap motel room in Van Nuys. I'm a fly on the wall during the encounter between Papa Lindstrom and his private dick and Molly

Lindstrom. The shouts and the tears are flowing freely when the pimp walks in. Bullets don't have names on them. The girl and the pimp get bundled into the dick's Caddy for a long, lonely ride to the landfill.

I don't have a shred of proof, but the fucking imagery is so vivid, eventually it eats away at me, plagues my waking hours. Lately, I'm convinced that nothing is real, so the unreality of this scenario assumes the same weight as anything else. Conway helps me into the suit I usually wear to funerals and drives me to the Lindstrom estate. I leave him in the car, tell him it won't be fifteen minutes, and then I hobble inside to say the awful things I've got to say.

Here's the test. Here's where I receive validation or comeuppance. Maybe it'll be both. For a moment I hesitate on the steps while a goon named Larry approaches. It is lush and green and sweetly humid. Not a glacier in sight—

—Lindstrom charges me with the knife brandished. I'm a step ahead of the game. I drop my cane and snatch the cavalry saber from its ornamental wall hooks. Coming in I'd expected mockery, perhaps indignant outrage, the threat of arrest, and certainly the risk of getting roughed up by one of the old man's goons. Hell, if they'd simply laughed and phoned the funny farm, it wouldn't have surprised me. What I don't account for is how fast the situation escalates into a killing. In retrospect, I can't blame myself for not entirely buying that the dreams were bona fide. Crazy people believe their own bullshit and so forth.

The snarl, the savage glint in his eyes, this is the murder in L.A. reprised. Man, it's not as if I'm a fencer, or anything. I make a haphazard swing when he gets close and there goes the knife and two of his fingers under a table. Unfortunately for both of us he doesn't take a hint. He leans down and retrieves the knife with his left hand and I hobble forward two steps and swipe at him again, both hands wrapped around the hilt. The sword cleaves through his neck without any trouble and his head plops onto the Persian rug and rolls onto its side so those devil-dog eyes are blinking at me.

"Oh, shit," I say.

The wife doesn't return and there's a hell of a mess in the parlor, so I leave. The goon doesn't intercept me on my way out the door. I do a spit check of my reflection at the car and don't see any blood on my suit. My hair is mussed and I'm sweating, but that's me these days. I smile at Conway and tell him to take us home. He doesn't suspect anything and I retreat into myself with alacrity. My brain wants to shutter the doors and call it a day. I roll down the window and breathe in the smells of grass and leaves.

A cloud swoops in and paces the car. The breeze gains an edge and snow begins to fall. My heart stops. But it's not snow, it's hail, and Conway hits the wipers and in a minute or two we're through it and gliding beneath glorious blue skies. I place my hand over Conway's and close my eyes and try not to make that transcendental journey to Alaska, or visualize Lindstrom's mouth working up a voiceless curse.

I figure if this isn't a dream, the cops will be waiting at the house. And they are.

FINAL GIRL II: THE FRAME
Daphne Gottlieb

Don't answer the phone.
Don't answer the door.
Don't do it.
No—really. Don't.

Too late.

Don't worry.
You will make it through this.
Stay calm. If you are reading this,
you are here.

You are here because you are in danger
and you are in danger because you are here.
You've got a bad case
of the captivity narrative.

This means you are a white female under 30,
and you haven't had sex or
you only do it with your husband or
you only do it by force.

THE CUTTING ROOM

None of this is your fault.
Someone did something that put you here:
Your forefathers raped the land.
Your husband stole America.
Your father oppressed the poor.
Your sister had sex in the house.

You will be taken from your home
or you will be forced to leave it.

If you hear music,
you are in a horror movie.
That means you get a knife to fight back with.

If you hear music
and the people holding you captive
are wearing jackets that say "ATF"
you are in Waco.
That means you are Joan of Arc.

If you are eating dinner with your husband
in early America
and there's a knock at the door
and it's Native Americans with weapons,
you're Mary Rowlandson.

If you are eating dinner with your boyfriend
in late California
and there's a knock at the door
and it's white people with masks and weapons,
you're Patricia Hearst.

If you are eating dinner with your boyfriend
in the living room
and he is killed by people with masks and weapons

FINAL GIRL II: THE FRAME

when you bring the dishes to the kitchen,
you're in a horror movie.

Here's how to survive:
Watch as everyone around you dies.
Scream until your eyes work.
They will work when you pick up a weapon.
They will work when something changes:
Maybe the Native Americans are just like you.
Maybe money, your father, is the great tyrant.
Pick up a weapon and gain sight.
You will fight back or die.
You will fight back.
You will become a girl who is a boy.

The story runs all the way
to daybreak, when you can be a girl
again and everything
will be returned home.
Even us.
Until then, everything
is electric projection
and we are
your captive audience.

ILLIMITABLE DOMINION
Kim Newman

Okay, you could say it was my fault.

I'm the one. Me, Walter Paisley, agent to stars without stars on Hollywood Boulevard. I said "spare a thought for Eddy" and the Poe Plague got started . . .

It's 1959 and you know the montage. Cars have shark-fins. Jukeboxes blare the Platters and Frankie Lyman. Ike's a back number, but JFK hasn't yet broken big. The Commies have put *Sputnik* in orbit, starting a war of the satellites. Coffeehouses are full of beards and bad poetry. Boomba the Chimp, my biggest client, has a kiddie series cancelled out from under him. Every TV channel is showing some Western, but my pitches for *The Cherokee Chimp*, *The Monkey Marshal of Mesa City*, and *Boomba Goes West* fall on stony ground. The only network I have an "in" with is DuMont, which shows how low the Paisley Agency has sunk since the heyday of *Jungle Jillian and Her Gorilla Guerrillas* (with Boomba as the platoon's comedy-relief mascot) and *The Champ, the Chimp, and the Imp* (a washed-up boxer is friends with a cigar-smoking chimpanzee and a leprechaun).

American International Pictures is a fancy name for James H. Nicholson and Samuel Z. Arkoff sharing an office. They call themselves a studio, but you can't find an AIP backlot. They rent abandoned aircraft hangars for soundstages and shoot as much as possible out of doors and without permits. At the end of the fifties, AIP are cranking out thirty to forty pictures a year, double features shoved into ozoners and grindhouses catering to the Clearasil crowd. They peddle twofers on low-budget juvenile delinquency (*Reform School Girl* with *Runaway Daughters!*), affordable science fiction (*Terror from the Year 5,000* with *The Brain Eaters!*), inexpensive chart music (*Rock All Night* with *The Ghost of Dragstrip Hollow!*), cheapskate creatures (*I Was a Teenage Werewolf* with *The Undead!*), frugal combat (*Suicide Battalion* with *Paratroop Command!*) or cut-price exotica (*She-Gods of Shark Reef* with *Teenage Cave Man!*). When Jim and Sam try for epic, they hope a marquee-filling title—*The Saga of the Viking Women and Their Voyage to the Waters of the Great Sea Serpent*—distracts the hot-rodders from sub-minimal production values and a ninety-cent sea serpent filmed in choppy bathwater.

The AIP racket is that Jim thinks up a title—say, *The Beast with a Million Eyes* or *The Cool and the Crazy*—and commissions lurid ad art, which he buries in hard-sell slogans. He shows ads to exhibitors, who chip in modest production coin. Then, a producer is put on the project. Said producer gets a writer in over the weekend and forces out a script by shoving peanuts through the bars. *Someone* has to direct the picture and be in it, but so long as a teenage doll in a tight sweater screams on the poster—at a monster, a switchblade, or a guitar player—no one thinks too much about them. Sam puts fine print into contracts that makes sure no one sees profit participation and puffs cigars at trade gatherings.

Roger Corman is only one of a corral of producers—Bert I. Gordon and Alex Gordon are others—on AIP's string, but he's youngest, busiest, and cheapest. After, to his mind, wasting half his budget hiring a director named Wyott Ordung on a 1954 masterpiece called *The Monster from the Ocean Floor*, Roger trims the budgets by directing most of his films himself. He seldom does a *worse* job than Wyott Ordung. Five critics in France and two in England say Roger is more interesting than Cukor or Zinnemann—though unaccountably *It Conquered the World* misses out on a Best Picture nomination. Then again, Mike Todd wins for *Around the World in 80 Days*. I'd rather watch Lee Van Cleef blowtorch a snarling turnip from Venus at sixty-eight minutes than David Niven smarm over two hundred smug cameo players in far-flung locations for three or four hours. You don't have to be a contributor to *Cayenne du Cinéma* or *Sight & Sound* to agree.

After sixty to seventy films inside four years, it gets so Roger can knock 'em off over a weekend. No kidding. *Little Shop of Horrors* is made in three days because it's raining and Roger can't play tennis. He tackles every subject, within certain Jim-and-Sam-imposed limits. He shoots movies about juvenile-delinquent girls, gunslinger girls, reincarnated-witch girls, beatnik girls, escaped-convict girls, cave girls, Viking girls, monster girls, Apache girls, rock-and-roll girls, girls eaten by plants, carnival girls, sorority girls, last girls on earth, pearl-diver girls, and gangster girls. Somehow, he skips jungle girls, else maybe Boomba would land an AIP contract.

The thing is everybody—except Sam, who chortles over the ledgers without ever seeing the pictures—gets bored with the production line. Another week, and it's *Blood of Dracula* plus *High School Hellcats*, ho hum. I don't know when Roger gets time to dream, but dream he does— of bigger things. Jim thinks of bigger *posters*, or at least different-shaped posters. In the fifties, the enemy is television, but AIP product *looks* like television—small and square and black and white and blurry, with no one you've ever heard of wandering around Bronson Cavern. Drive-in screens are the shape of windshields. The typical AIP just lights up a middle slice. Even with *Attack of the Crab Monsters*, *The Amazing Colossal Man*, and *The She-Creature* triple-billed, kids are restless. Where's the breathtaking CinemaScope, glorious Technicolor, and stereoscopic sound? 3-D has come and gone, and neither Odorama nor William Castle's butt-buzzers are goosing the box office.

Jim or Roger get a notion to lump together the budgets and shooting schedules of two regular AIP pictures and throw their all into one eighty-five minute superproduction. Together, they browbeat Sam into opening the cobwebbed checkbook. This time, Mike Todd—well, not Mike Todd, since he's dead, but some imaginary composite big-shot producer—will have to watch out come Oscar season. So, what to make?

In England, they start doing horror pictures in color, with talented actors in starched collars and proper sets. Buckets of blood and girls in low-cut nightgowns are included, so it's not like there's art going on. Every other AIP quickie has a monster in it, so the company reckon they're expert at fright fare. There's your answer. Roger will make a classy—but not *too*-classy—horror. Jim can get Vinnie Price to star. He'd been in that butt-buzzing William Castle film for Columbia and a 3-D *House of Wax* for Warners, and is therefore a horror "name," but his career is stalled with TV guest spots on debatably rigged quiz programs or as fairly fruity actors touring Tombstone on Western shows. After Brando, well-spoken, dinner-jacketed eyebrow-archers like him are out of A pictures. What Jim and Roger don't have is a clue as to what their full-color, widescreen spooktacular should be *about*. They just know *Revenge of the Crab Monsters* or *The Day after the World Ended* won't cut it.

Enter Walter Paisley, with a Signet paperback of *Tales of Mystery and Imagination*. No, it isn't altruism—it's all about the client.

Boomba's out of work and eating his weight in bananas every single day. Bonzo and Cheetah have a lock on working with Dutch Reagan and Tarzan, so my star is unfairly shut out of the town's few chimp-friendly franchises unless he's willing to do dangerous vine-swinging, crocodile-dodging stunts those precious primates want to duck out of. Therefore, I'm obliged to scare up properties suitable as vehicles for a pot-bellied chimpanzee. I ponder a remake of *King Kong*, with a chimp instead of a gorilla, but RKO won't listen. I pitch a biopic of Major Sam, America's monkey astronaut, but that goddamn Russian dog gets all the column inches.

In desperation, I ask an intern who once had a few weeks of college about famous, out-of-copyright stories with monkeys in 'em, and get pointed at "Murders in the Rue Morgue." Okay, so, strictly, the killer in that yarn is an orangutan not a chimpanzee—but every film version casts a guy in a ratty gorilla suit, so Boomba is hardly wider of the author's original intent. I know of AIP's horror quandary, and a light bulb goes on over my head. I dress Boomba up in a fancy suit and cravat and beret for the Parisian look and teach him to wave a cardboard cutthroat razor. I march the chimp into Jim and Sam's office just as Jim and Roger are looking glumly at a sketch artist holding up a blank board which ought to be covered with lurid artwork boosting their break-out film.

Tragically, Boomba compromises his employment prospects by crapping his velvet britches and grabbing for Sam's foot-long cigar, but my Poe paperback falls onto the desk and Roger snatches it up. He once read some of the stories, and thinks he particularly liked "The Fall of the House of Usher." Sam objects. The kids who go to AIP pictures have to study Poe in school and will therefore naturally hate him. But Jim remembers Universal squeezed out a couple of Poe pictures and racked up fair returns back in the Boris and Bela days. Then, Sam—who gives every appearance of actually having *read* "The Fall of the House of Usher"—says you can't make a horror movie without a monster and there's no monster in the story. "The house," says Roger, eyes shining, "the *house* is the monster!" Jim and Sam look at each other, thinking this over. Boomba is forgotten, chewing the cigar. Then, management buys Roger's line. The house *is* the monster.

Important issues get settled. Is there a part for Price? Yes, there's someone in the falling house called Roderick Usher. Is there a girl? Roderick has a sister called Madeline. Paging through the paperback, they discover Poe doesn't say Madeline *isn't* a teenager in a tight sweater. I suggest the thin plot of the eighteen-page story would be improved if a killer chimp escaped from the Rue Morgue and broke into the House of Usher to terrorize the family. No one listens.

Jim and Roger run with "The Fall of the House of Usher." They happily read out paragraphs in Vinnie Price accents. The sketch artist covers his board with a falling house, Vinnie lifting a terrified eyebrow, a buried-alive babe in a tight shroud, coffins, crypts, skeletons, an atomic explosion (which gets rubbed out quickly), and slogans ripped from Poe prose. "He buried her alive . . . to save his soul!" "I heard her first feeble movements in the coffin . . . we had put her living in the tomb!" "Edgar Allan Poe's overwhelming tale of EVIL and TORMENT!"

I see my slice of the deal vanishing along with Sam's cigar. Eddy is dead and long out of copyright, so there's no end for him. This cheers Sam up, since he'd been all-a-tremble at the prospect of having to buy rights to some horror book from some unwashed writer.

So, just when it would take a steam-train to *stop* AIP making *The Fall of the House of Usher*, I mention I am the agent for the Edgar Allan Poe Society of Baltimore and can easily secure permission—for a nominal fee—for the use of the author's name, which they have registered as a trademark. For a few moments, the room is quiet and no one believes me. Sam is skeptical, but I tell him the reason Poe's middle name is so often misspelled is to evade dues payable to the EAPSoB. He mulls it over. He swallows it, because it makes sense to him. He's ready to argue for going with *Edgar Allen Poe's House of Asher* as a title before Jim and Roger shout him down. Sam doesn't care about critics, but little slivers of Jim and Roger do, so they're ready to strike a deal on the spot. I have a pre-prepared contract, which needs crossings-out, as it's for a monkey as actor rather than an august body as trademark-leaser, but will still do.

As soon as I'm out of the office, I *found* the Edgar Allan Poe Society of Baltimore and start paperwork on trademark registration. It turns out I'm not even the first in the racket. Edgar Rice Burroughs and Mark Twain, or their heirs, have beaten me to it. The deal may not be 100% kosher, but AIP's check clears. Probably, they just want to shut me up, since I'm theoretically responsible for bringing them the property. Hey, it's my drugstore paperback. They offer me an "associate producer" credit, but forget to include it on the film. Maybe it's lost in the five minutes of swirling multi-colored liquids tacked on after the house has burned down and tumbled into the tarn. But, from then on, I'm part of the Poe package.

The Fall of the House of Usher—or *The House of Usher*, as it is called on the posters to save on lettering—is made in a comparatively leisurely fifteen days. Vinnie shaves his moustache, under protest as if he were Cesar Romero, and wears a white wig, which he likes enough to model in his off-hours along Sunset Strip. There are only three other people in the speaking cast, so the star gets first bite of all the scenery available for chewing. On set, Vinnie objects to the line "the house lives, the house breathes!" Roger tells him "the *house* is the monster," and Vinnie sells it with eyeball-rolling, velvet-tongued ham. In my capacity as "ass. prod.," I have Boomba pose for a portrait as a degenerate Usher ancestor. Floyd, the camera genius, doesn't get a good shot of it so you can't see the chimp's cameo in the picture.

This is how it plays. In some earlier century (no one's sure which), a brooding youth with a Brando sneer and a Fabian haircut travels through burned-out wasteland to a painted-on-glass mansion where Vinnie twitches at the slightest sound and rolls his eyeballs as if they were marbles. He has extra-sensitive senses, which are a perpetual torment to him, and looks severely pained whenever anyone drops a fork or lights a lamp. Our hero is searching for his missing girlfriend, Vinnie's sister. She flits about, showing cleavage, then faints and is buried alive in the basement. Girl claws her way out of crypt, irritated, and scratches out Vinnie's eyes as if he were making a play for her date at the record hop. A candle falls over and the House of Usher catches light like Atlanta in *Gone With the Wind*—indeed, some of the burning building stock footage might *be* offcuts from David O. Selznick's day. Vinnie and girl get crushed and/or burned. Our hero makes it out unscorched, and broods some more—presumably his agent has just told him how much he's getting paid and he's resolved to quit acting and become a producer so *he* can wave the foot-long cigars some day. A caption runs "'and the deep and dark tarn closed silently over the fragments of the House of Usher'—Poe." Just to make sure you know, Eddy's name pops up several more times during the swirly credits.

Against expectations, *Usher* is a monumental hit, boffo boxo, molto ducats in the coffers. Roger makes money. Vinnie makes money. Sam and Jim make more money than they can imagine, and Jim at least has a great imagination. Edgar Allan Poe, or the Baltimore Society in his name, makes money. Even Boomba gets residuals for the use of his unseen likeness. There actually *are* residuals and Sam has to find out how to pay them. The matter never came up with *Voodoo Woman* or *Phantom from 10,000 Leagues*. Naturally, being Hollywood, this means only one thing—sequels.

The first pass runs to pitches like *Return to the House of Usher . . .* only there's a stinking tarn where the old homestead used to be, so few dramatic possibilities not involving expensive underwater photography present themselves. I spin a story out of my head in which Roderick Usher's ghost crawls out of the tarn as a green monkey with flippers. Jim sees straight off that I'm angling a star role for Boomba and nixes the approach. It would be easy to take offense—after all, the chimp is a better actor than the ducktailed hoodlums AIP put ruffs, doublets, and floppy-tasseled hats on in subsequent movies.

Skipping through my now-dog-eared and broken-spined *Tales of Mystery and Imagination*, Roger gets excited about "The Pit and the Pendulum." The slavering sketch artist, about whom I'm starting to worry, draws a teenybopper in a tight sweater strapped down in a pit while Vinnie swings a blade over her bazooms. Jim and Sam love this, and are disappointed when Roger looks up the story and finds it's a *guy* in the dungeons of the Spanish Inquisition. Never mind, he says, the *pendulum* is the monster. By this, he means the torture angle is grabby enough without the added distraction of bazooms. The artist rubs out the bosomage, and puts in a manly chest—revealed through pendulum-slashes in a frilly shirt.

So, *Pit and the Pendulum* gets a greenlight. Even Sam sees one picture for the price of two is a better deal if it hauls in ten times the gross of the average four old-style AIP creature features. He quietly squelches Bert I. Gordon's *Puppet People vs. the Colossal Beast* project and Alex Gordon's long-cherished *She-Creature Meets the Old-Time Singing Cowboy* script, and pours added shekels into *Pit*. It's AIP's big hope for 1961.

Only problem is, "Pit and the Pendulum" *isn't* a story—just a scene. Guy in pit. Nearly sliced by pendulum. Escapes. Even Roger can't spin that out to feature length with long shots of dripping walls, gnawing rats, and Vinnie licking his lips. The problem is solved, unusually, by the writer. Dick Matheson takes his *Usher* script, changes the names, and drops the climactic house fire in favor of Pit/Pendulum business. This time, brooding youth—not the same one, though you'd be hard pressed to tell the difference—is looking for his missing *sister*, and she's married to Vinnie. But she's still buried alive—twice, as it happens. The *Usher* sets are back, with new painted flats and torture equipment to bump the House up to a castle. The establishing shot is a bigger glass painting, with crashing waves included. Vinnie keeps his moustache, which saves behind-the-scenes drama—and wears tights, always a big favorite with him.

One morning, I wake and find I've grown a moustache too. Plus I'm thinner, paler and more watery-eyed. And my wardrobe—which was once full of snazzy striped threads—runs to basic black. I don't think much of it, because the times they are a-changing. *Pit* is, if anything, bigger boffier boxo than *Usher*, and the walls start closing in.

Tales of Terror gets through *its* remake of *House of Usher* in the first reel, and calls it "Morella." Then, it runs through "The Black Cat" and "A Cask of Amontillado" (Peter Lorre and Vinnie compete in a face-pulling contest) for a second act, finishing up with "The Facts in the Case of M. Valdemar" (bad-tempered Basil Rathbone turns Vinnie into a "nearly liquid mass of loathsome—of detestable putrescence"). Since most of the pages are now torn out of my book, I venture the opinion we're using up doable Poe at an alarming rate, especially since AIP are cranking out more than one of these pictures a year. I try to get "Rue Morgue" back on the table, determined Boomba will have his comeback before the well runs dry. After only one-and-a-half remakes of *House of Usher*, everyone is bored again—the curse of success in this business, if you ask me—and trying to break out.

First, Roger sneaks off to do *The Premature Burial* at another outfit, with Ray Milland playing Vincent Price, but Sam and Jim buy into the deal, so Roger is sucked back in. *Premature* isn't quite as much of a remake of *Usher* as *Pit* and "Morella," but it *is* a remake of the scheme-to-drive-the-husband-crazy subplot Matheson padded out *Pit* with. Roger wants to hop-frog off and make, I don't know, socially significant movies about segregation. He winds up buried alive in Venice, California, in those standing Danny Haller sets. Decaying mansions with stock furniture. Tiny soundstage exteriors with false perspective stunted trees. Dry ice mist pooling over bare floor.

Piqued that Milland is daring to usurp his schtick, Vinnie hares all over the library, doing *Master of the World*, *Confessions of an Opium Eater*, *Twice-Told Tales*, *Diary of a Madman*, and *Tower of London*. In Vinnie's mouth, Verne, de Quincey, Hawthorne, de Maupassant, and Shakespeare somehow turn into Poe. Brooding youths. Velvet jackets. Buried-alive girls. Vinnie a-flutter. Crypt in the basement. House burns down. Swirly credits. The Shakespeare (*Tower of London* is *Richard III* translated into English) is directed by Roger, who swears he can't remember being on the set. He admits it's possible the film got shot during a blackout he had during a screening of a Russian science-fiction film he was cutting the special effects out of to fit around rubber monster scenes shot by some kid to see release as *Rocket Voyage to the Planet of Prehistoric Women of Blood*. Meanwhile, Vinnie is *muy fortunato*, lording it over the castles of AIP, hawking Sears-Roebuck art selections and cookbooks on the side.

Even the critics start noticing they get the same picture every time. Recalling that this happened before, I propose an ingenious solution. When Universal got in a rut with Frankenstein, Dracula, and Mummy pictures, they had the monsters meet Abbott and Costello. Comedy killed off the cycle. Once you've laughed at a horror, it's never frightening again. Since Lou has passed away, we can't get the team back, but I suggest it would at least triple the hilarity if Bud's new comedy partner is a rotund, talented chimpanzee . . . and AIP can launch a new series with *Abbott and Boomba Meet the Black Cat*. It'll slay 'em in the stalls when Boomba starts tossing loathsome, detestable putrescence at Vinnie Price's moustache. We can bill Boomba as "The Chimp of the Perverse."

Before I sell Jim, Sam, and Roger—not to mention Bud Abbott—on this, Matheson dashes off a *funny* remake of *House of Usher*, purportedly based on "The Raven." It breaks my heart to tell Boomba he's been benched again, but the "ass. prod." gig is still live and EAPSoB dues are pouring in. *The Raven*, for comedy value, casts Vinnie as the brooding youth in tights, makes the buried-alive chick a faithless slut, and has Boris Karloff play Vincent Price. The castle still burns down in by-now scratchy stock footage, which almost counts as a joke. Lorre is in it too, driving Karloff nuts making up his own dialogue. The juve is some piranha-toothed nobody who lands the job by spreading a false rumor he's Jim Nicholson's illegitimate son. When it comes out that he isn't, Sam swears the grinning kid will never work in this town again, though it's too late to cut him out of *The Terror*, yet another remake of *House of Usher* that Roger shoots in three days because he still has Karloff under contract. The twist here is that the house is washed away rather than burned down.

After sending the cycle up with *The Raven* and cynically hammering it into the ground with *The Terror*, there's no way this perpetuation of Poe can persist. So, relief all round, and a sense everyone can move on to better—or at least new—things in 1964. Jim thinks H. P. Lovecraft could be the new Poe, and buys up a ton of his stories. Yes, AIP lay out for film rights! Banner headlines in *Variety*. Having missed out with Verne, Hawthorne, De Quincey, and the other bums, I found the Howard Phillips Lovecraft Society of Providence. I pore through *The Outsider, and Others*, determined to find a tale with a good part for a chimp—the best I can manage is a rat with a withered human head in "Dreams in the Witch House," which should be close enough. But first up on AIP's Lovecraft schedule is *The Case of Charles Dexter Ward*. Only it's going to be *The Curse of Charles Dexter Ward*—*Curse*, which sounds like swearing and violence, is a better movie-title word than *Case*, which sounds like measles and bedrest.

For some reason no one can fathom, Roger wants the non-bastard Nicholson to play Charles Dexter Ward. He thinks up this scene where Chuck is possessed by his evil wizard ancestor and smashes an axe through a door to get to his terrified wife (Debra Paget) while shouting something from *The Tonight Show*. I know that will never work, but keep quiet. Vinnie, meanwhile, happily breezes off to play Big Daddy in *Sweet Charity* on Broadway, intending to conquer a whole new career as a musical comedy star. The velvet jackets go in storage. The burning-building footage goes back in the cans. As per HPL, this time, the *monster* is the monster.

Though I don't live anywhere remotely near a Witch House, I'm tormented by dreams—not of human-faced rats or green monkeys, but an angry Eddy. In my restless slumber, Poe comes at me with a long list of grievances that, in my official EAPSoB capacity, he wants presented to Congress, the publishing industry, drinking establishments long since gone out of business, the United States Army, and sundry other bodies and individuals. With his name writ large on panoramic magic lantern screens undreamed of even in the thousand-and-third tale of Scheherazade, he feels he has the attention of a general public who once gave him the shortest of shrifts—and wishes to plead for a redress of wrongs done long ago. I put these dreams down to the rich foods I'm able to afford thanks to "ass. prod." fees, and think hard about cutting down on lunches.

At the *Charles Dexter Ward* preview, we find out something mysterious and beyond imagining has happened during production. I settle into my seat, with a big bucket of popcorn Sam has made me pay for, certain that the HPLSoP is going to trash the EAPSoB in the coming fiscal year. The lights go down, the curtains crank open, and the projector whirrs. The AIP logo fills the screen. The opening title is not *H. P. Lovecraft's The Curse of Charles Dexter Ward . . .* but *Edgar Allan Poe's The Haunted Palace.*

There's a rustling, creeping, sussurating, terror-filled sensation in the house. The wet cigar falls from Sam's open mouth. Roger puts on dark glasses and starts to cry. Jim gets up and checks with the projectionist that this is the right film. I know now we're all cursed, that we'll never be free of Eddy Poe Rex.

The velvet jackets are back. The fog swirls on those same tiny sets. There's a crypt in the basement, where the monster lives. It's out of focus. Vincent Price, grieving for lost chances on the Great White Way, plods through a part written for a much younger, scarier man, bidding a bitter-sweet farewell to life as the New Rex Harrison (or the White Sammy Davis Jr.). Finally, as we sob in the screening room, the house burns down. It's another remake of *House of Usher.* After burning beams collapse for the ninth or tenth time, there's even a quote. "'While, like a rapid ghastly river, through the pale door, a hideous throng rush out forever, and laugh—but smile no more.'—Edgar Allan Poe."

We know how that pale throng feel . . .

In melancholy despair, Roger flees to Swinging England, vowing to make films about Oliver Cromwell and the Beatles. Unable to resist the fateful clutch of dread destiny, he shoots *The Masque of the Red Death* and *Tomb of Ligeia*—with Vinnie Price, buried girls, burning buildings, swirly credits, and end quotes. "The boundaries which divide life from death are at best shadowy and vague. Who can say where the one ends and where the other begins?" "And Darkness and Decay and the Red Death held illimitable dominion over all." There's nothing Roger can do. He hires Richard Chamberlain, Christopher Lee, Shirley MacLaine, or Jerry Lewis, but visits the star's dressing room on the first day of the shoots to find ashen-faced, quivering-jowled, red-eyed Vinnie Price having his eyebrows powdered and helped into another velvet jacket.

I wind up the HPLSoP and find myself shackled full-time to the interests of the EAPSoB, which has regional chapters in Boston, New York,

Paris, and Antarctica. The Society brings a massive lawsuit against NASA, claiming that the Apollo program is infringing the intellectual property rights of "The Balloon Hoax."

Boomba drowns in his swimming pool. At Hollywoodlawn, I march leaden-footed behind Cheetah, Bonzo, J. Fred Muggs, and Stanley (billed as "more fun than a barrel of teenagers" in Disney's *The Monkey's Uncle*) as they carry the child-sized coffin to the tiny grave. Judy, the simian slut who wormed her way into Boomba's affections then stole a plum continuing role on *Daktari!* from him, makes a show of honking bogus grief into her Kleenex. The wake is a gloomy, ill-tempered affair. I repress an urge to daub the sanctimonious surviving chimps with pitch, string 'em up from the beams at Ben Frank's, and set light to them.

Poe goes on. Roger, running in vain from the Red Death, takes a trip around the world in eighty pictures. *City in the Sea*, *The Oblong Box*, *The Conqueror Worm*, *Murders in the Rue Morgue* (finally—but with a goddamn gorilla suit and made in Spain!), *X-ing the Paragrab*, *The System of Dr. Tarr and Professor Fether*. All the Tales and Poems are consumed, so AIP start in on the *essays*. In *Eureka!*, a velvet-jacket philosopher is on the point of understanding how the universe functions when his buried-alive niece claws at his eyes and the house catches fire.

My hair long and lank, my cheeks hollow, my eyes red-veined, my moustache floppy—I realize I *look* like Eddy Poe. Considering he was found near death in ill-fitting clothes borrowed from someone else, it seems I even dress like the unhappy poet whose still-beating heart of horror I discern beneath the floorboards of my office or bricked up in the basement of my bungalow (which doesn't even *have* a basement). Everywhere I go, every mirror I look into, I glimpse the specter of myself, silently accusing, "Thou art the man!"

I *am* that "unhappy master whom unmerciful disaster followed fast and follows faster till my songs one burden bore—till the dirges of his hope that melancholy burden bore—of 'Never-Nevermore'!"

But I'm not alone in being by horror haunted, by Eddy ensnared, by Allan alienated, by Poe persecuted . . .

By now, it's not just Roger films and Vinnie vehicles. It's *everything* Jim and Sam put into production. Alongside remakes of *The House of Usher*, AIP are doing annual reunions of *Beach Party*—itself a thinly disguised remake of *Gidget*—with beach bums and bikini babes surfing and smooching to tunes from Frankie and Annette, plus comedy Hells' Angels led by Rocco Barbella from *Bilko*. Even in the first *Beach Party*, the first signs are there when "Big Daddy," who runs the hangout shack on the beach, looks up and turns out to be . . . Vincent Price. AIP try a James Bond skit and it comes out as *Dr. Goldfoot and the Bikini Machine*, with Vinnie Price using a razor-pendulum to part Frankie Avalon's hair. Soon, *all* beach pictures bear the mark of Poe—*Buried Alive Bikini*, *Beach Blanket Berenice*, *Muscle Beach Metzengerstein*. Annette spends more time in a shroud than a bathing suit, with a black cat entombed in her beehive hairdo. Rod Usher takes over the Hells' Angels, wearing a studded velvet jacket and a floppy-tasseled cap, and complains that the revving of bikes is torture to his over-sensitive ears.

We're all drinking heavily now, and choking on the poison. The *Hollywood Reporter* prints an item that Jim is on the point of marrying his thirteen-year-old cousin. *Variety* claims Roger is trying to raise funds for a Southern Literary Magazine when he ought to be shooting a motor-racing picture in Europe. At the Brown Derby, they say Sam is never seen without a raven flapping ominously after him, croaking whole stanzas. Vinnie lands a prime-time comedy special, but it comes out as *An Evening with Edgar Allan Poe*. My second-best client, a rare and radiant exotic dancer whom the angels name Lenore, flies from my agency door and I spend much time agonizing about her lost and lovely tassels.

Still, it continues. AIP try a war picture. It turns out to feature a brooding young commando who storms a Nazi castle in search of his missing girlfriend and finds Vinnie in a velvet SS uniform before inevitable torture, burial alive, and burning-down. With his producer's hat on, Roger sends some film students and the Nicholson kid into the desert to make a Western, and they come back with Vinnie as an accursed cattle baron, doppelganger gunslingers, and a cattle stampede flattening the ranch house in place of the fire. *Rocket Voyage to the Planet of Prehistoric Women of Blood* eventually sells to television with the hammer and sickle insignia on the spacecraft blotted out. It is somehow re-edited. A brooding young astronaut lands on a haunted world where

Mr. Touch-and-Go Bullet-Head (Vincent Price) rules a telepathic tribe of ululating bikini girls who are interred living within the tomb as doom-haunted dinosaurs set fire to the whole planet.

Then, it's not just American International.

The plague shows up as little things in little films. Two Cavalry troopers called "William Wilson" in *The Great Sioux Massacre*. A "Pink Panther" cartoon called *Dial "P" for Pendulum*. A premature burial in *John Goldfarb, Please Come Home*. Then, a descent into the maelstrom. The Red Death arrives during the revolutionary scenes of *Doctor Zhivago*, and the rest of the film finds Darkness and Despair descending illimitably over Omar Sharif and Julie Christie. *The Agony and the Ecstasy* features Charlton Heston laboring for decades over a small oval portrait of one of Roderick Usher's ancestors. *The Spy Who Came in from the Cold* winds up with Richard Burton clutching a purloined letter and ranting that the orangutan did it. Even a John Wayne–Howard Hawks Western turns on a Poe poem, *El Dorado*.

The curse is complete when movie theaters book *The Sound of Music* as a roadshow attraction and get *The Sound of Meowing*. In vast, empty, decaying haunted-picture palaces across the land, Julie Andrews climbs ragged mountains and pokes around a basement only to find Captain von Trapp (Vincent Price) has walled up his wife along with her noisy cat. At the end, Austria burns down.

My senses are more painfully acute by the hour. I can not venture out by day unless the sun is completely obscured by the thickest, gloomiest cloud and after dark can tolerate only the tiniest, flickering flame of a candle. My ears are assaulted by the faintest sound. A housewife tearing open a cereal packet two blocks away reverberates within my skull like the discharge of a Gatling gun. I can bear only the most pallid of foods, and neglect my formerly favored watering holes to become a ghoul-like habitué of the new McDonald's chain, where fare that tastes of naught save cardboard may be found at the expense of a few trivial cents. The touch of my secretary becomes as sandpaper upon my appallingly sensitive skin, and raises sharp pains, sudden dizziness, and then profuse bleeding at my pores. Few in the industry return my telephone calls, which is all to the good since I can of course scarcely bear the torture of tintinnabulation . . . of the bells—of the bells, bells, bells, bells, bells, bells, bells—of the moaning and the groaning of the bells.

Movies are only the beginning. Soon, Poe is everywhere. The *house* is the monster, and the house is the United States of America. The breakout TV hits of the next seasons are *The Usher Family*, *The Man from U.L.A.L.U.M.E.*, and *The Marie Tyler Roget Show*. Vincent Price takes over from Walter Cronkite, and intones the bad news in a velvet jacket, promising "much of madness, and more of sin, and horror the soul of the plot" in reports from Vietnam, Washington, and the Middle East. Sonny and Cher take "The Colloquy of Monos and Una" to Number One in the hit parade, followed by Procol Harem's "A Whiter Shade of Poe," Scott McKenzie's "San Francisco (Be Sure to Put Some Flowers on Your Grave)," the Mamas and the Papas' "Dream a Little Dream within a Dream of You," the Archies' "Bon-Bon," and Dean Martin's "Little Old Amontillado Drinker Me." Vinnie hosts *American Bandstand* too, warily scanning the dancers for a skull-face figure in red robes.

A craze for floppy shirts, ink-stained fingers, and pale faces seizes the surfer kids, and everyone on the strip has a pet raven or a trained ape. Beauty contests for cataleptics are all the rage, and "Miss Universe" is crowned with a wreath in her coffin as she is solemnly bricked up by the judges. The Green Berets adopt a "conqueror worm" cap badge. Housing developments rise up tottering on shaky ground near stagnant ponds, with pre-stressed materials to provide Usher cracks and incendiaries built into the light-fittings for more spectacular conflagrations. The most popular names for girls in 1966–7 are "Lenore," "Annabel," "Ligeia," and "Madeline."

In a kingdom by the sea, we are haunted. In the El Dorado of Los Angeles, white fog lies thick on the boulevards. The mournful "nevermores" of ravens perched on statues are answered by the strangled mewling of black cats immured in basements. And the seagulls chime in with "tekeli-li tekeli-li" as if that was any help.

During the whole of a dull, dark, and soundless day in the autumn of the year, when the clouds hang oppressively low in the heavens, I pass alone in a Cadillac convertible through a singularly dreary tract of country; and at length find myself as the shades of evening draw on, within

349

view of the melancholy House of Roger. I know not how it is—but, with the first glimpse of the building, a sense of insufferable gloom pervades my spirit. I try to shake off the fog, like the after-dream of a reveler upon mary jane, in my brain, and rid my mind of the words of Poe. Yet he sits beside me, phantasmal, fiddling with the radio dial, breathing whiskey and muttering in intricate rhyme schemes. I have taken the Pacific Coast Highway to Malibu, where AIP and Corman—flush with monies from the Poe pictures—have thrown up a studio in a bleak castle atop the jagged cliffs. From the road, it looks phony as a glass shot. The scrublands all around are withered and sere, and I'm not even sure what "sere" means.

The castle seems abandoned, but I gain access through a wide crack in the walls. In the gloom, I find the others. Roger, in dark glasses with side panels. Sam, with raven chewing on his cigar. Jim, haunted by the doppelganger who no longer claims to be his son. Vinnie, worst of us all, liquid face dribbling over his frilly shirt, eyebrows and moustache shifted inches lower by the tide of loathsome, of detestable putrescence. A few others are with the crowd—the embalmed, toothless corpse of Lorre; an ancient withered ape just recognizable as Boris Karloff; barely breathing girls and a teenage singer coughing blood into a handkerchief; an ignored brooding youth or two, hiding in the shadows and trying to avoid being upstaged.

All eyes are accusingly upon me. "Thou art the man," is written plainly on everyone's faces. I admit it to myself, and the plague-ravaged company. We have brought Poe back. Neglected and despised in life, to his mind cheated of the riches and recognition due his genius, he has been kept half-alive in the grave, plagiarized and paperbacked, bought and sold and made a joke of. No wonder we have raised an angry Eddy, a vindictive and a spiteful genius. This time, he has caught on and he will not let go, not of us and not of the world. This is the dawning of the Age of Edgar Allan, the era of Mystery and Imagination. We have *ushered*—ahem—it in, but we are to be its mummified, stuffed, walled-up victims, the sacrifices necessary for the foundations of even the shakiest edifice.

I have a new horror. It seizes my brain like a vulture's—no, a raven's—talons. I hear the faint whisper of nails against wood, the tapping of hairy knuckles against a coffin lid, that first gibber of fear before the awful realization takes hold. I can hear Boomba, and know that—through my neglect—I have suffered him to be *buried alive*. The gibber becomes a snarling, hooting, raging, clawing shriek. The tapping, as of someone gently rapping, becomes a hammering, a clamoring, a gnawing, a pawing, a crashing, a smashing. Wood breaks, earth parts, and long-fingered, bloodied, torn-nailed, horribly semi-human hands grope for the bone handle of a straight razor.

Jim and Sam want to know what to do, how to escape. To them, every contract has a get-out clause. Roger and Vinnie know this isn't true.

Without, a storm rages. The heavens rage at the sorrows of the world.

A door opens with a creak. The attenuated shadow of a chimpanzee is cast upon the flagstones, gleaming cruel blade held high. We turn to look, our capacity for wonder and terror long since exceeded.

Brushfires burn all around, struggling against the torrents. The crack that runs through the castle—the crack that runs through *California*—widens, with great shouts as of the planet itself in pain and terror. A million tons of mud is on the march, and we stand between it and the sea. The walls bend and bow like painted canvas flats. A candle falls and flames spread. A maiden screams. A burning bird streaks cometlike through the air.

The ape's clutch is at my throat and the razor held high. In Boomba's glittering, baleful eye I discern cruel recognition.

Vinnie, before the burning beams come down, has to have the last quote . . .

"'. . . the screenplay is the tragedy Man, and its hero the Conqueror Worm!'—Edgar Allan . . ."

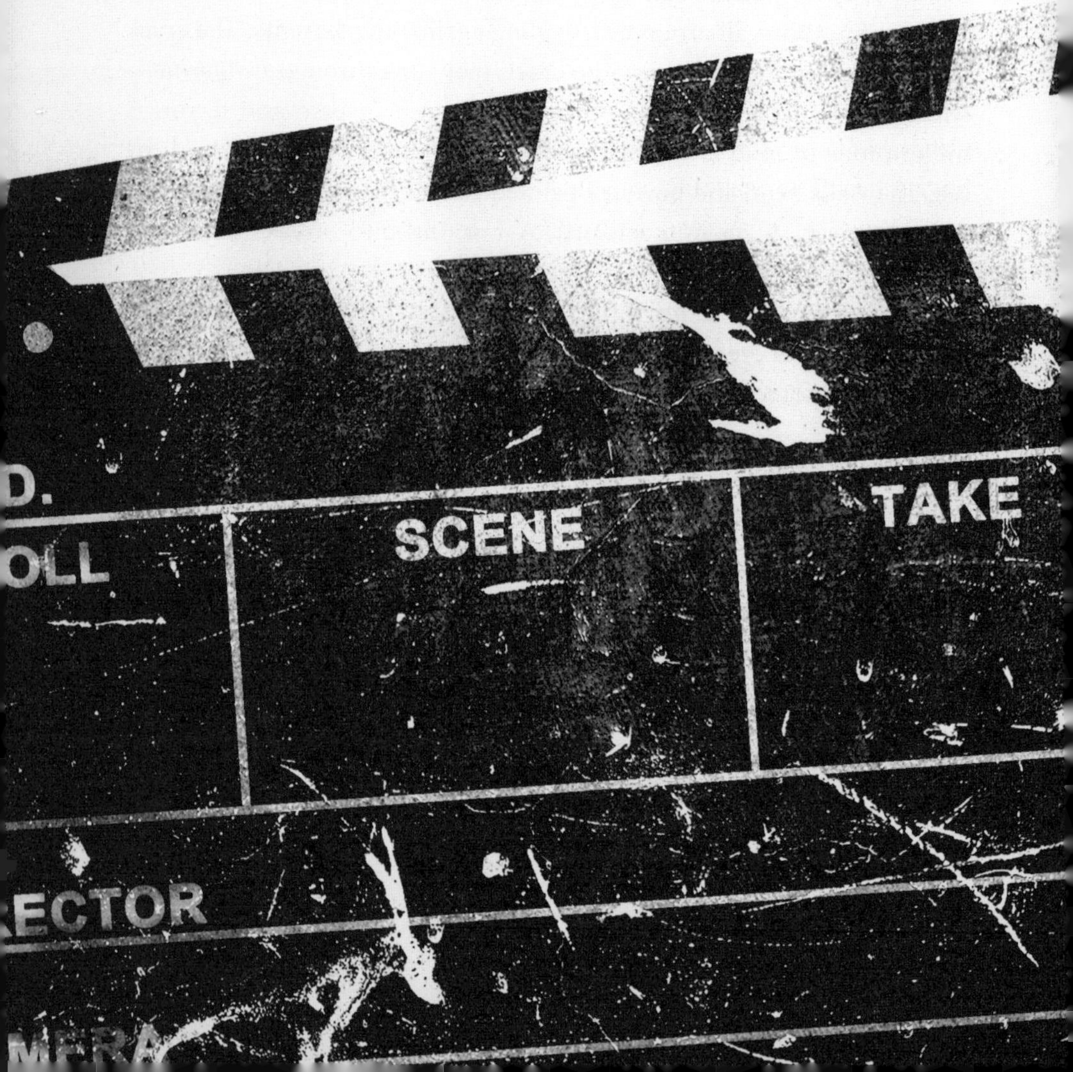
SCENE
TAKE

ABOUT THE EDITOR

Ellen Datlow has been editing science-fiction, fantasy, and horror short fiction for more than thirty years. She was fiction editor of *OMNI magazine*, *Event Horizon*, and SCIFICTION and has edited more than fifty anthologies, including the annual *The Best Horror of the Year*; *Fearful Symmetries*, an unthemed anthology of horror and the supernatural; *Hauntings*, a reprint anthology of ghost stories and haunted houses; *Lovecraft's Monsters*, a reprint anthology of stories, each involving at least one of H. P. Lovecraft's creations; *Telling Tales: The Clarion West 30th Anniversary Anthology*; *Nightmare Carnival*; and *Queen Victoria's Book of Spells: An Anthology of Gaslight Fantasy* (an adult anthology with Terri Windling).

Forthcoming is *The Doll Collection*.

She's won multiple World Fantasy Awards, Locus Awards, Hugo Awards, Stoker Awards, International Horror Guild Awards, Shirley Jackson Awards, and the 2012 Il Posto Nero Black Spot Award for Excellence as Best Foreign Editor. Datlow was named recipient of the 2007 Karl Edward Wagner Award, given at the British Fantasy Convention for "outstanding contribution to the genre"; has been honored with the Life Achievement Award given by the Horror Writers Association, in acknowledgment of superior achievement over an entire career; and has just been awarded the World Fantasy Life Achievement Award for 2014, which is presented annually to individuals who have demonstrated out-standing service to the fantasy field.

She lives in New York and co-hosts the monthly Fantastic Fiction Reading Series at KGB Bar. More information can be found at www.datlow.com, where she occasionally blogs. You can also find her on Facebook and on Twitter under the handle @EllenDatlow.

CONTRIBUTORS

Stephen J. Barringer's first publication was the short story "Restoration" in the Canadian SF magazine *On Spec*; he has since won first and second prizes in the long-running Toronto Trek/Polaris media convention's short-story competition and has written several gaming products for various RPG systems as well as a radio-play adaptation of E. F. Benson's "The Room in the Tower" for Canada's Dark Echo Productions. His story "Necessary Evil" will appear in *Kaleidotrope* sometime in 2015. A lifelong resident of Toronto, he is married to Gemma Files.

Laird Barron is the author of several books, including *The Imago Sequence*, *Occultation*, *The Croning*, and *The Beautiful Thing That Awaits Us All*. His work has appeared in many magazines and anthologies, including *The Best Horror of the Year*, *Blood and Other Cravings*, and *Lovecraft Unbound*. An expatriate Alaskan, Barron currently resides in upstate New York.

Gary A. Braunbeck is the author of twenty-four books, among them the acclaimed *In Silent Graves*, first novel in the ongoing Cedar Hill Cycle. His fiction has been translated into Japanese, French, Italian, Russian, and German. More than two hundred of his short stories have appeared in various publications, including *The Magazine of Fantasy and Science Fiction* and *The Year's Best Fantasy and Horror*. He was born in Newark,

Ohio, the city that serves as the model for the fictitious Cedar Hill in many of his stories. As an editor, Gary completed the latest installment of the *Masques* anthology series created by Jerry Williamson, *Masques V*, after Jerry became too ill to continue, and also co-edited (with Hank Schwaeble) the Bram Stoker Award–winning anthology *Five Strokes to Midnight*. Gary's work has been honored with six Bram Stoker Awards, an International Horror Guild Award, three Shocklines "Shocker" Awards, a *Dark Scribe Magazine* Black Quill Award, and a World Fantasy Award nomination. Visit him online at www.garybraunbeck.com.

Edward Bryant began writing professionally in 1968 and has had more than a dozen books published, including *Among the Dead*, *Cinnabar*, *Phoenix without Ashes* (with Harlan Ellison), *Wyoming Sun*, *Particle Theory*, *Fetish* (a novella chapbook), and *The Baku: Tales of the Nuclear Age*. He initially made his reputation as a science-fiction writer (winning two Nebula Awards for science-fiction short stories in the late 1970s), but he gradually strayed into horror and mostly has remained there, writing a series of sharply etched stories about Angie Black, a contemporary witch; the brilliant zombie story "A Sad Last Love at the Diner of the Damned"; and other marvelous tales.

Dennis Etchison's stories have appeared in magazines and anthologies since 1961. He is a three-time winner of both the British Fantasy Award and the World Fantasy Award and served as president of the Horror Writers Association from 1992 to 1994.

His collections include *The Dark Country*, *Red Dreams*, *The Blood Kiss*, *The Death Artist*, *Talking in the Dark*, *Fine Cuts*, and *Got to Kill Them All & Other Stories*. He is also a novelist (*Darkside*, *Shadowman*, *California Gothic*, *Double Edge*), editor (*Cutting Edge*, *Masters of Darkness I–III*, *MetaHorror*, *The Museum of Horrors*, *Gathering the Bones*), and scriptwriter. He adapted 150 episodes of the original *Twilight Zone* television series for radio in addition to writing original scripts for *The New Twilight Zone Radio Dramas* and Fangoria Magazine's *Dreadtime Stories*, and he wrote

Christopher Lee's commentaries for more than two hundred episodes of *Mystery Theater*.

Forthcoming work includes a career retrospective in S. T. Joshi's *Masters of the Weird Tale* series (Centipede Press) and a volume of new short stories, *A Long Time Till Morning*. Much of his backlist is currently available as e-books published by Crossroad Press.

"Deadspace" was originally published in *Whispers V*, edited by Stuart David Schiff.

Gemma Files was born in London, England, but is a Canadian citizen who has lived in Toronto, Ontario, for her entire life (thus far). She has been a film critic and a teacher of screenwriting and Canadian film history. In 1999, her story "The Emperor's Old Bones" won the International Horror Guild Award for Best Short Fiction. She is best known for her Hexslinger series of weird west novels, *A Book of Tongues*, *A Rope of Thorns*, and *A Tree of Bones* (all from ChiZine Publications), but she has also published two collections of short stories—*Kissing Carrion* and *The Worm in Every Heart*—and two chapbooks of poetry. *A Book of Tongues* won the 2010 Black Quill Award for Best Small Press Chill (both Editors' and Readers' Choice) and was nominated for a Bram Stoker Award in the Best First Novel category. Five of her short stories were adapted as episodes of the 1998–1999 U.S./Canadian horror television series *The Hunger*, for which she also wrote two screenplays. She is currently hard at work on her next novel.

Daphne Gottlieb is the author of nine award-winning books, most recently the nonfiction title *Dear Dawn: Aileen Wuornos in Her Own Words* (with Lisa Kester) and the poetry collection *15 Ways to Stay Alive*. She lives in San Francisco, where she works with the casualties of America's class war.

Stephen Graham Jones is the author of thirteen novels and four collections. Most recent are *Zombie Sharks with Metal Teeth*, *The Least of My*

Scars, and *Flushboy*. Up soon are the novels *The Gospel of Z* and *Not for Nothing* and the collection of flash fiction, *States of Grace*. Jones has had some one hundred fifty stories published, many included in Year's Best collections. He has been a Shirley Jackson Award finalist, a Bram Stoker Award finalist, and a Colorado Book Award finalist, and he has won the Texas Institute of Letters Award for fiction, the Independent Publishers Award for Multicultural Fiction, and an NEA fellowship in fiction. He teaches in the MFA programs at CU Boulder and UCR Palm Desert. Find out more at http://demontheory.net or by following him on Twitter (@SGJ72).

Garry Kilworth has been writing fantasy and science-fiction stories for almost forty years, and he still gets a kick when a fresh idea jumps into his head. *Attica*, his fantasy novel set in an attic the size of a continent, with three adventurers on a quest through a dangerous land terrorized by animated junk, is in production with Johnny Depp's movie company, Infinitum Nihil. *The Fabulous Beast*, his latest collection of short stories, has recently been published by Infinity Plus, and *Poems, Peoms and Other Atrocities*, a poetry collection created in a collaboration with his departed friend Robert Holdstock, is available from STANZA (PS Publishing).

Joel Lane was a British novelist, short story writer, poet, critic, and anthology editor. Although most of his short fiction could be categorized as dark fantasy or horror, his two novels, *From Blue to Black* and *The Blue Mask*, were more mainstream.

He received the World Fantasy Award in 2013 for his most recent collection, *Where Furnaces Burn*, and he won the British Fantasy Award twice. His short stories have been collected in five volumes. He died in 2013.

Gary McMahon is the acclaimed author of nine novels and several short-story collections. His latest novel releases include *Beyond Here Lies Nothing* (third in the Concrete Grove series, published by Solaris), *The End* (an apocalyptic drama), and *The Bones of You* (a supernatural mystery), and his short fiction has been reprinted in various Year's Best volumes.

Gary lives with his family in Yorkshire, where he trains in Shotokan karate and likes running in the rain.

Read more about him at www.garymcmahon.com.

David Morrell is the critically acclaimed author of *First Blood*, the novel in which Rambo first appears. He holds a Ph.D. in American Literature from Penn State and was a professor in the English Department at the University of Iowa. His numerous *New York Times* best-sellers include the classic spy trilogy *The Brotherhood of the Rose* (the basis for the only television miniseries to premiere after a Super Bowl), *The Fraternity of the Stone*, and *The League of Night and Fog*. An Edgar, Anthony, and Macavity awards nominee, Morrell is the recipient of three Bram Stoker Awards from the Horror Writers Association as well as the prestigious lifetime Thriller Master Award from the International Thriller Writers organization. He has also been nominated for two World Fantasy Awards. His writing book, *The Successful Novelist*, discusses what he has learned in his four decades as an author.

You can find out more about David and his work at www.davidmorrell. net.

Steve Nagy lives and works in Michigan. He spends his days providing phone support to newspapers throughout the United States and overseas. His evenings belong to his family. The dark hours after everyone goes to bed belong to his muse. His stories have been reprinted in *The Mammoth Book of Best New Horror* and *The Year's Best Fantasy and Horror*.

He maintains a website at http://stephenwnagy.wordpress.com/, where he usually blogs about writing and how it influences his life.

Kim Newman was born in Brixton (London), grew up in the West Country, went to university near Brighton, and now lives in Islington (London).

Newman's most recent fiction books include *Where the Bodies Are Buried*, *The Man from the Diogenes Club*, and *Secret Files of the Diogenes Club* under his own name and *The Vampire Genevieve* as Jack Yeovil. His nonfiction books include *Ghastly Beyond Belief* (with Neil Gaiman), *Horror: 100 Best Books*, *Horror: Another 100 Best Books* (both with Stephen Jones), and a host of books on film. He is a contributing editor to *Sight & Sound* and *Empire* magazines and has written and broadcast widely on a range of topics, including scripting radio documentaries, role-playing games, and TV programs. He has won the Bram Stoker Award, the International Horror Critics Award, the British Science Fiction Award, and the British Fantasy Award. His official website, *Dr. Shade's Laboratory*, can be found at www.johnnyalucard.com.

Nicholas Royle is the author of *First Novel* as well as six earlier novels, including *The Director's Cut* and *Antwerp*, and a short-story collection, *Mortality*. He has edited numerous anthologies, including *Darklands*, *Murmurations: An Anthology of Uncanny Stories about Birds* and three volumes of *The Best British Short Stories* (2011–2013).

A senior lecturer in creative writing at Manchester Metropolitan University, he also runs Nightjar Press, publishing original short stories as signed, limited-edition chapbooks, and works as an editor for Salt Publishing, where he has been responsible for Alison Moore's Man Booker–shortlisted *The Lighthouse* and Alice Thompson's *Burnt Island*, among other titles.

Robert Shearman has written four short-story collections, which collectively have won the World Fantasy Award, the Shirley Jackson Award, the Edge Hill Readers Prize, and two British Fantasy Awards. The most recent, *Remember Why You Fear Me*, was published by ChiZine. But he is probably best known for his work on the television revival of *Doctor Who*, bringing back the Daleks in an episode that was a finalist for a Hugo Award. He has also written extensively for radio and theater. He lives in London.

CONTRIBUTORS

Lucy A. Snyder is the Bram Stoker Award–winning author of the novels *Spellbent*, *Shotgun Sorceress*, and *Switchblade Goddess* and the collections *Sparks and Shadows*, *Chimeric Machines*, and *Installing Linux on a Dead Badger*. Her writing has appeared in *Strange Horizons*, *Weird Tales*, *Hellbound Hearts*, *Dark Faith*, *Chiaroscuro*, *GUD*, and *Lady Churchill's Rosebud Wristlet*.

She currently lives in Worthington, Ohio, with her husband and occasional co-author, Gary A. Braunbeck. You can learn more about her at www.lucysnyder.com.

Peter Straub is the author of eighteen novels, including *Ghost Story*, *Koko*, and *Mr. X*; two collaborations with Stephen King, *The Talisman* and *Black House*; and his most recent, *A Dark Matter*. He has also written two volumes of poetry and two collections of short fiction. He edited *Conjunctions 39: The New Wave Fabulists*, Library of America's *H. P. Lovecraft: Tales* and *American Fantastic Tales*, and *Poe's Children*. He has won the British Fantasy Award, nine Bram Stoker Awards, two International Horror Guild Awards, and three World Fantasy Awards. In 1998, he was named Grand Master at the World Horror Convention. He has also won WFC's Lifetime Achievement Award and the Barnes & Noble Writers for Writers Award. The University of Wisconsin and Columbia University gave him Distinguished Alumnus Awards.

Genevieve Valentine's first novel, *Mechanique: A Tale of the Circus Tresaulti*, won the 2012 Crawford Award for first fantasy novel. Her second, *The Girls at the Kingfisher Club*, was recently published by Atria. Her short fiction has been published in *Clarkesworld*, *Strange Horizons*, *Fantasy*, and *Tor.com* and in the anthologies *Federations*, *After*, *Running with the Pack*, *Teeth*, *Willful Impropriety*, *Nightmare Carnival*, and others.

Her nonfiction has appeared at *io9.com*, *NPR.org*, *Lightspeed*, and *Weird Tales*, among other venues, and she is the co-author of *Geek Wisdom*, a book of pop-culture philosophy from Quirk. Her appetite for bad movies is insatiable, a tragedy she tracks on her blog, genevievevalentine.com.

Howard Waldrop, who was born in Mississippi and now lives in Austin, Texas, is one of the most iconoclastic writers working today. His highly original books include the novels *Them Bones* and *A Dozen Tough Jobs* and the collections *Howard Who?*, *All about Strange Monsters of the Recent Past*, *Night of the Cooters*, and *Going Home Again*. He won the Nebula and World Fantasy awards for his novelette "The Ugly Chickens."

Waldrop continues to work on the novels *The Moon World* and *I, John Mandeville*.

British author **Ian Watson** published his first story in *New Worlds* in 1969 and his first, award-winning novel, *The Embedding*, in 1973. His many novels of science fiction, fantasy, and horror include *The Martian Inca*, *Miracle Visitors*, *The Fire Worm*, *The Flies of Memory*, and *Mockymen*. Among his twelve story collections are *The Very Slow Time Machine* and *The Great Escape*. He also wrote the first four novels to be set in the Warhammer forty thousand universe. His most recent major novel was the historical medical thriller *Waters of Destiny*, a collaboration with Andy West.

Watson has twice won the British Science Fiction Association Award and has been shortlisted for the Hugo and Nebula awards.

In 1990, he worked with Stanley Kubrick on what became *A.I. Artificial Intelligence* (2001), completed by Steven Spielberg after Kubrick's death.

Two collections, *The Best of Ian Watson* and *The Uncollected Ian Watson*, were recently published.

F. Paul Wilson is the award-winning, *New York Times* best-selling author of forty-plus books and many short stories spanning genres including medical thrillers, science fiction, horror, adventure, and virtually everything between. More than nine million copies of his books are in print in the United States, and his work has been translated into twenty languages. He also has written for the stage, screen, and interactive media.

His latest thriller, *Dark City*, starring the notorious urban mercenary

Repairman Jack and is the second of The Early Years Trilogy, following *Cold City*. *Fear City*, the last in the trilogy, is about to be published.

He currently resides at the Jersey Shore and can be found online at www.repairmanjack.com.

Douglas E. Winter is a writer and lawyer. He is the author of the novel *Run* and several critically acclaimed short stories and novellas.

Winter edited the horror anthologies *Prime Evil* and *Revelations* as well as the interviews collection *Faces of Fear*. His other nonfiction works include *Stephen King: The Art of Darkness*, *Faces of Fear*, and *Clive Barker: The Dark Fantastic*.

A. C. Wise was born and raised in Montreal and currently lives in the Philadelphia area. Her fiction has appeared in such publications as *Clarkesworld*, *Lightspeed*, *Apex*, and *The Best Horror of the Year Volume 4*, among others. In addition to her writing, she co-edits *Unlikely Story*, an online magazine publishing three unlikely themed issues per year. You can find her online at www.acwise.net.